About Ho

The Wild Hun. ___

Erotic paranormal ménage romance

*Winner of The Romance Reviews' **Best Book of 2011** award ~ There's a reason why Cherise Sinclair is on my auto-buy list: she writes fantastic erotic romances with great stories and wonderful characters. So, when I saw her newest release, I was intrigued that it was a departure from the kind of books that she normally writes. But, I am happy to report that she's done it again. Hour of the Lion was simply amazing. Hot hunky shifter men, a strong and sassy heroine, a gripping story, and some oh so lovely ménage action are just the tip of the iceberg in this phenomenal read!*

~ The Romance Reviews

First a Marine, then a black ops agent, Victoria Morgan knows the military is where she belongs…until a sniper's bullet changes her life. Trying to prove she's not washed up, she rescues a young man from kidnappers. When the dying boy transforms into a cougar—and bites her—she learns of an entire hidden society. He begs her to inform his grandfather of his death and to keep the secret of the shifters' existence. She can't refuse, but what if the creatures pose a danger to the country she swore to protect?

As guardian of the shifter territory, Calum McGregor wields the power of life and death over his people. When a pretty human female arrives in their wilderness town, he and his littermate become increasingly concerned. Not only is the little female hiding something, but she is far more appealing than any human should be.

While investigating the shifters, Victoria begins to fall in love with the werecat brothers and the town as well. For the first time in her life, she might have a real home. Her hopes are crushed when a deadly enemy follows her from the city, and the shifters discover she knows their secret. Now nobody is safe—least of all Victoria.

> *With a fantastic heroine, two yummy heroes and a whole host of fun side characters (I've already asked for a certain bear and wolfie to get books :D) this slick paranormal romance came at me out of nowhere and knocked my socks off.*
>
> ~ Scorching Book Reviews

Want to be notified of the next release?

Sent only on release day, Cherise's newsletters contain freebies, excerpts, and articles.
Sign up at:
www.CheriseSinclair.com/NewsletterForm

Hour of the Lion

The Wild Hunt Legacy: 1

Cherise Sinclair

VanScoy Publishing Group

Hour Of The Lion
Copyright © June 2011 by Cherise Sinclair
Print Edition
ISBN: 978-0-9837063-2-8
Published by VanScoy Publishing Group
Cover Artist: Hot Damn Designs

Acknowledgements

I want to extend my profound appreciation to the following people:

To the readers of my contemporary books for being brave enough to trust me in a different genre. I hope I haven't let you down.

For those of you who play on my Facebook page, bringing photos and jokes and perverse humor. You always brighten my day.

For Chelle Hicks for beta reading and—*sigh*—being right far too many times.

To my patient and loving family who chivvy me out of my writing cave and remind me there's a whole 'nother world outside. I love you all so, so much.

To Melissa and Dan Lowe for helping with Marine-speak. They—and I—send this message to our Service Members around the world:

"Stay safe, keep your heads down, and come home. We're praying for you."

Chapter One

*T*HAT WAS A *really bad dream*, Vic thought, though it had started well enough. Looking up at her father, trying not to fidget, she'd recited the marketplace gossip, and she'd remembered every detail too. He'd actually smiled and said he couldn't do without her. But somehow twenty years had passed, her boss stood over her hospital bed and was saying a disabled Marine wasn't any good to him. He'd walked away, leaving her there. Alone.

Even now, wide awake, she felt the aching loss in her chest.

Only...the ache was real. Her ribs really did hurt. This was more than a nightmare residue. Her sniper-damaged knee ached like a pulled tooth, and her skull throbbed like hell. Couldn't be a hangover. She hadn't tied one on since Wells recruited her into his estrogen-heavy, covert ops unit.

When she opened her eyes, light blasted through them like a frag grenade, and she barely managed to muffle the moan. Just the thought of turning her head had bile flooding her mouth. *Then don't move, Sergeant. Just assess.* She was curled up with her cheek resting on cold cement. An ugly feeling crept up her spine when she realized her hands were tied in front of her. Narrowing her eyes to slits, she took stock of the room. Exposed beams, cinder-block walls, and tiny rectangular windows near the ceiling.

The stench of feces and sickness mingled with a musty smell like mildewing socks. *Basement.*

A gray-haired woman lay nearby, her back to Vic. Familiar-looking. *That was it.* Her memory engaged.

Rescuing a woman who was trying to escape from a man. *Check.*

Didn't win. *Check.*

Now, tied up in a basement. *Check.*

Probably concussed, too, considering the speed of her thinking. Her day had definitely gone to hell. *I might as well be working.* Why the hell had she risked her life when a phone call to the police would have worked?

The answer to that really sucked. She'd acted all macho—and stupid—to prove she still had it. That she wasn't irreparably damaged. But she was. In the hospital, Mr. Show-no-emotions Spymaster had looked at her with pity; he didn't think she'd heal enough to return to duty. So she'd jumped right into the first fight she could find. *Act any dumber and I might as well be a guy.*

Well, with luck, her inept rescue could be salvaged. The idiots hadn't tied her legs.

Hearing footsteps, Vic froze, watching through dark eyelashes as the guy she'd fought appeared. Shaved head, built like a linebacker, all muscle. Ripped off sleeves showed tattoos: eagle, globe, and anchor; bulldog; skull and crossed rifles.

"Hey, BeastieBoy." The man walked to a metal kennel near the stairs. A naked teenager with shaggy blond hair huddled in the far corner of the cage. Shivering. Scared half to death. Eyes sunken, he was skinny, as if he hadn't eaten in weeks. Bruises and abrasions—even burns—marred his fair skin.

Vic's breath hitched. *Tortured?*

Baldy slapped the top of the cage with his fist, making the kid jump. "You ready for another session, pussy cat? Just tell me how to make new beasts, and I won't hurt you anymore."

"I won't tell you anything." The boy's voice cracked on the last word.

Brave kid. Vic cheered silently even as her stomach tightened in fear for him. And what did the asshole mean by making new beasts?

"Dumb fuck." Baldy raised a long rod—a cattle prod. The kid was as far back as he could get, but it wasn't far enough. He jerked at the shock of the prod, and the bastard didn't stop, kept jamming with the prod until the boy screamed.

Teeth grinding together, Vic yanked at her ropes.

And then the kid…blurred.

A huge tawny cougar stood where the boy had been. A chilling snarl ripped through the room, echoing off the concrete walls. The hair on Vic's arms rose.

What the hell? Kid one moment, the next, a…a mountain lion. She sucked in a hard breath, tried blinking her eyes. The big cat still paced the cage. *Am I drugged?* Like when Private Renner had a bad reaction to morphine and spent hours screaming about ghouls eating his heart. Or maybe she had a concussion. Yeah, this wasn't happening. She didn't believe in ghosts, ghouls, or people changing into mountain lions. Woo-woo stuff was for flakes and druggies.

"Cut the crap, Swane." A man said from the stairs. White, average height, heavy build. Older, in his sixties. Wearing a suit. Scarred knuckles matched his battered face, nose busted in the past, thin lips and dead-cold eyes. Might be in nice clothes, but the body inside said *thug*. "He can't talk in cat form."

"Not my fucking fault. I only tapped it," Swane said. When the cat swiped at the cattle-prod with three-inch claws, he used the prod until the cat shrieked in pain. "It's not gonna talk anyway." Swane tossed the device onto a table. "Fucking thing would rather starve. Look at it—it's dying."

"Dammit." The suit crossed the room to the cage where the

cat paced back and forth. "It's amazing he's still alive. He should have died the first week with what you did to him. The creatures are fucking strong."

"An' you really want to turn into that?" Swane spit on the floor.

Vic stared. The suit wanted to become an animal? Was he insane?

His face turned ugly. Brutal enough that Swane took a step back. "I'm not paying you to think. Just to get answers." He glanced over his shoulder. "What happened with the old bitch?"

Swane walked over and, with his foot, he shoved the woman onto her back. Hands and feet tied, she blinked blankly as froth trickled from her toothless mouth. "Another goner." Swane nudged her with his boot.

"Get rid of her."

"Will do." Swane's mouth pulled into a twisted smile as he set his boot on the woman's throat.

Before Vic could move, she heard the crunch of breaking cartilage, and then it was too late. Sucking air through her teeth, she tried to stay motionless against the fury rising inside.

Expressionless, Swane watched the old woman's strangling efforts to breathe, her death spasms. When her body finally stilled, pleasure shone in his eyes, and his filthy jeans showed his erection.

Sick bastard. Vic clenched her jaw. She should have done something, created a diversion. *I didn't save a helpless woman.* Her war-torn past stretched out behind her, littered with bodies—testaments to the times she hadn't moved fast enough, discovered enough information, or pushed herself hard enough. The ones she'd failed.

"You were clever to test this first, boss." Swane glanced at the body. "You could have ended up like her."

"Why are they dying, dammit? Why the fuck don't they

change?" The suit hit the table with his fist, then stared at the dead woman. "They've all been druggies, alcoholics. Maybe they're too unhealthy to survive being bit." When his gaze lit on Vic, he walked toward her.

She closed her eyes completely.

"Didn't kill her, Swane?" His voice held a thinly concealed taunt. "The bitch looks healthy enough. Let's give her a try."

"No. She's mine. I kept this piece of ass for me, not you."

Vic's skin crawled at the thick lust in his voice. Icy fear punched past the tight grip she'd maintained on her emotions.

"You can fuck her all you want...after." The man slapped her hard. "Still out. Toss her in the cage while I tranq the cat."

A second later, Vic heard the whap of a tranquilizer gun. Fuck, what were they planning? *Can't afford fear—push it aside.* When Swane grabbed under her arms, Vic made her move. Clamping her elbows to her sides, she pinned his hands and swung her legs up toward his head. She opened her eyes in time to ensure that her feet hit him in the face. The crack of impact felt infinitely satisfying.

Baldy toppled backward, releasing her.

Jaw set tight, she rolled up and onto her feet.

He rose, shaking his head, looking like he'd been raised on steroids instead of candy. Considering the Marine tattoos covering his neck and arms, his fighting skills might be as good as hers.

Vic took a step back, feeling cartilage grate. That kick hadn't done her knee any favors. She back-pedaled toward the stairs, trying to disguise her limp. As Swane advanced, she dropped into cat stance, the foot in front tapping the floor lightly, ready to kick him into never-neverland.

"Don't move, cunt."

Vic froze. The suit had the tranq gun in his hand, dart already loaded, aimed right at her chest. He motioned to the panther's cage. "Crawl in or Swane will stuff you in there unconscious."

She took a step back. In with the mountain lion? The rush of terror made her head spin. "No way."

"Open it," the suit said to Swane.

Scowling, Swane worked the combination padlock and half opened the door. "Stop dicking around and just shoot her. Better yet, give her to me for a while. When I get through, she'll beg for the cage."

If he tranked her, she wouldn't have a chance of escaping. Eyeing the groggy cat warily, she bent and entered the cage, feeling Swane's anger like a wave of heat as she crawled past.

The cat was on its side, head nodding, eyes glazed.

"Do it before he changes back." The suit slammed the cage door shut.

She turned, "Do what—" and the psycho shoved the cattle-prod into her stomach. Fiery pain blistered across her skin, and with a yell, she staggered backward. Right into the snarling cat.

She landed hard, tangled in its legs, scrambling to get away. Paws seized her. Its claws ripped into her back, and the mountain lion sank its teeth into her shoulder.

"God!" Agony tore through her. She kicked, nailing it in the stomach. The animal snarled viciously. She shoved herself free, its claws tearing her skin. Rolling away, she scrambled into the corner farthest from both the cat and the cattle-prod.

"That'll do." The suit picked her wallet up from the table and tossed it to Swane. "I gotta leave. Give your buddies on the force some green in case anybody asks about her."

"Got it."

The suit scowled at the lion. "Go ahead and do whatever you want to get answers out of the kid. He's dying anyway."

Swane's eyes lit and he smiled. "I need to pick up a few things to use, then I'll start. You'll have your answers."

Torture? Vic's stomach turned over. As they walked up the stairs, she realized they intended to leave her caged with the cougar. Vic pushed her face into the wire. "Let me out of here!"

The basement door closed, and the overhead bulb snapped off. The only illumination came from the tiny windows near the ceiling. Bad light for her, good light for a mountain lion. Her shoulder hurt like hell, and blood soaked her shirt sleeve, running down her back and sides. *Blood?* Just what she needed, a way to smell like a cat's supper. She turned her head slowly.

The cougar watched her, eyes slitted, ears back. The one cat in the world that didn't think she was its best friend. Even worse, it looked as emaciated as the kid had been. Its fur was dull and patchy and the golden eyes were sunken.

It looked really, really hungry.

"Nice, kitty," she murmured in a low voice. "We're stuck here together, so let's just be mellow about it, okay? My name's Victoria, but my friends call me Vicki." Her ops team had called her Vic, and right now, that was short for *victim*.

The cat watched as she sidled sideways toward the cage door. She knelt, checked the lock. Generic combination padlock. She could do this if her hands were free. And if the cat didn't decide it was hungry for human tartare.

To her relief, the cat's ears tilted forward and its eyes rounded. A second later, the cougar blurred.

Thinking her vision was screwing-up, Vic rubbed her face against her jean-covered knee, then raised her head.

The young man lay sprawled across the wire floor.

"Jesus-fuck!" She jerked back, falling against the wire. That was no drug-induced hallucination. Eyes narrowed, she studied the cage. There was no hidden door to pull a panther out and shove in a boy. Gritting her teeth, she stayed wedged in place. People didn't just turn into animals, and animals didn't turn into people. No fucking way.

The kid blinked at her blearily, ran a tongue over cracked lips, and said in a hoarse voice, "Nice to meet you, Vicki. Sorry about the clawing and uh, tooth-marks."

Vic's hands closed into fists. He was definitely no longer a mountain lion. "What *are* you?" she whispered.

He struggled to raise his head and gave her a pitiful smile. "Some people call us Daonain or *shifters*. Me, I prefer werecats." He glanced toward the stairs, and she could see him trying to hide his terror.

"A *shifter*," Vic said, staring at the battered young man. Up close, the poor kid appeared in even worse shape, she thought with a welling of pity. "Oh, sure—like in some Ann Rice novel or something?"

"She does vampires, not shifters, thank you very much," he said stiffly.

"Oh, yeah. I knew that." Vic pulled at her wrists. Swane had done a good job on the knots—there was no give there to exploit.

Suddenly, the kid's words registered—*people call us shifters*. "Us? *Us?* Like, there's *more* of you?"

"Well, duh."

"Jesus, take a nice, simple walk and blunder into the Twilight Zone. So what's with getting you to bite me?"

"Don't you watch TV? It's supposed to turn you into a werecat."

"You aren't fucking serious—turn me into a werecat?" Vic's breathing stopped. She turned her fear into a glare at the kid.

"I told them biting wouldn't work." His voice carried anger and guilt as he whispered, "I tried and tried to tell them." His gaze avoided the dead woman. "We're *born* as Daonain."

Her breath eased out. "There's a relief."

"Yeah, I bet."

Vic yanked at her bindings again, hissed as the skin on her

wrists tore. "Look, cat-person or whatever, do you think you can untie me without...um—"

A trace of humor appeared in his light green eyes. "Without having you for supper? Not a problem." He tried to rise and failed, his chest heaving as if he'd just jogged a mile. Looking even paler, if possible, he motioned her to him instead. "I only lose control when I'm drugged. Or suddenly hurt."

Bending to walk under the low top, Vic crossed the cage, her knee grinding with each step.

"Or, uh, scared."

She froze a few feet from him. "You turn into a cougar when you're scared?" The way her voice rose higher at the end was purely humiliating. She cleared her throat. "Yeah, well, you're not afraid of *me*, right? And not really scared this minute...right?"

He snorted. "I've been terrified since they caught me a month ago."

She didn't move. Cats can't see you if you don't move— she'd heard that somewhere. But probably, being only two feet away might ruin that effect.

His sigh was almost a laugh. "Get over here. I won't trawsfur—uh, change into cat form—unless they come back. Cross my heart."

The childish phrase pulled at her emotions; really, he couldn't be more than seventeen or so. Just a baby. And a very sick baby to boot. Where he wasn't bruised, sliced, or burned, his skin was an unhealthy yellowish-white. No wonder she'd managed to get away from him despite being tied.

It still took a fair amount of courage for her to turn her back on him so he could work on the rope.

A couple of extremely long minutes later, she was free. She hunched over her hands, trying not to scream as the blood began to circulate. It felt like she'd plunged her hands into a barrel of shattered glass. *Shit, shit, shit.* She sucked in air, breathing hard against the pain, while she opened and closed her fingers.

"Untying you won't do any good," the boy said. "We're still locked in."

"Not for long, buddy," she muttered. "What's your fucking name, anyway?"

"It's Lachlan—and you sure swear a lot."

"I'm planning to stop." She winced at his disbelieving look. "Really." And the assholes who grabbed her should get totally fucked for messing up her fucking good intentions.

"Gramps always says people only swear because their vocabulary is limited."

"'In certain trying circumstances, urgent circumstances, desperate circumstances, profanity furnishes a relief denied even to prayer,'" she said absently.

"What?"

"Mark Twain." Now, had they taken everything from her pockets or just her wallet? "Of course, compared to Kipling, he's a wussy."

He smiled. "Ya know, I think my grandpa would like you. I like you too." He looked shy as a little kid, and her heart ached. How could he endure all this and still show such sweetness?

She cleared her throat. "Well, uh, good." Card...card. She patted her back pockets, felt something stiff in one, and elation bubbled through her. "Look." She pulled the city transit ticket out of her pocket.

Lachlan craned his neck to frown at the little brown card. "Vicki? City transit is good, but I don't think the bus stops at this cage."

She laughed. "Watch and learn, young Skywalker." Carefully, she tore the card into a narrow strip, then ripped some more and folded it into an "M" shape.

"Origami?" Lachlan said doubtfully, "My grandfather might

enjoy it. He likes weird stuff." The, "*I miss him*" was so soft, she almost didn't hear it.

"How does Gramps feel about lock-picking?" She wrapped the heavy paper around one arm of the combination lock, wiggling and shoving the bottom of the "M" into the crevice until she felt the click.

"The Force *is* with us." She yanked the padlock open.

"Fucking A!"

"Don't swear," she said primly and shoved the cage door open. "Let's go."

When he tried to stand, his legs buckled, dropping him back on the floor. He kept trying anyway, struggling for air like a landed fish. Hell, the boy was so thin, she could see his ribcage jerk with each heartbeat. The bastards had almost killed him.

"Kid. Quit. You'll give yourself a heart attack."

"I won't stay here," he gritted out. Shoving his fingers into the wire, he pulled himself a foot toward her. His determination was appalling, yet awe-inspiring. "Even if Swane doesn't do it, I'm dead anyway."

"What the hell does that mean? No, don't tell me. Just shut up." She grabbed his arms and dragged him out, wincing at how the wire floor abraded his fragile skin. With awkward maneuvering, she got him into a fireman's carry. Skinny, yes, but he weighed a ton as she straightened. Pain stabbed into her knee and her head pounded hard enough to blow her skull apart.

The kid didn't move. Had she killed him? No, as the ringing in her ears died down, she heard him wheeze for air. He sounded like hell.

But hey, she wouldn't want to die in a cage either.

The stairs were a nightmare, even when she risked an arm to lean on the rail to keep her knee from buckling. "For someone so skinny, you sure are heavy."

"Sorry. And here I've been trying to lose weight for you."

She grinned. Wise-ass baby—reminded her of herself, cracking jokes when scared spitless. She glanced at the back door, then limped out the front. Her knee wouldn't put up with this abuse long.

The streetlights were coming on, circles of light spilling onto the dark, wet street. The drizzling autumn rain felt wonderful as it washed the sweat from her face. Now what? Steal a car? But there wasn't a vehicle on the street in this damned ritzy neighborhood. All locked away in their fancy two-car garages.

"Time to call the cops," she said, half to herself.

Lachlan jerked, almost knocking himself off her shoulders.

"Don't do that!" She rebalanced him, biting down the groan when his hip dug into her ripped-up shoulder.

"I can't go to a hospital," Lachlan said frantically. "Not me—I can't. I shift if I'm hurt. I'm such a loser," he whispered, the self-disgust pulling sympathy from her. Yeah, she'd felt that way as a kid, always doing something stupid, like when she used her left hand to pass food to an Iranian minister. Father had turned purple.

"Please, Vicki. No cops, no doctors."

"You're awful fussy," she muttered. She picked a direction and started to walk. Jesus, they were screwed.

But she was free. And hey, she'd experienced lots of *situations*, as Wells liked to call them. Trapped in a house about to be blown up, caught snooping by her Iraqi neighbor… "Hang in there, kid." Squeezed the emaciated leg hanging over her shoulder.

Worry bit into her guts as she realized his body had gone truly limp. He needed a hospital and to hell with his shifter paranoia crap. She'd bust him out later if she had to. She headed straight for the nearest house.

With no hands free, she kicked the door in lieu of ringing a doorbell. Politeness was over-rated anyway.

An outside light flipped on, and a man's face appeared in the small viewing window. "Who is it?"

"We were attacked," she returned. "Call an ambulance. Fast. This boy needs help."

After a long minute, the door swung open. "I don't think a robber would be bleeding so enthusiastically," the white-haired man said in a dry voice. "Let's get you out of the rain."

Legs shaking with exhaustion, she staggered after the man, and the room's warmth wrapped around her like a cocoon.

"Sit down, child." He waited until Vic dropped onto the sofa, then laid the kid down next to her.

As he disappeared, Vic slid her legs under Lachlan's shoulders so she could hold him. "Hey, kid."

His eyes blinked open, the unfocused gaze slowly clearing. He stared around the living room. "We got out," he whispered.

"Yeah." Vic couldn't manage more; her throat had tightened to the point of choking. Even awake, he looked bad. Really bad. "We're safe here. He's a nice old man."

"A human? Vicki—promise you won't tell him—tell anyone—about me. Or about shifters. *Ever.*" He clutched her hand, the veins in his neck stood out as he tried to sit up.

"Okay, fine, I promise. No one would believe me anyway."

"Thanks. That's good. This is good." His voice was so soft she had to lean down to hear him. "I really, really wanted to die free—not in a cage."

"I'd rather you lived, damn it," she gritted out as she brushed the drenched hair out of his face.

"I wish." His eyes were very green as he looked up at her. "My body pretty much shut down yesterday. It's a shifter thing; metal's bad for us, and that cage…" His mouth twisted in remembered pain.

"The docs will start IV's, give you blood, fluid, food—you'll be fine."

"No. But it's okay. I knew it was gonna happen." Regret filled his eyes, and he blinked back tears. "My grandfather—he'll be all alone now. He doesn't have anybody but me."

"Live for him," she urged. So many people had died in her arms, she couldn't face another. Not this boy—he wasn't old enough to die. Her chest felt raw and open.

"Not an option." His lips were blue, the color of death. "You got nobody either?"

She shook her head. "No." A couple friends on the other side of the planet. And Wells—could a spymaster be considered family?

"Now you will." He gasped in a breath. "Go to my grandpa, Vicki. In Cold Creek. Tell him what happened to me. Promise?"

"Promise. I'll bring him to you in the hospital." Yeah, she'd find the old man wherever he was. "But you *will* be there, you hear me?"

His forehead wrinkled. "How does it go?"

"What?"

He rubbed the scrapes on his shoulder. His fingers came away blood-streaked. "Fire in blood."

Raising his hand, he wiped his tear-streaked cheek. "Water."

"Lachlan?"

He pursed his lips, puffed on his wet, bloody fingers. "Air."

"What are you doing? Lachlan?" He didn't seem to hear her. Delusional? She'd seen it before with blood loss.

He touched her filthy face and smiled at the dirt. "Earth."

"Honey, I want you to rest," she urged. *Please don't do this to me—live!* For a second, his face blurred into her teammate, gasping her life away, and Vic's arms tightened. *Oh, please, not again.* "Just concentrate on breathing and—"

"And finally my spirit—that's the gift. I remembered it," he told her, pride in his young, young voice. "C'mere." He lifted his arm for a hug. She leaned forward and winced as his dirty fingers dug into her mangled, bleeding shoulder.

A second later, he slid his arm down for a true hug and pulled her close. "Tell Grandpa I gifted you…and you're my gift," he breathed in her ear.

Her arms closed around him. "Dammit, you'll tell him, Lachlan. You'll tell him."

But only silence answered her.

Gone. He was gone.

Vic slumped back on the couch. Her cheeks were wet. Even as she scrubbed her face with her hands, she felt more tears spill from her eyes. What was wrong with her? She never cried.

People died. All the fucking time. She hadn't even known this kid. Tears ran down her cheeks, falling like little explosions of her grief onto Lachlan's empty face.

Footsteps heralded the return of the old man. "I've got—" The rest of his sentence was cut short by the wailing of multiple sirens, approaching rapidly. "I'll go wave them in."

Vic could see the emergency vehicle lights through the thin front window drapes. She slipped out from under Lachlan's body, hesitated long enough to touch his cheek in farewell. His skin was already cooling.

She took a shaky breath and moved away.

At the window, she pushed open a crack in the drapes. Ambulance in front and a cop car across the street. What would law enforcement do with her story? Uncertainty churned inside her. Were Swane's police *buddies* out there?

Paramedics jumped out of the ambulance and were met by the old man. Over at the police car, a uniformed cop was talking with someone. The lights, still flashing, illuminated his grim face and that of…Swane. As the kidnapper talked, the cop nodded and turned toward the house, hand on his pistol.

Oookay. That answered that.

A minute later, as Vic eased over the back fence, she heard

Swane yell, "Where's the girl?"

The thwarted anger in his voice awarded her a moment of pleasure before she landed painfully on the other side of the fence.

Chapter Two

THE NEXT AFTERNOON, Vic steered the decrepit Jeep around a curve and entered Cold Creek. She sighed wearily. Between the slashes on her back and ribs, the bite on her shoulder, her aching knee, and the various blows she'd taken from Swane…well, maybe she'd felt worse the day the house in Baghdad was bombed with her in it, but not by much. God, she hurt.

She hadn't even gotten to beat the hell out of the assholes—that really burned.

Her head felt hot and gritty, like it was filled with desert sand. She probably should have tried to get more sleep, but Seattle didn't feel safe. Not with who-knows-who looking for her. Hopefully they'd stay too busy for a while to focus on her. After her anonymous phone call to the police, the bad guys should be scrambling to cover their tracks. And wasn't that hopeful thinking—they'd probably just abandon the place and the dead woman.

Oh shit. Was she brain-dead or what? That woman and others had died because Lachlan bit them.

Lachlan bit *me*. The good news: with him gone, no more victims would die. At least until they caught another cat-thing.

Bad news: I might die too. Her chest felt hollow. Dying for something so stupid wasn't how she'd planned to go. If she had to check out, it was supposed to be in a blaze of glory, saving her buddies or a bunch of civilians. Not shivering and puking from being used as a feline chew-toy.

Go to a hospital? She shook her head. Swane would watch for someone admitted with an animal bite. She might call Wells for help, but he'd expect the whole story. *Yeah, see, I got bitten by some shapeshifter thing?* She herself barely believed people could turn into animals, and she'd seen Lachlan do it. The old man dealt in cold, hard, provable facts. He'd figure she'd gone bonkers and put her in a padded cell. So, no hospital.

The suit had thought the bitees died because they were in poor health to begin with. *I'm not weak, not poorly nourished. And fuck this shit, I'm not gonna die.*

She gripped the wheel tighter and concentrated on driving. Already the sun was setting, sending its fading rays across the valley and turning the snow-capped mountains a bloody red. The traffic had dissipated after leaving Seattle. Not much going on in Cold Creek, according to the realtor. The town ordinances kept it from growing or even having a McDonald's. The realtor had sounded positively disgruntled.

Vic's smile grew as she drove through the downtown, maybe four blocks long with nary a stoplight in sight. Apparently, the residents had spent their money on the trees and plants in the center island and on antique street lights. People were strolling into the stores, sitting on wrought-iron benches in the shade.

"Toto, I think we're back in Kansas," Vic murmured, unsure if she was pleased or appalled. The peacefulness increased when she turned onto a small street with arching maple and spruce trees, brightly colored flower gardens, white picket fences, and wide front porches.

It was all very civilized until she looked upward to the dense green of an untamed forest. One mountain, then more and more, piling up on each other like blocks scattered by a child. Made sense that werethingies would hang out close to big forests and mountains, right? The thought sent icy fingers up her spine.

She pulled her gaze away and concentrated on following the realtor's directions. A block from Main Street, the sidewalks disappeared. There—*House for Rent, Cold Creek Realty, See Amanda Golden.* The sign was stuck next to a distinctive mailbox in the shape of an outhouse. Outhouse…she could definitely use one of those. That swing through Starbucks had been a poor tactical decision.

The rental was a small brown house with white trim and a wide porch. Unlike the other houses on the street, this place boasted no flowers. Instead, short bushes marked the property lines, and a widely branching oak tree dominated the small, well-trimmed lawn. Looked peaceful enough.

A hotel would have been easier, but who knew how long this might take. She should have asked the kid his last name.

And she'd have to be really discreet. Did the bad guys know Lachlan came from Cold Creek? Would the cops be alerted to watch for her? She wouldn't survive long if they found her. The suit had shown no remorse over what he'd done to the kid, and Swane had reveled in it.

She turned off the ancient Jeep—the only decent car in the cheapo car lot—and the engine died with an ominous sputter. A short, limping walk to the house left Vic out of breath, her legs quivering…and fear creeping into her gut. She'd lost too much blood, taken too much damage. Look at the way her hands were shaking. She couldn't defend herself against a five-year-old child, let alone someone like Swane.

Come to think of it, she wouldn't know who to defend *against*. She closed her eyes and shook her aching head. Coming here without knowing the score was like walking blindfolded into a fire zone. Even so, she wasn't going to leave. Lachlan had trusted her to tell his grandfather what happened.

God, she'd rather face a Bradley tank with a twenty-two pistol than notify someone their kid was dead. Would the old man break down and yell at her like O'Flannagan's parents had? Or be like Shanna's. Her best friend's mother had deflated as if her soul had shriveled away with Vic's words.

Why did people have to die?

At the memory of Lachlan and his courage, his humor, she had to brush the mist from her eyes. Dammit, stop. She could almost hear the drill sergeant's cutting voice, *"You gonna break down and bawl, Morgan? Pick up your weapon and act like a marine!"* She sucked in a breath, and straightened her shoulders.

On the white-railed porch, she glanced longingly at the cushioned wicker chair before rapping on the door. No response. She frowned at her watch. Five-thirty. Right on time. The blasted realtor better hurry, cuz, God, she really, really had to pee. Scowling, she looked around for a secluded nook that would serve for a latrine. Nothing.

Trying not to cross her legs, she studied the house. A screenless front window near the end of the porch was half-open—just calling to her. Really.

She shoved the window open all the way, wishing it was either set lower in the wall or her legs were longer. *Dammit, haven't I done enough calisthenics in the past twenty-four hours?*

Grabbing the window frame with one hand, she jumped up far enough to swing a foot over and grimaced when the movement painfully jostled every fucking owie she had. She tried to pull the other leg over and—dammit—her jeans caught on something sharp. A nail. *Stuck. Fucking-A.* She tugged, feeling the nail dig into her inner thigh.

Why does this stuff only happen when I need to pee?

IGNORING THE WOOD pixie chittering angrily in the oak tree,

Sheriff Alec McGregor silently stepped onto the porch, coming up behind the burglar. He tried not to laugh as the criminal squirmed like a paw-pinned mouse.

It'd been a boring week so far. The last excitement was a good four days ago when old Peterson, having indulged in rotgut tequila, tried to demonstrate how to tap-dance on top of Calum's bar…which he did about once a month.

At least a pinioned burglar had the dubious distinction of being unique.

He rubbed his chin, feeling the rasp of stubble. He'd noticed—being as how he was a guy—what was wiggling was a very fine, nicely rounded ass in tight jeans.

And being a guy, he felt the need to see the front of this dangerous perp who had one leg inside the window and the other outside. He moved silently across the porch and checked out the criminal's front side to see what else the evening might hold.

Evening is going well. Hair, the rich color of dark walnut, rippled across her shoulders, and her purple T-shirt was tight enough to reveal amazingly lush breasts for such a compact body. Since she was too occupied to notice his arrival, he could study her assets without being considered a macho pig. *Abundant.* Yes, that would be the word. He'd heard the *more-than-a-mouthful is wasted* saying, but when it came to breasts, he was a bit of a glutton.

Concentrating on freeing her leg from something, she was oblivious to everything else.

He thought for a minute and decided to speak up. And hey, he needed to see the color of her eyes—for the report and all.

"My jail is empty today," he remarked sociably. "In case you wondered."

She froze like a mouse hearing a fox. When huge copper-colored eyes met his, everything inside him came to a halt, like the day he'd been chasing a rabbit and got his leg caught in a steel trap. A hard painful grip, only this time it was his chest being squeezed.

The sound of her breath whuffing out, like she'd been pounced on, cleared his mind. *Cop—I'm a cop.* And she was a burglar. No pouncing on this little prey allowed…and wasn't that a damned shame?

"Oh, hell," the lady perp said, obviously having recovered fast. She now looked more pissed-off than concerned, and that just wasn't right. "Listen, I'm really just—"

He leaned his hip against the porch railing and crossed his arms. "It's called breaking and entering," he offered helpfully.

Her mouth dropped open. "No way. Hey, I talked to the realtor this morning and—."

"Um-hmm. It's good you've done your homework. Shows a certain pride in your work."

The sparks in those big eyes almost did him in. "I am not a burglar, dammit. I'm here to rent this place. Amanda Golden is supposed to meet me."

He studied her for a minute. She had the realtor's name right—'course it was there plain as could be on the rental sign.

A wisp of scent drifted past him. Blood. Fresh. "You're bleeding."

She blinked at the change of subject and he noticed with pleasure how her thick lashes feathered down against skin tanned almost as dark as her brown eyes.

"I'm bleeding?"

Herne help him, but she really was lovely—and he shouldn't let that pretty face suck him in. She probably wrapped every male she met around her *ringless*, delicate finger.

Besides, she was human. Some shifters enjoyed sampling human females, but he'd never understood the attraction.

He pointed to where a nail had snagged more than her

clothing, and blood darkened the leg of her jeans. "Looks like the previous renter overlooked a few nails from last season's Christmas lights. Let me get you down from there before I start on some serious interrogation."

Her eyes narrowed, then she leaned forward. Reaching out, she obviously intended to steady herself on his forearms, but the opportunity was too good to ignore. With a smooth move, he dropped low enough that her hands settled on his shoulders instead, and he grasped her around the waist. His fingers curled around surprisingly hard abdominal muscles—the female must work out regularly—and he lifted her up.

She gasped as he swung her onto the porch. Her grip tightened on his shoulders, lean hands, not soft, yet they felt very, very good on his body. Her hands would probably clutch his shoulders—just like that—as he slid inside her, filled her.

He shook his head. Where the hell had that image come from?

Her eyes were huge, and she smelled of pain and fear. He released her immediately. She was frightened. And he could tell it was more than just worry about being arrested. No, she was scared of *him*. The idea was insulting.

"Um. Thank you." Her voice was husky.

"My pleasure." After all, honesty was the best policy, and he'd enjoyed the hell out of getting his hands on her. Was looking forward to enjoying more, but…she was scared of *him*?

On the street, a white Taurus pulled up behind the Jeep. Amanda Golden slid out, briefcase in hand, hurried up the sidewalk, and onto the porch. "Hello, Alec. Ms. Waverly? I'm sorry I'm late. I got hung up at the title company."

"That's all right. I've been kept entertained," his ex-burglar said dryly.

"Well, damn, guess I have to let you go." And she would have decorated his jail cell so nicely too.

She shot him a nasty look, her appealingly full lips tightly compressed.

When she started to move, Alec tucked a finger under her belt to halt her. "Let's make sure you aren't hurt too bad," he said. "Nails can be nasty."

As he leaned forward, he realized the faint scent of blood wasn't just from the nail; it came from multiple places. She had dark red-brown spots on the back of her T-shirt. The gasp when he'd lifted her from the windowsill—had that been from surprise or pain?

He studied her closer. Meticulously applied makeup covered a bruise on the side of her face. There was maybe a lumpy dressing on her shoulder under the T-shirt, and something more than a bra wrapped around her sides.

Now, all that damage might be from a car accident. But that wouldn't explain why she was scared of him, the most likable fellow on this planet. So. He could be wrong—frequently was—but he picked the most logical explanation.

Someone had beaten the hell out of her.

"WHERE ELSE ARE you hurt?"

Why would the big sheriff ask that? Vic wondered, feeling a chill. She'd covered the blood and bruises adequately. Had her description and injuries been on an APB?

Dammit, he'd already given her one scare. For a nasty moment, she'd thought Swane had hired him until it became obvious he was just a small-town cop having himself a good time.

"Don't be silly," she said, deliberately misunderstanding. "A little nail scrape doesn't warrant all this concern."

Nudging his arm away, she shook hands with the realtor. "Ms. Golden, nice to meet you."

"Just call me Amanda." Tall, blonde, wearing silky black

pants with matching jacket, she was the epitome of a refined style that Vic had never mastered. After giving Vic's hand a firm shake, the realtor frowned at the cop. "Is there a problem?"

"You got here just in time," Vic said. "Your policeman was about to arrest me and haul me away."

Amanda's snicker wasn't at all businesslike. "Ah, yes. If his jail's not overflowing with criminals, Alec feels he's not doing his job." She leaned forward and whispered loudly, "Of course, it's only a two-cell jailhouse."

Vic smiled and glanced over her shoulder to see how the sheriff took being taunted. With one hip propped on the railing and a lazy grin on his tanned face, he didn't look too upset.

When his focus shifted from Amanda to Vic, his gaze intensified, as if he were trying to see inside her. She felt a quiver low in her belly, but from worry or attraction—she wasn't sure. Probably worry.

Towering six feet five or so with appallingly broad shoulders that narrowed to a trim waist, the man moved like a trained fighter. Not all spit and polish like a Marine though. His golden-brown hair brushed the collar of his khaki-uniform, and he'd rolled his sleeves up, revealing corded wrists and muscular forearms. She remembered how easily he'd lifted her, how those big hands had wrapped around her. He was damned powerful, despite the easy-going manner.

Yeah, the quiver was definitely from worry.

But then he smiled at the realtor, and a dimple appeared at one corner of his mouth. The laugh lines around his eyes emphasized a thin blue-tinted scar that angled across his left cheekbone as if someone had marked him with a pen. His voice was deep and smooth and slow as warm honey, and she felt her muscles relax. "You have a mean streak, Amanda," he was saying. "I'll have to warn Jonah."

"He wouldn't believe you," the realtor said as she worked on unlocking the front door.

The sheriff turned, letting that should-be-a-registered-weapon grin loose on Vic, and her temperature rose. "So," he said, "Ms. Waverly, will you be staying in Cold Creek?"

He was gorgeous, and he looked at her as if she was something tasty. "Um…" she said and his smile increased a fraction, just enough that she realized what an idiot she was. *You're losing it, Sergeant.* She scowled at him. "A while."

And the sooner she left this damn town, the better.

The breeze whipped his shaggy hair "Well, while you're here—" he started.

"I need to get my stuff," she interrupted. Anything to escape. Odd how the scare from the sheriff's appearance had wiped out her need to pee.

To her annoyance, he followed her down the steps. "You're going to enjoy Cold Creek," he said. Before she could dodge, he slung an arm around her shoulders, and she felt his fingers trace the thick gauze dressing covering the cat-bite.

"Thank you, but I can manage," she said, smoothly enough despite the way her heart was pounding. Then she looked up.

Dark green eyes the color of the mountain forests narrowed, and he studied her like she was a puzzle to be solved. A quiver ran up her spine as she realized the laidback manner and slow voice camouflaged a razor-sharp intelligence. Knives tended to come at a person in two ways: dark and hidden, or out in the open, all bright and shiny. A bright and shiny blade could still leave you bleeding on the sands.

She pulled away. "I'll be fine."

"Well then, I'll take myself off so you can get settled in." He waved at Amanda Golden and smiled at Vic, but this time the smile didn't touch his eyes. "I'm sure we'll run into each other again, Ms. Waverly. Cold Creek's a small town."

Cordial, polite. And Vic heard the threat underneath.

ALEC SHOVED OPEN the heavy door to the Wild Hunt Tavern, picked his favorite table in the back corner, and settled into the chair for some serious pondering.

That had been an odd meeting and an odd woman. Over many years of law-enforcement, he'd arrested a few wife-beaters and interviewed their battered wives. Ms. Waverly's injuries might have come from a fist, but she surely didn't give the impression of an abused woman. That glare she'd given him, for whatever reason, was almost lethal.

Actually, the woman's moods, within the space of ten minutes, had been as winding as a tornado. From being wary of him, to being attracted, to giving him a look like: *I'll cut your guts out with a rusty spoon.* She might be a foot shorter, but he had a feeling she'd be quite a wildcat in a fight. And in bed.

Now why did he find that so arousing?

"Excuse me, Sheriff, would you care for a beer?"

He looked up into the prettiest blue eyes on the planet and grinned. "Jamie, if you fetch me a beer, I'll have to arrest your thirteen-year-old butt and throw you into my jail."

She wrinkled a freckle-covered nose. "I won't bring it— Daddy will, so I guess you still won't have anyone in your jail tonight, huh?"

"Now that was a low blow," he conceded, winning himself a delighted smile before she trotted off to the bar, all legs and bounce like a half-grown cat.

A few minutes later, Calum set a mug of Guinness and a glass of wine on the table, then took the empty chair.

Alec tilted his head toward his niece as she danced her way between customers. "I envy you sometimes, *brawd.*"

His brother turned to look, and his gray eyes softened. "Indeed. She's a blessing." He sipped his wine, his gaze intent on his daughter. "And makes me afraid in ways I never thought I could fear."

Alec took a drink of the rich, malty beer before commenting, "You're not the type to shy from leaves blowing in the wind. What's up?"

"I summoned the Daonain to meet tonight."

Alec's hand tightened on the mug. Shifter meetings were rarely called. He bowed his head to the God-chosen leader of the shifters in this territory and said formally, "Cosantir, I'll be there."

THAT NIGHT, ALEC rested one arm on the fireplace mantle as he listened to the debate. Despite the chill of the evening, the tavern felt uncomfortably warm, and the scent of anger and sweat mixed with the wood smoke. Golden light from the brass wall sconces flickered over the people squeezed around the heavy oak tables and lining the back. Seemed like any adult shifter in the Northern Cascades territory had attended.

After Calum had told them about the outlawed steel-jawed game traps that shifters had found in the forests, and that Thorson's grandson had been missing for a month, the mood had turned ugly. No surprise there. Daonain were predators, after all. The werecats were the worst. A wolf or bear might fight if cornered; a cat would shred an opponent to bloody ribbons just for entertainment.

After Calum shot down Grady's proposal to attack any human entering the area—Grady was rather excitable—Angelina claimed the floor. Alec listened for a minute, grinning at his brother's careful lack of expression. Calum had little patience for stupidity, and Angelina's logic was as convoluted as a house-brownie's tracks on cleaning day.

"We don't know if the trappers are after us specifically or just poaching," Calum said, cutting Angelina off before she could digress further. He straightened from leaning on the bar, and the power of a Cosantir shimmered around him like heat waves. "If they're looking for us, I'll be happy to oblige them. After that, they won't remember why they were on the mountain at all."

The people laughed, and the level of hostility waned. Calum reminded them, "We've become lazy about observing the precautions. That needs to stop. Use the tunnels below the tavern. I want no humans to find piles of clothing at the edge of the forest, let alone to see one of you shift. Also, remember—"

The bar door burst open, and Joe Thorson shoved his way through the crowd to the center of the room. Deep lines and gray bushy brows accented his leathery face. Thin white scars covered his hands and arms—souvenirs of his younger days when he'd fought to win the females at Gatherings. Tears had tracked the dirt on his face.

Dread iced Alec's blood. What could possibly make the old werecat cry? *Lachlan?* He pushed his way to the maddened werecat. *To serve and protect.* The duty given to a sheriff by the law…and the duty given to a *cahir* of the clan by the God.

After giving Thorson a second to recognize his scent, Alec wrapped an arm around his shoulders. With only a token snarl, the old man allowed the familiarity, yet another sign of his distress.

"What's wrong, Joe?" Alec kept his tone calm as the raised voices hushed.

"My grandson—Lachlan," Thorson's voice was hoarse. "He's dead. Killed in the city."

The noise rose. Males lunging to their feet. Angelina's shrill scream. The Murphy brothers' curses.

Calum growled low, then snapped, "*Silence.*" The command with a Cosantir's power behind it quieted the room. "Tell us what happened, Joe."

In his usual jeans and white shirt, Thorson rubbed his face, streaking the dirt. "That shifter detective in Seattle—Tynan O'Connolly—just called. Like you asked, he'd watched for Lachlan in Seattle. He said…" His voice broke. "There was a young man's body in the morgue."

Alec raised an eyebrow at Calum, silently requesting permission to continue. Calum nodded.

"Go on, Joe," Alec prompted, squeezing his shoulder.

Thorson shook his head like a confused animal. "The cops haven't identified him, but they're trying, passing out pictures. Tynan emailed me one. It's my Lachlan." His words dropped like stones into the quiet room.

"Did you go to the morgue in Seattle?" Alec asked quietly despite the unease fingering the back of his neck. An autopsy wouldn't show the magic that created a shifter, but carelessness would. If Thorson's actions exposed the shifters, he'd be declared an enemy of the Daonain…and as a cahir, Alec would have to kill him.

"I never went near the station."

Relief loosened Alec's grip, and he pulled in a hard breath. "By the God, I'm sorry, Joe. Sorry for Lachlan, sorry for you, that you can never—"

"Never put claim to him or bury him. I know, dammit." Thorson stared at the floor.

Calum said, "I'll call Tynan for more information, but for now—has he discovered how Lachlan died?"

Thorson's head snapped up, his eyes burning with fury. Against his fingertips, Alec felt the tingle of imminent trawsfur. He shook the old man's arm. "Control yourself. We need answers, not claws."

When Thorson growled, Alec tensed, preparing to fight a berserk cougar.

After a moment, Thorson sucked in a breath, and the tingling receded, disappeared. As the wildness left his body, his eyes showed his shame. The old guy probably hadn't lost control like that since he was a cub. "Sorry, my friend," he said softly.

"It's all right," Alec answered, equally softly. "Tell us what you know."

Sorrow deepened the lines in Joe's face, and he had to clear his throat. "He looked starved. Ribs showing. Tynan said he was jaundiced from liver shutdown."

"Metal-induced?" Alec asked.

"Yes." The man's fingers curled, shaping claws.

Alec shared the need to slash and rend. The pain of that kind of death... Instead, he squeezed the tight shoulder under his hand. "Stay with me here, Joe."

A heavy breath. "He had burn marks, cuts, bruises. He'd been beaten. Tortured. Some of the cuts were in square patterns on his skin."

"Wire cage," Calum growled. His pupils had turned black with a Cosantir's rage. "That would explain the liver failure, too."

"They kept my boy in a cage!" The words burst from Thorson. "They tortured him, starved him." He moaned, "A cage, Cosantir, a cage ..."

"They will pay," Calum said quietly. "Was Lachlan penned up when they found him?"

Thorson shuddered, staring at the floor, and Alec knew the man couldn't bear much more. He needed the forest, to feel the trees and grass and scent of freedom, to have the Mother's love around him. "Tynan thinks Lachlan escaped," Joe said. "But too late. A man found my boy and a female on his doorstep and took them in, then called 911."

"Did—"

"When the police and ambulance arrived, Lachlan was dead. The female ran out through the back door."

"Hell," Alec muttered.

Finally, Thorson looked up at their leader. The old man had known Calum and Alec since they were boys sneaking reads of comic books in his store, but he showed no memory of that now. As close as he was to changing, he probably only saw the black eyes and the aura of power. "Cosantir, please. I need—"

"We can manage here, Joe," Calum said. "Purge your grief on the mountain. Alec, go with."

As Thorson stumbled toward the exit, hands reached out to him—carefully—to stroke in shared sorrow and friendship.

Alec led him into the cool, silent cave like a child. Without speaking, they stripped, Alec lending a hand as Thorson fumbled. Then, Alec called the magic. As the wildness enveloped him, his mind sank like a stone, deep into animal instincts. There was only *now*, and the sorrow at the youngster's loss was buried under the wave of scents and sounds. And this was why Thorson needed the forest. His grief would return when he returned to human form, but…less.

As his paws hit the earth, Alec felt the touch of the Mother as Her love flowed into him. Raising his head, he sniffed the air. Already in cougar form, Thorson stood in the doorway. Alec butted his shoulder affectionately and led the way out of the tunnel.

The light of a pale, cold moon shone down outside the cave, and the scent of the pine needles under their paws rose around them. Alec looked back to see the gleam of cat eyes and then sprang forward into the dark forest. Joe followed.

VIC WOKE, DIDN'T move while she assessed her surroundings. Warm, smooth fabric over and under her, a faint lemon scent—sheets. She lay in a bed. A bed was good, much better than concrete.

Where? The new rental. Lord, her brain was moving slow. The house stood silent. No stench of gunpowder or sweat or blood. Things were looking up. She opened her eyes…and winced. The curtains glowed in the morning sun, the print a garish display of lions and tigers and bears.

"Toto, we really gotta get out of this place," Vic muttered and slid her legs over the side of the bed with a loud indulgent groan. Jesus fuck, she hurt. She rubbed her face. Was she really planning to look for people who turn into animals? In the light of day, the idea sounded insane. She didn't believe that shit, did she? Then again, the bite and claw marks on her body offered pretty good proof.

And speaking of claw marks, it was time to take inventory; easy to do when you sleep commando:

One: a headache throbbing like a ghetto blaster with the bass on high. The room felt like a sauna. Great, she had a fever.

Two: her left shoulder felt like some lion had ripped a chunk out of it. *Oh, wait—that's what had happened.* Considering the way her week had been going, she probably had gangrene. She pessimistically peeked under that bandage. Well, halleluiah, no putrid green gunk, but the surrounding redness showed a brewing infection.

Three: Under the gauze wrap, Lachlan's claw marks on her back and sides looked like a red-streaked geometry lesson: *parallel lines do not intersect*. And wouldn't *those* be cute scars…but they weren't infected.

Four: She sucked in a deep breath and groaned as unseen knives stabbed into her left side. Cracked ribs. Alas, no cure for them except time. And *revenge*. She looked forward to a rematch with the ape called Swane—and they would meet again, count on it—when she'd kick *his* ribs in.

Five: her right knee ached, but thank you, God, she could put weight on it and not fall-down-go-boom like some spastic cripple.

I'm alive. Life is good.

As she headed across the bedroom, she snorted a laugh. The same maniac had bought both the curtains and wallpaper. On the walls, deer and elk wandered through the forest like *Bambi gone wild.* "You'd better hope the lions stay on the drapes or you're all breakfast," she warned the herbivores, then shook her head. Bad enough to be talking to herself. Conversing with the wall? Next stop, psycho ward.

A shower cleared her head. She ignored the rainbow trout swimming along the bottom of the blue shower curtain. Thank God the sunny kitchen and living room lacked the wildlife obsession. No coffee though.

"Must go shopping." She couldn't do anything without a full load of caffeine—and some ibuprofen for the pain and fever.

First, she needed to call her handler. The old man got cranky if he didn't know where his agents were, even the ones on medical leave. Taking a chair at the small kitchen table, she pulled out her new cell phone and punched in the numbers.

"Wells." Voice low but edged. Typical Wells—speak softly, then gut them with a sharp knife.

Didn't it just figure that he'd actually answer his phone this time? She'd have preferred voice mail—recordings never asked awkward questions. "Sir." A nonchalant tone, that's the ticket. "I'm getting out of the city and heading into the mountains. Might be out of touch for a while."

"Is there a problem, Morgan?"

"No, sir. Well, come to think of it…" Excellent lead-in, not too pushy. "Perhaps one thing."

"Go on."

Here it got tricky. Dammit, she'd never lied to him, and doing so felt like gravel in an open wound. "I had a drink with an old buddy from Afghanistan. She told me about an ex-marine named Swane."

"Swane." She heard the scratch of his pen as he wrote the name. More anal than a proctologist, Wells jotted everything down. Hell of annoying at first, until she'd learned other people often forgot stuff…like the moron last year who'd forgotten the GPS quadrants for the pickup zone and her best friend had died. She swallowed. *Stay on track, Marine.*

"What is the problem—I assume there is one—with this individual?" Wells asked.

"Seems he's torturing homeless people and using a cop contact for the cover-up. Doesn't look good, sir, to have a screwed-up marine loose in Seattle." After a few scandals involving recently discharged Marines and violent altercations, the military was walking on eggshells. Although this wasn't in Wells' area, he'd still do something.

A grunt. "No, that's not good. Your buddy's name is…?"

"I'd rather not say, sir. I don't want to betray a confidence."

Silence. She knew what he was thinking. Duty to your country outweighed any other loyalty, including what you owed to your friends. But she'd made a promise to Lachlan. Unless the shifters were dangerous, she wouldn't put them in Wells' sights.

"All right, Sergeant. I'm not in-country, but I'll look into it when I return."

In spite of the pain, she grinned. Getting Wells onboard was siccing a pit bull on a poodle. "Thank you, sir. I'll be in touch. Good—"

The line clicked. Wells never said *goodbye.* He thought it sounded like a curse, so he saved his *farewells* for his enemies.

"Goodbye, Swane," she said cheerfully. "Bye-bye, Mr. Asshole-Suit. 'Parting is such sweet sorrow'."

Yeah, if anyone could find these guys, Wells could. The first time she'd seen him, she'd been doing sit-ups to burn off her anger at being turned down for combat duty. She looked up at this man. Older than her father. Sharp nose, icy clear blue eyes, tailored clothing like some English aristocrat. He'd watched her for a minute, before giving her a thin smile. "I hear you want to join the fighting in Iraq."

She'd frozen halfway through a sit-up as he said, "If you don't mind wearing civilian clothes, I can promise you all the danger you'll ever want, and that your work will make a difference." He'd won her over with his final words. "I need you, Morgan."

He'd kept his promise then and always. She could safely leave the kidnappers to him.

Time to go shopping. But when she rose from the table, her headache went ballistic. Then dizziness hit, a riptide sucking at her consciousness. Dropping back on the chair, she shook her head. Oh, this wasn't good at all. Fucking-A, was she going to die like that old woman?

As she staggered into the living room, sweat broke out on her skin like she was in the fucking desert. But her legs crumbled under her, and she hit the floor hard. God! Everything hurt so bad she didn't know what to hold first. *Just shoot me now.*

"LORD, LOOK DOWN on Thy Servant! Bad things have come to pass.

There is no heat in the midday sun, nor health in the wayside grass.

His bones are full of an old disease—his torments run and increase.

Lord, make haste with Thy Lightnings and grant him a quick release!"

AFTER A MINUTE of not moving, she groaned and tried to push to her feet. Her stomach turned over, bile flooding her mouth. Werecat bites—not for the faint of heart.

Chapter Three

WELL, WELL, WELL, Alec thought as he strolled down Main Street. *Here's an unanticipated gift.* In front of the bookstore was the pretty woman he'd almost managed to arrest last week. Not being in any particular hurry, Alec stuck his hands in his pockets and leaned against a wrought-iron streetlight to enjoy the view. Seemed like that long, wavy brown hair was just begging for a man to bury his fingers in it. The silky strands rippled against her tightly rounded butt, something else that would fill his hands nicely.

The same breeze ruffling her hair brought him the scent of illness, a tad acrid, yet sweet. So she *had* been sick. He'd wondered…

He'd driven by her house now and then over the past few days. Leaves had built up on the hood of her car. If the lights inside hadn't moved from room to room, he'd have worried she'd died in there, so it was a relief to see her, not only alive, but out and about.

Yet, even as she innocently perused the bookstore display, she made his instincts twitch like a mouse scenting a wolf in the underbrush. He'd even run her name last week, but no priors had popped up. Hell, *nothing* had come up. So if she'd been beaten up by a husband or a mugging, she hadn't reported it.

Then, again, maybe she wasn't innocently perusing, maybe she was casing the joint, planning to break in. Make off with all of Thorson's cherished classics, or even the steamy romances favored by ninety-year-old Miss Evangeline.

Couldn't allow that kind of crime in his quiet town. *As a dedicated officer of the law, I must take action immediately.* Pushing off the pole, he wandered closer, still enjoying the sight of her backside, at least until he looked up.

She was studying his reflection in the bookstore window. Herne help him. How long had she watched him ogle her ass? Maybe she'd just caught sight of him?

She turned and the decidedly unfriendly expression on her face killed that hope.

Brazen it out? *Good afternoon and I couldn't help admiring your ass?* Unfortunately, she didn't seem to be a female who'd appreciate that type of honesty. He held his hand out instead. "We meet again, Ms. Waverly. How have you been?"

She didn't look any more thrilled this time than she had the last time they'd met. This outright dislike could give a man a complex.

"Good afternoon, Sheriff." She didn't answer his question, obviously hoping to stop the conversation dead. Now, that might work…if he was anyone but Alec McGregor, renowned for never being at a loss for words.

He tilted his head slightly. "It's good you didn't say, 'I've been fine', since you don't seem like you've been fine at all." And that wasn't bullshit. She looked like hell. Her pallor had turned her dusky complexion almost yellow. She had dark circles under her eyes. Lost a few pounds too, leaving her high cheekbones standing out like boulders in a meadow. "Have you been ill?"

Despite the annoyance in her eyes, she gave an inaudible sigh and answered, "I apparently picked up some flu bug. This is my first day out of bed."

"Now, that's a shame. New to the town and you probably didn't have anyone you could call to help you out." He'd seen no other cars in front of the rental house.

"I managed," she said, briefly and added an insincere, "Thank you." She turned her gaze back to the store, obviously hoping he'd take the hint and leave.

A pity he wasn't skilled in the nuances of polite society. He leaned against the plate glass. "You planning to break into the bookstore now? Continue your life of crime?"

"Listen, I wasn't breaking in. I rented that house, remember?"

He scratched his neck, worked up a befuddled look. "Oh. I forgot."

That might have been a curse she muttered under her breath before saying, "Well, since you're here, I wanted to buy a book—and what kind of business name is this anyway? BOOKS."

Alec grinned. "Thorson, the owner, doesn't believe in fancying things up."

"No shit." She scowled. "None of the lights are on inside. It's three o'clock on a Saturday. I've heard of short business hours, but this is ridiculous." The edge of annoyance in her voice was sharp as a blade.

"The owner's out of town for a couple weeks. Need a book, do you?"

"Well, duh," she muttered. "Yes. I like to read. Any suggestions?"

"Weeell," Alec drawled, just to see sparks glint in those big brown eyes like solar flares that'd fry anything in their path. The woman needed to mellow out a tad, or her pretty hair would turn gray. "The library is open Monday through Friday."

"That doesn't exactly help me today."

"Baty's Grocery usually has a few books."

"Five—count'em—five paperbacks off the best-seller list, and I've already read four and wouldn't read the last if you paid me." She stopped and considered. "Not even then."

"Now, Seattle would have a dozen bookstores—"

"My Jeep's dead."

"Not been a good day for you, has it?" he said, sympathetically.

"Hell, it's been a crappy *week*," she exploded. Then she laughed—the first time—and his heart slammed right up against his ribcage. Damn, but there was something about her that yanked at him.

"The auto shop will have my car running by tomorrow." She sighed. "But I don't have a television or anything to read. I can survive without a TV, but no books? I may die."

"Have a dead body cluttering up my streets? Can't be tolerated." He could only wish that needy expression had been for his attention, dammit.

He moved to stand beside her, unsurprised when she unconsciously stiffened. The girl had rigid lines defining her personal space. Too rigid. Leaning forward, his shoulder rubbed pleasantly against hers as he pointed toward the end of Main, then up-slope to the Wild Hunt. "My brother lives above his tavern and has several walls of books. If you sweet-talked him,"—he fixed her with a stern look—"not, I add, like the poor effort you've shown me so far, you might wangle a loan of a couple of books."

"Thank you, Sheriff," she said, surprised, but sincere. Then she smiled and added in a sultry, way too suggestive tone, "I'll try my best to sweet-talk your brother."

"Oh, hell," he muttered. Why the hell had he scheduled an interview in five minutes?

Her laugh was low and throaty as amusement turned her

copper-colored eyes to gold.

He was a dead man.

VIC STOPPED JUST inside the Wild Hunt Tavern to let her eyes adjust from the bright afternoon light. After a moment, she could see the round oak tables scattered across the wide room. An alcove off to the right contained a couple of pool tables and a jukebox with the usual garish lights. Two couches sat in front of a massive fireplace on the left wall. A long dark bar ran the length of the back with a mirror behind it. Automatically she catalogued escape routes: picture windows at front and sides, the back wall to the left had a doorway to the restrooms and kitchen and exit.

Not a bad place. No blood stains were visible on the dark hardwood floor, the jukebox was playing soft country music, and the smell of beer vied with the appealing scent of roasted peanuts.

Trying to ignore the ache in her knee, she strolled past a center table seating three rednecks, probably the drivers for the rigs taking up most of the parking lot. Two men were playing pool. A young college-aged couple by the fireplace held hands and talked quietly, totally enmeshed in their own little world.

Vic frowned and checked the room again. Where was the sheriff's brother? Or a waitress at least. She slid onto a wooden bar seat. And waited a full minute. Then grabbed a handful of peanuts as a reward for being patient and all that shit. But she owed the deceptively easy-going sheriff a thank you for giving her an excuse to meet a local. It didn't usually take long to get to know who had information in a town, and who liked to talk. This was an excellent start.

As she cracked peanuts and practiced patience, two of the truckers tossed several dollar bills onto their table and left.

Vic drummed her fingers on the bar. Didn't anyone work in this joint?

Finally a youngster hurried out from the kitchen, wiping her hands on a white apron worn over faded jeans. Sun-colored hair and a British Isle's complexion, and—Vic frowned—no way was this kid over twenty-one. The girl checked the room, stopping to talk with the people by the fireplace.

The remaining trucker, a big man with a florid face, pushed himself to his feet with a grunt of effort. After a furtive glance at the underage waitress, he picked up the money left on the table and lurched toward the door.

The girl looked at the table, and her mouth dropped open. "Hey! You took my tips!" She ran after the trucker and circled to stand in front of him, a chihuahua confronting a rottweiler.

He glared. "Didn't do nothin'.Get outta my way, kid."

"Give me back my money." Hands on hips, the girl had the bravado of a child who'd never been seriously hurt.

That kid was about to learn a really hard lesson. Vic scowled as she eased off the bar stool and crossed the room. And how dumb was this? She hadn't even healed up from the last fight.

The bastard actually swung at the girl.

Almost too late, Vic slammed her forearm into his, knocking his punch to one side. The kid squeaked in shock and back-pedaled quickly. 'Bout time.

So. Stand down and let him go? Naw, letting the asshole steal from a baby didn't sit right. "Give the kid back her money, and your afternoon won't be ruined," Vic said softly.

"Get the fuck out of my way, or I'll smash your face." He waved a beefy fist at her.

Vic pushed the little girl farther away and out of the field of fire. Across the room, the other bar occupants were moving to assist.

She didn't need or want help. "Oooo, now I'm scared."

His face turned beet red as his anger overcame his brain—whatever brain he had. Probably not much bigger than his dick. He let out a roar and swung.

Perfect. Vic moved six inches.

His fist hit the door. "Fuck!" Shaking his hand, he reeled back.

While he was distracted, Vic plucked the money out of his undamaged hand. After opening the door, she stood in the opening, waving the dollar bills tauntingly.

He lunged at her. "Bitch, you're gonna—"

That widdle brain probably couldn't think of a word nasty enough, Vic figured, and she moved out of the way again. Well, almost out of the way. She did happen to stick her foot out. And maybe lift it a little to improve the guy's dive.

What a great dive. Face first into the pavement. "Ouch," Vic said sympathetically, leaning on the open door. "I bet that hurt."

"Yes, I would assume it did," said a deep, cold voice next to her.

Her hands coming up in a defensive move, Vic spun to face the man. Black clothing, leanly muscular, chiseled features, forbidding expression. *Mr. Tall-Dark-and-Deadly.* She hadn't even heard him approach. Dammit, nobody moved that quietly.

He eased two steps back. "Pardon me. I was simply admiring your work. Bloody fine job."

Vic was taken in by the calm tone until she met his gaze. His pupils were black with fury.

"Well. Thank you." A little unnerved, she turned to check the trucker, but he was alive although staggering.

The girl peeked out of the door, saw her assailant retreating, and grabbed Vic around the waist for a hug. As her ribs threatened to cave in, Vic managed not to scream—somehow—though the world spun like a top.

"Oh, thank you! I was, like, really, really scared," she babbled as Vic tried to escape. The girl had a grip like a plumber's wrench.

"Here's your money," Vic gasped, handing over the dollar bills in exchange for being released.

"Jamie." The man said the girl's name, uninflected, just the name, and, shoving the money into her pocket, the child turned to stand military straight in front of…her father?

He was a good six-three, with black hair and a dark complexion where Jamie was short and fair. The kid's features looked nothing like his, and boy, her impulsive attitude was nothing like his. The man was like a volcano filled with molten magma controlled by thick rock walls. The trucker should be grateful Vic got to him first—this guy would have *incinerated* him.

Jamie stared at her feet. "I'm sorry, Daddy. I just wanted my money."

"Indeed. And did confronting a drunk work well for you?"

"I—I didn't think he'd get so mad." Her voice was only a whisper. "I was scared."

Just when Vic had decided the father was a real asshole, he wrapped the little girl in his arms. "So was I, Jamie, so was I."

Vic bit her lip as her insides turned to mush. Fucking-A, she'd turned into a wimp. Time for a quiet retreat. She glanced at the shaken young couple in the middle of the room, received a thumbs-up from the pool players closer to the door. Rubbing her ribs, she eased away.

The mission had been fun, but not exactly a success—no books, dammit. After letting the door close behind her, she made it partway across the parking lot when she heard the man's voice. "Stop." The "please" that followed seemed to an afterthought.

Vic hesitated. Aftermaths, thank yous, and all that shit tended to suck.

But the kid moved faster than a cockroach in the light and

planted herself square in Vic's path. "Daddy wants to talk to you."

Vic sighed. Knocking munchkins ass-over-teakettle just wasn't done. She reversed direction with Jamie skipping beside her.

The man held his hand out, his dark eyes intent on hers. "My name is Calum McGregor. This is my bar." His fingers were callused, firm, and very strong. "Thank you for helping my daughter."

"I'm Victoria Waverly. And she shouldn't be left alone in your bar," Vic said bluntly.

"No, she shouldn't." Narrowed eyes the color of slate turned toward his daughter.

The kid's head went down again. "I'm sorry, Daddy. I saw the men leave and I wanted my tip. I didn't want that man to take my money."

"Jamie, he nearly flattened you."

"I'm sorry," she whispered.

Vic smothered a smile. Neat trick the girl had, turning a man into a marshmallow. *I should take notes.*

"We'll talk at supper tonight," he said as Jamie pulled the door open. Just when the girl probably thought she'd escaped reprisal, he added, "Before then, please determine what punishment you think would be appropriate."

Heaving a sigh, Jamie disappeared inside.

"She wasn't expecting that one," Vic said in approval.

"Indeed." The man tucked his fingers under Vic's arm, steered her firmly across the room, and settled her at the bar. "What can I get you to drink?"

"Just water, please."

He set a bottled water and glass in front of her and leaned his elbow on the counter. "Is there a way in which I might repay you for saving my daughter?"

Vic almost asked for a book, then reconsidered as she opened the water and took a sip. She needed information about the shifter beasts. She needed to find Lachlan's grandfather. What better place to do recon than the local—and only—tavern? "I'd like a job."

"A JOB?" CALUM felt as if the little female had punched him.

Hire a *human*? In his tavern? He'd offered repayment for balance. The *Law of Reciprocity* had to be observed, even if with a human. He'd expected her to wave his gesture away or name a monetary amount. But employment? He was trapped in a net of his own making. "Let me think."

She nodded and sipped her water peacefully, the least anxious job applicant he'd ever seen. He studied her for a minute, taking in the diminutive body—maybe five-four—trim, but shapely with especially fine breasts. Big eyes, long hair that made a man want to tangle his fingers in it, full lips…a lethal little package, in more ways than the trucker had discovered.

He opened a bottle of water for himself, buying time. Two problems arose. The first—the door to the forest tunnels was in the hallway. Would she notice shifters using it? Probably not. She'd spend most of her time in the main room, and the hall also held the restrooms and back exit so there was a reason for people being in that area.

Secondly, how would his shifter customers react to a human employee?

A handful of shifters—especially the older ones—hated humans. Unfortunately for them, unless they wanted to live completely isolated or in Elder Village without amenities, they had to rub shoulders with humans. He looked across the room to where Tom and Pedro were playing pool. They would be no problem. In fact, most of the Daonain wouldn't care what species the waitress was so long as the drinks arrived in an expeditious manner. They might even be pleased since he'd been short-handed since Tiffany had returned to college last month.

For the human haters… It helped she was female. With the scarcity of female Daonain, women were revered, and that regard would likely be extended to this human.

"Miss Waverly," he said, drawing her attention. "I don't have any need for kitchen help. However, although I already have a waitress, I could use a part-timer." He hesitated and cautioned, "The bar can occasionally get rather rough. Perhaps—"

"It sounds perfect." She toasted him with her bottle. "Waitress and bouncer combined in one."

His jaw dropped. "You do not understand. That was a warning."

She tilted her head, and her lips quirked.

He brought to mind the efficient way she'd dealt with the trucker. No noise during the altercation, no hysterics after. "Indeed, what was I thinking? Your hours would be seven to eleven on Tuesday and Wednesday, four to two-thirty on Friday and Saturday. I pay standard wages; you keep all your tips."

She held out her hand. "Works for me."

He took her hand, feeling the calluses on the delicate fingers. She was no stranger to work…or to fighting. "Where did you learn to fight like that?"

"I studied martial arts for a while."

"Apparently you were an excellent student. Yes, I believe we have an accord. You may start Friday."

"Great. Now that's out of the way—is there any chance I can borrow a book?"

WHAT AN EXCELLENT day—some fun beat-up-the-bad-guy exercise, a new job, a good book. With a wiggle of content, Vic settled herself in the comfortable swing on her front porch and picked up her paperback. A Clancy. Amazing how much the author knew, considering he'd never done covert ops. Maybe she should take notes.

She put her good leg up on the railing with a grunt of pain and sat back carefully. Her ribs were fine until she moved, then it felt as if someone was shoving a buck knife into her side.

Oh, well. She had coffee steaming on the adjacent small table, a book, a comfy swing, and the sun was warm on her legs. The scent of damp grass mingled with a cool piney breeze off the looming mountain, and she didn't start work until tomorrow. Aside from the fact she had a battered body, had lied to her boss, still had to tell some old guy his grandkid was dead, and needed to investigate weird beastie things that looked the same as normal people, life was perfect.

Taking a sip of coffee, she swirled it in her mouth and hummed in pleasure. Coffee and chocolate—the inventor of mocha should be sainted.

As she tipped the cup up, movement in the big oak tree caught her attention, and she tensed, then relaxed. Not a sniper—branches weren't thick enough—but what was it? No flutter of wings, no bushy tail. Maybe a cat?

Keeping a wary eye on the tree, she set the swing to gently rocking and dropped the book into her lap. Despite all her preparation, she couldn't concentrate on reading. Too much hung over her head.

Could Lachlan's remains have been returned to his family? The local police and ambulance crews had been on-site, so she doubted Swane could spirit Lachlan's body away. The coffee turned bitter on her tongue as guilt slashed through her. *You don't abandon your teammates, dammit.*

But she wasn't a Marine now. In black ops, there were no teammates.

Concentrate on finding Lachlan's grandfather. Surely the people here would talk about the kid, whether they thought he was missing or knew he was dead. So just listening might work, even if it took longer.

And what better place for gossip than a bar? She grinned. That had been righteous good luck, being in the right spot to play hero and score a job. It had been good luck for the little girl as well. Vic's gut tightened at how the trucker had swung at Jamie. *I should have drop-kicked his balls over the nearest truck.* Then again, his face had met the pavement hard enough to turn it into hamburger. That would have to do.

Forcing the tension out of her muscles, she tilted her head back. The puffy white clouds above were piling up against the mountains and growing darker. Probably would storm tonight. Did werecats run around in the rain?

She sure didn't know. *How the hell am I going to do this?* Okay, she could track mountain lions in the woods, but when she found one, how could she tell if it was a shifter or a real cat? She touched her still-tender shoulder and grimaced. Considering she'd discovered, up close and personal, just how friendly mountain lions were when pissed off, that didn't sound like the plan of the week.

Hunting cougars in the woods is out.

How about searching for shifters in their human form? Not much easier. Like she could run around with a cattle prod and zap townsfolk until one turned all furry? She snorted. Aside from upsetting the local populace, that overly clever sheriff might not warm to the idea. He was already too focused on her and her business.

She remembered too well how he'd studied her with those dark green eyes… Hell, he'd watched her like a kitten watched an ant, waiting for the right moment to pounce.

She pulled in a long breath at that thought—the sheriff

pouncing on her, pouncing and then bouncing, that firm mouth on hers, that long muscular body. Just the way he moved—like a warrior—set her insides quivering. Guys like him were hell in a fight and totally the best in bed.

After a sigh, she sucked down some coffee. *Been a long dry spell, eh, Vics?* She hadn't had any fun since…when had it been? Ah, the hunky intern in Walter Reed Hospital. Too young to maintain a decent conversation, but *ohh-rah*, he was built, and that was all she ever looked for.

Funny how that worked. A close call left her with this…need…to prove she was alive. And nothing demonstrated that faster than sex.

But not this time. A quick fuck with the sheriff might win some information, but would be as dangerous as poking at a rattlesnake. She had a feeling his curiosity wouldn't diminish with a bout in bed. Probably the reverse.

Ah, well. With a disappointed sigh, she picked up her coffee. Damn but being a good Marine sucked sometimes.

Okay, cougar baiting, whether human or kitty, was out. She'd just have to treat this as a straight information-gathering mission. Let the gossip, the facts, everything flow in without trying to divert it in any one direction, and then filter out the good stuff and see where it led. Lachlan had said there were more shifters here. If so, eventually she'd get an idea how to track them down.

So. I have a plan.

And hey, she had an actual job too. She glanced over at the mountain and tried to locate where the tavern perched just above the town. It was right about—Something in the oak tree rustled the leaves again. The nearest branches bent down, almost touching the porch, and as she watched, a tiny hand the size of a dime snatched an acorn and disappeared.

Chapter Four

L ATE FRIDAY AFTERNOON as the sun sank behind the mountains, Vic hurried across the sparsely filled parking lot and shivered as the frigid wind went right through her clothes. Damn cold town, especially after sunset. She needed to buy herself a jacket.

She pulled open the heavy oak door of the Wild Hunt, and groaned happily as warmth wrapped around her. The room wasn't too crowded yet. A few scattered people sat at tables. The small couches by the fireplace were both occupied. She gave the blazing fire a wistful look before scanning the right side. Three skinny guys with spiked hair and untucked T-shirts acted goofy by one pool table; two older men with John Deere caps and plaid shirts were at the other. The sound of a ball hitting the pocket was drowned out by a whoop of joy. Looked like the tavern wasn't all that busy, despite it being a weekend. Good. How long had it been since she waited tables?

Her new boss stood behind the bar, mixing a drink with his back to the room. His shoulder-length, raven-black hair was tied back with a leather cord which was a pity. Looked like it'd be fun to play with. He had a really nice ass too…and she shouldn't be noticing this kind of thing.

Did you forget the investigation, Sergeant? But when he

turned, she noticed that his black eyebrows had a cynical arch she really liked. And the deadly way he moved, even stuck there behind the bar—hell, he should have a flashing sign in front of him: DANGER

He watched the room, she noticed, never completely relaxed. His head lifted as he spotted her by the door. When his dark eyes trapped her—held her—heat burst in her gut like a detonating missile.

Fucking-A. She ripped her gaze away and crossed the room—slowly—to give her ears time to stop buzzing. Her hormones must be acting up. And of all the men in town, she had to get horny over a cop and her new boss. *Duh, Vic.*

After setting a drink in front of one customer, Calum met Vic at the end of the bar. He gave her a disappointingly impersonal nod. "You're right on time." Hell, she'd forgotten how deep his voice was with a low rumble that reminded her of an Abrams tank.

"Thank you. What now?"

"Let me show you around, and then you can start waiting tables." He took her arm, tucking his fingers under her elbow in a disconcertingly firm grip. His hand was hot against her bare skin, and she shivered, this time not from cold.

Jesus, get over it. First, she'd angsted about what to wear like some vacant-headed Barbie. Now she felt pissy he hadn't even eyeballed the goods under her low-cut knit shirt. How fucking female could she get?

He led her down the back hallway and motioned to restroom doors on the right. "Part of your job will be to check the women's room at intervals and resupply as needed. A janitorial service handles the cleaning."

"Good to hear." *Latrine duty is for losers.* Her shoulder rubbed against a rock-hard chest when he effortlessly turned her. Damn, he made her feel small. Feminine. Talk about unsettling.

Across the hall, a wide door stood open. "This is a token kitchen only, nothing fancy. We serve peanuts and popcorn." A small table and chairs were angled into one corner. He handed her a black apron, notepad, and pencil from the wall shelves. After explaining the popper, he pointed to the massive dishwasher and sink in the back. "Filling and running the dishwasher is one of your duties. I'll show you how later tonight."

As they reentered the bar, she turned and looked down the hallway, checking lines of retreat. Just in case. Five doors. Kitchen. The far end with an EXIT sign. One with an OFFICE plaque. One open to a stairwell leading upward. The last door was noticeably heavier than the others and boasted an expensive electronic combination lock. Odd. Did he keep money or valuables in that room? Why not in his office?

In her experience, locked doors hid all sorts of interesting things. And what kind of reaction would she get for asking? She pointed to the door. "What is that—"

"I believe you are ready to begin," he interrupted. He nodded toward the fireplace area. "Start with that table."

A few feet away, she stopped and frowned. The damn man had the unconscious authority of an officer, one that assumed others would do as ordered. She snorted. They probably did. Just look at the way she'd reacted.

Of course, she'd been in the military for years. Her obedience didn't surprise her—but never before had a commanding tone made all her girlie-bits tingle.

ALEC WANDERED INTO the Wild Hunt about eleven that night. A cold beer would go down good right now.

He'd have arrived earlier if two human teens hadn't stolen Devlin's beloved Mustang for joy-riding. Dev had jumped into his pickup and pushed them off the road, unfortunately denting the Mustang's door. Alec had arrived just in time to keep him from shifting into cat form.

Herne help him, it had been a close thing. There was a reason Daonain lived only in small towns or villages—they rarely had enough control to live in a city. Tynan O'Connolly was one of the few living outside shifter territory, and most people figured he was a little crazy to go play cop in Seattle.

Far better to be the sheriff of a sparsely populated, mountain county. Smiling, Alec pulled open the tavern door and was engulfed by the scent of fresh popcorn and the sound of Rosanne Cash. Every table was taken; a normal crowded Friday night. In the clear space by the jukebox, three college-aged women tried to line-dance, their boots so new the toes still gleamed.

When he saw a couple snuggling on the fireplace couch, envy washed away his pleasure. When was the last time he'd shared the enjoyment of a crackling fire with a female?

As he raked his hair back, he puzzled on it for a moment. Sex during Gatherings was just sex and didn't count. There had been that time with Tina, but she'd merely wanted to warm the sheets. He fingered the ridges still healing on his neck; a screamer and a scratcher—she might as well have been in cat form. That wasn't what he called snuggling by a fire.

He shook away the unreasonable loneliness and decided Calum's new waitress would be an excellent diversion. Not only a pretty female, but one who'd aroused his curiosity. He glanced at the barmaid's station. The adjacent stools were occupied by two men in their twenties. Red eyes. Acrid stench. Obviously stoned as well as drunk. Now, would Calum be annoyed at losing paying customers?

Alec grinned. He hadn't pulled his littermate's tail in a while. Assuming his favorite I'm-a-bad-ass-sheriff expression, he crowded into the men's personal space. As a cop, he knew the risk, but hell, he hadn't had a good fight for days.

The man nearest the barmaid station scowled without turning around. "Get lost, asshole.

His friend puffed up belligerently, and then caught sight of the sheriff badge. And suddenly, Alec had possession of two fine bar stools.

"You should be ashamed of yourself," a husky voice said just behind his shoulder.

He turned with a grin, already knowing who spoke. "Me? I didn't lay a hand on the lads."

She frowned at him, pushing her full, dark red lips together, luring him into running a finger over her lower lip. Velvety soft and—

There was nothing soft about her glare.

"Oops," he said mildly and stuck both hands into the air. "No excuse for that, Ms. Waverly, but it does bother me to see you frown. Your mouth—" No, not a good topic. "You're a lovely woman, and you do pull at a man." A shame he couldn't add that her forbidding expression didn't match the fragrance of her attraction to him. A person's scent didn't lie, and hers was pulling him to her like a dog on a leash. Odd that a human's scent could be so attractive.

However, he really had overstepped the bounds of politeness. "I'm very sorry, ma'am."

She made a sound in the back of her throat, almost a growl. "Call me Vicki. You make it hard to stay pissed off, you know."

"There's a mercy. I'm Alec." He took her tray and set it onto the bar, then patted his newly acquired stool. "Take a break. Give your feet a rest."

"In this crowd? Fat chance."

After glancing at the orders on her tray, he slid the tickets down the bar to his brother. Calum gave him a narrow-eyed look, but held silent.

"It'll take him a few minutes to make those fancy wine coolers up," Alec said. "Must be from that bunch of yuppies by the window."

"Dead on." She eyed the stool with such longing it broke his heart. Forgetting she wasn't Jamie, he moved to pick her up and set her there. She knocked his arms away with a pair of hard cross-blocks.

"Ow."

She winced. "I'm sorry. My ribs are sore, and… I didn't mean—"

"Who beat you up?" The words escaped before he could recall them, and damn, he hadn't even had a beer yet to act so addle-pated.

She slid onto the barstool slowly, obviously stalling. "No one. I was clumsy and had a bad fall."

Sure she did. "Now I don't mind being told, 'That's none of your business.' But I've been a cop a long time, and the one thing I truly hate is being lied to."

Flushing, she turned away.

Having made a bit of a study of liars, he appreciated that she didn't protest her innocence like a chronic liar would do. "Thank you, Ms. Vicki," he said softly.

She shrugged, set up her tray with the new drinks, and waded back into the crowd.

As he watched, she dispensed the glasses, each to the correct person, and took more orders. Her gaze danced across the room, the tables, and he could see her calculating who needed a drink, who to check on next. He'd known from the quickness of her responses to him that she was smart, but now, he realized she was cannier than he'd figured.

He frowned. The expert fighting skills Calum had mentioned weren't easily acquired and showed she had discipline and determination. Apparently she hadn't been anxious about getting a job. She had no family here.

What's she doing in Cold Creek?

AFTER LOCKING THE cash into his safe, Calum walked back into the main room. Almost done for the night. Only the little human waitress remained.

She'd managed her first day quite nicely. As he wiped down the bar, she picked up the last few glasses from the fireplace mantle. Moving rather stiffly, wasn't she? He felt a twinge of guilt. He'd had her start on the busiest day of the week. Then again, she'd been invaluable. Rosie couldn't have kept up. The waitress had staggered out an hour ago, muttering about retirement in her rough voice.

Calum drew two beers and cleared his throat. When she turned, he said, "Let us celebrate your first successful evening. Come." He led the way to the fireplace. A fire elemental lay curled on the glowing coals. The salamander looked up hopefully, but Calum shook his head slightly. He wouldn't be adding more wood this late.

After setting their drinks on the table, he sat on one couch.

She took the couch across from him and picked up her beer. "This is a nice way to end a busy evening."

"Indeed. After this much activity, it can be hard to settle." He studied her before taking a drink. "Have you been a waitress before?"

"Oh, I've tried my hand at some of everything," she said lightly. She had a low voice like brushed silk, pleasant to the ear.

And he could recognize evasion when he heard it. Would she recognize persistence? "Are you a native of our state?"

Her eyes narrowed a little. "'Fraid not. I was an ambassador's brat. Lots of states, lots of countries, lots of homes."

"That's a hard life for a child. I've heard it's even harder for the mothers."

She shrugged. "My mom died when I was young and we didn't have any family, so my father dragged me with him anytime he couldn't hire a housekeeper to leave me with."

Motherless, homeless—had her father filled the gap? A man dedicated to a political career. Doubtful. "Then you were exposed to many cultures growing up?"

"Exposed? That sounds nasty. But yeah."

She might fit in better than he'd anticipated. The question was how would the human-haters in town react? He picked up one of the checkers pieces and noted a spark of interest in her glance. "You play?"

"It's been years."

"Then it is time." He set the game up. "What brought you to Cold Creek? We don't get many tourists this time of year."

She shoved her first piece forward. "I've always wanted to live in the mountains."

That sounded like truth…but not all the truth. "We're high enough that the weather here can be rather nasty." He slid a piece forward.

She played a canny game, surrendering pieces reluctantly, but sacrificing where needed. Aggressive, focused on the goal, much like Alec's style. Even his questions didn't distract her.

But her answers stayed ambiguous. Worrisome. She tossed them off with a carefree voice, but he could almost hear her mind racing for the best response. As Alec had said, the little human was a puzzle.

He won the game. Barely.

"This was fun." She tucked the checkers into the table slots. "It *was* a good way to unwind. Thank you."

"My pleasure."

With their empty glasses, she disappeared down the hallway. A minute later, he heard the dishwasher start up. Smart little human—only needed to be shown something once. Did she know how rare that was? He followed her to tell her so.

Across the kitchen, she was hanging up her apron, and then, hands over her head, she stretched. Her close-fitting shirt outlined the tight muscles of her stomach, the jut of her lush breasts, her muscular biceps. The harsh kitchen light acquired a glow as it rested on her skin, emphasizing high cheekbones, full lips, and the long line of her throat.

His pulse picked up, and his hand tightened on the door frame.

Lowering her arms, she touched her side gingerly as if it hurt. Spell broken, he blinked. What was he thinking? She was *human*. Inter-relations were not forbidden, but wisdom dictated avoidance, both physical and emotional.

Daonain weren't attracted to humans anyway—they didn't have the right scent. Normally. Unfortunately hers was bloody appealing. Not wild as a shifter's would be, but clean as the mountain air with a hint of flowers and feminine musk.

He cleared his throat, and she spun around fast, almost cat-like, taking a defensive stance. Her eyes displayed no fear, just a readiness for battle.

If he'd moved...but he didn't. He leaned against the door frame and crossed his arms, waiting.

"Fuck, you're quiet," she spat out, easing back.

"Please excuse me for my...silence." He studied her for a moment. Her mouth drooped slightly, her eyes looked weary, and her fingers trembled. "I should not have kept you up. I fear this evening has been more tiring than you anticipated."

She shoved her hands in her jeans pockets. "I'm fine. I had the flu last week so I wear out fast. Couple of days and I'll be back to normal."

"Then you are content with your employment?"

"Are you sure you and the sheriff are brothers? You don't

sound at all alike."

"Ah. I was raised in the British Isles; Alec joined relatives in the south."

She laughed. "In that case, I'm surprised you can even communicate with each other. Speaking of communication"—she gave him a narrow-eyed look—"next time, *I* get to lead the interrogation."

He tilted his head. He might well learn more from her questions than her evasive answers. "Next time we'll play chess."

TONY VIDAL SAT at his desk. Fatigue made him feel as if he weighed several hundred pounds. His left hand held a pen—and trembled. He laid his right over it, pressing down, willing the shaking to stop as fear knotted his stomach.

Parkinson's. A slow decline into helplessness. That was not for him—Tony Vidal—who'd crawled his way up the ladder, leaving dead bodies in his wake. Years ago, he'd gone from being the Bull's most feared enforcer to slitting the drug lord's neck and taking his place. Then using his rival's little daughter as a lever, he'd forced Garcia right out of Seattle. Hell, he'd even given the kid back—a little scarred up, but alive. He'd been on top for years. People answered to him, money flowed in as the drugs flowed out.

No fucking way would he let himself turn into a drooling idiot and have some ambitious son of a bitch slice *his* throat. He released his left hand and it lay quiet. He didn't shake constantly—he still had time to find the answers.

The fucking werecats held those answers. He knew it.

He leaned back, remembering the village where he'd grown up. All the rumors he'd heard—people who changed into animals, who never aged, who never got sick. He'd laughed at the fairy tales…right up to the time he'd seen one of his teachers transform into a mountain lion.

His family had moved away shortly after, and he hadn't thought much about it. Until his diagnosis. Until the doctor had said there was no cure for Parkinson's, merely a delay in the inevitable. The sickly curl of fear never left him. But he'd known what he had to do. Become one of the beasts. Live forever without any sickness.

If he could only find out how to do it.

He drummed his fingers on the desk. What was Swane doing all this time, diddling himself? Worthless bastard—Vidal didn't have forever to wait. He punched in Swane's number.

"Yeah," Swane answered.

"What's going on?"

"The fire investigator could tell it was arson, and they found what was left of the old woman's body in the basement, but the investigation's stalled. We're clear," Swane said smugly. "What do you want me to do now?"

Vidal scowled. Dumb fuck. However, the ex-mercenary could be trusted to carry out orders without screwing up...if the sadistic asshole didn't get carried away like he had with the kid. "Find me another creature."

"Like how? The traps where we caught Beastie-boy are empty. And a few are gone. Want me to move them to a new spot?"

"Let me think." Walking over to the huge bay windows, Vidal stared out at the drizzling rain. For some reason, the place where he'd grown up had turned into a ghost town, but the rumors had mentioned other places with werecreatures. One was somewhere in the mountains northeast of Seattle—he'd remembered that because his uncle lived in Seattle. He knew they were up there. Catching the boy proved that. "Leave some traps where we got the kid. Then find the closest town and set traps around it—stay off the hiking trails though. If you need to hire someone, tell them you've been contracted to trap a mountain lion."

"Got it."

"Call me in another day." Vidal shut the phone off and scowled at the open folder on his desk. He picked up the driver's license lying on top. Victoria Morgan. The bitch was pretty. And clever. She'd disappeared fucking thoroughly. But her ID had led him to the Marines, and then he'd called in favors to get the rest of the information. She worked in a covert unit under an Agency big shot. No wonder she'd slid through their fingers so easily.

The CIA. Nothing he wanted to fuck with. But she'd seen him and Swane.

He didn't want to kill her though—not right away. If the cunt was alive, he'd find out whether the bite had turned her into a werecreature. Besides, the kid might have talked to her, even told her where the creatures hid.

If she had any information… Well, Swane enjoyed women. By the time he finished, she'd be begging to tell them all she knew.

AS VIC STEPPED out onto her porch, she took a long breath of moist air, heady with the fragrance of fallen leaves and snow from the mountains. Did snow have a smell? Her coffee supply was running low, so she'd decided to walk into town like everyone else did around here. Her knee would tolerate an easy stroll.

As she walked down the steps, she glanced at the tree in the front yard. A quiver of uneasiness wiggled in her guts like a worm. She'd watched the branches for the past week, and no more little hands had poked out of the foliage. But sometimes the leaves rustled—against the wind.

As if shapeshifters weren't enough to deal with. Scowling, she stared up. Another couple of weeks and maybe her ribs wouldn't kill her when she climbed up there. Then she'd examine every fucking inch of that tree.

And she'd take her Glock with her.

Nothing showed. Each day, yellowing leaves drifted down to cover the lawn, but plenty remained. More than enough to hide a squirrel or something. *Something.*

She glared. Two weeks ago, she'd have laughed at anyone talking about…nonexistent creatures. Now? "You know, little bastard, if I knew what you were, I might leave out food for you to eat. Squirrels like nuts, right?" Or maybe it was a rat—in that case, all bets were off. "Maybe I should get a rat trap instead." She slapped the tree trunk.

As she walked away, something hit between her shoulder blades. "What the hell?" She spun, looked around. An unshelled walnut rocked back and forth on the ground.

A walnut? The tree was an oak. The day was calm with no wind, and she stood several feet out from under the canopy. A chill inched up her vertebrae as she had a visual of a squirrel winding up for a pitch. *Nah.*

Well, whatever-it-was would have to wait until she healed up a little more. Giving the tree branches her best I'll-be-back stare, she sauntered away.

Chapter Five

THE TAVERN HAD closed an hour earlier. As Calum walked Victoria to the door, he smiled at the disgruntled look on her face. Although she'd won the first chess game last week, he had recouped and was now ahead in games. But so far, she'd stymied him in another way—he still had no idea why she'd come to Cold Creek. Nonetheless he thoroughly enjoyed the verbal sparring. The little human had a keen mind and a delight-fully wry sense of humor.

After opening the door, he let her out into the night. "Are you sure—"

"You always ask that. I can walk myself home, thank you very much."

"As you wish." In spite of his better judgment, he moved closer, noting the first faint whiff of female arousal and the dusky rose color that tinged her cheek. Why did this feisty human have to be so appealing? With an effort, he stepped back and smiled down into eyes the amber-brown of sherried Scotch whiskey. "Having witnessed you in a fight, I should be more concerned for your opponents."

"Now you're talking smart." As she left, she touched her fingertips to her temple in a jaunty salute.

A salute? Uneasiness raised his hackles. Daonain stayed far

away from anything having to do with the military. After all, if the government ever learned of their existence, the probable outcome would be genocide for the shifters.

As Calum watched the human cross the parking lot, he smiled. The way her round ass moved in those tight jeans…truly, a less Marine-like movement he couldn't imagine. He'd like to bend her over, take her hips in a hard grip… Arousal purred to life inside him.

He took a slow breath to calm himself and scented Alec. His brother appeared, detouring to the edge of the lot to speak with Victoria. They chatted briefly, and then Alec ran a finger down her long hair, tucking a loose strand behind her ear. The scent of interest and arousal—from both of them—drifted downwind to Calum.

That was damned odd. Shifters weren't interested in humans any more than a dog wanted to breed with a cat. Even if that wasn't true, a Daonain couldn't afford to get involved with a human.

By the time Alec approached, Calum still hadn't figured out what to say. How could he lecture his brother when he himself felt the same? "She's a pretty human, isn't she?"

Alec turned, his eyes on Victoria's slim figure as she disappeared into the night. "Way too pretty, and a sore trial to my restraint. Why does she have to smell so good?" His upper lip lifted as he sniffed the air. "Smells like she's testing your control too, eh, brawd? A shame she's a human. It's been a while since we shared."

"It has." Nothing felt as right as pleasing a woman with his littermate beside him.

As Calum flicked off the last lights in the bar, Alec went down the hallway and unlocked the heavy portal door.

The small sitting room was tidy enough. Alec fingered long gashes on one couch. "Who clawed this up?"

"Rebecca's daughter, Lindsey, when she shifted early. Brawd, am I getting old or do our children have initial trawsfur younger these days?"

"According to the news, puberty arrives earlier for humans; apparently Daonain aren't any different." Alec paused, and then grinned. "But yes, you're getting old."

"Bugger you," Calum said mildly. He opened the closet door.

Alec stepped in. Behind the hanging garments, he pressed two panels at once, moved his hands, and did two more. At the almost inaudible click, he shouldered open the door to the cave with a grunt of effort. No human would be able to open it by himself.

Calum followed, breathing in the cold, damp air that smelled of dirt and minerals. Downstairs in the cave, he stripped and tucked his clothing into the carved-out niches. The urgency, the *need* to trawsfur, tightened within him. With a sigh of relief, he opened the portal in his mind. Wildness blew into his soul like wind through an open door. Magic coursed across his skin, sank deep into his bones, tingling, changing him. He let himself drop forward and landed on his front paws.

Alec was still undressing, as easygoing in this as he was in all things. Calum yawned, curling his lip back and exposing his fangs in a not-so-subtle hint.

His brother only grinned. "With your type A personality, you'll probably have a heart attack before you reach seventy."

As air from outside wafted into the cave from the three tunnels, Calum caught the heady scent of a rabbit and the end of his tail twitched. With an effort, he kept his mind from sinking too deeply into the wildness. They had things to do before they could hunt.

Finally, Alec shifted. He rumbled in satisfaction and shoved his golden-furred head into Calum's shoulder. Typical Alec affection, Calum thought, as the love he felt for his brother mingled with feline acceptance of a littermate.

Calum rose to his hind legs, grabbing Alec with his front paws. They tussled until, with his distinctive chirp of enjoyment, Alec sprang down the left tunnel. Calum followed, then took the lead as they ran up the mountain to one of the few roads in their forest domain. It was unmarred by tracks; no vehicle had passed since the last rain. They moved to check the next road.

The waning moon had risen in the black sky before they reached the most distant road. After this, they could hunt, and Calum's anticipation rose when his ears caught the scrabble of a shrew in the brush.

Overhead, the moon fought free of the clouds, illuminating fresh tire tracks. Calum's claws unsheathed as anger welled inside him. Although ostensibly owned by a lumber company, this forest belonged to the Daonain. With an effort, he fought his way free of emotions. For now.

Alec's muscular shoulder thudded into his, and Calum heard a harshly suppressed snarl as his brother spotted the tracks.

Calum padded silently into the forest, moving parallel to the road. The ruts continued for another mile. Near a small clearing, he caught the scent of humans and the cacophony of odors that accompanied them: deodorant, shaving lotion, leather, laundry soap, bath soap. He paused, letting his nose filter the information.

Two men. From the faint stench of dung and urine, they'd only arrived a few hours ago. No fire. A cold camp implied they didn't want to be found. He flicked an ear at Alec, and his littermate turned, slinking silently to the right of the camp. Calum moved left.

Sitting with his back against a pine tree, the human on watch held a shotgun across his knees. The other man snored in his sleeping bag, black hair poking out through the top. Metal gleamed in the moonlight showing a pile of animal traps for large animals. Rage welled up inside Calum like molten lava. This was *his* mountain; they were hunting *his* people.

Why? What did they know?

He pulled power and drew on a Cosantir's awareness of his territory. Dev, Rosie, Angie, Ben...seven Daonain total roamed the mountains right now. He needed to drive the intruders away and destroy their traps. But carefully...very carefully.

Having Alec arrest them for trespass and illegal trapping could backfire if the hunters questioned how the sheriff found them in miles of wilderness. The Daonain survived by not drawing any attention.

Alec appeared from the underbrush, anger obvious in his tight muscles and glowing yellow eyes. A tingle, a blur, and he was in human form, hidden from the camp behind brush and trees. Calum followed suit.

"S'pose you're not gonna let me rip their guts out," Alec growled.

"Regretfully no." Calum fought his own need to shred the hunters into little pieces. "They might have been hired to set traps without knowing why. Any other ideas?"

"Actually, yes." Alec leaned against a cedar and scratched his back on the trunk. "I saw Ben's spoor. Fresh."

Ben? Recently laid off from his construction job, the shifter was enjoying his vacation in animal form. "Spook them out of their camp?"

Alec's face had the innocent expression that his friends knew to distrust. "Every hunter knows how troublesome bears are, especially ones that have learned to scavenge. Why, I've heard bears think any container is filled with goodies."

Calum's gaze rested on the big cooler...undoubtedly full of food, and the packs and boxes scattered across the clearing. He rubbed his cheek, feeling the harsh scratch of stubble. The night was getting old.

He moved his mind to a Cosantir's awareness. Ben was very close. "You have a wicked soul, brawd."

A COUGAR SNARLED nearby.

From the shadows, Alec watched the man with the shotgun startle, his head thumping into the tree he'd been leaning on.

When the underbrush rustled, Alec grinned. Calum must be rubbing against every bush in the area. A loud snarl, even closer.

The guard jumped to his feet. The other man frantically struggled out of his sleeping bag and snatched up a tranquilizer gun. The two moved out of the clearing quickly and quietly.

Ten minutes later, Ben rampaged through the empty camp. The big bear enjoyed itself, clawing open boxes and backpacks and leaving litter strewn everywhere. Behaving exactly like a normal hungry bear.

Ben had saved the best for last—the three-foot-long ice chest. The bear clawed the cooler open, gouging the hard plastic. After a few slurping noises, Ben straightened. Half of a massive salami jutted from his jaws like a cigar.

Voices approached, and Alec stiffened. The hunters were returning, grumbling all the way. Calum had managed to lead them quite a ways before losing them.

"Hey! Hey, dammit!" The first man stepped into the clearing, holding the thirty-aught-six like he knew how to use it. "Somebody trashed our camp!"

Get the hell out of there, Ben.

Ben rose to his full height and let out a roar that halted the hunters in their tracks barely long enough for him to put a rockfall between him and the men. A shotgun blasted, echoing through the mountains. Sparks shot off the granite.

Without speaking, one man moved to check Ben's trail while

the other hung back, rifle poised at his shoulder.

Alec's gut tightened as he watched the way the pair functioned. The quickness of their response, even the hand signals they used, pointed to military experience. And Lachlan had been tortured. The threat to the Daonain might be deadlier than anyone had realized.

Chapter Six

THE RUN FROM the parking lot through the rain and into the Wild Hunt left Vic drenched. As icy water trickled down her neck, she turned to scowl at the downpour. In the last two weeks, the season had definitely settled into a cold wet autumn. The desert was looking better and better. After all, what were a few grenades and IEDs between buddies?

"Raining out there?"

She glanced around as Alec left his friends and moved close enough that his appealing scent tantalized her: clean clothes, a hint of aftershave, and musky male.

Mmmmh If she swayed any nearer, her breasts would rub his chest. *No, Vic.* She retreated a step and leaned against the doorframe. If she didn't keep her distance, her clothes would start to steam from the heat growing between them. Jesus, maybe she should go back outside, have a cold rain shower. "Uh, yeah, it's pouring like a son-of-a-bitch."

"Must be. You're soaked, darlin'." His smile could brighten the gloomiest day. Dammit. "You're pretty early. You didn't walk here, did you?"

"Hardly." She watched a wave of rain advance across the parking lot like strafing fire. In the west, the setting sun had turned the dark clouds a sullen red. "And it's Friday—I start early on Friday and Saturdays."

"Gonna be a long shift." He lifted a strand of her hair, frowned as water dripped onto the floor. "Calum has some towels in the kitchen. Dry off before you catch your death."

"Yes, Daddy."

"*Daddy?*" His gaze moved down her body like a warm hand and returned to where the wet fabric molded to her breasts.

Her breath caught as everything inside loosened.

He rested his palm on the doorframe over her head and leaned in. As he inhaled, his nostrils flared. "Vixen," he murmured, so close his breath warmed her cheek.

She should stop this… His lips were tantalizingly near. At the heat in his dark green eyes, she felt her skin flush. Sensitize. She was caught, every cell inside her longing for his touch. Her face turned up, and she brushed her lips against his.

He froze. The muscles in his jaw hardened into granite, and he took a step away. "I'm a fool…and I'm sorry, Vicki." He turned and walked out in the rain, muttering, "Herne help me."

Trying to tell herself she was relieved, Vic watched him cross the parking lot with his long-limbed, easy gait, and her lust felt as if it radiated outward in hot waves. How the hell did he make her feel like this? Like she'd give anything to wrap a fist in his shirt and pull that lean body down on top of her. She could almost feel his weight on her, the way he'd take her mouth, tease her into kissing him back, then—

Holy fuck-doodle. If she didn't get her act together, she'd melt right here in the doorway. She shook her head, sending water *splatting* against the floor. At least, she was warmer than when she'd come in. A lot warmer.

And an idiot. Just because she felt as if he was a friend—a teammate. Like many of the Marines she'd fought with, he held the same dedication to duty. Add in that warped sense of humor and…that body? Hell, how could she resist?

With a curse, she slammed the door shut, pleased to see customers jump at the noise. As she made her way across the sparsely filled room, a table of uniformed forest service workers watched her. One younger guy muttered, "Looks like Alec's caught himself a female."

A gray-haired, darkly tanned man answered, "She's easy prey."

Prey? The asshole thought of her as prey? She slowed, considered knocking a chair-leg off the old goat's chair, let him land on his ass. But hell, they were just *men*—another term for clueless—and they hadn't been speaking to her.

She veered toward the hallway and caught another fragment: "…strangely appealing, anyway." That was more like it. Why their voices were so loud, she didn't know. Come to think of it, the entire room seemed awfully loud, like a TV with the volume turned to high. Her hearing felt as sensitive as after a night downing shots of tequila. Only she hadn't been drinking.

"Hey, Vicki!" Jamie slammed the dishwasher closed and ran across the kitchen to bestow a hug.

Thank God her ribs had healed. "Ah …" Dammit, she'd know what to do with a teammate's one-armed embrace, but this was a girl. A baby. After a second, she lifted one hand and patted the kid awkwardly.

"Jeez, Vicki," Jamie frowned up into Vic's face. "When somebody hugs you, you hug them back."

"Oh. Okay." Wrapping her arms around the skinny shoulders, she could only marvel at a child so well loved, who would know that lack of a hug wasn't from dislike, but from inexperience. She blinked rapidly against the prickling in her eyes and held the girl a moment longer to be sure the tears didn't show.

When the kid released her and looked up with a smile, the brightness in her face dimmed. Vic got another hug—a very gentle one.

"Jesus, all this mushy stuff," Vic muttered. *Pity.* She'd just been pitied by a fucking baby. She stepped away and noticed her clothes had left the kid wet. "I need to dry off before I flood the place." Crap, that sounded like she was planning to cry. "I mean—"

But Jamie had trotted over to the shelves and snagged a towel.

"Thanks, kid."

"We get to work together today." Jamie perched on a stool by the sink and beamed. "I'm working 'til six tonight, Daddy said, since you'll be here to make sure nobody…" She frowned. "Um…nobody makes some advances."

Didn't that just sound like Calum? "Nobody makes an advance."

"Yeah. That's it."

After tossing the towel on the washing machine, Vic pulled her shirt away from her chest. The dampness made it too tight…and too cold. Glancing down at her tits, she groaned. Alec had not only seen her nipples, but must have been able to count every crinkle around them. No way could she serve tables like this.

"Very attractive, however I'm not running a brothel," Calum said in a dry voice.

Vic jumped. Now she knew how her buddies had felt when she'd snuck up on them. Then his words registered. He found her breasts attractive? Her cheeks heated, and she turned her face away. God, two men in one day had made her blush. Worse—were making her hornier than an off-duty Marine in Taiwan. What was the world coming to?

"My clothes are soaked. Do you have any suggestions?" she asked, trying for an even voice.

"I have a sweater in the office. Jamie, please go and take orders for drinks. Tell people I'll be out in a minute after I finish dressing our waitress." His gray eyes glinted as his gaze ran over Vic's body, all too much like his brother's had.

And having Calum look at her breasts turned her on just as quickly.

Dammit, now she was wet inside as well as out. With a huff of exasperation and desire, she crossed her arms over her chest and surprised a rare grin out of Calum. The flash of white teeth in that tanned face sure didn't do her hormones any favors.

Jamie trotted out the door, already singing along with Waylon Jennings on the jukebox.

Calum didn't move. Although his grin had faded, the crease along one lean cheek remained, making her want to run her fingers over his face. Over everything. The bulge in his black jeans showed he was equally interested. *Bad idea, Sergeant.* She bit her lip. "Sweater? Remember?"

"I do. You remain here while I find it." As he left the kitchen, his voice trailed back to her, "Your company right now would be an appallingly bad idea."

Without her permission, her feet started after him. *No, Sergeant.* She stopped. She was here to investigate stuff, not to scratch an itch. Or two. *Mmm, two men.* Alec's kisses, Calum's hands. *No no no.* She thumped her head against the wall hard enough to pound that idea right out of her brain.

AT A LULL later that night, Calum glanced around the room, feeling the glow of satisfaction. The tavern, gathering home of the Daonain since it first opened in eighteen eighty, was thriving under his care. Not only shifters liked the Wild Hunt, but OtherFolk and even humans enjoyed the warmth of companionship here.

Most of them. He eyed a table with three human females. Two were pleasantly drunk and soaking up attention from the human males. The third female nervously watched a couple of older shifters seated nearby.

Calum frowned. Only yesterday, Thorson had returned from the mountain where he'd gone to ease his grief. Tonight, he was single-mindedly trying to get intoxicated. Unfortunately, his drinking companion was Albert Baty, another human-hater. Sober or alone, the men posed no problem. Put them together, and their anger merged and increased.

After Rosie had gone off duty earlier, Calum had served the men himself so Victoria would have no reason to go near them.

Other customers had also required special service. He glanced at the corner table by the kitchen door and saw the dwarves' glasses were empty. Already. With a sigh, Calum built two more black and tans and carried them over. The satisfaction that the discriminating local dwarf population found his beer good was offset by the danger of having them frequent his bar, especially on busy nights.

Like many magical beings, the dwarves generated a *you-can't-see-me* aura. The RESERVED placard on the table and the slightly antagonistic waves coming from them repelled most humans…unless they were very drunk, like the old rancher last week who'd plopped himself down on Gramlor's lap.

And Alec—Alec had been laughing so hard he almost failed to wrench the axe away from the dwarf before Gramlor split the human's head open.

At the table, Calum kept his back to the room and bowed. "Gentlemen, your drinks. I trust everything is adequate?"

Nurxtan smoothed his beard. "You still have fine beer, Cosantir. I haven't visited here since your dam's lifemate passed on. My condolences."

"I thank you." He set a mug in front of each dwarf.

The other dwarf who came in often nodded his thanks.

Nurxtan's attention turned away. Alec had just walked in,

and his progress to the bar was hindered by greetings on all sides. "Your brother appears in good health."

"He is that."

The dwarf frowned. "He scatters his seed to many, many, yet has no formal lifemate. And neither have you, Cosantir."

"My mate died."

"Time has passed. Find another. Bonded Daonain are safer for all."

Calum's jaw tightened. Dwarves didn't lie, didn't hand out compliments, didn't have any tact, and those long noses of theirs poked into everything, including people's personal lives. "I–"

Nurxtan interrupted. "And this time, share with your brother."

No point in discussing it. Calum rendered a tight nod and stalked back to his bar. Bollocks. Lenora had been frail and her timidity had kept her from accepting Alec, warping their mating to only her and Calum. Alec had understood, but guilt still rode Calum's shoulders, even so many years after her death. Putting it aside, he returned to working the taps.

From the waitress station, Vic waved and caught his attention. "I need three white wines and a Bud Light," she called. As she reached for the water pitcher, her full breasts rested on the bar top like a prize to be gathered. With an effort, he averted his gaze, closing his hands around a cold wine bottle instead. *Three wines. Right.*

Despite the noisy conversations, he still heard his brother's snicker from the far end of the bar. Obviously Alec had seen where his attention had lingered. Calum shot him a look of frustration, and Alec raised his glass in a toast of perfect understanding.

"Your order is complete, Victoria." Calum placed the drinks in front of her.

"Thank you." She set them on her tray and gave him a smile

that flooded his system with testosterone. Her face was flushed, her eyes sparkling, and he couldn't help but wonder if she brought all that delightful energy to mating.

"Ring them up to the Howard account," she told him and hefted up the tray.

The ease with which she carried the heavy trays hinted at strong muscles hidden under her smooth female padding. She had the prowling gait of a shifter, he noticed again. He turned and met Alec's look. After drawing a Guinness, he moved down the bar to hand it over. "Here."

"Thanks." Alec took a gulp. "A human shouldn't affect us this way."

"Some trick of the pheromones. Shifters do bed humans, after all."

"Only because they're convenient—not because of any real appeal," Alec pointed out. "I don't know about you, brawd, but I'm damned attracted."

"As am I." Too attracted. The God was teasing him, keeping her constantly in his sight. Within his scent-range. But he knew it wasn't wise for a shifter to get entangled with a human. "After the Samhain Gathering, we should visit elsewhere."

"And check out some new females? Maybe even find a life-mate?"

"Precisely." His relationship with Lenora had been incomplete. Next time he'd be able to share his mate with his brother.

VIC'S EYES WERE going wonky, she decided. In her peripheral vision, she could see two short guys sitting near the hallway. But when she looked straight at the table, it was empty.

Hadn't she seen Calum deliver two drinks? He'd stood a while and then returned to the bar with empty glasses. Had he sucked down two glasses of beer by himself?

She averted her gaze, and in the corner of her eyes, saw the two guys reappear at the table. Very, very short men with waist-length beards. They looked almost like... She snorted. *Nah. No way.* Then again, she was looking for *werecats.* So, maybe, maybe, right here and right now, she had two mini-men who were escapees from the casting room of Lord of the Rings. *Dwarves.*

That had been a great movie, but the operative word was *movie,* not real life. God help her, was she going to have to investigate dwarves next? This task Lachlan had given her was turning into a complete cluster-fuck.

She set the tray down on the women's table with a thump that rattled the wine glasses. Forcing a smile, she said, "Here you go." After setting out the drinks, she glanced around the room. It was too busy right now to investigate that corner table. Rosie had gotten sick and left work early, leaving Vic the only waitress in a packed tavern.

And who had put on an Elvis Presley tune? Blue Hawaii—in Washington? That was just wrong.

Who needed a drink next? First, clear off the table by the fireplace. Then swing by the pool room. Most of the people in the main room should be okay for a while. Her gaze lit on the table nearest the door and the two older men who Calum had been serving. One man was pudgy and short with drooping jowls like an overweight bulldog. The other was over sixty, but looked like a junk-yard dog—just plain mean and with the scars to prove it.

The two glared at her as if she'd keyed their favorite pick-up. She checked the bar, but it was surrounded by people, which meant Calum couldn't see their pitcher of beer was empty. Apparently, the table was her responsibility. *Duty calls.*

She made her way over. "Gentlemen, what can I bring you to drink?"

"You can't bring me bird droppings, monkey face," the pudgy one said in a low voice. "Get away from my table before your stench makes me puke."

"Well." Considering she was supposed to also be the *bouncer*, maybe Calum would let her toss the asshole out the door to see if he'd bounce. *No. Be good, Sergeant.* Besides, starting a fight wasn't exactly considered covert. "Fine, then. If you need something, please go to the bar to get it."

He didn't answer, just slammed his almost empty mug down so hard that beer splashed across the table.

Stepping back hastily, Vic bumped the other guy's knees.

Junk-yard Dog shoved his drink away and rose to his feet, his deep-lined face distorted with rage. "I don't want you in here. Not you"—his maddened gaze turned toward the table of three women—"and not them either." Snarling like a rabid dog, he lunged at the wide-eyed college girls. "Get out."

"Oh, fuck." Vic tossed her empty tray on the table and caught the man by his collar. With a hard yank to pull him away from the shrieking women, she whirled, intending to push him out the door.

Rather than pulling away, he slammed himself backwards and elbowed her in the gut.

"Oof." She lost her grip on his shirt. He took two steps, and back-kicked, trying for her gut.

Jesus. She jerked sideways, and he missed. That was a very fast old man just spoiling for a fight. She grinned as adrenaline bubbled into her veins. A chance to play? *Mustn't kill him.* When he tried again, she grabbed his foot and twisted sharply.

Not wanting her to dislocate his knee, he hit the floor, rolled onto one shoulder, and kicked at her with his free leg. She let go before he could break her fingers.

Sneaky move. With a respectful nod, she stepped back. Had he gotten the venom out of his system yet?

She glanced over her shoulder to check her six. The other SOB had a knife.

He lunged at her, the blade coming in fast. She sidestepped. A quick punch to Pudgy's face yielded a satisfying flash of blood. God, this was fun. A sweep of her foot took his feet out from under him, and he landed heavily on his side.

The bitter old guy regained his feet all too fast, moving faster than a SEAL on speed, and dammit, her gut still ached from his elbow. He circled around her, looking for a hole in her defenses. She heard Calum's deep shout and ignored it. There were a ton of people between the bar and here.

She studied Junkyard Dog, waiting for his move. His eyes didn't look right—he wasn't just drunk; he was crazy mad. When he sprang for her, she dodged without retaliation. He recovered fast and spun around. Fucking-A, but he really wanted to kill her. Now what? Her job was to keep the peace, not send drunken assholes to the hospital.

The indecision cost her, and his fist slammed into her face in a blast of pain and light. She fell against a table, sending people spinning backwards with angry shouts. Mugs and glasses shattered; liquids spilled everywhere.

Flushed with shame, her cheek hurting like hell, she rolled out of the tangle and back to her feet. The bastard smirked at her, damn him. She sprang at him, faking a high punch. His block left him open for a side-kick to his gut and an immediate hard follow-through to his face with the same foot. The impact ran up her leg, and he flew like an overweight bird, landing on another table.

She winced. More damages. Calum would be royally pissed-off.

The pudge was up, and somehow, he'd regained his knife. Even as she tensed, Calum grabbed him, yanked his head back by the long stringy hair, and curled his fingers around the thick neck neck. "If I must rip your throat out, I will have an intolerable mess, and I will be even angrier than I am now."

Pudge froze, his eyes widening.

"Well, hell, brawd, are you saying I can't gut this one?" Crouching, Alec had one knee on Junk-yard Dog's neck, and a knife poised above his belly. The sheriff's face was cold and hard and furious. He looked fully ready to disembowel the older man.

Whoa. A bar-fight around here got deadly awfully fast.

Calum sighed, and his gray eyes lightened. "I find intestines as unappealing as blood. Alexander, do please recall you are sheriff of this county."

"Well, hey, that did slip my mind." Alec took an audible breath, and tension flowed out of his body. He spoke to the old guy, "Thorson. Looks like you get to enjoy the hospitality of my jail. I need a word."

The man's voice was hoarse, not surprising considering Alec's knee was wedged against his larynx. "My word is given."

"Albert?" Alec's frozen gaze turned to pudgy.

"My word is given," Pudge repeated.

As Calum released his captive, Alec hauled Thorson to his feet and pushed him sideways so the two drunks stood together.

Standing in front of them, Calum crossed his arms. "I will forgive your debt to me, but this woman works for me and was doing only what she was hired to do." His words were soft and sheened with ice. "She offered no insult to you, yet you've done her damage. By the law of reciprocity, she is owed." He looked around his bar.

Puzzled, Vic followed his gaze. Two men and the college girls appeared confused. So did the young couple by the fireplace and a man seated at the bar. Everyone else in the place stared at her with expressions ranging from coldly angry to assessing. A second later, heads bowed slightly, and a murmur came from the room. "She is owed."

What the hell was going on? Vic opened her mouth to ask and reconsidered. Right now, Calum looked nastier than her first drill sergeant after a recruit dropped his rifle in the mud. When his gaze lit on her, she almost snapped to attention.

Thorson's mouth tightened into a bitter line as he stared at Vic, repugnance streaming from every pore in his body. But he answered quietly, "We will discuss the compensation with you, Cosan—uh, Calum."

"Indeed, I think not." Calum nodded at her. "Your discussion will be with the one who is owed. I've found her honorable and fair for a—I believe she can determine her own recompense to achieve balance. Let us say, this Monday, your bookstore at one o'clock. Miss Waverly, does that meet with your approval?"

"Sure. Sounds fine." What exactly had she approved? Feeling blood running down her face, Vic swiped a hand across the gash on her cheekbone and saw rage flash into Alec's eyes. The situation felt too volatile, and retreat seemed the best solution to defuse it. "Excuse me while I get cleaned up."

She moved through the room, her eyes fixed on the kitchen door to escape the stares. Her face hurt, and the humiliation hurt worse than her face. That old guy shouldn't have been able to lay a finger on her. He'd not only kicked her, but had actually gotten in a punch. From the look of him, he had to be approaching seventy.

Seventy. *God help me, I'm already over the hill and not even thirty yet.* And what was all that about being owed? Some mountain custom or something? Calum had a few questions to answer.

In the kitchen, she dropped into the chair by the setup table and worked on releasing the lingering adrenaline.

Unfortunately for her state of mind, less than a minute later, Calum stalked into the room, followed by Alec. And didn't they both look like they still wanted to kill someone. Her, probably. She'd handled the men badly and disrupted the whole tavern.

She raised a hand, realized her knuckles were bleeding on Calum's clean floor. *God, I can't win.* "I'm sorry, guys. I didn't—"

"Shut up," Alec said, the shortest sentence she'd ever heard from him. Yeah, he was pissed off. He yanked a paper towel off the roll, stuck it under the water.

Fine, okay, shutting up. But Calum stood on her other side, and she really needed to tell him how sorry she—

"Look at me," Alec said.

She turned back, caught the full effect of blazing green eyes. He knelt in front of her, so close she could see faint scars across one cheek. Parallel lines. She stiffened—lines like the ones around her ribs. Claw marks.

He grabbed her chin, his fingers firm. Warm. "Hold still. This is gonna hurt, baby." He pressed the cold, wet paper towel against her cheekbone.

"Ouch," she murmured.

"Listen," he said, "there—"

"Move." Calum nudged Alec over with his knee. He yanked a chair closer with one foot and seated himself before taking her hand. His gray eyes were almost black, his mouth tight. Muscles flexed under his white shirt—he was ready to wade into a fight, all right.

"I didn't mean—"

"Shut up," they said, almost in chorus. Calum held out a small bottle to Alec. "Put iodine on that rag."

"Hey, no, wait." Her grab for Alec's wrist was a little too late, too weak. He forced her hand down on her thigh and pressed the cloth to her face. It burned, napalm in a bottle. She'd hated the shit since she was a kid. "Jesus, I survived the fight and now you're trying to kill me," she muttered. "What kind of archaic medicine is this?"

Alec grinned, and his grip on her hand eased, turned to almost a caress. "You're too tough to die, woman."

A compliment? His words slid through her humiliation like the sun through fog. She glanced at Calum, just in time to see him dump half the bottle of iodine on her knuckles. She yelped. "Shit! Fuck!"

Whups. Not a diplomatic way to talk to a boss. She bit down on her lip, ignored Alec's snigger. "Um. Sorry."

"I do hope you refrain from that language when my daughter is present," Calum said mildly. His eyes had returned to gray, and his lips twitched upward.

She relaxed back into the chair with a whuff of relief. Calum used a finger to smear antibiotic ointment on her knuckles, and then handed the tube to Alec. They acted like she'd been broken into pieces instead of barely dented.

Both of them were intent on making sure she was okay. Nobody'd ever done that before. Oh, in the Marines, a buddy would slap a field dressing on you. But when undercover, she handled her own injuries. Funny how she'd gotten so used to the protocol: *If you're caught, you're on your own. We won't know you. No rescue, no aid.*

Alec grinned at her. "Want me to kiss it and make it better?"

She snorted. But as she looked at them and saw the very real concern in their faces, something seemed to snap inside her. As a child, she'd heard that if she swallowed a watermelon seed, one would grow in her stomach. She'd spent a week, patting her belly, waiting…for nothing.

But now, looking at Alec and Calum, she could feel something deep inside start to unfurl and grow.

THE RAIN HAD stopped, and the crescent moon rode the clouds like an ancient drawing of Herne, the horned god of the hunt. Cold air flowing down the mountain slopes into town brought the scent of snow, of pine trees, of tiny damp glades and the deer that stepped silently through them.

But tonight Alec felt no hunger to run the wild. Tonight, his hunger was for the young female quietly walking beside him. A female both beautiful and deadly.

During the fight in the Wild Hunt, he'd been terrified for her. Worse, he'd almost lost control and shifted, something he hadn't done since a teenager. He glanced down at his small companion and shook his head. His fear for her had been sadly misplaced; he should have worried for her opponents.

When Thorson had kicked at her, Vicki had actually grinned, her delight obvious. He'd been shocked—hell, he was still shocked. Female shifters fought only for home or family and went straight for the throat or belly every time.

What kind of female enjoyed brawling? And got herself in a deadly fight and still pulled her punches. Even as he'd shoved his way through the customers to her, he'd seen how she'd moved her target to a jaw rather than the thorax and then softened a kick. She could have killed either of them.

Alec grinned. Once he sobered up, Thorson, with his years of brawling, would know that too. Wouldn't that pull the old werecat's tail?

When they reached the corner of Cumberland Street, Vicki looked up at him, her eyes a golden-brown in the moonlight. Would they brighten even further with passion? "You really don't have to walk me home," she protested again. "I'm fine. Shouldn't you head for the jail to take care of those men?"

"I'm in no particular hurry." Alec stuffed his hands in his pockets to keep them out of trouble. "They'll be more polite after the alcohol has worn off."

Muttering, "I doubt it," she started down the sidewalk. A breeze ruffled her hair as fallen leaves whispered across the pavement in an autumn song. "Alec?"

"Um-hmmm?" Her skin was a flawless ivory in the pale light of the moon, and the need to touch was almost unendurable.

"Why did those two men want to kill me? I've never seen

them before."

Oh, this wasn't right—beautiful, deadly, and *smart* too? The Mother had been very generous with Her gifts. "Well, now, seems like they'd just had too much to drink. You've seen bar fights before."

"Alec, you're blowing smoke up—um, you know full well that wasn't a normal bar fight. I didn't do anything to get them upset, and neither did the three college girls." A frown line appeared between her pretty arching brows, made him want to rub it away.

"You really shouldn't worry—"

"The only time I've seen anything like that was when a bunch of White Pride guys started a fight with a black Marine. They wanted to kill him."

This was too close for comfort. "What happened? Did they succeed?"

"Against a Marine? Get real." Her husky laugh was as compelling as a gurgling spring on a dry day. "But Alec, those men tonight had the same look. Hatred, but not for what I did, but because of something I represent. Something...hmmm." Her voice trailed off.

"What?" Worry crawled up his spine like a line of ants, and then he relaxed. She couldn't possibly know anything about Daonain. "So, where did you learn to fight like that?" he asked. Time to yank back control of this conversation.

"Oh, my daddy insisted his little girl be able to protect herself, especially since we traveled so much." The fact she let him change the subject was a tad worrying. Like watching an alley cat deliberately letting a mouse go. What *did* she know?

She resumed walking. "I've had years of karate lessons."

He could smell the scent of honesty, or rather the lack of nervousness indicating a lie. But she was, perhaps, not telling all the truth. She was obviously accustomed to full-out fighting. He scowled and bit back the need to push harder. It had been a long evening, and even if she'd enjoyed the fight, she'd collected a few knocks. But tomorrow, all bets were off.

They walked up to the house and stopped at the porch steps.

"Thanks for the company," she said.

"The pleasure was mine." He gave in to the urge and ran his hand over her skin—every bit as velvety as it looked. When he threaded his fingers in her long silky hair, her breathing picked up.

"Do you want to come in?" she asked.

Yes. "No." Somehow he managed the lie with a straight face. A noise made him look up to see a sprite, awakened by their conversation, scowl down from the tree. "No, Vixen. If I come in, we'll be indulging in some serious physical activity, and I think you're a tad bruised for that."

Her mouth dropped open.

He stepped closer, bathed himself in her feminine fragrance and the growing scent of arousal, his and hers. How could she have the smell of a human...yet almost like a shifter? What strange chemistry produced that?

Once more, he drew his fingers across her uninjured cheek and down, feeling the hammer of her pulse in her neck. His control slipped. He curved his arm around her firm waist and pulled her close enough to slide his hand up under her shirt. Under her bra.

"Oh God." She held herself stiff for one second, then melted against him, all lush female.

Nuzzling the fine hair at her temple, he cupped her breast, so firm and soft at the same time, and rubbed his thumb over its tightly puckered nipple. When her breath hissed in, he nearly laid her down and took her right there in the grass.

Instead, he released her—although it felt as if he was ripping his insides out—and brushed his lips across hers. Teasing, light. Her mouth was tender, full, enticing as she opened to him. Her hands slid up his chest, twined around his neck and she pulled him—the female had muscles—against her. His sex pressed against her stomach even as her breasts flattened on his chest, and the sensations shot through him like he'd fallen full into Gathering time.

He ran his hands down her back and took one sweet ass-cheek in each palm. "Herne, I've been wanting my hands right here since I met you," he whispered, squeezing gently, feeling a quiver course through her body. He angled the kiss—and bumped her cheek.

She winced, hissed in pain.

"Oh, hell." His fingers did not want to relinquish their prey, but he let go and gripped her shoulders to move her away. "You're hurt. And this is not the time."

And not the person. Herne help him, he was charging straight for misery, no doubt about it. She wasn't a shifter, dammit. Daonain weren't all that attracted to humans, so why now? *This must not happen.*

"When is a good time?" Her voice was throaty, like she'd just woken up, just had sex, just—

He gritted out, "Go. Now."

"Oh, fine."

If she stuck out that delectable bottom lip, he'd have to bite it.

She merely huffed and turned away. But then, as she moved past him, she stroked one hand up the front of his jeans.

Vicious, evil female. He tightened so hard he almost groaned. Gritting his teeth, he watched her waltz up the steps and into her house.

And then, somehow, he managed to walk back to the jail.

Chapter Seven

THE FOLLOWING MONDAY, Vic watched a black-tail deer spring up the winding mountain trail to disappear into the pines. She yawned and shook her head. Not much sleep, thanks to how the sexy sheriff had said good night. The way he kissed, the feel of his hard hands, even his smell—God, she'd wanted him. Good thing he'd kept his head. *Not smart, Sergeant, wanting to have sex with someone in the target population.*

What bothered her now was that this afternoon, she'd see Calum. Over the past few weeks, she'd come to know him. He had a dry humor that didn't come close to masking that lethal aura of power and authority and intimidating self-confidence. The way he studied her, seeing more than she wanted to show. He was as honorable—and protective—as Alec. In an entirely different, but frightening way, he turned her on just as much. That was against the unwritten code—lusting after brothers, and so not like her. It was unreal.

Almost as unreal as her stroll through the woods. Sighing, she watched a little tree-person run along a pine branch, pause to stare down at her, and disappear.

Vic planted her butt on a convenient log and frowned. She'd seen four *tree-things* on her walk. Or, maybe three—would a tree-thingie be considered the same as a bush-thingie? The bush one had looked smaller, its long fingers tipped with claws that had snagged her hair as she'd pushed past some blackberry bushes.

Her eyes widened. No damn way—as a youngster, when blackberry thorns had caught her hair and clothing—had it really been a bizarre bush-person?

Nah. Even as a child, she'd have spotted any bush-thingie grabbing her clothes. They seemed to live just in this area. Why this mountain was so populated with strange creatures she didn't know, but dammit, she'd figure it out…starting with the shifters.

Damn shifters. It would be convenient if one would obligingly pop out and say, *"Hi"*. She glanced around hopefully.

No luck. Then again, she hadn't really expected to find a fuzzy werebeast slinking past. She'd just needed to get out of town for a while. Those two guys who'd attacked her. She had to wonder if they'd done it because of her…would it be her species? Would shifters be considered a separate race or species?

Yeah, she bet the two drunks were shifters. They'd been too fast and strong, especially the old guy who should be in a wheelchair instead of trying to put his boot in her gut. Rising, she headed toward the sound of trickling water. After two sunny days, the drying pine needles underfoot crackled slightly as they released a tangy scent. It was so quiet she could hear the branches overhead rustle in the wind.

The desert seemed a long way away. But there were some nasty similarities. In Iraq, the question was: is that person a terrorist? Do they have a bomb underneath their clothing? Here, she had to ask: does this person turn into something with claws and whiskers in their spare time?

Alec had scratch scars across his face. Did that mean he'd met a shifter…or was one? What would he do if she asked him about Lachlan's grandfather?

She shook her head. *No, don't bring it up with him for now.* She already had suspects to stake out. Yeah, a couple of *human-*

hating…things who in animal form would probably devour her for breakfast. After biting her into tiny pieces.

God, Lachlan's request was so not fair.

Thinking of fairness, what was all this '*owing*' business anyway? These people sure had weird customs. She'd have to ask Calum before they met her two attackers today. Breathing in a moist green scent, she discovered a tiny stream almost hidden by underbrush. She knelt and dipped her hand in the icy cold water. Such a pretty place, maybe she should—*Wait*. She stared at her knees. *I knelt?* When had the pain in her knee disappeared?

Slowly, she rose to her feet and touched her leg. Rubbed her knee. No pain. She did a snap kick, a side kick, and lunged, putting all her weight on it. No agony, no weakness. Healed. She was healed!

"*Ohh-rah!*" She did a victory dance from one side of the clearing to the other. A second later, she whipped out her cell phone. The reception was barely adequate, but she dialed anyway.

"Wells." Her boss wasn't one to waste words.

"Sir. It's Morgan. I'm ready to return to duty."

"Sergeant." His voice warmed. Now that was a shock. "You believe you are *fully* recovered?"

"Yes, sir."

"Not that I would ever doubt your word, Sergeant, but I need a doctor's confirmation. Are you still in Washington?"

"Yes, sir."

She heard scratching sounds, shuffling papers. "I'll send the paperwork for a physical to Lewis-McChord. See Doctor…ah, yes, Dr. Reinhardt. I will accept no other physician's okay, is that clear?"

Hell, another one of his unbribable people. "Clear, sir. I'll call him tomorrow."

"Good enough. As to the matter you'd mentioned before—"

More paper shuffling. "Yes. The ex-marine named Swane. I'm back in the States now, and I've started some inquiries. Do you have any additional information for me?"

This was her chance to bring up shapeshifters... She remembered Lachlan's terrified face and sighed. *I gave my word.* "No, sir. That's it."

"Then, I'll talk to you after I have Dr. Reinhardt's report in hand."

"Thank you, sir."

Her grin faded as she closed the phone. Once again she'd dodged telling Wells about the shifters. Dammit, she needed to return to Baghdad where the issues were clear and she knew her ass from a hole in the ground. And where she wasn't getting sucked into people's lives and lusting after civilians.

But her mission wasn't over. She had to find Lachlan's grandfather. And be certain the werebeasties posed no danger to normal, unfurry people, or no matter what she'd promised Lachlan, she'd turn over the investigation to Wells. Her promise to the American people came first. *Hell.*

As she scowled, she saw something skitter across a branch, then a tiny face peered down at her. Another of those tree-thingies? She pointed a finger at it. "Whatever you fuckers are, do not—I repeat—do not follow me to Baghdad."

JOE THORSON SQUINTED against the bright afternoon light as he stepped out of his bookstore. His twisted knee burned like fire, and the massive purple bruise on his jaw had turned shaving into a hellish exercise.

He deserved every bit of it.

Nodding at Al Baty who waited on the sidewalk, Thorson eased onto the ironwork bench by the display window.

"You look like you got caught in an avalanche." Al took the

matching chair. He grinned, fingered his chin. "The human packs a punch."

"Does she," Thorson said in a dry voice.

"At least—"

"Shut up." His soul felt tattered with humiliation. What had he been *thinking* to attack a *female*? No matter the species, it was wrong.

He waited silently as Calum and the human strolled down from the tavern. As they approached, Thorson stood and waited. And watched, noting how Calum's eyes darkened, his posture turning protective. Surely the Cosantir hadn't formed an attachment to this...human.

Thorson turned his gaze on the female. Pretty enough, he supposed, but lacking—his eyes narrowed—actually, she wasn't lacking. She had a werecat's grace although not the wild scent of one who'd run the forests. He could see why she might, possibly, have attracted Calum. Still, any relationship with a human would be as doomed as an air sylph trying to mate a fire salamander.

"Calum," he said, nodding to the Cosantir, then grudgingly tilted his head to the female. "Miss."

She was silent, an unusual trait in a human. One to be appreciated.

"Victoria, this is Albert Baty. He owns the grocery store," Calum said. "Joe Thorson owns Books."

Her gaze was cool, her voice husky. "Great name for a bookstore." No tedious, *pleased to meet you*, or *how are you* niceties from her.

"Have you suggestions for reciprocity?" Calum asked. Strictly business was the Cosantir, especially when something raised his ire. He wasn't one a shifter wanted to rile up. Although he'd never wanted the God-given title, he'd led them with wisdom...and power that had become legendary.

Al stepped forward, his gut leading his chest by a good few

inches. He needed to get into the forest more, run some of that flab off. "First, Miss Waverly, I'd like to say that I'm sorry. I was drunk…and stupid."

Her eyes narrowed. "I've dealt with stupid drunks before. Never seen one try to knife a person in the back."

Al cringed like a whipped dog. Thorson barely repressed a snarl.

The grocer's face turned red enough to match the broken veins in his nose. "I-I."

The woman sighed. "Do me a favor. If you want to drink, leave the weapons at home."

"Yes, miss. I will," Al said.

By Herne, if Al had been in wolf form, his tail would be under his belly. Thorson really needed to rethink his friends, or, at least, avoid submissive werewolves.

Al continued, "My thought to balance the debt is free meat from the grocery for you as long as you live in Cold Creek."

The human's eyes widened. She glanced at Calum.

The Cosantir considered, then nodded. "A fair exchange. Let it be so." He turned to Thorson, his pupils very close to totally black. Not a good sign. He obviously held Thorson to blame for the fight.

"My apologies also, Miss Waverly," Thorson said stiffly. He wouldn't—couldn't—crawl like his dog of a friend. Not for a *human*, even a female one.

She tilted her head, studying him. "Why do you hate me?"

The question came like a slash to the jugular. *Because you're one of them who killed my boy. Human.* Images of Lachlan flooded his memory. The day the boy arrived, his mother dead, his little face so white. Giggling under a pile of books dislodged when he'd tried to climb a bookcase. His wonder at his first trawsfur. His body lifeless on a steel table. Killed by *humans*. Thorson choked on hatred. His hands closed into fists, tingling with the beginning of trawsfur.

Calum pulled the human back a step and moved in front of her. His eyes, black as night, met Thorson's, and power edged his voice. "No, Joe."

The impending change fled; the anger did not. Lips closed over a snarl, Thorson turned his head away and struggled for control. He heard Calum speaking…"lost his grandson. Grieving…not himself." And hearing, he regained his composure. No one apologized for him.

He turned back to the female. "I'm sorry." Her face was whiter than the snow-capped peaks, her eyes shocked. Did grandchildren not die where she came from?

"I… Fucking A, you're…" She swallowed and raised her voice and her chin both. "I'm sorry for your loss, Mr. Thorson."

"Thank you." He inhaled, his chest sore from more than the fight. "Calum. I haven't thought of a way to achieve balance. Since you know the fem—ah, lady, have you suggestions?"

"I have an idea that might serve," Calum said smoothly. The faint smile on his face had the hackles on Thorson's neck rising. Last time he'd seen that smile, Calum had crippled the recipient. "I would suggest you give Miss Waverly free rein in your bookstore." Calum glanced at Al and added, "As long as she resides in Cold Creek."

The Cosantir had lost his mind. How could free books compensate for Thorson's attempt on her life? But by Herne, the female clasped her hands together, and the look on her face could only be described as bliss.

Calum raised an eyebrow at Thorson.

An unfamiliar human underfoot in his domain? The towns-folk he knew were bad enough. Thorson choked a little, and then spit out the traditional answer. "The balance is fair. Accepted."

ENGULFED IN THE aroma of books, leather, new paper, and a hint of dust, Vic was unable to keep the smile off her face. She'd begun to wonder if the place was ever open. Bookstore withdrawal—who would suspect such a thing existed? But she'd get her fix today. The store was even better than she'd hoped with a great selection of new and used books, including military sci-fi.

Joe Thorson had taken up position behind the small counter, watching her, his expression somewhere between amused and furious. Furious wasn't good. This probably wasn't the smartest thing she'd done, entering a pissed-off panther's lair.

Then again, this lair had *books*.

And she didn't blame him for attacking her, not after Calum's explanation. The old man *had* to be Lachlan's gramps, and if he'd learned how his grandson had died, it was no wonder he hated humans.

Turning her back on him, but keeping her ears open, she did a quick survey of the place. Like everything else in this town, the building was old. The counter was by the left wall. The door behind it probably led to a back room. Towering wooden bookshelves created a maze on the hardwood floor. The right wall held a table and ladder-back chairs before a fireplace. Useful, but not very friendly. She noted the two windows framing the fireplace as possible exits.

Wandering around the room, she discovered a shelf of recently released books. *Yes!* A new Guy Gavriel Kay went under her arm. She thumbed through a Bujold and kept it also. But there was a new Crusie, dammit. No. With a lingering sigh, she forced herself to walk to the counter.

He eyed her and her choices.

"I expected you to take more," he said patronizingly. His voice was sandpaper rough, like someone had crushed his larynx in the past. White lacework scars covered his tanned forearms, so maybe the same person had tried to rip him apart. Considering his personality, quite understandable.

"I limit myself to two books at a time," she said. No need to mention how delaying to pack books had almost gotten her blown up. "I'll be back in a couple days for two more."

"I see." He held out a hand. "Let me put them into the system so my inventory remains correct."

He scanned in the barcodes and pushed them across the counter to her.

"Thank you." She gathered them up.

"Balance," he said, his mouth flattening slightly.

Earlier, on the way to town, Calum had explained the balance-reciprocity stuff was a local custom. It sure gave new meaning to the phrase, 'paybacks are hell'. But he'd offered only that in explanation and trying to get information out of him was like pumping a dry well. The man had even more control over his words and expressions than spymaster Wells did.

"See you soon," she said to Thorson.

With a short nod of dismissal, he turned away and bent over the small desk tucked in a corner.

Nice meeting you too, she thought to his back and—*oh, God.* A picture of Lachlan stood on the desk. The kid stood on a mountain peak, wind ruffling his hair. Laughing. Healthy. The grief that ripped through her stopped her breath.

She opened her mouth to tell the old man about his grandson, how fucking brave he'd been, how—

No. I can't. Lachlan's grandfather would have to wait until she finished investigating. She'd sidestepped telling Wells about these…creatures and now the burden was on her to be certain they didn't present a danger to the rest of the world, or at least to the United States citizens she'd promised to protect.

Joe Thorson was obviously a shifter. A really unhappy, vengeful werecat. If she revealed information about Lachlan's murder, the old guy would probably try to kill her again. Once was plenty for that dance.

As isolated as the town was, if they kicked her out—or killed her—getting another agent in place would be very difficult. She was here. Investigation first, then Lachlan's grandfather.

He glanced up from his paperwork, eyebrows raised.

She gave him a curt nod and left.

Chapter Eight

S HE FINISHED HER two books in three days and headed
back to the bookstore, zipping up her new fleece-lined, jean
jacket. At least she'd gotten in some shopping after seeing the
base doctor yesterday. Reinhardt thought her knee was healed,
but wouldn't commit himself until the lab and x-ray reports
came in. Perhaps that was good—she needed time to finish up
here.

Leaves crackled under her boots. The last few days had been
brisk and dry, and she'd hiked the forests by day and snooped
around the town at night. Without any results. Damn sneaky
furballs.

As she reached downtown, she noticed an awful lot of people around. Had she missed a parade or something? She nodded
at Angie, the owner of the diner and smiled at Warren from the
hardware store.

When she spotted Calum and Alec across the street, all the
blood in her veins carbonated and fizzed like a dropped Pepsi.
Dammit. The bastards had haunted her dreams. Alec's lazy grin,
Calum's penetrating gaze. Alec's leisurely stride almost concealing a powerful fighter's movements. Calum's silent prowl.

She wasn't the only one attracted to the men either. Women
flirted them up in the tavern and—Vic frowned as a frigid-

looking blonde stopped to talk with them and trailed a hand across Calum's chest. Who the hell did she think she was?

Another woman with huge breasts stared at the two men assessingly, as if she wanted to pull out each guy's dick and weigh it on a scale. Maybe Vic should inform her that, having rubbed against Alec's package, she would vouch for him in the size department.

When Vic's gaze shifted to Calum's crotch, she caught herself. *You're losing it, Sergeant.* Scowling, she crossed the street to Books. "Afternoon," she greeted Thorson.

He sat on a stool behind the tall counter, head bent over an open book. "To you," he rumbled, not looking up.

Vic headed for the science fiction shelves. A SF craving could be worse than needing chocolate and harder to satisfy. But only a few minutes later, she was back at the front.

"Hey!" She shoved the new Honor Harrington book under his nose. "I've waited months for this release."

The corner of his mouth rose an infinitesimal degree. "Then this is your happy day. Congratulations."

He took the two books for the barcode scanner.

"Speaking of happy days..." Vic leaned an arm on the counter and frowned out the window. "What's with all the strangers in town? Is something going on?"

From the sudden stillness in his face, she had her answer. Definitely something. He gave a token glance at the street. "Just city folks here to look at the leaves."

"Oh, well, that explains it," Vic said politely and took her books.

"Enjoy your reading," he said, equally politely.

Vic managed to suppress the urge to shake him until his secrets spilled out like coins from a vending machine. This place was getting to her. Overseas, everyone was against her and she knew it. Here... Here, she'd gotten sucked into their lives.

Jamie's hugs, Calum's hand wrapped around her arm, Alec's teasing. What if the two men were shifters? Hell, they probably *were* shifters. She didn't know whether to go forward or to pull back.

I don't want to pull back.

As she stepped out the door, she saw Alec and Calum talking with yet another woman. Vic's free hand closed into a fist. The hefty blonde wouldn't look nearly so pretty with her nose squashed all over her face.

The visual was satisfying; the urge was not. Vic sighed and shook her head. Neither man was stamped with a "property of Vic" sign.

"I hope you'll honor me tonight," said a man's voice.

Vic turned. Three Yuppies wandered down the sidewalk, one man on each side of a butt-ugly brunette, another guy a step behind. The men were focused totally on the woman.

Vic spotted a group across the street with one woman and four men, all giving the woman the devoted attention of starving dogs circling a bone.

Was this a test of a new pheromone perfume? Spray it on and every man in the area will be at your feet? "I want some too," she muttered.

VIC NEVER HAD figured out what was going on. After consoling herself with her new book, Vic ventured out as usual after sunset. Hands in her jacket pockets, she sauntered here and there, scuffling through the leaves on the sidewalks. The surfeit of people had disappeared from Main Street. She kept walking...and wasn't it odd she ended up at The Wild Hunt?

Even odder, the sign in the window said, "CLOSED", but cars filled the parking lot. It looked like a party, and Calum hadn't invited her. She sniffed indignantly, trying to ignore the

I've-been-left-out ache under her ribs.

She paused. Should she walk on? Did she really want to discover the answers, considering she'd begun to think they might be unpalatable? Nonetheless, it was her duty. *Move out, sergeant.*

As she crossed the lot, she noticed they'd lowered the window blinds. Usually Calum only put them down to block the glaring afternoon sun. Well, hell, snooping might be tougher than she'd figured. She tilted her head, trying to hear what was going on. Generalized babble, laughter, an occasion shout—nothing ominous.

The scuff of a footstep spun her around.

"Well, now, here's a pretty female." A tall, bulky man in his thirties circled a car, his eyes intent upon her. Another guy with flaming red hair and freckles walked behind him.

Caught like a first-year spy. Embarrassment heated her cheeks and deepened her voice. "Um. Good evening."

"And to you, miss," the redhead said. "Are you unaccompanied?"

"I—"

"Not for long," the tall man said. "My name is Duke, that's Tim, and let's just say that you're with us." He grabbed her hand and pulled her to his side.

She could have flattened him, but here she'd found the perfect way to get inside.

As they entered the tavern, Tim leaned in to brush her hair away from her face and audibly sniffed.

Now that was just rude. She wasn't wearing perfume. Did she stink or something? She scowled at him.

He took a step back. "A bit slow getting started, huh?"

"There's no hurrying a female," Duke said, keeping his arm around her.

A few paces into the boisterous room, Vic gawked like a new fish on the first day in combat. As she studied the milling people, she realized there were a lot more men than women. The women were sitting on the bar, on the tables, even on Calum's prized pool tables and men crowded around them, talking loudly over the lively country music.

The hallway door that led upstairs was propped open, and a couple emerged with the satisfied, flushed look of recent sex.

At a nearby table, the snooty-looking blonde who'd run her hand across Calum's chest had two men next to her; one stroked her shoulder, the other kissed her fingers.

With an effort, Vic closed her mouth, tried to look blasé, but Jesus fuck, was this some kind of orgy? Calum was into this? She hadn't thought he'd be so… Dammit, she liked him. *This is way confusing.*

The redheaded guy from the parking lot smiled at Vic. "So miss…" He leaned in and ran his hand over her butt.

Not a chance. She slapped his arm away and gave him a look that should have fried him in his shoes.

He shrugged. "Oh, well. Come on, Duke, let's find one that's interested."

They walked away, leaving her standing alone by the door. A second later, she realized that a lot of men were looking at her. Assessingly. *Oh, fuck. Time to leave.*

Too unnerved to take her eyes from the room, she groped behind her for the door handle. A big hand closed on her fingers.

"A little out of your element, Ms. Waverly?" Alec slid a hard arm around her waist.

"Yeah. Very." *Thank you, Jesus.* "I was walking and got dragged in here by a couple of guys. What's going on?" She tried an innocent look, but as Alec pulled her closer, she gave it up. God, he felt good. Watching all the sexual displays was like…contagious…and now she was horny as hell. When Alec ran his hand up and down her back, every nerve fired, and each stroke made her skin more sensitive.

Unable to resist, she turned into him. His other arm went around her, and he curled his fingers under her butt, squeezing and pulling her up against his thick cock, lifting her slightly so her pelvis slid down against the hardness.

"Alec." Her voice came out husky.

His face was flushed, and his eyelids heavy. "You really, really shouldn't be here," he said and took her mouth as if he'd been doing it for years.

Everything inside her burst into flame as his tongue swept in, dueled with hers. He leaned in, pinning her against the wall. As his broad chest crushed her breasts, she gripped his shoulders, reveling in the rock-hard muscles under her fingers.

"To hell with common sense," he muttered. He slung her over his shoulder like some demented cave man.

"What the fuck?" She thumped him with her fist.

He made a chortling sound. One big hand squeezed the back of her lower thigh to hold her in place. His other hand slid high between her legs. She could feel the heat of his fingers so close to her sex, igniting a burn. His finger stroked over the crotch of her jeans, and she wiggled uncontrollably. He laughed.

As he climbed the stairs, people brushed past them. She heard husky laughs. When a man ran his hand down her leg, she felt rumbles under her stomach as Alec growled like an animal.

An animal? She stiffened. *Wait.*

He walked down the hall into a small room, bent, and dropped her. She fell onto softness. Pushing up, she realized that silky green cushions covered the floor. A fireplace sent out heat and enough light to see Alec's expression.

ALEC LOOKED DOWN at Vicki as she pushed to a sitting position. He hesitated. Sex with a human. Sex with a human during a Gathering. This was a bad idea. It shouldn't even be happening, dammit. Daonain weren't attracted to humans.

But as his head explained everything to him quite clearly, the scent of her arousal wrapped around him, heating his blood, and urging him to possess her, take her. *Now.*

He'd already had two females, but it didn't make any difference. Not with his Vixen sitting like a prize, right here in front of him. His cock hardened until it pulsed with every heartbeat. Logic lost out to the animal inside him.

He dropped to one knee to take her mouth again, and her soft, full lips opened for him, her tongue twining with his. He took her breath in, gave her his, then pulled back long enough to kiss down her neck to the curve of her shoulder. By Herne, the little sounds she gave, deep in her throat, were going to kill him. Wanting—needing—more, he undid the top buttons of her jacket.

Her hands closed on his arms as if she wasn't sure whether to pull him closer or push him away. Holding her gaze with his, he unhurriedly opened her jacket far enough so his fingers could trace the edge of her bra through her shirt.

Her breath hissed in, her eyes going unfocused. Her scent intensified, fragrant, compelling. Overwhelming. *Hell with it.* After shoving to his feet, he ripped his shirt off. A hail of buttons thudded against the wall. She inhaled sharply, but her golden gaze never wavered from his body. He flung his shoes and pants to one side and knelt beside her on the cushions.

She willingly moved into his arms, all female and fragrant. Her long hair spilled over his skin in a silken kiss. *Oh, yes.*

"Alec," she whispered, "this isn't wise."

"I know," he murmured, burying his face in the crook of her neck where her scent was strong and wild. He bit the muscle there, lightly, laved it with his tongue, bit again. "But right now, this minute, you're mine."

VIC RAN HER hands over his bare chest, ruffling the crisp golden hair covering his hard pectorals. This was crazy, but oh, God, he felt so good.

"You're overdressed, Vixen," he whispered and flicked open the remaining buttons on her jacket. "Wouldn't want you to overheat." He slid her coat off and fondled her breasts through her T-shirt, teasing her hardening nipples with his fingertips. The stroke and squeeze of his big hand sent heat straight to her groin, and she couldn't find a *no* in her when he pulled her shirt and bra off, then her shoes and jeans.

His eyebrows rose at the knife she wore strapped on one calf. Then, he efficiently stripped it off along with the rest of her clothes.

She was naked before she knew it. Giving a short laugh, she murmured, "I do love competent people." But that made her think of other things. "I'm on birth control and tested recently. You?"

He frowned for a second as if not understanding, then shook his head. "No diseases."

Feeling too exposed under his intent gaze, she pulled him down to cover her like a massive muscular quilt. He moved slightly, and his cock settled between her thighs, the head teasing her folds. *Oh yes.*

He nibbled on her lips and then took her mouth, his lips firm, his tongue wicked.

She kissed him back, threading her hands through his thick hair, holding his head while she sampled him. She traced a finger over the tiny ridged scar on his cheekbone before biting his jaw. His skin tasted of salt and man and a shiver ran up her spine.

He hummed when she kissed his corded neck. His back muscles tightened into granite when she licked the hollow above his collarbone. God, she wanted to just rub herself against him. Instead, she ran a hand down his flank and grasped his cock.

He slowly pulled away and sat back on his haunches.

Startled, she pushed up on one elbow. "What? You're stopping?"

A dimple appeared with his slow smile. "My momma taught me to savor my desserts." His eyes were like molten heat stroking across her body; his hands followed. His fingertips ran over her collarbone, her shoulder. He paused, and in the dim light, she saw his eyes narrow as he traced the shiny scars from Lachlan's bite. His gaze on her body, he unerringly found each remnant of past battles: right bicep and forearm, knife scars; left thigh, shrapnel; left hip, bullet. How well did he see in the dark anyway? Her muscles tightened. Would he ask—?

"You've had a rough life, sweetheart," he said before nuzzling each scar gently. She relaxed, worry replaced by something...softer, an unfamiliar feeling as tender as his lips.

Then, with a sinful smile, he started to explore anew. Her stomach muscles quivered at his light touch. He traced a line up between her breasts, circling each mound with teasing fingers...circling until her skin felt needy. Hungry. Her nipples bunched, aching for more. When his lips finally closed on one peak, electricity arced straight to her pussy, and she gasped for air, arching off the cushions.

His mouth on her breast was hot, his tongue hard and ravenous, teasing unmercifully. His hand possessed her other breast, and the deluge of sensations sent her senses whirling. Her fingers clenched in his hair—probably painfully—to pull him closer, and she couldn't seem to release her hold. His scent wrapped around her, a sunlit forest, pine trees. Male. Very male.

Her hips rose, rubbing her pelvis against him as she ached with emptiness. "Alec—please—" Her legs parted, inviting him in.

"Ah, I might have known you'd get all urgent on me." One big hand stroked down her inner thigh, pushing between her legs. *Yes. Now.* Her insides quaked in anticipation of a hard, fast hammering.

To her surprise, he moved back and kissed his way down her body. A bite for her stomach that made her squeak. His tongue circled her belly button. His breath puffed hot against her pelvis. There he settled. He grasped her thighs, pushing her legs apart, and opening her fully to his gaze. "Oh, yes," he murmured. Bending his head, he nibbled on the tender skin of her inner thigh.

The muscles in her legs tightened uncontrollably, and her hands curled into fists in his hair. *No.* She'd done this before, and she didn't want this. Fast hard sex, that's all she wanted, sex where she could control how much she felt. Not this way, lying before him so exposed…so intimate. "No, Alec." She tugged on him. "I want you inside me. Now, dammit."

"Not just yet, baby," he murmured.

When she tried to close her legs, his broad shoulders kept her thighs spread. His head lifted, and he studied her as if he saw more, much more, than she wanted him to see. As if he could see her fear as well as her arousal.

His steady gaze released her, and he kissed between her hip and pussy. "Don't worry so much, Vixen. This is making love, not war." His fingers pressed her folds completely open, and she felt cool air touch her, the slight rasp of his stubbled cheek, and then his tongue slid lightly, tenderly over her sensitive skin. She moaned, her vision blurring, and her legs falling open.

When he nibbled and tongued her inner folds, she tensed even as her hips pressed upward for more. "Alec—"

He gave a growling laugh and nipped her thigh. A wave of heat hit her and her head dropped back. God, it was too much, felt too good. She was losing control; her mind drowning in the surging of her body. In the determined gentleness of his touch.

The heat of his tongue circling her clit made her moan. She

felt swollen down there, too tight. Burning for more. And then one hard finger eased inside her. She gasped as nerves wakened within her. His thick knuckle rubbed against her opening, sending sensation unfurling.

She couldn't catch her breath as her hips jerked with every slide of his finger, of his tongue. His finger stroked her inside; outside, his tongue never left her clitoris, circling the spot, never touching the top.

Her whole world wavered, tightening, tightening, suspended in the black space of need.

And then his lips closed over her and he...sucked. His tongue slid over her clit, the very top, and a grenade of sensation turned the room white and blew her to pieces.

HIS VIXEN WAS a screamer, Alec thought as she spasmed around his finger, her hips bucking against his face. Under his tongue, her clit softened, and he teased it, enjoying the way she clenched with each stroke. She hadn't wanted to lose control—he'd seen that clearly—but when she did, she was glorious.

As her shuddering slowed, he eased his finger out, smiling at how slick she was and how her scent had sweetened with her climax. "By Herne, you taste like the finest honey." After a final lick that elicited only a tiny quiver, he moved back up her body.

Her arms lay limp at her sides, and he grinned, his scalp tender from her tugging on his hair. He'd never enjoyed anything so much in his life as sliding past her desire to control everything...and making her come. He kissed her lightly. "You're beautiful, Vicki," he whispered.

When she blinked in surprise, then smiled in pleasure, his heart squeezed. Her tough attitude covered up such tender feelings. The discovery made him want her all the more.

He settled between her legs and pressed his cock lightly against her slick entrance. By Herne, he needed to be in her. Her eyes widened, and then he sheathed himself, all the way home in one move.

Back arching, she clenched. "Oh God!"

"No, just Alec." She was hot. Tight. He closed his eyes, not moving, simply savoring the squeeze of her pussy around him, letting her accustom to his size.

"I like how you feel." Her voice was husky, the sound pulling him down to take her mouth and pillage those soft, swollen lips.

When he rubbed his chest across her breasts, her nipples hardened to points at the friction. Finally, unable to hold out any longer, he started to thrust, the feeling rich and good.

She ran her hands up his back, played with his hair, obviously starting to regain her senses. Couldn't have that. He kissed her again, smiled against her lips, and raised his hips enough to allow his hand down below. When his fingers touched her clitoris, she gasped, and her inside muscles tightened around him so quickly he almost lost control. Herne help him.

As he set up a hard rhythm, her eyes unfocused. Her hands closed on his shoulders. With each thrust, he slid a wet finger across her sensitive flesh, and suddenly her hips were pumping with real urgency.

"God, Alec, I don't need... I already..."

Oh, but he needed. He needed to feel her spasm around him, to see her overwhelmed again. "Shhh." He took her mouth and drove hard as her heat tightened. She met him thrust for thrust, pressing him to go faster. Too fast. Gripping her ass, he slowed her rhythm, rotating his hips instead. Her muscles quivered, and he surged deeper.

Her breath puffed hot and fast against his neck as little moans escaped her. He gritted his teeth and slowed further, feeling each inch going in, each inch withdrawing, the finest sensation known to a male. Again, and again.

Her fingers dug into his shoulders. "Alec, please... Please..."

Her thigh muscles were quivering, her pussy tight around him. She was close. Pulling her hips up to meet his, he plunged, deeper, harder, and her wail filled the room.

As she spasmed, every muscle in his body tightened. His balls drew up tight to his groin as if someone had them in a firm grip. Another hard thrust and his release blew through him, white-hot pressure from deep inside as he poured himself into her. As her hips lifted up to him, her pussy billowed against his shaft, drawing out the last drop.

Heart pounding, he rested on his elbows, studying her flushed face and the pulse hammering in her neck. She was warm around him, soft under him. Just another female...yet this joining felt different. Her body under his hands felt just right, his release more satisfying. Fulfilling. How could that be?

He kissed her gently. They were yet joined when he rolled, placing her taut little body on top where he could let his hands stroke over her soft, damp skin. A mountain rescue of two young hikers had left him exhausted, but after a short rest, he damn well intended to have her again and collect some sweet screams.

"COSANTIR, WE NEED your help." The whisper came from outside the small Gathering room where Calum lay sprawled over Ursula's naked body. Although he'd felt oddly unenthusiastic this Gathering, Ursula had nagged, and he'd finally relented and brought her upstairs. The scent of her arousal had sparked his own, and the joining had been adequate, if not fulfilling.

She murmured drowsily as he withdrew and rose. After pulling on his clothes, he slipped out of the room.

Karen waited in the hallway, her face shiny with sweat, almost whining with impatience.

"Tell me what is wrong," he said in a low voice.

"A fight, Cosantir," she choked out. "Farrah went outside with the two males she had chosen, Chad and Patrick. An out-of-territory male followed them to the south clearing and started a fight."

She grabbed his arm. "They're fighting as animals, and the guy's a grizzly and Chad's only a little wolf. He's hurting him."

Bloody hell. Calum ran down the stairs. The normally locked door to the portals stood propped open for Gathering. Down into the cave, out onto the mountain. The night wind blew cold against his skin, still warm from mating.

Growls and pain-filled yelps came from ahead. The males were indeed fighting in animal form.

When he reached the clearing, he snarled. Up on hind legs, a seven-foot grizzly swung its arms at a wolf. Near the trees, Farrah was crying hysterically and clinging to Patrick. Karen ran across to join them.

The scents of anger and fear—and blood—hung heavy in the air. The wolf limped from a badly mangled hind leg and tried to retreat, but the stranger kept advancing. Wanting the kill.

Not on my mountain. "By Herne, you will *halt!*" The command backed by the God's power hit the two animals. Stunned, they dropped to their haunches, shaking their heads. Calum motioned for Patrick to pull Chad out of danger.

The unknown grizzly remained in the center of the clearing, trying to regain its feet.

The bear growled when Calum grabbed it by the scruff of its neck. "Trawsfur," Calum ordered, sending power into the animal. The tingle of shift and the touch of Herne mingled and then he threw the naked stranger, now in human form, sprawling on the ground.

The man was big, well-muscled, with dark hair and dark

eyes. He pushed to his feet, wobbling slightly.

"Karen, the Healer's inside. Get him, please," Calum said, then stared at the stranger. Rage tightened his voice. "Your name?"

"I'm hurt," the male whined, holding out an arm with bite marks across it. Shallow punctures, Calum noted. Chad had obeyed the Law of the Fight and done no permanent damage.

"Name," Calum repeated, and his anger finally registered, for the stranger dropped to his knees.

"I… Andy. Andy Schoenberg. From Rainier Territory."

"Do the Elders in your Territory not instruct their clan in the Laws?"

When Schoenberg cringed guiltily, repugnance roiled in Calum's gut. Had the shifter no pride?

"I see you know the Law. Look at your opponent." Calum pointed across the clearing. The wolf's savaged leg was black with blood, and exposed bone glinted in the moonlight. "Do you have aught to say in your defense?

"She was ignoring me. I-I just wanted… I thought she'd choose me if I won." His shoulders sagged. "No."

"Then this doom I pronounce upon you. Marked as outcast, you will be shunned by shifters and OtherFolk until the marks of banishment are gone."

Chapter Nine

S OMEONE RAN PAST the door. Vic roused. Beside her, Alec slept, sprawled over the green cushions. The reddish glow of the dying fire highlighted the long line of muscle down his back, the tight curve of his buttocks. He was absolutely beautiful.

And she was absolutely terrified. *What the hell have I done?*

A quick fuck wouldn't have been a problem. No strings, no regrets, no future. This…this hadn't been a simple fuck. He hadn't permitted her to keep it that—and he'd not only satisfied her as no man had before, he'd touched a part of her she kept well-hidden. He'd created a tie between them, a connection where she'd had none. He'd become more than just—

In the hall, a woman spoke, and Vic tilted her head, trying to hear. "…need you. Chad's been hurt. His wolf was no match for a werebear. Calum's out there now."

Vic's breath hitched. *Wolf? Werebear?* Lachlan hadn't mentioned other animals. God, what *were* these people? A chill ran through her body, driving the sweet lethargy away. She glanced at Alec. They'd had a…fun interlude, but it was over.

Dammit, she should have told Wells. But she hadn't, so it was up to her to investigate. Her duty stood before her.

Duty sucks. With a silent sigh, she rose and soundlessly pulled on her jeans and shirt. She froze as Alec's breathing paused and resumed.

The hall was empty. Shoes in hand, she tiptoed down the stairs and followed the footsteps that seemed to have headed toward the back exit. But before the end of the hall, the door with industrial-strength locks stood open, and candles lit the tiny room. She stepped inside and pulled the door closed behind her. A gun safe occupied one corner of a small sitting room. Over the couch, a moose's antlered head held two weapons. Vic walked closer and stopped, stunned. One was an antique Enfield that probably dated back to the Civil War, and the other a black-powder Shenandoah from even earlier. Lovely, lovely rifles.

No wonder Calum kept the room locked. Not only to keep his customers from stealing, but also for Jamie's safety. Nothing ... *otherworldly*...was in here. The relief was like a wave of warmth in the Arctic, and with it came the urge to climb back up the stairs and join Alec for a—

No, this didn't explain that conversation upstairs. As she frowned, a cold draft whispered against her face...in a windowless room with the door closed? She moved toward the closet, breathed in the frigid, dank air, and saw an opening in the back behind the hanging clothing. A secret door.

Oh hell, Calum must be part of this shifter stuff. Would have to be. Disappointment sliced through her heart like a dull knife.

No. An agent doesn't have a heart; Wells had told her that again and again. A spy has only duty, and that duty now compelled her feet down the stone steps and into a cave as cold as the hollow left in her chest.

Pale moonlight spilled over the forest outside the cave. After a quick glance, Vic stepped out cautiously. No one was around, although anyone could lurk unseen under the dark trees. So where was the action?

As the chill wind tugged at her hair and clothing, she listened. *There.* Voices, not far away. After smearing dirt on her too-white face, she headed in that direction, grateful the carpet of pine needles silenced her footsteps. The moonlight brightened, washing over the people inside a clearing. Vic crouched behind a tree, edged out far enough to watch, and saw Calum. From the look on his hard face, he was royally pissed-off. *Now why do I think I'm not going to like the end of this party?*

He stood over a naked man with a bleeding arm. Under the trees, a man and two women bent over a—*oh, fuck, damn, shit*—over a *wolf.* The animal lay on its side, panting. Dark blood covered one gray-furred leg. *Some orgy you throw, Calum.*

But this party had gone seriously bad. Calum's face had set in dangerous lines, and when he spoke—damned if he wasn't acting like some judge. Not only did the others let him, but the shivering wussy actually knelt. Calum grabbed the man's hair and said, "Trawsfur" in an icy voice that sent shivers through Vic.

The man blurred—Vic's teeth clenched. She remembered that weird shimmer. *Oh God. A bear.* The man had turned into a fucking grizzly bear. Vic stuffed her fist against her mouth to keep from whimpering like a terrified puppy. She'd seen men beaten, knifed, blown up, but this turning into animals was waaaaay out of her league.

Calum stripped, and her momentary admiration disappeared when his figure blurred. *Oh, please, not again.* A huge panther took his place, one that made Lachlan's animal seem a midget. The cat's short-haired pelt was brown, paler on the belly. Its tail lashed back and forth; its eyes flashed gold in the moonlight. Vic closed her eyes, opened them, her lips silently moving, "No, this is so not happening."

She jumped when Calum—the cat—slashed the bear's muzzle open. The poor bear just took it. As the grizzly staggered across the clearing, all the people-shaped people turned their heads away like they didn't even see the animal. Vic felt a second of pity. She knew how it felt to be on the outside. The bear silently disappeared into the forest, and Calum changed back.

Vic's fingernails had dug into the bark of the tree. Not surprising. Well, she'd found the shifters, and a lot more of them than she'd figured. She pulled her hand open with an effort. Just how many werebeasts lived on this mountain?

The thought made the tiny hairs on her nape raise. What if one was watching her now? Why the fuck hadn't she worn her Glock? Of course, Alec might have noticed that little accessory as he stripped her.

Alec. Alec was Calum's brother so, oh God, he must be a shifter-beast too. Horror iced her skin, dried her mouth. She'd kissed him—he'd been *inside her.*

Get the hell out of here. She rose to her feet, her legs shaky. If she returned through the tunnel, she'd risk being spotted by the fuzzy creatures—or worse, running into Alec. She'd better circle around, go into town by a different route.

She eased one foot back, then another, glanced at the clearing and saw Calum lift his head and sniff. He turned…and looked straight at her.

Oh, fuck.

Before she could run, someone grabbed her from behind, tangling his fingers in her hair and yanking her head back. No words, but the sharp cold metal laid gently against her throat froze her better than any spoken threat.

Why the hell had she even gotten out of bed this morning?

ALEC HELD THE knife against Vicki's throat, unable to find any words to say. Heat rose from her skin, twining with the scent of her. Part of him wanted to throw the knife away and take her in his arms. The other part wanted to slice deep and spill her life's blood onto the forest floor.

Had she only mated with him to get information? If she'd ripped his heart out with her bare hands, it wouldn't have hurt this much.

"Cosantir," he called, not bothering to raise his voice. Even in human form, a shifter's ears were almost as keen as a cat's. "You have a spectator."

"I scented her a minute ago. Bring her here."

With one hand fisted in the human's hair, knife at her throat, Alec guided her into the open area.

Having pulled on his clothing, his brother waited in the center of the clearing. His nostrils flared. The slight wind undoubtedly carried the scent of Alec on Vic and vice versa—the distinctive smell of sex. Anger darkened Calum's eyes.

Alec's jaw clenched. What had he done? Self-loathing rose like vomit in his throat, and his hand tightened in her hair so hard she made a tiny sound of pain. He stopped her in front of Calum, his body a wall behind her to keep her in place.

Near the trees, a huddle of people hovered near a small gray wolf. *Chad?* The healer knelt beside him, and Alec winced at the sight of the wolf's injuries.

Following his gaze, Calum frowned. "Farrah, prepare one of the mating rooms. Patrick, carry Chad for the healer."

Farrah murmured her obedience. Patrick dipped his head. "Yes, Cosantir."

As the others headed for the cave, Calum's attention turned to Vicki. Alec felt her muscles tighten under the impact of the Cosantir's black gaze.

"Kneel, Victoria," Calum said softly.

She stiffened, her chin rising. Alec pressed the knife harder against her throat until a thin line of blood appeared. He had to suppress a shudder. Stubborn female had enough courage that she'd die before complying. And he couldn't...couldn't.

Well then. Fisting his hand tighter in her hair, he slammed his boot into the back of her knees, yanked her off-balance, and shoved her down.

VIC LANDED PAINFULLY on her knees. She snarled, fighting the urge to struggle. *Bastard*. She'd have rather died than kneel. Her anger burned away some of the panic icing her guts.

Her scalp hurt from his controlling fist. *Asshole*. This wasn't the Alec she knew. Dammit, this was why she never let herself be sucked into relationships. If she survived this, she'd cut her losses and get the hell gone.

She raised her gaze to the man in front of her. His pupils were as black as the night sky behind him. Fear slid into her again, sharp as the knife against her throat as she realized that she might not leave this place alive.

Not a good thought. As dread compressed her chest, she struggled to breathe normally, fighting the rigidity of her body. *"Jest roll to your rifle and blow out your brains An' go to your Gawd like a Marine."* She was a Marine; death happened. Her muscles loosened slightly, her breath slowed.

"We accepted the small amount of information you offered when you arrived," Calum said. "Questioning people isn't our way. But now perhaps we should ask a few. What *really* brought you to Cold Creek?" Shirt still unbuttoned, he crossed his arms over his chest.

The damned knife hadn't moved from her throat; Alec waited immovable behind her.

Probably her best bet would be to play stupid. Pretend to be an inquisitive woman, innocent of anything more threatening. She opened her mouth and…the words wouldn't come. Somehow the thought of lying to Alec, and even Calum, hurt deep inside for no reason. But why? She'd spent the last years living untruths—why should she find it so hard this time?

Calum could probably tell anyway, she thought, meeting his

penetrating gaze. A second later, she realized she didn't have to lie at all. The lump in her stomach disappeared. "I was looking for shifters."

Behind her, Alec stopped breathing.

"Were you now?" The icy menace in Calum's voice made her shiver. *Dammit.* He continued as if he hadn't noticed, "How exactly did we catch your attention?"

"A boy named Lachlan died in my arms." Just saying the words tightened her throat. *Failure. Grief.* She blinked furiously and took in a long, controlled breath.

Alec said incredulously, "*You* were the female with him?"

"Yes. I-I was there." Her voice cracked.

Calum paced away from her then back. Having seen him shift, she recognized where that graceful prowl had originated, but the overwhelming confidence?—oh, that was all his own. "Why didn't you tell anyone?"

"Tell someone?" The knife no longer pressed against her neck. She rubbed the burning slice, letting the pain anchor her. "Oh, sure, like I'm going to walk up to you and ask, *'Hey, are you one of those people who turn into cats?'* Get real."

A glint of humor touched his eyes. "Ah, no, that wasn't what I meant. Why haven't you told anyone about Lachlan?"

She scrubbed her face with her hands, stalling for time. It would be better to escape this emotion-ridden location, achieve a stand-down. Knowing how the kid died wasn't going to make a shifter feel very kindly toward a human, even a woman. "Listen, can we discuss this somewhere else? My knee can't take kneeling for long. And I'm bleeding."

Alec grunted as if she'd hit him.

Calum hesitated, then nodded. "Lachlan's grandfather needs to hear this." He gave her an assessing look. "Unless there is a reason he should not be present?"

Oh, great. "It's not a pretty story, but he's the reason I'm here." She had two men who now hated her guts, one of whom she'd slept with, and next would talk with an old man who'd tried to kill her. The night just kept getting better and better.

A LONELY BEER sat on the small patio table beside him, only half-empty. Thorson had lost his taste for drowning his sorrows after trying to kill the little brown-headed human. A *female*.

He shook his head, still shocked—*appalled*—at how uncontrolled he'd acted that night. Neither grief nor anger could excuse such behavior. She wasn't even that bad of a human, he'd realized. She'd choose her books and leave quietly. No silly blather, all business. And she was a good waitress according to his friends. He admired competence, no matter the species.

He glanced up the hill at the dimmed light of the Wild Hunt. There'd been a time he'd never missed a Gathering, but he'd grown old and needed his sleep.

Not that he slept very long these days. He tended to get up and prowl around the house, avoiding the rooms where grief lay like dust in the corners. Sometimes the boy would join him out here in the back. They'd lean back, put their feet up on the deck railing, and watch the clouds attempt to dominate the sky.

Under the light of the full moon, the yard seemed very empty. Maybe he'd return to bed and try to sleep.

As he stepped inside the kitchen, someone pounded on his door. His mouth tightened. No good news arrived in the wee hours of the night. Then again, nothing could be that bad—his worst fears had already come to pass.

After winding his way through the dark house, he opened the door and saw Alec's face in the tree-dappled moonlight. "Alec. Is something wrong?"

"We need to talk to you, Thorson. Can we come in?"

We? Thorson stepped aside. Alec walked in, followed by

Calum and the brown-haired human. Alec led the way into the living room and even presumed to toss another log on the dying embers in the fireplace.

"What's all this about?" Thorson let the irritation show in his voice, but giving the female the respect due her, he censored the profanity.

Calum pulled her to the couch near the fire, and then he and Alec sat down beside her, one on each side like unmatched bookends.

Or guard dogs.

Thorson crossed the room to stand before the mantle, putting his features in shadow and theirs in the light. Alec smiled, and oddly enough, he saw the same understanding of the technique on the human's face. "Well?" he asked.

"Victoria has a story to tell us," Calum said. He turned to put his hand on the female's forearm and not in a particularly friendly way.

Alec leaned forward. "Joe. We just heard this ourselves. Vicki was with Lachlan when he died."

The words clawed deep into Thorson's chest, and he choked on a breath. "She—she was the female who disappeared?"

"Aye." Alec laid a hand on her other arm.

Thorson frowned. She looked more trapped between the two than supported by them. He wasn't drunk, and he had an aversion to females being manhandled. "Are you here of your own volition or not?"

Her gaze dropped to one restrained arm, then the other, and a wry smile graced her face. "Pretty much. I'd been trying to figure out how to talk with you anyway—without a fight this time."

The realization that he himself had kept her from his door was galling and turned his voice thick and bitter. "You're here now. Tell me."

"It's not a pretty story," she warned. His jaw clenched, but he gave her the nod she waited for. "All right, then. I was walking down a street in Seattle when I heard a scream …"

AS VICTORIA'S TALE continued, Calum watched her. She talked about her brutal captors, and her face darkened with anger. When she spoke of how Joe's grandson had died, she blinked back tears. Obviously, Lachlan's death had hurt her badly. Some of Calum's worry eased. And she'd known about the Daonain for weeks and hadn't betrayed the knowledge.

She'd come here to honor her promise to a young man, the actions of an honorable person. A touch of guilt made him frown. He'd been harsh with her tonight.

Then again, she *had* been sneaking around, following them.

She finished her recounting with, "…and I slipped out the back door, jumped the fence, and found a place to hole up for the night. I arrived here the next day." With a scowl at each brother, she pulled her arms free and wrapped them around herself. Calum could see Alec's desire to comfort her. He felt the same.

Instead, he considered her story. "They deliberately threw you into Lachlan and didn't leave until he bit you."

"Uh-huh."

"Trying to make more shifters," Alec murmured. "Won't work."

"Lachlan said that." She pushed hair out of her face. "So what happens now?"

"We'll investigate further," Calum said. She didn't need to know more than that.

"Right. But what happens to me?"

Calum caught Alec's worried gaze. She did bring out a male's protective instincts, didn't she? "How many people have you told about us?"

"Nobody."

"Why not?"

"I promised Lachlan I wouldn't."

"And if we'd scared you?" Calum trapped her gaze, waiting for her answer.

She said reluctantly, "If I thought you were dangerous, I'm not sure what I'd do."

"Do you think we're dangerous?" Alec asked and tugged on her hair.

She snorted. "You guys are damned scary. And I have to wonder, if I'd just blundered into you in the forest, what would you have done?"

"Would Alec have slit your throat, you mean?" Calum asked.

"Ah, yeah, something like that."

Thorson's eyebrows went up. They hadn't mentioned the events in the clearing.

Calum studied the little human for a minute. Her hands had gripped together so tightly her knuckles were white. More worried than she wanted them to realize. And so he answered in greater detail than he had planned. "A Cosantir has the ability to blur a person's memory of the previous few hours. This has been our primary defense for generation upon generation. We are *usually* careful that a human doesn't discover us," he added with a hard stare at Alec who gave him a rueful look.

"A messed up memory would be horrible," Victoria said slowly, "but at least you're not murdering people."

Calum tilted his head without answering—for death could indeed be a penalty. A shifter whose actions exposed the clan was killed, either at the hand of his Cosantir or a cahir like Alec.

Her brows drew together. "I've known about shifters for longer than a few hours. How would you deal with me—if I wasn't such a nice person and all?"

Awkward question. The mind-wipe ability was called that for

a reason. Reluctantly, Calum said, "Then a longer period of time is…destroyed. As far back as is necessary."

"Leaving big holes in a person's mind, and they wouldn't know why?" She shuddered. "I'd rather die."

"Well, you are not dead," Calum said, "but you do look exhausted." And still worried. An edge of pity slid under his defenses, and he ran his knuckles down her soft cheek. "You acted honorably, Victoria. Your memories are yours to keep."

However, the rest of their discussion should be conducted without a human in attendance. Rising, he held his hand out to her. "I'll escort you home so you can sleep."

CALUM WASN'T HIS usual smooth self this evening, Vic thought, as he paced silently beside her. He tried to hide it, but ever since he'd heard how Lachlan died, anger had simmered inside him. When a streetlight illumined his face, she saw his pupils had gone back to black. Must be some shifter thing, although no one else seemed to change their eye color like that.

He caught her look and smiled slightly, setting his hand on her back below the edge of her coat. Funny how he could terrify her one moment and make her feel so safe the next. If Alec was like a comrade in arms, Calum was the best kind of officer, one who took to heart any harm to the ones under his command.

His warmth, his nearness was both comforting…and disconcertingly arousing.

He walked up onto the porch with her. After she'd unlocked her door, he lifted her chin to study her face in the moonlight. "Will you be all right tonight?" he asked softly.

"No problem." Her voice came out uneven. The feel of his warm fingers, the sure way he touched her sent her insides into quivers.

His eyes lightened to a silvery gray. "Never admit to any

worries, do you, little human?"

Human? *Little?* The insult lost its sting under his affectionate tone. He stood close enough she could feel the heat of his body, and his scent surrounded her, brisk and clean and wild, like the wind from the mountaintops. "Um." What had he asked? "No."

A vertical crease in his cheek accompanied the amusement in his eyes. "I'll bid you good night then." His fingers cupped her jaw as he bent and took her lips. With an arm behind her, he drew her closer. No teasing kisses for him, just smooth possession. His lips were far too knowledgeable, his mouth demanding, and her world began to swirl. When he lifted his head, her arms were around his neck.

She pulled them down with a gasp and pushed him away— or tried to. His arm didn't loosen. God, in bed with Alec just hours ago, now kissing his brother? What kind of skanky whore did that make her? "Let go of me."

He regarded her, brows pulled together, as if confused by her about-face. "Why?"

She pushed again, even though her body wanted to move forward, to melt against him so thoroughly that nothing could separate them. And that was just wrong. Dammit all. "Calum, your brother, Alec and I…" She swallowed. Why the hell was she tongue-tied? And her tone came out nowhere near as cold as she might have wanted. Maybe because she was radiating heat to rival the sun. "Alec is interested in me," she finished finally.

"As am I." His confusion remained for a moment, then understanding glimmered in his eyes, and he smiled at her. "A human. Why is that so easy to forget with you?" He kissed her lightly, ignoring her words completely.

Her body betrayed her, softening, yearning toward his. As if he could tell, that slight smile came and went on his face. "You look tired, Victoria. Take this weekend off from work." He ran a finger down her cheek, leaving heat in its wake. "Sleep well, little female."

Using all her willpower, Vic stepped away from him and into her house. After closing her front door, she leaned back against it. *Fuck, what a night.* Her body hummed with arousal from Calum, and yet her insides ached wonderfully from how Alec had taken her.

And she still had jitters from having a knife to her throat. She held her hands out, watched them tremble. God, she hadn't been so close to death since she'd been caught in that firefight in Baghdad.

Quite the evening, hey? A party, sex—*great sex!*—almost getting her throat slit, and for a grand finale, getting her hormones boosted sky-high from the wrong brother. *There's nothing like an exciting, event-filled life.*

She scowled, remembering how she'd gotten caught skulking. If Wells ever heard, he'd rip her a new asshole, even though Calum's being able to scent her didn't seem fair. Surely that broke one of the spy rules or something.

Shaking her head, she crossed the living room to the fireplace. As she built a comforting fire, she couldn't stop thinking of all the unanswered questions she had. Like where had the shifters come from? Was this some mutation thing or what? As sparks shot up the chimney, one flame blazed higher, swirling in a unique dance. And...*are those eyes?*

Jesus! She jumped back, shivering despite the heat.

Bush-thingies, tree-thingies. Now fire-thingies? *I'm only here to check out shifters, dammit.* She frowned. Maybe she should return to Thorson's house and see if she could hear something. The way Calum had hustled her out like a five-year-old being sent to bed told her they planned to talk more.

Or I'll just stay here. Someday, maybe, she'd forget the deadly look in Calum's eyes when he caught her spying on them. She touched her throat, tracing the thin scabbed line where Alec's knife had cut.

Alec. He'd been hurt, thinking that she'd used him. God, as if anyone could. She closed her eyes as warmth flooded through her. Great sex was a cold term for what they'd shared, how he'd held her and watched her with those dark, dark green eyes. He'd seen her, past the smart mouth and tough attitude to the needy person inside—and he hadn't taken advantage. No, he'd grown even more tender and insistent about giving her pleasure.

She rubbed her stomach. Yeah, her thoughts made her guts hurt—she glanced down and her hand stilled. She wasn't rubbing her abdomen, but her chest. Over her heart. *God, get a grip. And needy? My ass.*

She jumped to her feet, paced across the room. So anyway, they hadn't killed her. She'd fulfilled her oath to Lachlan by talking with Thorson. She was healed. Tomorrow she'd call Doc Reinhardt and kick his ass until he'd okayed her return to duty.

Staying was…not a good idea. She'd gotten far too involved with these kitty-cat brothers. Caving in to Calum's firm grip and demanding kiss. Swept away by Alec's hands on her body, his smooth voice murmuring to her, his eyes so intent—she shoved that memory aside. It had been great sex—nothing more.

Instead think how Wells would ream her out if he heard she'd laid a local. *It's time to blow this pop-stand.*

CALUM HAD LEFT with the female, and Alec had gone to sit on the porch, leaving Thorson by himself. He tried to wrap his mind around the dangers to the clan, but his thoughts pulled away to follow their own path. Resting his elbows on his knees, he watched a salamander curvet in the blazing fire. It danced upward into the chimney before diving into the coals in a flurry of sparks. One ember landed, bright on the cold stone of the hearth, then its glow faded to dull black.

Lachlan hadn't been alone when he died, and he'd had comfort from the human. Oh, she hadn't said as much, but as she'd tried to recall Lachlan's words, she'd curved her arms as if around a person. Yes, the boy had been held and comforted at the end.

It eased his grief to know that. And even at the end, the boy had thought of his old grandfather with worry. With love.

Lachlan hadn't told the female, "Call Gramps." He'd deliberately sent a human to Cold Creek, a Daonain-inhabited town. Why?

Thorson looked up as Calum and Alec walked into the living room, deep in a discussion already. That the Cosantir and the head cahir would include him in their plans was a gift, an acknowledgment of his grief and need. Silently, he rose and served each a beer.

"Two men at the house. One in a suit—but she called him a thug—and one was ex-military." After a smile of thanks for the drink, Alec dropped onto the couch. "Remember those trappers we drove away? Looked like they'd had military training. The one with a shaved head was probably Swane."

The wind gusted the windows and the house creaked, settling even as Thorson settled his old bones in his favorite chair.

Calum took the seat opposite. "The man tried to create more shifters with Lachlan, for whatever reason, and failed. Now he's lost the one shifter he had."

"So they're trying to catch another," Alec said flatly. "The poachers arrived after Vicki and Lachlan escaped. And they were a hell of a lot closer to Cold Creek than the ones we found before."

"It doesn't sound as if Lachlan gave them any information, but his belongings…or logic…directed them here. Now I wish we'd questioned them, rather than driving them off," Calum said. "Even if I had to gut their memories afterwards."

Thorson heard his regret and guilt. "You couldn't know if they were guilty or not." He shook his head. "You were correct in what you did, Cosantir."

"He's right, Calum," Alec said.

Bitter lines around his mouth, Calum stared at the fire for a minute, and then scrubbed his face with his hands. "What's done is done. I fear we have another problem beyond poachers. Since the man thinks a bite will transform a human, he'll search hard for Victoria."

"Hell, brawd, you're right." Alec straightened, his eyes chilling. "First step is to find out who owned or rented that house. I'll start there."

As the cry of a wolf trailed down from the mountain, Thorson felt the coldness of worry creeping into his old bones. Were those humans setting traps in their forests even now?

"I'll ask Tynan to access the military files and search for an ex-marine named Swane," Calum said, taking a sip of beer. "We might get a current address from that. We cannot act until we find them."

"And then?" Thorson gritted out.

Calum slanted him a look that told him fury burned in the Cosantir as hotly as it did within him. "And then, we will treat these murderers as they deserve."

Chapter Ten

THE NEXT DAY, Vic pulled the phone away from her ear and stared at it. No way. This was enough to make her believe Wells really was as psychic as some of his agents claimed.

"Sir." She cleared her throat. "Did you just say you wanted me to fly to Washington D.C.?"

"If your hearing is that faulty, I'll put you back on medical leave."

Fuck, he sounded like he hadn't had his coffee today—or for a week or so. "And once there?"

"Report to my office."

A meet? Her stomach slid greasily to the floor. She might avoid the subject of shifters on the phone, but in person? Concealing information from Arthur Wells was as futile as hiding a sin from God. Or trying to lie to Calum.

"I was looking forward to returning to my assignment in Baghdad." *Weak, Vic, weak.*

But his voice softened slightly, if that were possible for a voice sharper than a blade. "I realize that. However, I'm scheduled for China next week, and I want to see you in person before I leave. Five days, Sergeant. Can you manage?"

Trapped. "Have I ever not?"

"No, you always come through," he said quietly and made it

all worse by adding, "I've missed you, Marine. I'm pleased you're coming back to us."

She managed to hang up before she broke down and bawled like a baby. He was the nearest thing to a family she had. And she had concealed information he really should have.

But why the meet? Had he gotten a hint of what the guy in the suit was hunting—the shifters. Slumping lower in her chair, she moaned. How the fuck was she going to handle this?

IN THE AFTERNOON, Jamie decided that cold weather needed something hot like Italian food. Calum had hesitated, wanting action. His instincts hammered at him to fight to protect the clan, but he had no opponent to attack. He'd sent shifters into the forest, searching for traps and poachers. Tynan and Alec were hunting through military and Seattle databases. Pacing around the house like an irritated cat would help nothing.

So he and Jamie walked into town to pick up the ingredients for lasagna. As they carried the groceries out of the store, he took a deep breath of the biting cold air and smiled at his daughter.

With her mother's slender build and her nose and cheeks pink, she bounced along the sidewalk like one of Santa's elves. "Did you see that gnome?" She pointed to the beady eyes peering from the sidewalk gutter. "He made a face at me!"

Calum suppressed a laugh and asked reasonably, "How can you tell?"

"Honestly, Daddy. I know they're ugly, but he stuck his lips out and—" she demonstrated, and he did laugh.

"Ah, well, the cold makes them ill-tempered."

"Yeah, even the pixies are grumpy. One threw an acorn at me yesterday, and I hadn't done—hey, look, there's Vicki!"

Through the bookstore's display window, Victoria could be

seen talking with Thorson. Before Calum could refuse, Jamie grabbed his hand and pulled him into Books.

Although Victoria didn't smile, pleasure lit her eyes when Jamie gave her a happy hug. Over the past weeks, Calum had enjoyed watching the repressed little human deal with his daughter's exuberant affection.

"I haven't seen you forever!" his daughter complained and cast Calum a disgusted frown. "Daddy doesn't want me in the bar when people start really drinking."

"What a mean guy," Victoria agreed, giving him a look that, if she were anyone else, he'd call uncertainty. Of course, only a couple of days before, Alec had almost sliced her throat. Then she'd come close to having her memory wiped by Calum. And he'd kissed her goodnight. That might be enough to unnerve even this self-confident female.

With a straight face, he asked, "Victoria, you appear tired. Have you been sleeping well?"

Thorson barked a laugh.

A wry smile curved her full lips. "Too many strange noises at night, I guess."

Calum grinned. Bloody tough female there. One he wanted. By Herne, he felt like pulling her into his arms and taking possession. His cock hardened in agreement.

As if she could tell, her gaze heated…and then she edged away, even as he reminded himself that she was human. "Are you two here to get a book?" she asked Jamie.

"Can we, Daddy?" Jamie implored. "I've read all mine."

"Jamie, I don't know—"

Thorson grinned and interjected, "You want your daughter to be literate?"

"Reading is very important," Victoria agreed solemnly.

Quite outnumbered. "Fine."

Jamie handed him her grocery bag and disappeared into the

stacks. "One book," he called after her.

"Two books would be better." Victoria pushed the two books she held across the counter to Thorson.

"Some people are cheapskates," Thorson commented loud-ly.

"Thank you for the support. I'll have you know, her paper-backs are pushing mine off the shelves, and I'm probably one of your best customers, you bugger."

"Sounds like you're a little off your feed." Thorson picked up Victoria's books and set them on his desk.

"Cranky," Victoria agreed, talking to Thorson as if Calum wasn't standing right next to her—standing close enough to breathe in her unique spicy fragrance, feel the heat from her body.

And cranky was a term for children who hadn't had their naps. With a frown, he looked down. Their eyes caught...and held. Humor danced in her eyes and curved her lips, and he couldn't suppress a laugh.

It was a rare female who could tease him out of a...cranky...mood. Even rarer to find one who made him harden and laugh at the same time. Why did a human have to be so attractive?

"Here." Jamie crowded between Calum and Victoria and pushed her selection across the counter.

"Two?" Calum asked dryly.

"I don't want anyone to call you a cheap—uh, something, so I thought I'd better get two books like Vicki said." Jamie gave him such an innocent smile that no one could possibly doubt her sincerity. No one but a very experienced father.

"Hmmm. An extra book. That would mean an additional night of washing dishes, I believe?"

She wrinkled her nose at him. "Oh, okay."

"I need to get going," Victoria said, and although she smiled, her brown eyes looked so sad that Calum's heart wrenched.

"Aren't you getting any books today?" Thorson actually frowned at the little human.

"No. I just wanted to bring those back."

"Wait." Jamie grabbed her sleeve. "You want to come to dinner? We're making lasagna."

Calum stiffened. Was the God testing him, setting this female in his path at every turn? The time they spent working together and cleaning up after closing had been hard enough on his control. Even worse was when they'd share a beer afterwards, watching the fire die down while discussing politics and cultures and books. She shouldn't attract him at all, and he certainly should not ever have kissed her. Yet, as Alec had said, Gatherings and danger brought out the animal in a shifter.

But to continue this foolishness?

He'd hesitated too long, and Victoria shook her head. "I... No, Jamie, I need to—" she paused, obviously at a loss for a good excuse.

He should have let it go, but the hurt in her eyes was like a knife in his chest. "We are experts at lasagna-making, and it would be a pity not to share our superb culinary skills with others. We'll expect you at seven."

She frowned at him. So unsure—something he rarely saw in this woman. But after looking at Jamie's pleading eyes, she sighed. "Well, all right. I love lasagna."

FUCK. SITTING AT his office desk, Vidal crumpled up the paper he'd just signed and flung it at the wall. His signature had always been a fat scrawl. Now it was small, a pencil's width, the letters all crammed together because his fingers wouldn't loosen any more. And he'd lost his balance again this morning.

Fear crawled around inside him like a cockroach in his guts.

His time was running out—the fucking Parkinson's was winning. *Diseased.* Furiously, he swiped his arm over his desk, sending everything crashing to the floor.

He glared at the sound of a knock. "Yeah. What?"

Swane opened the door and walked in. His cold brown eyes flickered over the mess. "Got something." He set some papers down on the desk.

Forcing his anger down, Vidal looked them over. "Medical reports?"

"Uh-huh. Military. For a Victoria Morgan who's recovering from a knee injury."

"Alive? Son of a fucking bitch, she survived!" His hopes leaped. Had she transformed? Was she a werecreature now? He looked through the pages and scowled. "The report don't say nothing about bite marks."

"The doc called'em: *various healed scars*. But see here"—Swane flipped to the back page—"The bitch wanted a copy, so she gave them her address."

Vidal squinted to decipher the small type. "She's living in Cold Creek?"

"Now doesn't that put your shorts in a wad?"

Vidal shoved the papers away. "Get her. And find out if she's changed into one of them."

"Just like that, huh." Swane snorted. "Go ask her, "Hey, Miss Morgan. Eating more red meat lately?"

"Cut the crap." Vidal leaned back in his chair, trying to keep his excitement from exploding. "Just get her. But be careful. She's seen your ugly face."

"No problem. I got some merc buddies who need a few extra bucks. They can take point; I'll do backup."

Vidal frowned. More people in on the information. "I don't—"

"They'll never know what's going on. They'll just tranq her

and toss her into the van—they won't see her turn into a cougar. If she even can."

Swane's last remark hit Vidal hard. *She must have been transformed. She had to have.* "Good plan." Vidal listened to the rain against the window. "When you spot her, grab her right then. No matter what. With her fucking background, she could disappear completely if anything sets her off."

"Got it. You know, if she's hanging out in Cold Creek, it's cuz the kid clued her in. She knows something." Swane's smile didn't reach his dead eyes. "Give me a day with her, and she'll be happy to tell you every fucking detail."

THAT NIGHT, VIC veered across the parking lot to the right of the Wild Hunt where a tall wooden fence enclosed the tavern's side and back yards. As she opened the gate, a chill shook her like a cold hand stroking up her spine. The last time she'd gone through a wooden fence to a back yard, she'd been knocked out, tied up. And then had a mountain lion munch on her. Hopefully this evening would end better.

Or not. It's not like she had an appetite. *I hate goodbyes.* Leaving a message would be far, far easier. But the kid wouldn't understand. Vic remembered the times her father left for overseas stations without telling her. As she'd cried, whatever housekeeper he'd hired would give her his note. It had never helped.

So tonight, she'd tell Jamie goodbye in person. And hopefully, Calum wouldn't get upset about losing a part-time barmaid.

A few steps past the gate, she stopped and stared. *Wowsa.* After the barren parking lot in front, she hadn't been anticipating…this. The brick path down the side was overhung with lilacs. Roses climbed over the wooden archway at the entrance, and the late blooms lent sweetness to the air. In the backyard, a knee-high rocky waterfall splashed into an oval pond. Gold and red koi flashed just under the water's surface hoping for a handout. Crumbs scattered beside a tall-backed bench showed someone liked to feed them.

Herbs filled the corners adding the scents of rosemary and oregano. Vic turned in a circle. What did this place look like in the summer? She felt a stab of envy. Must be nice to plant something and be around months later to see it blossom.

Still seemed as if a werecat should have a chicken house, not a garden. God, there was so much she didn't know about them.

The path led to steps climbing to the second-floor landing. As she put her foot on the first step, her heart rate increased with her anticipation…of seeing Calum. Oh, man, coming here was stupid, stupid, stupid. Growling under her breath like some wacko released from a psych house, she stomped up the stairs. There were two doors, not one, as if even the damned entrances were saying, 'choose one brother or the other'.

She pounded on the one with Calum's name.

"She's here!" Jamie's voice rang out. The door was thrown open, and Vic got her second hug of the day. She'd had more hugs this season than in several years. Scary thought. "Hey, munchkin." The feel of the kid's skinny arms filled Vic with fondness…just fondness. Nothing more.

Vic pulled back, shoved her hands into her jeans pockets. "Nice garden you got here, kid."

"Did you see the fish? The red one is Peter and the gold one with orange marks is Wendy. And there's a big guy with black patches—he's Hook." Jamie put her hands in her pockets like Vic. "Of course, I named them when I was just a little girl."

"Of course," Vic agreed solemnly. As she smiled, she saw Calum watching from the door. The way his eyes softened when he looked at his daughter squeezed her heart. Then his gaze met hers. Heat seared her skin in a blast of fire. Oh, this was such a bad idea. "Hey," Vic said weakly.

"Welcome to our home." His lips curved as if he could see her worries. "Come in, Victoria. We're eating lasagna tonight, not little humans." As he disappeared into the kitchen, Jamie grabbed her hand and dragged Vic after her like a pull-toy.

Calum checked the oven, then turned. "What can I get you to drink?"

"Beer if you have it." The heady smell of garlic filled the large kitchen, and her stomach rumbled.

As Jamie laughed, Calum smiled, poured Guinness into a mug, and handed it to Vic. "Don't worry. As soon as the bread is browned, we'll eat."

"I didn't realize I was hungry."

Calum took a sip of his own drink, a dark wine. As he studied her over the top of the glass, his gaze felt like a hot sun against overly sensitive skin. "You should eat more," he said. "You're underweight."

"That's rude, Daddy. I think Vicki is perfect," Jamie said loyally.

Laughing, Vic swung an arm over the kid's shoulders and frowned. "Have you grown? Weren't you shorter yesterday?"

"Scary, isn't it," Calum said in a dry voice. "She'll have her first trawsfur soon and the thought terrifies me."

Vic's jaw dropped open. "Jamie will?"

"Daddy!" The girl turned to stare at Vic. "You told Vicki—"

"Ah, I forgot to tell you, dearling, Victoria knows about us."

CALUM GRINNED AT his daughter's bug-eyed look, and Victoria looked quite as startled as she stared at Jamie.

"You never thought of young shifters?" he asked.

"Um, no." Victoria touched Jamie's cheek so gently that his heart squeezed. "Will you turn into a cat? Like your dad? Is Alec a cougar too?"

Jamie giggled. "I'll probably be a cougar. And Uncle Alec is too."

"God, I bet you'll be beautiful," Victoria said, the wonder in her voice sending a pang through him. "So what happens the first time you change? Is it anything special?"

Jamie answered in such a serious tone that Calum was warned. "Well, sparks come out of our hands, and we make a big boom—"

Victoria's eyes widened.

He snorted as his evil offspring burst into giggles.

Victoria blinked, then gave her throaty laugh. "Little monster, you had me. Way to go." She turned to Calum. "I take it the first shift is nothing special?"

"Much like you've seen. The major difference is a youngster's lack of control." He tried not to think about the children unable to trawsfur back, the ones that went feral, or those so overwhelmed and terrified that they ran themselves to death. His Jamie was level-headed. Smart. She'd get through it fine.

Jaw clenched, he turned away under the guise of removing the garlic bread from the oven. He handed the basket to Jamie. "Let's eat."

As they sat at the round oak table, he saw Victoria glance at the fourth place-setting, and answered her unspoken question. "Alec usually gets off around—" Before he could finish, the back door opened and slammed shut.

His brother appeared in the kitchen doorway. "Damn, that smells good. Did you eat al—" When he caught sight of Victoria, his words sputtered to a close, and he stared.

Bugger it. Having her here, in their home, had been a mistake. He was asking for pain for himself...and Alec...and even Victoria. He shoved out a chair with his foot. "Alec. Sit and eat before the food gets cold."

Alec took the seat beside Victoria. "I'm in shock. We usually only have one lovely lady at our table."

Jamie giggled. "I invited her, Uncle Alec."

"Good job, kiddo." He served himself up huge helpings of salad and lasagna and added a piece of garlic bread. "Sorry I'm late. Had to ticket a couple of city boys for looking ugly in a 'no-ugly' zone."

Victoria's brows drew together. "Are you serious?"

"Weeell." Alec leaned back in his chair. "If I don't like the looks of someone, we just keep an eye on them, make sure they're not here to cause trouble. If needed, we'll give them a nudge to move along."

Calum smothered a smile. Alec had perfected the good-old-boy, we-hate-outsiders sheriff routine when he'd lived in Texas.

"I keep forgetting you have a nasty side," Victoria murmured, looking more impressed than not. She popped a bite of lasagna into her mouth, stilled, and then hummed, her lids half-closing. Lost in pleasure. *Herne help me.*

Calum's breath turned ragged as did Alec's. Their eyes met in perfect understanding. *Want this female for us.* But she was human. They both looked away.

"We"—Calum cleared his voice to remove the huskiness—"We encountered Victoria in the bookstore today." He smiled at her. "I noticed Thorson looks less unhappy. Did you talk more with him?"

She nodded. "He asked me to tell"—she glanced at Jamie and amended—"to talk about old times. He seems so lonely. Not many people come into his store."

"He misses Lachlan," Jamie said. "I miss him too. He was always fun."

"Does Joe have no one else?" Victoria asked.

Alec shook his head. "His sister died years ago, and she'd had only two children. Lachlan is her daughter's child. When Lachlan's mother and her lifemate–um, spouse—were killed in a car accident, Thorson gave him a home. Technically, he's Lachlan's grand-uncle."

"No kids of his own?"

"None he knows about," Alec said. "He enjoyed the fight too much and never took a lifemate."

Victoria stirred her fork around in the remnants of her meal. She'd eaten heartily, Calum was pleased to see. "How old is he anyway?" she asked.

Jamie spoke before Calum could stop her, "He's gonna turn a hundred in two years."

Victoria choked, swallowed. "Very funny, you rat. You got me twice tonight. Really though, how old is he?" She studied Jamie's face. "You weren't joking."

Jamie shook her head.

Copper-colored eyes settled on Calum's face. "Another shifter thing?"

He nodded, hoping she wouldn't take it any farther.

No grace was given. "So how old are you?" she asked.

There was a reason very few humans were allowed to know about Daonain; this was one. But he didn't lie. "Alec and I are in our late fifties."

"Damn." She eyed him and Alec, her gaze like dancing sunlight. "You carry your age well, guys. How long do shifters live then?"

"Around a hundred-twenty or so." Alec winked at her. "No immortality, I'm afraid."

"There's a relief. A hundred—I almost got my butt kicked by a centenarian? Some bouncer I am." Her face sobered. "Speaking of being a bouncer, I'm giving you notice, Calum."

"What's that mean?" Jamie asked.

Calum forced himself to take a breath. "You're leaving me—us—Cold Creek?"

Her lips curved ruefully. "Yeah. I've kept my promise to

Lachlan. And my knee's healed up, good as new, according to the doc, so I need to get back to a real job."

Jamie pushed to her feet and threw her arms around Victoria. "I don't want you to leave," she wailed, giving voice to Calum's feelings as well.

Victoria hugged Jamie, blinking hard. "I know. But my people need me a lot more than your dad needs a barmaid. I go where I'm needed."

TO VIC'S RELIEF, the evening ended early. They'd shared some wine in the living room, but Jamie was moping, Calum was quiet, and Alec... God, the unhappiness in his eyes wrenched her heart.

We screwed once, she reminded herself, as she went into the kitchen to get her coat. *Once.* Hell, he'd held a knife to her throat—what kind of relationship was that? She picked up her coat. Besides, if he... She blinked. The dinner dishes were piled by the sink, the table wiped clean of all spills.

She turned in a circle, but the place stood empty. Nobody had done the clean-up; they'd been in the living room. Surely Calum didn't have a maid. Not a crumb littered the floor, although she spotted a small bowl of milk and a tiny piece of frosted cake on a plate in one corner. Did werecats keep domestic cats?

"Do you really have to go now?" Jamie stood in the doorway.

"Yeah, I need to pack." Like she had much of anything to worry about. Vic nodded toward the corner. "I didn't know you had a cat."

"Oh, we don't. That's for the—" Calum's hand on Jamie's shoulder stopped the girl.

As he turned Jamie back to the living room, Vic sighed. Another fucking secret.

"Alec will walk you home," he said, his smile not reaching his eyes. Oh, hell, he couldn't be unhappy too, could he? But she thought of the evenings they'd spent talking, arguing over politics and books, the late night chess games. Simple pleasures. His quiet companionship had filled a hole she hadn't realized was there. Both he and Alec had made her realize how alone she usually was...and would be again.

Yeah, this was why people shouldn't get attached to each other—because it hurt like hell to leave.

Alec waited by the front door, tossing his car keys up, and catching them.

She just looked at him. Wanting. Those large hands had stroked her body, that clever mouth had... *Inhale, Vic.* "Alec, I can get home by myself." She shook her head at him. "I need a quiet walk, and you and quiet don't go together at all."

Jamie snickered.

Alec's smile was tight as he ruffled the kid's hair. "You are a nasty lass, little niece, and Vixen is a bad influence on you."

His use of his special nickname made her chest tighten. Without speaking, Vic stepped past him and out, closing the door behind her. The chill wind whipped at her hair as she went down the steps. Night had fallen and the fountain was silent.

Chapter Eleven

THE NEXT AFTERNOON, Thorson ignored the tinkling doorbell as a customer entered the store. He scowled at the paperwork on the desk. By Herne's Holy Antlers, he'd added the numbers three times and gotten different sums each time. If he came up with a fourth sum, he was going to—

"Heads-up, dude." A throaty contralto. A spicy scent. The little, book-loving barmaid.

Thorson spun his chair around. Vicki waved a travel cup in the air and offered it.

"What's that?"

"Coffee," she said. "I've had yours; mine's better."

He rose to his feet, vaguely disgusted with his manners that he hadn't done so at once. What in Herne's name was wrong with him these days? "Fine, give it here."

She handed it over. Steam from the tiny drinking hole teased his senses with the rich fragrance of coffee. It definitely didn't smell like his normal bitter brew. He took a sip and felt every taste bud in his mouth start to sing in praise. Another sip and he eyed her over the top of the cup. "You trying to bribe me for some reason?"

Her low laugh reminded him of Lachlan, and his lips pulled into an unaccustomed smile.

"No bribe. It's a goodbye present." She turned to look at the long shelves of books. "I'm going to miss this place...might even miss you a little."

His legs seemed to weaken—old joints, undoubtedly. He dropped into his chair. "Are you leaving us, girl?"

She leaned on the counter, resting her weight on her arms—maybe her legs were shaky too. "My knee is healed, so I'm going back to the job I had before. It's overseas, and I travel light."

He drank his coffee and studied her without speaking. If she'd been a shifter, he'd have put money on Calum and Alec snagging her for a lifemate. Even for a human, she was all right.

Her eyes met his steadily in the way he'd come to respect. No back-down in the girl. Plain-spoken. He'd have called her cold if he hadn't watched her with Jamie. Or seen her trying not to cry when she told him about Lachlan. "I might miss you a little too," he managed.

Her lips curled into a half-grin. "Well, let's not get all mushy here." She bent over and with a grunt of effort set a...thing onto the counter.

"What the—what is that?"

"This is your goodbye present. It's a coffee-maker and it grinds the beans too. The cup of coffee was just to show you what you're missing."

"You expect me to use that?"

She shoved the behemoth toward him. "Yeah. Listen, Joe, in the cities, every corner has a Starbucks. Since there's nothing like that in Cold Creek, I figure people might come in here on these freeze-your-ass-off days—like today—just to have a decent cup of coffee."

Not a bad notion, really, but... He frowned at the machine. "And they'd want me to make them fancy-pants latte or mocha or some such?"

"Naw. The mountains don't have helpless city folks. Just put out good coffee and have extras like chocolate syrup and whipped cream and all that sitting on the table. Let'em make their own."

He could see it. Maybe change the fireplace chairs to comfortable ones. Have this contraption over there. People would straggle in all day long. His store wouldn't be so lonely. That was what she'd planned, wasn't it? "Pretty sneaky, girl."

Looking a little lost for such a spirited female, she touched his hand. "I think Lachlan hoped I'd stay. He said...'*Tell Grandpa I gifted you...and you're my gift*'. Kinda like he entrusted you to me or something. I have to go, so I thought this..." She moved her shoulders, gave him a wavery smile, and hurried out into the cold and rain.

As he stared after her, silence closed around him. He'd thought of Lachlan as a gift from the Mother. But then the boy had died. Now apparently the gods were taking this gift also.

DAMN BUT IT sucked saying goodbye to people, and maybe she'd grown old, because it seemed much harder this time around. Vic figured she hadn't hurt this much since she'd lost her buddy, Shanna, in Afghanistan.

And I don't even like that old man.

Icy fingers of rain drizzled down her face bringing back the chill feel of Shanna's hand as her blood drained into the sand. Vic closed her eyes to force the memory and the pain away. That was then; this was now. *Move on.*

Always moving on. Would she ever stop?

She crossed the street and looked into the grocery store. Maybe she should pick up some diet Cokes for the road. The bright lighting made it a cheerful oasis under the gray sky. As Al waited, Mrs. Neilson piled the counter with canned dog food for her poodle, so old and fat it could hardly walk. Vic tried to smile. Failed. Damn, she'd miss this place.

Forget going in the grocery. *Go back to the house. Finish packing. Leave.* There, she had a plan.

Behind Vic, the door opened, and Mrs. Neilson instructed Al, "And don't forget to order the food for senior dogs next time."

Vic looked over her shoulder. The stout woman patted her thick wool coat closer like a chilled bird ruffling her feathers. Farther down the sidewalk, a man turned abruptly to look at the hotel window.

The hotel didn't have a display. What kind of idiot stood in the rain, staring at nothing?

The muscles in Vic's shoulders tightened. A person's subconscious—or monkey brain—noticed the oddest details. Something out of place, behavior that didn't make sense. Too many people where there should only be a few. She resumed walking, brushed straggling wet hair away from her face, and spotted two men across the street, paralleling her course.

She faked a stumble and knelt to retie her shoe so she could scope out her six. Behind her was the hotel window loiterer and an additional man. All wore dark coats with scarves or pulled-up collars, rendering them anonymous in the steady rain.

They walked with none of the animal grace displayed by Calum or Alec—or even Thorson. So they probably weren't shifters. Well good. She'd rather fight humans than werecritters any day of the week. As adrenaline upped her pulse and tightened her muscles, she rose and continued down the sidewalk. They followed.

Yep, she was being hunted, pretty aggressively too. Wasn't life just full of surprises? Were they buddies of that asshole Swane? Seemed logical. How the hell had they found her?

Think about that later. If she continued going straight, she'd leave the downtown area, and in this weather, the residential streets would be pretty empty. Undoubtedly the men's plan. *Need to turn around.*

She stopped. After pretending to rummage through her pockets and not finding what she wanted, she retraced her path. Past Angie's Diner, the hotel, Baty's Grocery. The one guy remaining on that side saw her coming and ducked into the store. Vic crossed the street and felt the net of men contract. They planned to grab her in the middle of town? Damn.

She was moving fast as she went into the bookstore.

Thorson looked up. "Forgot someth—?"

"Where's your back exit?"

His brows lifted. "Rear of the storeroom." He pointed to a door behind the counter.

"Stay out of this," she snapped, darting behind the counter and through the door.

Darkness. She tripped over something. *Dammit.* She fumbled for the penlight on her key ring. The tiny beam showed her a huge room filled with boxes and a winding path to the exit.

She'd just reached the exit when shouts broke out in the store. A yell of pain. A growl. Oh, fuck, why had she picked Thorson's place instead of somewhere else? That junk-yard dog wouldn't sit quietly while thugs tried to follow her. She yanked the knife from her calf sheath and dashed back across the storeroom.

The knob was already turning, so she waited until the door opened a crack, and then gave it a hard kick. The heavy oak slammed into the guy's face with a thud she felt in her bones.

He dropped like a rock, a tranq gun clattering to the floor. *One down.*

She whipped through, jumped over the body, then paused to map out the situation. One bastard just entering. One had closed on Thorson, and she grinned. Joe would take the poor sucker apart.

The third rushed her, saving her time. She sidestepped, then kicked him and took his knee out. As he fell, she used his greasy hair to whack his head against the counter and winced as his skull fractured. *Two down.* Nice of Thorson to use solid oak for his door and counters. She glanced at him.

His opponent had pulled a knife. Thorson knocked aside his arm, plucked the blade from his hand, and jammed it into his chest. The man crumbled into a heap. A gleeful grin appeared on the old man's face, then the sharp retort of a pistol split the air, and Thorson staggered backward against his desk. The splattering blood turned his paperwork a garish red.

No! Vic spun around. The gunman stood just inside the door. With a snarl, she flung her knife.

With a choking sound, he dropped his weapon to grab frantically at the blade in his throat. Blood sprayed across the wooden floor as he went down to his knees. Spasming, he fell forward.

"You play rough, little female." Thorson was standing, one hand pressed to his shoulder. Blood streamed between his fingers.

"Jesus, I thought he'd killed you!" Giddy relief soared through Vic, and she grabbed his grizzled head to plant a kiss. One second of joy, then she dropped her jacket on the floor to strip off her T-shirt.

Wadding it up, she shoved the makeshift bandage against the bullet hole. "Does nine-one-one work here? Are you allowed to go to the hospital?"

"Yes and I am." Thorson's knees buckled, and he dropped into his chair.

"Stay," she ordered like he was a dog, which was just wrong. She pulled her jacket on over her bra before grabbing the desk phone. As she punched buttons, she watched the door. If she'd have planned this, she'd have someone designated as a backup. More bad guys might be coming.

"What is the nature of your emergency?" came the voice.

"A robbery at the bookstore in Cold Creek. The owner got shot."

The operator gasped—were they allowed to do that?—and then returned to her monotone, "I'm sending the police and ambulance. Please stay on the line until they arrive."

Near the storeroom, the man she'd hit with the door groaned and tried to roll over. She dropped the phone long enough to walk over and slam his head against the floor.

A grin appeared on Joe's face, pushing aside the lines of pain. "You *were* pulling your punches during our bar fight. I knew it."

How could a guy remind her of her father, a drill sergeant, and her teammates all in one? Ignoring the ache in her chest, she scowled and snapped, "Just shut up and keep pressure on that wound."

When a siren wailed its approach, she almost cheered. The cavalry had arrived.

A second later, the young deputy burst into the store and stopped dead at the carnage.

With adrenaline still pumping in her veins, and relief threatening to choke her up, she took it out on him. "You fucking idiot! I told nine-one-one the owner was shot. Have you ever heard of checking things out first?"

In the corner of her eye, she saw Alec doing just that, standing to one side, looking through the window. He entered silently and gently pushed his deputy aside before kicking the pistol away from the dead guy. His dark green eyes flickered over Vic and the downed men. When he looked at Thorson, his mouth tightened. "You're gettin' slow, Joe. Is it bad?"

"Nah, missed the good stuff." Thorson moved his shoulder and grimaced. "Hurts less than a clawing."

"Oh, sure it does." Alec looked around again, his face impassive, so coldly competent that Vic wanted to fling herself into his arms, and how wrong was that?

His gaze returned to Thorson. "What're they after? They don't have the scent of druggies."

Thorson tilted his head. "Her."

She'd already begun edging toward the storeroom door when Alec's eyes pinned her to the spot. "Talk to me, Vixen."

Looking out the window past him, she saw a dark car crawl down the street. One man. The backup. She retreated another step. "I need to get out of here."

Alec turned, spotted the car.

An ambulance passed it and screeched to a stop with two wheels on the sidewalk. Joe would be okay. *Thank you, God.*

Frowning at her, Thorson jerked his head at the back. "Git."

"Jenkins, take Thorson outside. I'll lock the store behind you," Alec ordered and elaborated, "If they ask, say a guy attacked Thorson, trying to get money, and escaped as you arrived." He flashed a grin. "No need to mention the dead bodies or the short, skinny female."

"Got it." The deputy nodded, raised his eyebrows at Vic. "Thanks for the advice on reconnoitering. Now get out of here, short, skinny female."

They seemed awfully blasé about dead people.

With a sigh, she pulled the body blocking the storeroom away, then opened the door.

Alec stepped up behind her, tucking his fingers under her belt to halt her. "I'll bring the car around to the park. Wait for me by the big oak." He handed over her knife, then strolled out the front.

Indecision gnawed at her as she hurried through the back door. Make for the trees or let him help? Everything in her said go it alone. Teammates only got in the way or got hurt. If anything should happen to Alec... The thought stole her breath.

But as she crossed the park, the tall, wet grass flattened beneath her feet, leaving an indelible trail. They'd know exactly where she went. But she could manage. She'd almost reached the tree line when she spotted the big oak.

Guilt tightened her jaw. However Swane had found her, she'd targeted this town for him. Even worse, if she left a trail to the forest, his men would comb the mountain and might run into unprepared shifters.

Dammit. She'd have to do this the hard way—and accept help. Forcing herself to turn, she walked over to the oak and watched Alec's car slide around the corner and up to her.

LESS THAN AN hour later, Alec stood in the tunnel entrance with his brother and Vicki. He frowned. The rain had turned to sleet. Up higher, it would be snowing heavily, and there wasn't much daylight left.

Vicki shook her head. "I still think I should just let them trail me out of town."

"No," Calum said flatly. He turned to Alec, "I'll join you in a couple of days. Will you be all right?"

In other words, could he manage hiking with a human up the mountain rather than running in cat form? Alec grinned and patted Vicki on the head. "We'll be fine. She's a tad on the short side, but she's got heart."

Her golden-brown eyes shot sparks, and he choked on a laugh. If she'd been a werecat, he'd be drawing back a mangled hand about now. After buttoning his heavy coat, he shouldered the pack of emergency supplies and clapped Calum on the shoulder. "Check on Thorson before you come up, would you? He was pretty hard hit."

"Aye." Calum ran a finger down Vicki's cheek and murmured, "Little human, you've shortened my life by several years." He gave Alec a brief smile. "Be safe, you two," he said and headed up the steps.

As if mesmerized, Vicki stared after him, and Alec grinned. His brother had that effect on females. "Let's go, Vixen. This isn't an easy climb."

She turned and looked at the mountain, her big eyes filling with misery. "I brought this mess on you all."

"True. Of course, Lachlan shouldn't have let himself be caught. Or he shouldn't have run away in the first place. And Joe should have been more understanding so he wouldn't have run away, and—"

"Okay, okay, I get the point." She hefted her pack and followed him as he took the most direct path upward. "Where is this cabin anyway?"

He pointed toward the mountaintop. "Straight up there."

"Oh, God," she said resignedly. "Mountain climbing in a blizzard at night. You cat-people sure know how to show a girl a good time."

"WHAT DO YOU mean, you lost her?" Vidal scowled and pressed the cell phone closer to his ear.

"Four of my men walked into that bookstore. None came out. Gotta figure they're dead." Swane's cold voice could barely be heard through the static. "The old fart—the owner of the store—went to the hospital. Cops are saying a man tried to rob the bookstore and escaped after shooting the owner. No mention of Morgan or anyone else. Definitely a cover up."

Incompetent bastards. Vidal swore under his breath. "Go on."

"I asked around quietly, and she works at the town tavern, only she's using the name Waverly."

"Check out the bar," Vidal agreed. "Is she at her place?"

"No. Her house is empty, but her car is still parked there. She's not at the tavern either."

Worse and worse. Morgan would be a fool to return to the town. And they'd alerted the werecreatures.

However, their target area was obviously Cold Creek. Dammit. "How could one old man and a woman kill off four men?" *Bungling fuckups.* Vidal kicked his wastebasket across the room and halted, shocked at his own actions. He never lost control. Ever.

"I'm not sure," Swane said. "But I got an idea. I want to grab someone who can tell us about the town. Not a creature—just a person who'd know what's going on. About the shifters...and their families."

Vidal sat down in his chair. Carefully. "What good would that do?"

"Leverage, boss." Swane's laugh made Vidal's skin crawl. "Beastie-boy sure as fuck would've talked if I'd been skinning pieces off his sister."

"Do it."

FUCKIN' A. VIC was freezing. She hadn't been this cold since a mission in the mountains of Afghanistan. She shivered so hard her bones hurt. But that was good. When a person stopped shivering, death was right behind.

And she knew some of the shivering was from what she'd done. She'd killed. The feeling of shattering bone, the sound of the man choking on his own blood, the blank look of death—she swallowed as nausea rose again. Wiped the tears from her face...again.

The snow increased the higher they went, sometimes whipping into her face like sand and sometimes falling straight down, piling up so she could no longer see the tree roots and obstacles underneath. She had the bruises to show for it, having flattened her length out on the trail a few times. *Grace incarnate, that's me.*

The sun was gone, the moon wasn't up, and even if it was, nothing would penetrate the dark clouds overhead. Her wimpy-ass penlight had died an hour ago.

Why the hell am I here? She should have stayed in Cold Creek, taken out the backup people, then found Swane and the business-guy and wiped them out. Then—maybe—she wouldn't feel so guilty. Her mouth tightened as she remembered Thorson's wound, the blood on the desk, his pain. God, so stupid. Why had she ever tried to escape through his store?

Too late to do anything now. The bad guys would be long gone. She'd have to wait for Wells to give her the information on Swane she needed—and then, no matter what, she'd finish this.

Wells. Oh fuck. She was due in Washington D.C. She felt like hitting her head against a tree. Could her life get any more screwed up?

"We're almost there." Alec's voice reached her.

Oh, sure, and he'd been saying that for over an hour. That fine body of his had moved steadily up the mountain—never faltering, never tripping, never falling. If she'd had the energy, she would have planted a boot right where the sun don't shine.

"Ah. There we go," he said.

Concentrating on the lousy footing, she ran into his stationary figure. "Oomph."

"Sorry." He pointed to something undistinguishable in the darkness. "We're here."

She squinted. Nothing. "How can you tell?"

"Cat eyes, baby, cat eyes." Wrapping an arm around her waist, he urged her across a small clearing to a building.

"There *is* a god," she breathed, and Alec chuckled.

"Hold on a minute." He shoved open the door and went in.

A lantern flickered alight.

Taking that as an invite, she pulled the door shut behind her. There was no heat, but the escape from the wind made the place seem almost warm. Teeth chattering, she looked around. An authentic, one-room cabin with a fireplace on the far wall, wood and kindling next to it. A rough-hewn table and stump chairs on the left. Pots and pans hung from nails, and dishes were stacked on a rustic shelf. Wooden bins were built into each wall.

Alec set the lantern on the table and started building a fire. He nodded at the bin. "There's blankets and some sleeping pads in the box. Why don't you haul them out? Put them here in front of the fireplace."

Wool blankets, foam pads, quilts. By the time she'd piled them in the center of the room, the fire blazed with enough heat to make her numbed fingers tingle.

Alec set a snow-filled pot on the grill, then rummaged through a metal-lined bin filled with canned foods and freeze-dried meals. A few minutes later, they had mugs of hot chocolate.

"Nice place," Vicki murmured, risking her lips to sip the scalding chocolate. She swallowed and closed her eyes to savor the sensation of heat bursting inside her.

Alec toasted her with his mug and a smile. "We keep it stocked for emergencies like this, and for shifters who get hurt and can't make it back to town."

He added another log to the fire and settled onto the pile of blankets. "Whoever uses the place reports to Calum, and he sends up whatever is needed to restock it."

"Carry supplies up that mountain?"

"That's why Herne invented teenagers."

She snorted a laugh and settled herself in the other blanket pile. The shivers had lessened, and she gazed sleepily around the room. "No windows?"

He shook his head. "Prevents any telltale glow at night. There's enough trees overhead to disperse most of the smoke, and as you saw, getting here isn't for the faint of heart."

"No shit." Two narrow ledges, hopping from stone to stone across creeks. "Were you following a path?"

"A variety of animal trails. We never use the same one twice, and if one starts looking too obvious, it's abandoned for a season or two."

"How can you tell if someone's used a trail recently?"

He tapped his nose. "People leave a scent."

"Even in person form, you have cat eyes and noses, huh?" She frowned remembering Jamie tripping over a bottle in the dark parking lot. "Jamie doesn't see well at night."

"Not yet. After her first trawsfur, she will. And as she spends time in animal form, the more she'll acquire animal senses." He grinned. "There are theories about why. Personally, I think we get used to seeing at night and using our noses, and our human bodies adjust."

"Huh." Her eyes drooped, and she jerked her head up as she realized she was nodding.

Alec took the cup from her hand. "Go ahead and sleep. You're safe now, Vixen."

Safe? The man was out of touch with reality. The world held no safety. As her eyes closed, she felt a blanket being tucked around her.

Chapter Twelve

THE NEXT DAY, Thorson heard footsteps approaching Calum's guest room—well, his room for the moment. He looked up gratefully, needing a diversion from his worries. For once, reading wasn't working.

"You are quite the stubborn bastard, you know," Calum remarked as he pulled a chair closer to the bed. "Why not stay in hospital? You have enough control to not trawsfur when you're hurting."

Thorson marked his place in the book and set it down. "Only way a hospital keeps me is if I'm unconscious."

"If I had known what it would take, I would have arranged it," Calum said drily.

Thorson barked a laugh. "Wouldn't put it past you." A gust of wind hurled spatters of snow against the window, and he frowned as worry stewed in his head. The storm that had settled over the mountains yesterday showed no signs of easing. "You think they're okay?"

Calum followed his gaze, mirrored his frown. "Alec is strong." His words were clipped with concern.

"You're worried about something though."

"About your attackers. Bugger the bastards." Calum rose and paced across the room. "I had the deputy take fingerprints before disposing of the bodies. The prints didn't show up in the databases that Alec has, so I sent them to Tynan. His contacts can run the information through the various agencies."

"Sounds slow."

"Too slow." Calum steepled his fingers. "Victoria suggested we use her for bait—see if we could draw them in and this time, keep one alive." He frowned at Thorson. "You and Victoria are too efficient at killing."

Thorson ignored the compliment. "You're not going to use a female as bait."

"No. I refused. So we'll keep her safe, and I'll wait for Tynan's ID and follow it up the line."

Thorson rubbed a finger across his book's leather binding. "This is senseless. If they wanted to kill a witness, they'd have sent an assassin, not a team to capture her."

"Aye. But they had Lachlan bite her. They probably expect her to turn into one of us."

"Maybe we should hand her over and deflate that notion," Thorson said, knowing they'd do nothing of the sort.

Calum's lips curled into a thin smile. "Indeed. And by handing her over, we might decrease their numbers by a significant amount."

"There's an idea. She's a deadly little female, isn't she?"

"What was she doing in your store anyway?" Calum asked, gazing out the window at the falling snow. "I thought she was leaving."

"Came to say goodbye." A pang shot through Thorson's heart as he remembered the glimmer of tears in her eyes. "Seemed to think she was letting Lachlan down. Apparently he'd told her…" He closed his eyes, searching for her words, *"Tell Grandpa I gifted you…and you're my gift"*

Calum spun around. "*'Tell Grandpa I gifted you'* He said that just before he died?"

"That's what she—" Thorson halted as the words took on a different meaning. He pulled in a shocked breath. "Could the boy have performed the Death Gift?"

Silence. After a minute, Calum rubbed his face wearily. "She said he got confused at the end and was babbling. But the ritual to an outsider might seem—"

Thorson finished. "Like the lad was out of his head. *Earth, Air, Fire, Water.* You think she's one of us?"

"If she is, she's hiding it well. The little female appears to have more secrets than a pixie has winter stores. I believe it is time to unearth some of those acorns."

VIC BLINKED AWAKE and assessed the situation. No gunfire. No murmur of voices. Soft blankets under her, more piled on top, and only her nose exposed. All warm and snuggly. Her muscles ached slightly from the hike, but a good ache, as after a hard P.T.

And hey, she was still on this earth. There was no feeling like that in the world. Knowing she could have been snuffed out yesterday, but through skill and muscle and courage, she'd won. *Yea though I walk through the Valley of Death, I shall fear no evil, for I am the baddest M-F in the valley.* She grinned, stretched, the joy of being alive singing in her like a ripple of music, and she wanted to share the song.

It just happened she knew a really good way to celebrate life…

Alec lay beside her, stretched out on his back under his own bunch of covers. He'd obviously tended the fire during the night—a big log burned cheerfully on a pile of glowing coals, and the cabin felt warm enough to slide out from her blankets and under the ones next to her. Alec's covers.

Deeply asleep, he didn't move as she snuggled up beside him and laid her head on his shoulder. He'd discarded his jacket and wore only a flannel shirt. The buttons slipped easily out of the holes. Yeah, he really had a great chest. She ran her fingers over the hard planes, traced out the six-pack ridges of muscle on his abdomen, and followed the thin line of hair down his lower stomach. Halleluiah, he was fully erect and rock-hard.

"Good morning," she breathed out and tipped her face up to nibble at his chin.

"Mmmmh." He rolled over, flattening her under him. He smelled absolutely incredible, like the deep forest with a masculine musk all his own. She could probably tell him and Calum apart just by scent. Weird.

He nuzzled the hollow below her ear and purred his pleasure when she spread her legs to cradle him. "I can smell your arousal," he murmured, his breath warm against her cheek. His hand pressed her pussy, and a searing jolt of heat made her hips lift. "I am going to…" He stopped, his muscles tightening under her fingers. "No. I'm not."

"What?" She rubbed her breasts against his chest and heard his breathing stop.

"By Herne, I want you, Vixen," he muttered. He kissed her, long and slow and deep. But then, with a low curse, he pushed himself away and stood up.

She stared up at him. What had just happened?

"Listen, Vix." He put a hand on her shoulder.

"Nah." Obviously he didn't feel the same as she did. Fine. The ache of his rejection hurt though, and she turned her face away so he couldn't see. "No worries. I just woke up feeling horny. No big deal."

"Uh-huh." He knelt on one knee beside her. "Considering how much I want to grab you, strip you, and bury myself inside you, you're not the only one aroused."

His words took her breath away. She sat up, clasped her hands together to keep from reaching for him. "But—"

He stroked a hand down her hair, and she looked at his intent green eyes, so clear it seemed as if light shone through them. "I'm a shifter, and you're human. It's extremely bad judgment to get involved. Hell, Daonain are almost never attracted to humans—the scent is wrong or something. Only yours isn't, dammit."

"But we...did it before. Remember? The Wild Hunt party?"

"Let's just say that your appearance at the Gathering was more than my self-control could bear."

Yeah, that made sense considering all the screwing going on that night. The sex-laden atmosphere had messed with her head too. "Go on."

"So, although an occasional encounter is overlooked, shifters don't get involved with humans. We—I am very close to caring for you more than I should," he said with a wry smile. He leaned his forehead against hers. "And I want you so badly I'm shaking. Let's not sit here and chance temptation."

She was very willing to give in to temptation, but could see it would cost him. In a funny shifter way, Alec was a highly moral man...cat...whatever.

He rose to his feet. "I'll get some breakfast prepared."

God. He hadn't buttoned his shirt, and his chest was thickly muscled. The man was lethally sexy. Her body quivered with need, and there was no cold shower in sight. "We got an outhouse somewhere, or do we use an available tree?"

"A tree." He grinned, a flash of white that curled her toes.

She closed her eyes. She fought a losing battle here; everything he did turned her on more. Outside in the freezing snow was where she needed to be. "I'll be back in a minute," she muttered.

Several minutes later, after she'd struggled through the foot-deep snow, fumbled her coat and shirt out of the way to undo her jeans, froze her ass off, and buttoned everything up with numb fingers, sex was the very last thing on her mind. Just let her hang out close to the fire and she'd be a happy camper. She rushed back inside.

He handed her a mug of steaming coffee. "This'll help."

Her hands were shaking with just that brief outing. "It's really cold out there."

"Temperatures can drop to under zero up here at night. It'll warm up a little during the day."

"A little, huh." She slugged back some coffee—crappy-tasting instant, but it burned all the way to her stomach and started filling her veins with caffeine. Only a fool would complain. A few more sips, and she felt almost normal. Settling on one of the stump chairs, she set her cup on the table. "Now tell me about shifter-human relationships."

He held up a freeze-dried packet of scrambled eggs and grimaced. "Maybe I should trawsfur and go hunt us up some real breakfast."

"No." She snatched it out of his hand. "Talk."

"Are you always this bossy?" he asked curiously.

She opened the packet with one wicked slash of her boot knife, and he winced.

"That's a nasty temper you have there, female." He mixed the eggs with water. "Basically, shifter-human matings are sterile. No children. And for various reasons, our numbers are declining. So shifters need to mate other shifters."

"Ah. Like a Muslim marrying a Catholic, huh?" A jagged ache made her chest throb.

"Something like that, only the Muslims won't die out. We might." His gaze was level, yet held regret. "I'd planned to talk with you, but then you said you were leaving, and I didn't think it mattered." He sounded like they'd had something…real …going.

"Geez, Alec," she made her voice cold. Hard. "I just wanted

sex, not some damned relationship."

"Yeah." He put his hand over hers, his fingers hot against her icy skin. "I knew that."

She felt her lips tremble and pressed them together. God, she had to get out of here, away from him and his fucking pity, before she burst into tears and embarrassed them both. "I need some air."

Yanking her hand back, she stalked out the door and into the snow-filled wilderness, heading anywhere, just as long it was far from the cabin. From *him*. This was stupid, stupid, stupid. How had he come to mean so much to her? Hell, she'd planned to leave, hadn't she?

She leaned against a giant pine and listened to the snow hissing down through the branches, the soft groaning of the trees swaying in the wind. Thin gray clouds trailed across the sky, blotting the sun's warmth, and the air was so cold it hurt her lungs. Alec would probably come out to check on her if she stayed here much longer. He never seemed to leave her alone for—

She thumped her head against the trunk. Had she subconsciously hoped he'd chase after her when she left Cold Creek? God, she was such an idiot.

Well. She exhaled slowly and watched her breath hang in the air before the breeze took it away. At least that idea was killed dead. Absolutely no hope of a relationship. She shouldn't have let Alec talk her into coming up here. And damned if he'd keep her from going back down. If Swane had people watching her house, well, wouldn't it be too bad if she had to disable a few? Break her heart, it would.

Fine, then. Get breakfast and some coffee, bundle up, and move out. She had a plan. Shoving her icy fingers under her arms, she headed back to the cabin.

She stepped inside and stopped at the sight of Alec near the fireplace. Buck-naked. Washing himself off with a sponge. The light from outside glowed against his skin, highlighting the hard muscles, the tight curve of his ass, his long, lean thighs, and glinted off the golden-brown hair at his groin and chest. Her breath strangled in her throat, and every little hormone that had finally cooled down flared up again like she'd been napalmed. Growling, she backed out and slammed the door behind her so hard the cabin shook. An avalanche of snow from the roof hit her, and something thudded on her boot. She looked down.

It was a tiny doll, the size of her hand. On the roof? Probably some boy had teased his sister by throwing her dolls up there. She'd get Alec to return it to whomever.

She turned the toy over, smiling. Naked. Anatomically correct with small high breasts. Pointed ears? An elf doll?

It moaned.

"Fuck!" Vic dropped it, caught it in midair, and felt it move slightly within her grasp. It was one of those tree-thingies. She shoved the cabin door open. Naked or not, Alec needed to answer more questions. "Yo, cat-boy!"

The irritated look on his face was a pleasure to see. He'd donned his jeans and was pulling on a green flannel shirt that matched his eyes.

She held up the doll-that-wasn't-dead. "What the hell is this thing?"

He walked over. "Oh, shit." Cradling the doll-thing gently in his hands, he squatted next to the fireplace. "Toss more wood on, would you?"

With another log, the fire blazed higher. She dropped down into the pile of blankets beside him. "What is it?"

"She, not it." Alec held it closer to the heat. "She's a wood-sprite. A forest pixie."

"Oh, well, I knew that," Vicki said sarcastically. "What's wrong with it—*her*?"

"They hibernate during cold spells. She probably came out for some sun and got caught by the storm. Didn't make it back to her hole."

"Will she be okay?" The little thing looked dead.

"Should. We'll bring her out of hibernation and take her to her tree. She'll need food. Here, hold her while I get something for her to eat."

He handed Vic the tiny body before she had a chance to object. "But—what do I do? Jesus, Alec, I don't know what to do!"

"Hold her close enough to the fire that your fingers feel toasty. Try not to drop her." When he grinned, she wanted to slug him, but he stood out of reach.

Staying motionless, Vic felt the chill leaving the pixie, and it took an occasional breath. It really was alive. *Fucking-A, I'm holding Tinkerbelle.* When it quivered in her hand and opened pale green eyes, sheer wonder filled her. A pixie.

Alec returned with a four-foot pine branch and a handful of evergreen spriggets. "Not the finest cuisine, but it'll do."

The pixie blinked at him, and he smiled at her. "Hey, sprite."

"Does it speak English?" Vic whispered.

"They don't talk much more than a squirrel does, but they understand quite a bit." He held up a tiny piece of fir and laughed when the pixie sat up and snatched it out of his grasp. Vic stayed steady as it perched on her palm, nibbling on the greenery. "It's warm."

"*She*—and that's good." Alec propped the large branch against the wall, securing the base with chunks of firewood. "There. She can hang out in here and finish warming up."

Vic leaned over and extended her hand. The pixie dropped the greenery and leaped, disappearing in the foliage. "Cool."

Alec piled the pine and fir sprigs next to the branch. "Good eating, pixie. Have at it."

A tiny hand reached down and snatched up a piece."

Vic stared at the branches. "It's just like the pixie-thing living in the oak in my front yard. It keeps throwing things at me."

Alec picked up his coffee. "Mmmmh, she's been pretty bad-tempered ever since old Bert died, and the new owner turned the house into a rental. Pixies are offended by change."

"Me too." Like having little things appearing all over the place. This whole mountain was weird. She settled back into the blanket pile. "You know, I—" With his cup halfway to his mouth, Alec stared at her as if she'd turned into some freakish pixie-thing.

"What?" she snapped.

"It didn't even register—you can see her."

"Well, duh, she's there, isn't she?"

"No. Not to humans." Alec scowled. "I keep forgetting you're not Daonain. You have the Sight."

"Do I look blind?" He was acting really bizarre. "What did you put in your coffee? Whiskey? I want some."

He rose and filled her cup again. She sniffed it. No alcohol in hers. Didn't that just figure.

Silently, he settled beside her, close enough for her to feel his warmth. Close enough that she wanted to crawl into his lap and share lots of warmth.

"Are you okay?" she asked.

"Not hardly. We need to talk about this, Vixen. How long have you been seeing pixies?" From the look in his eyes—so much darker a green than the pixie's—he really was upset.

On her part, she felt pretty fine. What a major relief to know he saw mini-people thingies too. Maybe she wasn't a candidate for a psych hospital after all.

"Vicki? Answer me."

"Oh. Sorry. Pretty much since I got to Cold Creek. At first I only saw flickers, maybe a hand sticking out…" She trailed off as a pixie hand poked out of the branches and grabbed more food.

"After you arrived? Not before?"

"After. I saw dwarf-looking people in the tavern one night. What other strange critters do you have in this area?"

"In this area? What—" He broke off and tilted his head, listening. A second later, Vic heard the scrunching of snow under someone's feet.

Alec was at the entrance before she even stood; the man could move when he wanted to. He cracked the door, then opened it wide. "I didn't expect you today."

"Something came up." Calum clapped his brother on the shoulder and stomped snow off his bare feet. Without even a blush, he walked into the cabin, bare-ass naked. Okay, yeah, she'd seen him stripped before. In moonlight. Now, by the light of the lanterns and fire, she couldn't drag her eyes away. Hell, no woman breathing would have been able to look away. He must have exerted himself running up the mountain for every muscle on his darkly tanned body was pumped and rippling. And his body was *all* muscle. She swallowed.

To her regret, he dressed quickly in a black sweater and jeans from the wooden bin. After pulling on a pair of thick woolen socks, he finally looked over at Vic and pinned her with those dark eyes.

She saw an accusation in them and stiffened. Whatever it was, she hadn't done it. Well, maybe she had, but she was leaving. It didn't matter. "What now?"

When his gaze finally released her, he noticed the branch and glanced quizzically at Alec.

"Vicki found a frozen pixie," Alec said. "She *saw* it."

"Interesting." He put a tea bag in a mug and added boiling water from the pot.

Alec narrowed his eyes. "You don't sound surprised."

After seating himself at the table, Calum set his cup to one side. "I think you'll understand in a minute. Victoria, join us, please."

His low authoritative order made her feel like a two-year-old. Annoyed, she tossed another chunk of wood into the fireplace. They might be used to this weather, but Iraq's climate was a lot warmer. She took a chair across the narrow table from Calum.

Alec sat beside her.

"When you said goodbye to Thorson, you told him Lachlan made you a gift," Calum said.

She felt Alec freeze beside her and started to turn toward him.

Reaching across the table, Calum cupped her chin in his hand, his fingers warm, but firm. "No. Talk to *me*." His deep voice held the authority of a master sergeant.

"Yes, sir. What do you want to know?"

"Just before Lachlan died, did he do or say anything strange? Give you a reason to feel he wasn't thinking clearly."

"Well…"

"Victoria, I realize you tried to save Thorson pain, but I need to know it all, ugly or not."

She pulled back. "The kid was trying to think of something and couldn't remember it. Then he said…um, something about fire and blood. He got blood on his hand…" She stared down at the table. Remembering…

He touched her filthy face and smiled at the dirt on his bloody fingers. "Earth."

"Honey, I want you to rest," she urged. Please don't do this to me—live! "Just concentrate on breathing and—"

"And finally my spirit—that's the gift. I remembered it," he told her, pride in his voice. "C'mere." He lifted his arm, like for a hug and she leaned forward, winced as his hand came down on her bitten shoulder and dug in.

"…but he didn't-didn't live. He was—" She blinked furiously, her throat tight, her arms remembering the feel of the boy as he went limp. Why did bodies get heavier when the soul had flown? Flown, God, she was getting all sentimental. She pulled in a shuddering breath, gave up the pretence, and roughly rubbed the wetness from her cheeks.

The silence finally registered. Alec was never quiet. She looked up to see him staring at her as if she'd grown horns. Calum had an intent look on his face, a finger tapping his lips.

She slapped the table hard enough to make her fingers sting. "Tell me what's going on. Now!"

Calum glanced at his brother, one eyebrow slanting up.

"He performed the Death Gift? For Vicki?" Alec's voice was ragged.

She made a fist. If they didn't explain, well, she was going to have to hurt them.

Calum took her hand and gently opened her fingers. His gaze held…pity? She stiffened.

"Victoria, just listen to me. First of all, Daonain are descended from the Fae." He noticed her blank look. "The Sidhe? Fairies?"

"You come from something six inches high with wings? Pull my other leg." She attempted a laugh and failed.

Alec snorted. "Not Disney fairies. More like…ah, the elves in Lord of the Ring. Tall, slender, magical. Lived in woods. Didn't like iron."

Metal—she could hear Lachlan's weak voice, "My body pretty much shut down yesterday; I've been on borrowed time since. It's a shifter thing; all that metal, you know."

Calum continued, "Before they abandoned our world—oh, a couple of thousand years ago—the Fae occasionally had offspring with humans. Some of those Fae were shapeshifters, so their mixed-blood children inherited the ability along with the other fairy traits. When Daonain mate, new shifters are born."

"Yeah. Alec explained that part." That heavy feeling crawled into her chest again.

"Did he now?" Calum's gaze went to Alec and returned to her. "There is one *other* way to create a new shifter. We call it the Death Gift ritual."

Ritual? She had a bad feeling about that word. She tugged at her hand, but he didn't release his grip.

"Like the Fae, shifters are partly magical," Calum said. "The Death Gift is *pure* magic. All Daonain learn it and know it is ours to use if we so choose…at the time of our passing."

She stiffened, shook her head. *No.*

"Yes. Lachlan wasn't confused. He invoked the ancient ritual to make you a shifter."

Relief rushed through her. "It didn't work, then. I'm no werecritter." She turned her hand over within his grasp. "See? No fur."

"And none on me."

Oh, shit. She stared at him, remembering how he'd blurred, then been a mountain lion, all power and grace.

"How long have you seen pixies?" Calum asked.

"Soon after she got to Cold Creek," Alec said. "Dwarves, too."

What did that have to do with being a furball? "I see what's here, and this mountain has pixies and dwarves all over it." She had the urge to hunker down as if a 'ma deuce' had just opened fire.

"So that's what you meant." Alec shook his head. "Vicki, there are sprites all over the world."

Her jaw dropped. "No. I never saw them before…"

"One of those fairy traits," Calum said, "is the Sight—the ability to see the OtherFolk."

"Oh, hell." This was so not good. She pulled her hand away

from Calum's grasp and hugged herself. The entire world seemed to have transformed, like flying from the arctic to the tropics, only much, much worse. *Pull it together, Vic.* "So, am I going to suddenly burst into claws and whiskers?" She tried for sarcasm, but damned if it didn't come out a whine.

Alec stood and wrapped his arms around her waist, pulling her back against his hard chest. And oh, she needed that—so much so that she tried to pull away. His embrace tightened, forcing her to accept his comfort.

"To trawsfur, you have to want to shift. It doesn't happen by accident," Alec said. "There's a place in your mind—some think of it as a door. When you're ready, you open that door and step through into the wildness."

And if she locked the damn thing? What was this going to do to her life? "Thorson told me stuff about being a shifter. Every month you need to shift into a werecat for a few hours."

Alec nodded.

Wouldn't that go over well in Baghdad or even some Iraqi village? "Lachlan shifted when he didn't want to."

Calum frowned. "That happens mostly in the first year, before control is achieved. Or sometimes later, if the shifter is very frightened or threatened."

"Uh-huh." So a grenade goes off, and suddenly I'm a cat?

"You have a problem with metal too, right?"

"Being surrounded by metal for long periods can overwhelm our systems. Magic and iron—" Alec stopped at the look on her face.

No transcontinental flights? Hell, she'd just walk to Iraq, right? And once there, she could stay out of hummers and tanks? What about cars? Damn, was that why so many people in Cold Creek walked?

"It has to be a pretty long period of time, Vix, before it's a concern," Alec said. "Otherwise it's just uncomfortable."

"Listen, I'm assigned to—" She closed her mouth, shock freezing her like an icicle through the guts. She'd almost blurted out what she was. Standing, she pulled out of Alec's embrace. "I don't want this fucking gift."

Calum rose too. "I'm sorry, Victoria. We've overwhelmed you with explanations. You need time to take all this in."

"Forget taking it in—can I give it back?"

The lines deepened in his face. "If you never trawsfur, then the magic will eventually fade away, and you'll be purely human again. Even the Sight will slowly leave you. However you might—"

VICTORIA RAN OUT the door, slamming it behind her so hard the cabin shuddered, and snow slid off the roof. The branch in the corner rustled as the pixie buried herself deeper. Calum shook his head. The little female had a powerful arm. His chest tightened as he fought the urge to go after her. To offer comfort.

Face set in unhappy lines, Alec picked up his cup and moved to the blankets by the fire. "Well, I think that went well, don't you?"

Calum grunted agreement. "We should be grateful we are far from her car."

"Now, that is a blessing." Alec took a sip of his coffee. "Did you have any idea about Lachlan's Gift?"

"Not a one. Although she is abnormally fast and strong…and sensitive, I assumed it was due to her martial arts training."

"Me, too. I'd never have thought Lachlan would be clear-headed enough to remember the Death Gift ritual. Not then."

"They had a bond between them. That's obvious." A dying lad, a woman who couldn't save him. The child must have been terrified and in such pain… Calum's fingernails dented the table as he fought the fury boiling in his veins. He took a breath filled with fire and released it slowly. "He'd have worried about Thorson being alone."

"Makes sense." Alec glanced at the door and voiced Calum's hopes. "She's a shifter, brawd, or can be one. She's strong, brave, spirited..." He smiled. "Fun to be with. Passionate. Blunt."

"And very vulnerable right now. Scared." But his lips turned up. "But we'll do our best to keep her for the clan...and for us."

WHAT THE HELL am I going to do? Vic stomped through the snow away from the cabin. *A shifter.* She'd saved the kid's butt, got him out of the cage, and he not only died on her, but turned her into some freakish cat-thing. Fuck, if he were here now, she'd kill him.

That thought and the stabbing memory of his pale lifeless face snapped her out of her tantrum. How could she think a thing like that? She would have defended him to her last breath. Slumping against a tree, she scowled at the darkening sky. Not a glimmer of sun escaped the thick clouds; it seemed as if her whole life had been washed of color, turned into shades of gray.

Just like her choices.

She wanted—needed—to return to duty. Being here, isolated from everything she'd known...it wasn't right. The job over there wasn't done. She needed to go back. But not if she'd turn into a cougar person.

She remembered when Calum had turned into a mountain lion, how his whole body had seemed to glory in the transformation. Maybe she should try... *No.* She had a feeling that trying on a cat shape would be like taking crystal meth—addictive with one taste. Once she'd done that, she could never return.

Had Calum told her the truth?

As if she'd summoned him, he appeared between the trees,

making his way down to her with his silent, predatory grace. "Victoria."

"Why do you always call me that?" she growled. "You're the only one."

He ran warm fingers down her cold cheek. "I find I like calling you something no one else does."

His gaze was as warm as his hand, and Vic took a step back. "Calum, look, I'm not going to—"

"Alec and I have been discussing your problem."

He said that as if her problem was something he could fix. *Not.* "I don't—"

"I need to visit Elder Village," he broke in. "It's a mountain town with only shifters, mostly the older ones wishing to avoid humans."

If he didn't stop interrupting her, she'd gag him and leave him for Alec to release. Then again, she'd seen him take Baty down, and also the speed with which he'd slashed the bear's muzzle open. She might not win a fight against him. "I'm listening." Dammit.

"Before we…disposed…of them, we took fingerprints and photos of your assailants. A contact in the city is gathering information, but discovering who employed them might take some time. In the interim, Alec and I think you should go with me."

"Excuse me? You want me visit a bunch of wereanimals."

"Precisely." He smiled as if she'd won the spelling bee. "The farther you are from these men, the better. In addition, you need space and time to think about what has happened to you. Finally, I'd like the Elders to meet you, even if you decide to refuse the gift."

His phrasing hurt. As if she was rejecting something special that Lachlan had… Well, she was. And yeah, she did feel guilty.

Tough.

Then he just had to put one last argument out there. He cupped her cheek in his big hand and murmured, "And I would very much enjoy having your company."

Oh, God.

Chapter Thirteen

THAT NIGHT, VIC rolled her eyes as Calum motioned her forward. Into a cave. When he'd said they'd stay at a way station, she looked forward to another nice warm cabin. But a cave? *Cold. Damp. Moldy. Ugh.*

A small rock wall niche near the entrance held candles. He lit two and handed her one. "We go farther back," he said, leading the way through a winding tunnel, veering to avoid holes and rocks. The damp air smelled of minerals.

After they entered a larger space, Calum set about lighting more candles, and soon flickering lights danced on the rock walls. The place was immense, the candle glow not reaching the top. And the ground... She lifted her candle higher. "I'll be damned."

"Quite likely," Calum agreed. "The church does not welcome shifters."

"No, not that," she said impatiently. "This." She pointed at the rippling ground. The back fourth of the cave held a small lake. "How deep is it?"

"Mmmmh, about three feet on this side. The far side...no one knows."

She shivered. "The way my life is going, there's some Loch Ness beast in there that eats people."

"Ah, now that would be interesting. But no, you've probably seen most of the magical creatures." He squeezed her shoulder reassuringly. "Daonain, dwarves, various pixies. There's probably an undine or two living in here. But salamanders dislike the damp, and—"

"Where are we sleeping?" she interrupted hastily. *Undines? Salamanders? God help me.*

"Over there." He pointed to a tiny fireplace and two wooden bins, and then continued, "Sylphs prefer the outdoors. There's no hellhounds or demons on the mountain. Not since—"

She punched his arm and bruised her knuckles on his rock-like deltoid. "If you're joking, stop."

"But—"

"If you're not joking, then definitely stop." She gave him a dirty look and headed across to the bins. *Demons.* If the world had demons in it, she didn't want to know.

Just like at the cabin, one bin held food and the other blankets. Tossing bedding on the ground, she kicked them into a pile. Then rethought and divided them. She realized she was sweating. "Calum?"

He walked over, glanced at the separate beds a fair distance apart, and quirked an eyebrow at her.

"It's hot in here. Is that my imagination or some creepy shifter thing?"

"Neither." His smile flickered. "The lake is fed by a hot spring. Would you care to bathe?"

"Are you serious? Really?"

His dark, rough laugh echoed as he motioned to the water. "Indeed. The shallower end is cool. Go deeper for hotter water."

She felt so dirty. She'd been filthy before, especially in the desert countries with sand everywhere and in everything and bathing was more of a mudbath. But God, she wanted a bath right now.

He must have seen her answer in her expression. Stepping closer, he tucked a finger under her chin and studied her face. "You look better, less on edge."

"It took a while for everything to sink in." She curled her fingers around his hand, met his gaze. "Is that why you stayed so quiet on the hike here?"

"Aye." He kissed her fingers. "The silence of the mountains serves me well when I am troubled. I hoped the peace would help you also."

He'd made her a gift of quiet understanding with no attempts at persuasion or arguing. Damn, why did she have to like him so much? She managed to smile at him. "Thank you."

"You are welcome. Of course, not being Alec, remaining silent wasn't a great hardship." Brushing her hands aside, he unzipped her jacket.

"Calum, I'm not a kid."

He tilted his head. "No, you are not. Even so, there are times you will allow another to care for you, cariad. This is such a time."

That sounded wrong, and still sent a wave of warmth through her. "I can manage by myself."

"I think there has been too much of that in your life," he said. When she frowned at him, he smiled. "Go. Enjoy your bath."

"I will." The jacket dropped. She unlaced her shoes and pulled them off. Halfway to the water, leaving a trail of clothing in her wake, she got down to her tank top and briefs and stopped. *Oops.* She turned.

Calum was leaning against the cave wall, watching her, and smiling a little.

"Um." What could she say? Turn your back? Go outside into the cold?

"I'll join you in a while." He paused, lifted that damned eyebrow. "Will it worry you if I indulge also?"

"Um. Fine." Maybe stay in her underwear? But they were damp and crusty with sweat. Hell, considering how incredibly male he was, he'd undoubtedly seen naked women before. She went to the opposite side of the cave, finished stripping, and walked in. It was like entering a hot tub. As the heat penetrated her skin, reaching deep into her, she let out a moan of joy.

Ergh, that had sounded way too provocative. She glanced over her shoulder. He was still leaning against the wall. Fine. At least over here, with only the candlelight, he wouldn't see much.

SHE WAS MAGNIFICENT.

As she rose out of the hot water into the cooler air, the candlelight glowed off her wet skin, highlighting each curve and shadowing like an artist's brush between her legs. Her chest muscles formed a lovely base for high, full breasts, the nipples pebbling. Her hair was a dark waterfall, spilling down to her sweetly rounded butt. He smiled—she didn't realize how well a shifter saw in darkness.

Using hard-earned control, he kept himself from getting erect. The disruptions in her life might have changed her interest in him. If his attentions no longer aroused her, he'd know by her scent, by her movements. And that would be that.

But if she remained interested, sex served as a quick way to remove barriers. A way to learn to trust. Victoria didn't let people close. She kept herself contained, rarely showing any emotion except anger. Jamie had shown him the little human had a tender heart, but why so well hidden?

If she decided to stay with them, she needed to trust in order to survive her first trawsfur. And, he admitted to himself, he wanted her trust for other reasons. Before this, she had desired him, welcomed his hands on her…his will over hers.

He stripped and went to the side of the cave near her. Ignoring how she dropped down into the water as he approached, he strolled past and to the wall. A tin container in a hollowed-out shelf contained soap. He sniffed each ball to pick one that suited her. Not that it would cover up her own scent—one that made him want to growl and purr at the same time. By Herne, he wanted to take her, make her come, and bury himself deep inside her.

WHY DOES HE have to so fuckingly virile? Vic watched him getting something by the cave wall, standing under one of the candles he'd lit. She tried to tell herself the heat rising inside of her came from the hot water.

But just look at him. Dark all over, his skin color more like her olive than Alec's golden tan. His black hair brushed his shoulders as if sampling the feel of the hard muscles. The backs of his thighs had a scattering of short black hair. Between his legs, his testicles hung, large and heavy. Very male. His frame was less bulky than Alec's, but his hard muscles were more defined, and her need to run her hand over his chest had grown to almost a compulsion.

But...he wasn't erect. Here she was, naked in the water, and technically a shifter now, and she didn't excite him. Hell, he wasn't even checking her out.

Deflated, she let her body sink below the water's surface and exhaled in a snort of bubbles. She was being an idiot. She'd bedded his brother and would like to again. Messing around with Calum would be wrong. She and Alec weren't a pair or anything, but she mustn't cause friction between the brothers. *No.* She popped back up and sucked in a breath of chill air.

Calum wasn't standing by the wall anymore. Regret washed through her, followed by relief. Yes, she'd better lock it down and keep her horny little body to herself.

"May I offer you some soap?"

She jumped, spun around. Holy fuck, he was not a foot from her.

The corners of his eyes crinkled as he repeated, "Soap?"

"Um." His chest was a matt of dark curling hair with water trickling down between the sculpted pectorals. After a moment, she yanked her gaze to his face. "Soap?"

"The substance used for cleansing?" he prompted as his smile creased one cheek. "Let me show you." He rubbed his hands together, forming froth that smelled like strawberries.

Without waiting for her agreement, he ran his palms down her neck, her shoulders, her arms. His touch was firm and cool against her overheated skin. Stunned at the way his touch felt on her body, she stood still. Picking up her limp hand, he washed her fingers with the foam, then massaged the plump part of her palm just below her thumb.

"Did you know this is called the Venus mound for the goddess of love?" He nipped the spot and sent a wave of lust up her arm and straight down to her groin.

"Calum …"

He stroked the soap over her biceps, massaging her muscles as if he was a well-schooled bath attendant. "Turn, little female," he murmured, guiding her until she faced away from him. She should protest, but he wasn't trying to grope her breasts, he was...

Hard fingers dug into her aching shoulders. "Oooh, God."

"Your backpack was too heavy." He'd argued with her before they left the cabin, wanting to carry their gear himself. Like that would happen.

"Mmmmh." He could scold all he wanted if he just kept his hands pressing away the soreness.

"Stubborn." With a soft laugh, he squeezed her trapezius muscles to the point of pain, then released his grip. As the blood flowed back into the relaxed tissues, she couldn't suppress a moan. His fingers traced the scars from Lachlan's bite, and he kissed the spot before continuing.

She couldn't move. It was like he'd cast a net over her with his sure touch, rendering her helpless. When her legs wobbled, he wrapped a hard arm around her waist, his hand resting just below one breast.

"We're not finished, Victoria." He nipped the nape of her neck, sending a jolt of electricity straight to her pussy.

And yet, the surge of heat wakened her from the spell. Her mind—and conscience—flicked on. He intended to have sex. She pulled away and turned. "Calum, no. This isn't right. Alec—"

"Victoria, Alec knows we will make love." He moved close enough that the stiff peaks of her breasts rubbed his chest, then cupped her chin in his steady hand. "Look at me, *cariad*."

Her gaze lifted as if compelled. *Don't let him talk you into this, sergeant.* "What does cariad mean?"

"It means darling." His thumb stroked her lower lip. "Alec and I often...share...our women. Alone or together."

Two men? *Oh God.* A wicked lick of heat swept through her body. She pressed her hands against his chest and hesitated, disconcerted by his rock-hard muscles. "No. I don't believe you. I won't risk hurting him." Her body throbbed with the need for sex, but hurting Alec wasn't something she'd do.

"It pleases me that you worry about my brother's happiness." His determined hands closed over hers and lifted them to his face. His beard shadow scratched her palms, sending an odd excitement through her. He smiled slightly and dragged his jaw slowly across her palms. When his gaze lowered to her breasts, as if imagining how his beard would feel against the tender skin, her body melted.

"No," she whispered and tried to step back.

His grip never loosened. "Victoria, I give you my word that Alec approves of you being with me." His steady gaze met hers.

Somehow she knew down to her bones that he wouldn't lie to her. "That's just…"

"It's a shifter thing, and we'll talk about it later."

She opened her mouth, and his eyes darkened. "Later, little female. I have things I wish to do to you now."

The hard, slightly rough statement eradicated her resolve. Her knees almost gave out. "But…"

"Shhh." He nipped her fingers, the tiny pains erotic, and then put his big hands around her waist and set her onto the hip-high rock ledge at the side. The surface of the water rippled over it and the flat stone was warm under her bottom.

He pushed her legs open and pulled her forward until his very hard erection pressed against her heat. She gasped, feeling her control slipping.

"That's right, cariad. You needn't think." He grasped her nape, guiding her lips to his, holding her as his tongue plunged inside to echo the rocking of his cock at her entrance.

His free hand covered her breast, cupping and stroking in such a way that when he finally reached the nipple, she was taut in anticipation. With only one calloused finger, he touched the peak, his touch so light, she arched into him for more. He chuckled, and his fingers closed, pressing gently on the tip. Like an electric shock, desire shot in a sizzling line to her clit.

She gasped and he took advantage, taking his kiss even deeper. His fingers rolled her nipple, the pressure growing past pleasure, bordering on pain, and yet her body shook with arousal. As her breast throbbed, he moved to the other, teasing until it swelled to match the first. Until her sex pulsed in time with her breasts.

Her head spun, and she clutched his shoulders. The hard muscles under her fingers lured her hands to stroke up his back.

He rumbled his pleasure. When he released her mouth, she felt as if she was melting right into the hot water. He regarded her for a moment, then smiled. His hand pressed on her sternum. "Lie back, cariad."

Unable to fight him, she reclined onto the warm rock. The silky water lapped at her sides and her pussy, heating her skin.

"Pretty little female," he murmured. His thumbs gently pulled her folds apart, then he bent, and his tongue slid over her sex. Like Alec had done. A tremor ran through her.

"No." She tried to sit up, "I don't want that." Too intimate, too vulnerable, giving him too much control. "Just fuck me."

His head lifted. He met her gaze, and his eyes narrowed as he studied her. His face softened, although she saw a crease appear in his cheek. "All right then."

With ruthless hands, he flipped her onto her stomach. Her legs dangled down, and his thighs moved them apart. A hard hand slid under her pelvis, and he lifted, tilting her hips up to him. A second's pause. His cock pressed against her, slickening in her wetness, and then he entered her with one hard thrust.

"Aaaa!" So big. Her fingers clawed at the rock as she struggled to adjust to his size. She'd asked for this, only she hadn't expected to feel…taken. That he'd stolen the control from her even more.

He didn't move, his groin against her bottom. "Breathe, little female."

She inhaled. Again. "Okay," she said, trying not to sound breathless. "Go ahead."

His deep voice flowed over her like honey as he said, "Oh I will, cariad." To her shock, the fingers under her pelvis moved down into her pubic hair. He tugged on the strands, creating tiny pinpricks of sensation. The whole center of her body was turning into a massive ache, and his cock wasn't moving.

He touched her entrance where she was stretched so tightly around his shaft and ran one of his slickened fingers over her throbbing clit. She jerked at the blast of sensation.

"What are you doing?" Her blood was singing in her veins.

"Exactly what I want to." His finger slid over and around her clit, ruthlessly driving it into hardness, until it was so engorged it hurt. When she wiggled, he set a hand on her bottom, holding her in place as his other drove her mad.

Her mind started to go fuzzy. "Calum, no."

"At this point, cariad," he murmured, "you do not command. You may beg, if you feel the need."

Fuck. Goddamn. He knew just where to press, sliding his finger in to join his huge cock, and up over her clit until her entire pussy felt like one throbbing nerve. And there he held her until she whimpered, her hips tilting to get his touch...there. She was panting, little moans, unable to think, to protest as he drove her higher. If he'd just touch—

Instead, he pulled out and inexorably back in. With the slow slide of his cock, pleasure vibrated through her system. Her eyes felt like they were rolling back in her head. Her vagina clamped around him, her thigh muscles trembled as his light touch moved closer to her clit and then farther away. The pressure coiled tighter and tighter, and somehow knowing he wouldn't let her escape, sent her even higher until nothing remained in her mind except the slow thrust into her vagina and his circling finger.

"That's right," he said softly. "I'm teaching you that you do not need to control everything. Let go, cariad. I will take care of you."

She wanted to—she did. So she tried one last time to move, to resist. His hand held her in place. As she gave in, a whimper escaped. A whisper. "Please."

He kissed her neck, his lips warm and gentle. "Little female, I would be happy to please you." His merciless hands closed on her hips, yanking her bottom higher, just as his shaft drove in hard. Deep. Over and over as everything inside her gathered into one place…and exploded, a massive bomb blowing molten fragments of pleasure through every nerve in her body. Her hips tried to buck against his ruthless grip, and the feeling of being controlled sent another wave of sensation pulsing upward. *God, god, god.*

With a rough, sexy laugh, he hammered into her in short hard strokes, and then pressed deep. She could feel his erection jerking inside and the increased slickness.

He played with her after, fingers teasing, his cock rocking in and out, until he'd drawn every last spasm out of her, until she was sensitive to the slightest touch, and she laid limp, heart pounding in her chest, covered in a hard sweat. When he turned her over and lifted her in his arms, she could only moan. She swallowed, and her voice came out in a whisper, "You bastard."

He smiled and carried her to the edge of the water. After drying himself, then her, brushing aside her attempts to help, he set her on the bedding. He knelt beside her. "You were far too quick, cariad," he murmured. He ran one finger down her cheek. "This time, we'll draw it out a little."

When her eyes widened, he wound his fingers in her hair, held her for another kiss.

HOURS LATER, CALUM lay beside her in the blankets, watching her breathe. He stroked his finger down her neck, damp with sweat, the tiny pulse still hammering. Her eyes were closed, the lashes dark smudges on her smooth skin. His body hummed with satiated pleasure. Once she'd finally relaxed into his control and care, no longer building barriers to protect herself, she was a responsive, generous mate.

He circled her swollen nipples with one finger. The satiny skin had turned a dark red from his sucking and bites.

Her eyes opened, still slightly glazed from passion. "Surely you aren't planning to start again, are you?"

He had taken her…many times. He smiled. "No, cariad. I think you have had plenty." Enough that she had winced with his last entry, although she had been too close to coming to want him to withdraw. He cupped her cheek and kissed her lightly. "I simply like touching you."

Her lips curved, and she leaned into his hand, much like a cat. His heart squeezed. The need to care for her, to make her his own had grown mountain high.

"So what are we doing tomorrow?" she asked, her voice slightly hoarse. The last two times, she had given him everything, inhibitions gone, and her screams of release had echoed through the caves.

"You'll meet the Elders, I will warn them in case the shifter-hunters come farther than I expect. We'll spend the night and return to Cold Creek, ready for battle."

"You said these people live isolated so they don't have to be around humans." Her brows drew together. "Because they hate humans or because they're afraid?"

Her brain rarely stopped working, it seemed. "Mostly fear and…" How could he put this? "When living amongst humans, a shifter must be ever cautious, not just in trawsfurring, but in speech and habits as well. It's a strain, and as the Daonain age and become more forgetful, they find it a burden."

"I suppose people might react badly if they knew about you."

He felt his jaw tighten, his hand close in a fist, and realized that as her barriers had disappeared, so had his.

"Calum?" She pushed up onto one elbow. "What… Something happened to you, didn't it?"

He stared at the rock wall until she stroked his shoulder, drawing his attention back. Her eyes were soft, worried—for him. How odd to feel a female's concern and desire to share sorrow. He'd never had that with Lenora.

"I was lifemated—married—many years ago." He set his palm over her small hand, keeping it against his face. "She was an only child. Shy. She painted. Much like a sprite, she lived in the moment. She'd often forget to cook—or burn the food when she did, and would disregard the rules about using the portals or shifting near trails."

He stopped, not wanting to share the horror, but Victoria's eyes stayed steady on his. This female wouldn't shy away from pain. "The wildflowers had bloomed, and she trawsfurred to visit the alpine meadows. As far as we can tell, a human saw her shift back. When she didn't return, I went to look for her." And found her body far too near a hiking trail, her eyes looking up at the sky as if wondering why help had never arrived. The man had used her own blood to—"The murderer had written DEMON on her chest. We discovered later that he was rabidly religious."

His jaw clenched as the memory kindled his fury. He'd tracked the killer through the darkening forest, and his fabled control shattered the moment he'd smelled Lenora's scent, seen her blood on the man. By the time his sanity had returned, the ground was soaked with blood, the human's body mangled beyond recognition. The man's shrieks haunted Calum's nightmares for years. "I...lost control and killed him." It had been the last time he'd allowed emotions to rule his actions.

Calum braced, waiting for Victoria to pull away, to show her horror.

"Of course you did. Good job." She patted his cheek.

Well. After a moment, he remembered what Alec had told him about the bodies littering the bookstore. This female was nothing like Lenora—perhaps like none he'd known before. In a wolf pack, she'd be the alpha female.

And that made her submission to him all the more meaningful. An alpha female submits only to her mate. He cleared his throat. "So we fear individual reactions as well as the government's reaction. We'd either be studied like lab animals or simply exterminated."

"That seems a little..." Her mouth pulled down, and she sighed. "Actually, that's probably what would happen."

"Aye. That's why we have a law that if a shifter reveals the Daonain to humans, he is put to death."

Her gaze turned to the dark water, her jaw tight, and Calum set his hand on her shoulder. How could he have forgotten she was so new? She turned to him, attempting to smile.

"Come, cariad. We should sleep. Tomorrow will be long." He pulled her closer, nudging her head down in the hollow of his shoulder. After a second of stiffness, she softened and cuddled with him, filling the holes in his soul with her mere presence.

Chapter Fourteen

I T WAS APPROACHING noon the next day when Vic followed
Calum down the tiny trail and into the "village" of scattered
cabins. "This looks like one of those old west towns in the
movies."

"Very close. We bought the property from a mining consor-
tium and fixed up the abandoned cabins."

Deep within the mountain range, the village nestled at one
end of a small valley under a light layer of snow. Vic frowned.
Things didn't look right. There weren't any real streets, for one.
"Where's the Main Street? The stores and all that."

"None." Calum stepped down onto a ledge and turned to
help her.

She ignored his hand and jumped. "Where's the power lines,
electricity, cable?"

"None."

"Too bizarre," she muttered. The scent of wood smoke
wafted past. "And everybody has to walk to get here?"

He dropped back to pace beside her on the wider trail. "It
doesn't take as long in animal form," he said. "A dirt road gets as
close as the nearest cliff. In the winter, we use snowmobiles to
get that far."

"Grocery? Bookstore?"

"We bring them supplies every few months."

"Damn." Although the sun was high, the air still held a nasty bite. She eyed the tree-covered mountains. "At least they won't run out of firewood."

His hard hand gripped her nape, and he drew her close enough to take her mouth in a long, thorough kiss. Her knees sagged. Pulling back, he ran a finger over her swollen lips. "I will keep you warm, cariad, never fear."

Cariad. It sounded more intimate than *darling*. She sighed. The night she'd spent with him had been terrifying. He'd taken control and kept it, satisfying her with hands and mouth, taking her hard and then gently, again and again. She'd never experienced anything like it, the way he pushed her one moment, cared for her the next. Why had she let him? *Let him?* Hell, admit it, she'd totally gotten off on doing whatever he commanded, surrendering her will to his. And he'd reacted as if he'd both expected, yet treasured, how she'd…submitted.

Fuck, she'd *submitted* to him. Like a whipped dog. She pulled back and glared at him.

His eyes narrowed, and he studied her, slowly, his gaze moving over her face, her body. "Little cat, what has you upset?"

"I'm not a dog." He wasn't getting it, so she added, "I don't go belly-up for a man."

"Ah. This is about last night." His lips quirked. "No, I doubt you've ever gone…belly-up…before." The utter confidence in his expression, in his whole body, sent a quiver through her. "I'm pleased that you would surrender to me, Victoria. Did you not enjoy making love?"

He'd broken down her defenses until her emotions had been as open to him as her body. He'd made her beg, dammit. She averted her gaze.

His hand cupped her cheek, turning her back to face him. His voice held an officer's stern determination with that thread of tenderness that undermined all her resistance. "Answer my question, little cat."

She'd never wanted to lie so bad in her life. But aside from the necessities of the job, she didn't. Dammit. "Yes. I enjoyed it." She turned her head. "Too much. I don't like that I liked it."

"Look at me." Gray eyes should be cold, but his were warm. So warm.

"This isn't who I am, Calum."

"You only surrender to me because you trust me. And because you want to." He brushed a kiss over her lips. "This is who you are when you sheathe your claws. You don't have to stay on guard all the time, Victoria."

Her mouth flattened. *Yes, I do.*

He smiled slightly, then started them back down the mountain, leaving her more confused than before. Sometimes when he looked at her with that penetrating gaze, it felt as if he'd touched her soul.

The man scared her spitless.

As they walked past the houses, Vic saw a guy step out of one, bare-assed naked. Without looking around, he shifted into a bear and lumbered up the steep slope. Damn, right out in front of God and everyone.

Calum rapped on the door of a larger cabin.

Vic scowled. Being with Calum was one thing—meeting a bunch of shifters? Entirely different. She didn't know how to act around them. Deep breath. Things change—deal with it. At least he'd knocked; they obviously observed a few human courtesies.

An old guy, as tough and stringy as a piece of jerky opened the door. "Cosantir, we weren't expecting you." His nostrils flared, and his brows went up as he looked between her and Calum. "Well, well. Come in."

Calum let Vic precede him into the house. She checked the exits: front door, two front windows, and another on the left, door at the rear to a hall leading somewhere. They were in the living area with a woodstove radiating glorious heat. Unlit lanterns hung from hooks on the wall, and woven rugs brightened the wooden floor. Looked like a hunting cabin but without any mounted animal heads or antlers.

After helping her out of her jacket, Calum said, "Victoria, this is Aaron. Aaron, meet Victoria. She has an interesting story for the Elders."

Vic nodded politely. Great, she'd spend the day being interrogated. She'd been insane to come here.

The old man opened the woodstove and poked at the fire. "Are you staying for a bit?"

"For tonight. One room will serve for us."

God, just announce to the world that we're having sex. Vic gave him a nasty look.

Calum's eyes lit with amusement. He ran his hand down her arm, a touch that soothed even as it sent a wave of heat through her. Those hands were… She stepped back and scowled at him. *Sneaky cat.*

Aaron cleared his throat. "I'll summon the Elders." He inclined his head in a slight bow to Calum, smiled at Vic, and left the cabin.

The small meeting room at the back of the house contained a round oak table with eight chairs. The first Elder to arrive was a wizened old woman.

"Maude, you look in good health," Calum said.

She smiled and thumped him affectionately along the ribs. "And you also, laddie. Gi' me a squeeze."

He hugged her, having to bend almost in half to reach her. Turning, he said, "Maude, this is Victoria. Victoria, Maude who is an Elder of this territory."

"This territory?" Vic repeated. "There are others?"

"Of course," Maude said. She studied Vic with sharp blue

eyes. "What area are you from?"

Good question. Vic glanced at Calum.

"Mine, Maude." Calum seated the old woman. "I'll explain when the others arrive."

Even as Aaron appeared with a pot of coffee and cups, three more came in. Abigail, Leland, and Perry. All with leathery faces seasoned by sun and wind, keen eyes surrounded by an abundance of wrinkles, and the stringy leanness of barn cats or coyotes.

Aaron took a place at the table and so there were five Elders. Calum pulled out a chair for Vic, and she joined them reluctantly. Whoopee, stuck at King Arthur's Round Table. She glanced at Calum out of the corner of her eye; at least the king was a hunk.

"You summoned, Cosantir. We're here. Spit it out." Leland was taller than the rest and had the bowlegged stride of someone who'd spent time on a horse.

"First, let me finish introductions," Calum said. "This is Victoria, a new shifter who has not yet experienced her first trawsfur."

With their impassive expressions, Maude and Leland must play poker, Vic decided. The rest stared at her in blank shock.

"At her age? How can this be?" Aaron asked.

After Calum explained, Maude had tears in her eyes. "I taught the lad in his First Year. Filled with pranks. I didn't think he'd paid attention, but he remembered when the time came. Well done, Lachlan." She lifted her cup. "Goddess willing, he will return to run with us again."

The rest raised their drinks, saying, "As She wills."

Calum smiled at Vic. "Lachlan has brought us a strong woman; she rivals Alec both in courage and sheer stubbornness." As the Elders laughed, he said seriously, "I bring Victoria, a werecat, to be Seen."

There was silence as the Elders studied her. Their eyes seemed to burn deep inside her, exposing her weaknesses, the darkness in her spirit, even the men she'd killed.

She wanted to slink down in her chair, to disappear under the table. So she firmed her spine, straightened her shoulders, and stared back.

The Elders spoke together. "We See Victoria."

Calum raised his cup again. "Rejoice, Daonain, the clan increases."

And cups clinked.

THAT EVENING, VIC lay on one of the twin beds in the room and watched Jamie pull clothes out of a backpack. To everyone's surprise, Alec and Jamie had shown up an hour before, having driven as far as possible and hiked the rest of the way. Vic and Calum would have a ride back to Cold Creek tomorrow.

"What kind of a party will this be, anyway?" Vic asked. "I didn't bring any nice clothes."

Looking between two T-shirts, Jamie said, "It's not a fancy party, not like we have in Cold Creek or anything. Nobody here has dress-up stuff."

"Well, that's a relief. So this is all right? Jeans and a shirt?"

"Yeah." Jamie finally picked up one shirt—a blue one that matched her eyes—and pulled it on. "Everybody will bring stuff to eat, but we don't have to since we don't live here."

Vic grunted. "Good thing. I'm not much of a cook. That's a nice color on you, Jamie."

"Thanks." The kid looked up from under her lashes. "I'm glad Lachlan made you a shifter. I didn't want you to leave."

Vic blinked as warmth enfolded her like a hot bath. "Well. I—" She sighed and let the words spill out. "I would have missed you, munchkin."

"Were you going to miss Daddy too?"

Look out, Sergeant. This conversation is booby-trapped. With relief, Vic heard a door open and cheerful voices from the living room. It sounded as if more people arrived. Oh, wonderful, she had two no-win options: being polite while strangers stared at the new freak shifter, or discussing a this-can't-happen relationship with a man's daughter—or niece—and wasn't this so totally screwed up?

She chose the least dangerous option and said with a groan, "Guess we'd better get our butts out there."

Jamie snickered. "Oh, Vicki, it won't be that bad."

"Easy for you to say."

Jamie took her hand and pulled her off the bed. "I'll take care of you. It's not a Gathering, so nobody's gonna fight."

"No fighting? What's the point?"

Giggling, Jamie dragged her into the living room. To Vic's horror, people surged through the front door like ocean breakers.

Aaron trotted over and handed her a big mug of hot chocolate. "I made this for you, young lady." He gave another one to Jamie before hustling away.

Vic stared at the mug. *No beer?* Dammit, she really wanted a drink. With a sigh, she sipped, then choked as it burned all the way down, not from the heat, but from the amount of peppermint schnapps Aaron had added. "Good God."

She pulled Jamie's cup out of her hands and sniffed it. No peppermint, just chocolate. "Okay, you can drink it."

Jamie took it back with a suspicious look. "I bet yours is better."

"And when you're twenty-one, you'll get to find out, won't you?" Vic answered. "Um. What are we supposed to do now?"

"We mingle and…and schmooze." Jamie frowned. "I'm not sure what that means, but it sounds cool."

"Come, come, let's introduce you around." Aaron popped back and chivvied Vic and Jamie forward like a hyperactive cattle dog. He stopped beside two women in their thirties seated on the sofa. "Victoria, this is Sarah and Gretchen. They're here visiting their mother until Samhain."

They offered chill nods.

Vic recognized Gretchen as the woman in Cold Creek who'd run her hand over Calum's chest. She was tall, slender, and fucking gorgeous with porcelain skin and French-braided platinum blonde hair. Her sister looked completely unrelated with a curvy build, dusky complexion, dark brown eyes, and wavy black hair. Also beautiful. "Nice to meet you," Vic lied.

"Jamie, Maude's grandson is here. He's just your age." Aaron dragged Jamie away. *Traitor*, Vic thought at the child, then sighed and took a chair. Although the women looked at her like she'd crawled out of a garbage can, she managed a polite smile.

"So you arrived here with Calum?" Gretchen asked, obviously already knowing the answer.

"That's right." Should she mention the attackers? God, someone should have briefed her before this party. "Um, we hiked up from Cold—"

"Hiked?" Sarah interrupted with a thin laugh. "Why didn't you trawsfur? You made the Cosantir walk like a stinking human?"

Vic considered being polite for all of two seconds and discarded the idea. They disliked her, for whatever reason, and the feeling was mutual. She rose and without one swearword—truly a miracle of self-control—walked away.

"Well!"

Vic didn't look to see who had spoken. Next stop? A mess of older people, including the Elders, mingled on the other side of the woodstove. Three middle-aged men stood by the door. A handful of women had taken over the kitchen. Jamie was engaged in a vehement argument with two boys about her age. No Calum, no Alec. *Damn them.*

Maude disengaged from the Elder group. "Come, child, there's food in the kitchen, and people want to meet you."

Vic glanced back at bitch one and bitch two. "Sure they do."

Maude tracked her gaze and gave a womanly snort. Tucking a hand under Vic's elbow, much like Calum's habit, she guided her into the kitchen. "Perhaps I should say *most* want to meet you. Some unattached females, well—"

"I usually have to *do* something before someone gets all huffy."

Maude laughed. "Oh, you did, Victoria, you did."

What had she done? Vic had no time to think as she was introduced to Heather and her mother, Helen. Round and soft with kind blue eyes, Helen smiled and took Vic's hand in both of hers. "We're delighted to have another woman for our Clan. Welcome, child, welcome."

"Thank you," Vic managed.

The woman's daughter laughed. "Every female is a stray chick to my mama, no matter how old they are." Heather was a tall, lanky woman about Vic's age wearing a russet sweater that matched her hair. She handed her mother a plate of sandwiches. "Here. I saw Leland looking in a few minutes ago. Of course, I'm not sure if he hungered for food or for you."

Helen flushed and frowned in mock disgust at her daughter. "Such notions you get." But she took the plate and Vic noticed, headed straight for the tough old Elder. He looked at her like a starving man spotting a McDonald's."

"Looks pretty gone on her," Vic commented.

Heather leaned back against the kitchen table and grinned. "The poor male's tried to get her into his cabin for years. He'd lifemate her in a heartbeat, but she wants to stay unattached for a while."

"Ah." Lifemated was the same as married, right? Why in the world hadn't Alec or Calum provided a furball dictionary?

Heather tilted her head. "You having an up-close-and-personal encounter with culture shock?"

"I'm past culture shock and well on the road to a major melt-down." Vic glanced at the crowd. "Is there a way to tell which shifter turns into which animal?"

Heather shoved a package of broccoli toward Vic. "Why don't you cut those up and we'll put out some dip." She started slicing up carrots. "The werecats, like Calum and Alec, usually have a prowling kind of gait. Maude and Aaron and Mama and my brothers are all bears; their walk is more bouncy. A wolf's gait isn't as distinctive."

"But if your mama is a bear, then how come you're a wolf?"

Heather rolled her eyes in a *duh* response. "My father or his ancestors must have been one. Me and my brothers are Gather-bred, so we're not sure of our fathers. But it's simple genetics, just like red hair or blue eyes."

Fathers? Before Vic could ask, a commotion at the door got her attention. Alec and Calum. Her spirits lifted so fast it was frightening. The men were quickly engulfed in greetings, but after a minute, Alec looked around, spotted Vic, and headed into the kitchen.

"Hey, Heather," he said, snatching a carrot from under her knife. "How's it going? You still CEO of that company?"

Heather gave him a thin smile. "You bet. We're raking in money hand-over-fist."

Alec shook his head, grinned at Vic. "Wolves. Nobody's better at teamwork, and they know right when to close in for the kill." He plopped down in a chair beside Vic.

Just needing to touch, she stepped closer and patted him on the head, trying not to notice how silky his hair was. The way he smelled of pine forests and masculine musk made her want to nibble on his neck. "Where'd you guys go? The party started a while ago."

"The village has bathing springs." He tucked his big hand around her leg, his fingers warm against her inner thigh. His thumb inched up to press on the seam of her jeans—right over her pussy.

She almost cut herself with the knife. Flushing, she glared and tried to move away.

He pulled her closer.

Heather snickered. "Oho, so that's the scent in the wind. How's Calum feel about this?"

What exactly was *this*? Vic glanced down at Alec. Surely Heather wasn't meaning some *relationship*.

He had a lazy smile on his face. "Oh, Calum is all in favor."

"Well, damn. About time." Heather presented Alec with a carrot as if awarding a prize.

God, she hated being ignorant. "Okay, guys, I'm confused. What are you—"

"I've noticed some gaps in her education," Heather said, frowning at Alec.

"No time. And"—he gave Vic an appeasing smile—"we didn't want to scare her to death."

"Scare me? What would—" A squeal from the doorway interrupted her.

"Alec!" Sarah, bitchy-sister-number-two, rushed in and pulled up a chair beside Alec. Her wide hips were balanced by equally large breasts, and she'd placed herself where Alec couldn't miss seeing all that cleavage.

Feeling positively puny, Vic concentrated on her cutting. She didn't care. She was leaving, wasn't she?

Heather's eyes held sympathy. "Mom and I are making cookies tomorrow. We could use some help. Stirring without an electric beater is tiring."

Vic managed a smile. "I'd like that."

"Good. Around ten or so. The house has a blue door since Mom had a feng shui kick a while back." She picked up the broccoli Vic had sliced and dumped it on the tray. "If you bring the dip, we'll take this out to the living room."

"Hey," Alec protested as they left him.

"That woman reminds me of kudzu," Vic said, glancing back. "Whatever it wraps around will suffocate and die."

"Good description," Heather agreed. "And Alec is so polite with women, he won't tell her where to take herself. Should we go back and rescue him?"

All that cleavage—he probably doesn't want to be rescued. The thought made her voice harden. "He's a big boy. If he wants to turn down what's being offered, he knows how to do it."

Going into the living room provided no escape, for there was Gretchen chatting animatedly with Calum, one fragile hand on his arm while she gazed up into his eyes. Seeing the guys with other women hurt, dammit, like someone was slicing her chest open, and that didn't make any sense. Sure, she'd slept with Calum, slept with Alec, but hell, she didn't own them. Not even close.

Heather set the tray down on a coffee table in front of the Elders who had taken over the couches. "The dip?" She held out her hand, then followed Vic's gaze. "Oh, girl, you've got it bad."

"It's not like that. I-I'm not even sure I'm staying. We'll probably never see each other again."

"Well, honey, you just keep telling yourself that." After setting the dip down, Heather looked around the living room. "Meantime, hmmm …"

"What?"

"You know, when I was a teen, and we first learned to trawsfur, Alec and Calum would leap out of the trees and pounce on me. They almost scared me to death." Heather's lips curved into an evil smile. "Although, I did bite Alec once, that's not nearly enough payback for all the misery they caused. A delayed revenge is much sweeter, don't you think?"

"Mmmmh, I guess I'm more of a kill-them-now sort of person." Would anyone notice if she escaped to her bedroom?

"I'm not. There he is... C'mon, I want you to meet my brother."

Vic hesitated and then followed, shaking her head. Men usually talked sense—women could be totally incomprehensible.

Heather's brother was a whopping big dude, Marine-sized, with keen brown eyes, shaggy brown hair, and a mouth made for laughing. She liked him immediately.

"Now look at what my little sister brought me today," he said, taking Vic's hand and holding it to his very muscular chest.

Heather cleared her throat. "Excuse me, Daniel, but I'm still here. And you're only my big brother by all of ten minutes. Victoria—"

"Vic or Vicki; nobody calls me Victoria. Almost nobody," Vic corrected. Although it didn't sound wrong when Calum said it.

"Vicki, then." Daniel kissed her fingers before releasing her hand. "I'm Daniel, crippled from being raised with this evil woman." He grinned at his sister.

"Oh, sure. And all those scars you and Tanner gave me after you learned to trawsfur? The way you'd swing at me with your giant claws, and you call me evil?" Heather punched his arm, grinned at Vic. "I left a six-pack of beer outside, want one?"

"Something cold and alcoholic? You bet."

Heather wrinkled her nose at her brother. "She sounds just like you." She took a step, then touched Vic's arm and whispered, "He's completely healthy and entirely single, in case you wondered."

Vic stared after Heather. No, she hadn't wondered, and although Daniel was exactly the type of man she enjoyed, she sure didn't need any more guy problems.

"You look like a lost lamb," he said and linked his hand with hers. "C'mon, we'll find a corner to commandeer and avoid the wolves…and cats. In fact, I think I'll keep you to myself for a bit."

"That won't be possible," a cold voice said from behind Vic. Calum moved in, standing close enough that his hip and shoulder brushed hers.

Daniel lifted her hand, pushed her sleeve up to her elbow, exposing the bare skin. "Well, now, doesn't appear like she's lifemated. Are you lifemated, Vicki?"

"I'm not sure I know what it means, but I don't think so."

"Oh, you'd know," he assured her, although his steady gaze never left Calum's.

Alec appeared on her other side, just as close as Calum. She was beginning to feel like a t-bone in front of starving animals.

When she heard an actual growl coming from Alec, Vic turned to stare at him. *What the fuck?*

"Vixen," Alec wrapped his big fingers around her biceps. "Let's go over—"

Oh, right. The minute she found someone to talk to, they're all over her like bees on honey. Not happening. She pulled her arm out of his grasp, and her hand from Daniel, and glared. "Excuse me, Sheriff, but I think you have some cleavage—I mean Sarah—to see to." Before he could react, she spun to face Calum. "And I'm sure the Ice Queen desires your presence."

When Daniel laughed, she lost it completely. The hell with it if her behavior wasn't very rational. And weren't they lucky she didn't have her Glock? She stepped out from between the two brothers, pausing to smile at Daniel. "Maybe some other time when I'm in a better mood. I'm partied out."

As she walked away, she heard Daniel say plaintively,

"Mommy, I want that one. Can't I—" and then he choked and groaned.

Reaching her bedroom, she shoved a chair underneath the door handle and flopped down onto the bed. What a wussy, abandoning the field to Cleavage and Ice Queen. Very bad strategy.

AS ALEC WATCHED, his brother stalked past the stunned guests and escaped outside. "Well, that was a surprise," he murmured. Calum's famous control had snapped with a vengeance.

"By Herne's horns, he hits harder than you do," Daniel wheezed, still hunched over his stomach. "You know, you two used to have a sense of humor. Especially about women."

"Not this time." Spotting Aaron's glare—*no fighting inside*— Alec pushed Daniel out the front door. The frigid air slapped against his face, restoring his equilibrium.

"Yeah, I get that." Daniel waggled his eyebrows. "She's incredibly appealing. Does she even realize you're trying to court her?"

"No, she doesn't," Calum said. He was leaning against the wall. "Forgive me, Daniel. I did lose control."

Daniel laughed and slapped Calum on the shoulder. "Good to know you're not perfect, buddy. And though it's been thirty years or so, you still throw a wicked punch."

"Indeed. I see you can still provoke a fight faster than anyone in the territory."

Daniel gave a mock bow. "Thank you, my son, thank you. So what's the story with the little lady? She looked lost as a heifer without a mama."

"That's a disgusting analogy," Alec said. "I take it you and Tanner are still running the Summerland in Rainier Territory?"

"Yup. Aside from the hellhounds increasing—we lost a new

shifter to them last month—we're doing good." Daniel brushed the snow off a wooden chair and sat down, propping his boots up on a protruding log of the cabin wall. "Are you going to tell me about Vicki? I'd like—"

"No you wouldn't," Calum said flatly.

"Got it." Daniel shook his head ruefully. "I heard she joined us by way of the Death Gift. What form is she?"

"Lachlan was a cat," Alec said, "so she must be one too."

Daniel stared. "Must be? She hasn't shifted yet?"

Calum sighed. "She was not completely certain she wanted to be a shifter."

"Hell, littermate, be honest. She knew she didn't," Alec said. The thought of her leaving chilled him faster than the air outside. "I'm not sure she's changed her mind, especially after meeting"—he snorted, remembering her words—"*Cleavage* and the *Ice Queen*."

Daniel's laugh sounded like a bull's bellow and echoed off the mountains. "You should have seen your faces, like she'd kneed you in the balls."

"She was angry with us for some reason," Calum agreed. "But—"

"Damn, you're blind, man. With anybody else, you'd see it. The girl's jealous of you both." Daniel gave a snort of disgust. "If she hadn't shown me that, do you really think you could have kept me from her?"

Alec managed to close his mouth. *Jealous?* He saw the slight smile appear on his brother's face. "We're idiots, all right," Alec said.

"I'm gonna go get some sleep." Daniel stood up and stretched, then glanced at Alec and Calum. "The way you both arrived within seconds of me touching her, I'd say the jealousy goes two ways, wouldn't you?"

"Yeah, well, we knew that," Alec said, then saw the blank look on Calum's face. "Or not."

Chapter Fifteen

V IC ESCAPED THE house before breakfast. She needed a break from all the people and emotions. These last few days, her emotions had turned as topsy-turvy as a B-15 with a drunken pilot.

After hiking the village, she followed a stream into the forest. The breeze whipped around her, blowing a fine dust of snow off the pine branches, and clearing her mind. Last night hadn't been her finest moment. Then again, what the hell had the guys been growling about? All three men stiff-legged and snarly, and that wasn't something she'd expected to see from Alec and Calum. Especially Calum.

Vic sighed and leaned her back against a tree. The mountain was so quiet she could hear snow plopping to the ground from the branches, the wind sighing through the pines, the little gurgle of the half-frozen stream.

Yeah, the guys had been pushy. She hadn't shown much better. What had possessed her to make those waspish comments—Cleavage and Ice Queen? Alec would razz her forever, and Calum might not say anything, but oh, he'd know she'd been jealous. She thumped the back of her head against the trunk. *Crap.*

Jealous. The thought made her want to run away. But it was

too late. She was here and entangled. And a shifter if she wanted to be.

Do I? At first, the thought had horrified her, but now, it didn't sound that bad. Everyone she'd met seemed pretty normal. Running around as a big cat? How cool would that be?

If only being a wereanimal didn't have so many downsides, like not being able to return to duty. No way could she pop into fur skin every month—not in Baghdad where people lived cheek by jowl. Or, what if she got shot? Might she wake up in a zoo rather than the hospital?

But how would she earn a living otherwise? All her skills were for war. Give up being a spy to work as a barmaid? Or a housewife? Did these guys even marry? She frowned. *Don't want to go there.* She needed to keep her times with Alec and Calum light-hearted. Fun. If it got more serious, well, who would she choose? Calum with his deep, commanding voice, who stole the control from her? Or Alec with that mouth she just wanted to bite and nibble, and who could make her laugh. Who she understood right down to the ground as another fighter.

Damn men. Didn't they know that one guy was supposed to call dibs and the other back off? No matter what Calum said, she felt guilty to have fucked him. It would be wise to just plain get away from them.

Yet the thought of leaving was so painful, she turned around and started back to the village.

Halfway there, she met Helen hiking up with a large basket over her arm. "Vicki, how nice to see you this morning." She raised her basket. "I'm hoping the squirrels left me some nuts. There's one lonely walnut tree just over this rise." Helen's face was nipped pink with the cold, her eyes a bright blue under a furred hood. "We're making cookies in an hour and expecting your help."

Vic grinned. "I'm there."

"That's my girl." Helen patted her on the shoulder. "If you're a good child, I'll let you take some back to your men. They both love their sweets, Alec especially."

Oh, yeah, she'd seen that. But—"They aren't mine."

"Of course not. Whatever came over me to say such a thing?"

Vic gave Helen a suspicious look.

Helen's eyes danced with laughter. "You can give them cookies anyway—and Jamie also. We'll bake extra. You change out of those wet clothes when you get back." She patted Vic and continued up the trail.

Vic watched for a moment, feeling unsettled. Would her mother have been like Helen if she'd lived? Would she have taught Vic to make cookies? And scolded her now and then?

Walking slowly, Vic had just reached the edge of the forest when she heard Helen scream.

"SHE A WOMAN yet?" Maude and Calum stood in the doorway of her house, watching Jamie play tag with the other teenagers.

"For about two months." His baby was almost grown up. He felt a pang of mingled pride and grief.

"So her first trawsfur will be any time now." Maude pursed her lips. "With all the problems down in Cold Creek, you should leave her up here with us, Calum."

"I've considered it. But I'm the one she's worked with. She responds to my voice." Fear squeezed his chest as he remembered the child last year who'd panicked and lost the ability to return to human. "What if something went wrong and I wasn't here?"

Maude opened her mouth, and Calum cut her off. "I can't stay. My responsibility lies in Cold Creek, especially now. I need to remove that human before he draws attention to us. Or harms another of mine."

"I understand, Calum. It's an evil time when a child has to be fearful in her own town."

"Aye." He handed Maude his cup. "I'll see you at Aaron's in an hour. We—"

A woman's terror-filled scream ripped though the quiet village and echoed off the mountains. Silence reigned for a few seconds before the noise began.

HELEN! VIC SPRINTED up the trail, cursing the heavy coat that slowed her speed. Before she'd gone far, two mountain lions flashed past, then a bear, leaving her behind so quickly she felt as if she wasn't even moving.

Vic pushed harder. With each harsh breath, the cold knifed into her lungs. She passed the stream and followed the tracks in the snow. She fell once and scrambled back to her feet as she heard a cougar's snarl.

At the base of a slope, she burst into a meadow and spotted the lonely walnut tree, then Daniel, Calum, and Alec. Naked and in human form. Helen lay sprawled on the ground, unconscious, and something had ripped her up bad. Red splotches marked the snow, the smell of blood metallic and ugly in the pristine wilderness. Anger and fear tightened Vic's throat as she saw bites and claw marks.

"I need something to stop the bleeding." Alec pressed his hands over a long laceration. He scowled at Helen's coat, the leather thick and useless for bandages.

"I'll go back," Calum said.

"No. Here." Vic shrugged out of her jacket, yanked off her flannel shirt, and tossed it at Daniel. As he ripped off a length of material, she took off the long-sleeved Henley she'd worn under it. Using her boot knife, Vic cut off strips and handed them to

Alec.

"She must have covered her head with her hood and arms." Calum examined Helen's face and neck with gentle hands. "She didn't panic."

Helen's coat was sliced to ribbons, but it had mostly protected the fragile skin underneath. Not her legs. Multiple gouges went through muscle almost to the bone, and she was bleeding badly. The men worked quickly, tying pressure bandages over the worst of the wounds.

As Vic pulled off her coat and bent to wrap it around Helen, Alec and Calum moved aside.

Calum bent to examine the red-flecked tracks leading away. "It's a feral." He looked at Alec, his voice level...and sad. "I'm sorry, cahir."

Alec bowed his head slightly. "Your will, Cosantir."

"Let's get going." Daniel lifted Helen in his arms.

"Go." Alec turned to Vic. "You're shivering, baby. Where's—" He glanced at Helen, saw the coat around her. "You're a treasure, Vixen. Now haul that precious ass of yours to where it's warm."

Vic hesitated. How could she leave?

Calum put his hand against her back and gave her a nudge. "We'll be taking turns carrying her down as fast as we can. Will you go ahead and find Aaron? Tell him what has happened and to prepare for us. Medical kit, heated blankets—he knows what to do."

Vic nodded with relief. "I'm on it." And then she ran.

WHEN CALUM EVENTUALLY finished his duties and returned to Aaron's cabin, he looked for Victoria. She wasn't in the kitchen where Aaron and Maude were stitching up Helen. The living room? There, tucked into a chair. He frowned. Although they'd returned almost an hour ago, she sat by the woodstove shivering, her face still pinched with cold.

Calum poured out some thick black coffee from the pot on the woodstove and held it out to her. "Drink. It's vile, but hot."

Giving him a pale smile, she tried to take the cup, but trembled so hard that coffee sloshed over the side.

Calum took it back and set it on the end table. "Stand up."

She gave him a confused look. Her wits were definitely chilled, or the obstinate little female would have argued with him.

When she stood, he took her place in the chair, pulled her onto his lap, and wrapped his arms around her. She wore a sweater, and he felt as if he held a fluffy icicle.

She relaxed against him. "God, you feel wonderful."

"I believe you have said that before," he murmured in her ear, "In the cave." He hardened at the memory.

She squirmed, then stilled as she felt his erection. "Sorry."

"I shall live." With his free hand, he picked up the cup of coffee and held it to her lips. "Drink, cariad."

She sipped, shivered, sipped. "I feel like a baby," she muttered.

He chuckled at the resentful tone. "Ah, you begin to recover."

"Damned cold mountains."

"They are indeed." He wrapped his arms tighter around her, enjoying the feel of a female's softness and the surprisingly firm muscles underneath. He rubbed his cheek over her silky hair, breathing in her scent, marking her with his.

"Sometimes people call you Calum and sometimes Cosantir. What's a Cosantir?"

Calum grazed his lips over a scratch marring her high cheekbone. "I am guardian of this territory." He knew what she'd ask next. "That would be the Northern Cascades."

"Huh. Big area. So, did you run for office or something?"

"Ah, no. I fear this isn't an elected position. The God chooses."

Her breathing stopped for a few seconds. "Oookay. Right."

When her lovely, cinnamon-colored eyes rose to his, he barely stifled a laugh. It had been a long while since someone looked at him like he had gone stark, raving bonkers.

"God picked you out of the herd, huh. And you would know this how?"

He nipped the back of her neck as a reprimand. "It is risky to taunt Herne, Victoria. And I know this because certain powers come with the title."

Rubbing her nape, she scowled at him. "You're so full of—"

As he opened himself to the God, power surged through him in an unstoppable wave. From the way she froze, his pupils had probably turned the color of night and even a sense-blind human could feel the hum radiating from him.

She swallowed. "That's why you played judge for that bear guy?"

"Aye," he sighed. He'd never wanted to be a Cosantir. He'd been a lawyer—a damn good one—living just inside the territory lines. But one does not refuse the call of a God. With his acceptance, Herne's power had fallen upon him like an avalanche, sweeping his past life away.

"What's a feral? Is that what got Helen?"

Bloody hell. "Aye," he said reluctantly.

"Feral means wild. So did a real mountain lion attack her…or one of you?"

How badly would this aspect of shifter life terrify her? "One of us."

She glared at him. "Pulling answers out of you is like getting information from a Su—is really difficult. Tell me, do shifters just go around attacking their buddies for fun?"

"Hardly for fun. We are stronger, live longer, are immune to human diseases, but we're still half-human, Victoria. If a Daonain becomes unbalanced mentally…" He shrugged, hoping she wouldn't continue.

Her brows drew together. "But humans don't turn into wild animals when they go nuts. Can it happen to anybody? Are *you* liable to turn feral?"

"I fear there is no easy answer to your questions," he said carefully. "Daonain do occasionally decide to live in animal form and simply become wild. However, attacking humans is an aberration." One that occurred all too often.

"How many ferals have you seen in the last…oh, five years?"

Stubborn wench. "Maybe ten or so." He felt her stiffen.

"That's…that's a lot." She shivered, and he didn't know whether from cold or from horror. Why couldn't she ask his silver-tongued brother these questions? Alec could make a visit to hell sound like a tropical vacation.

"Well, when you guys go hunt this feral, I want to go along. I'm a good shot. Someone can loan me a rifle and—"

"No."

"Dammit, Calum, Helen is my friend and—"

"There will be no hunting party with weapons."

She shoved off his lap and stood up, legs braced. "You're going to just let that thing go? Let it attack some other old person?"

"Victoria, you do not understand. We do not—"

After giving him a scathing look, she retreated to her bedroom.

Bloody hell.

THE DAY WAS almost over when Vic trudged through the village with a pot of stew. Alec had disappeared. Then Calum had carried Helen to her home and not returned. Vic wasn't sure if she was disappointed or not. Arguing with Calum…hurt, and being angry with him made her feel sick. *Damn him.*

When she'd finally left her room, Aaron had looked up from his game of Scrabble with Jamie and asked her to carry the stew to Helen's house.

Vic took a deep breath of the clean, cold air. She could hear the people in the scattered cabins, chatting, making supper, laughing. A wave of loneliness rolled over her. Would she ever have a place to call home? Somewhere she'd fit in?

"Vicki!" Heather came from the side of her mother's house, arms full of firewood. "Are you coming here?"

Under Heather's welcoming smile, the feeling of loneliness lifted like a morning fog. "I am. Aaron sent you guys some stew."

"Excellent. Mac 'n' cheese is the pinnacle of my cooking abilities." Heather shoved open the front door with one hip. "C'mon in."

Like Aaron, Helen had a log cabin, but where Aaron's home was rustic, hers looked bright and cheerful. A chair and couch were covered in vivid floral upholstery and colorful knitted afghans were tossed here and there. A small forest of African violets crowded next to a southern window.

"Feels like a summer garden," Vic said.

Heather dumped the firewood next to an ornately decorated woodstove. "Makes you forget the snow outside, doesn't it? Why don't you put that pot on the stove to warm and sit for a bit? I want to talk with you."

Vic did as she asked, then took a seat at the table. "What's up?"

"After Calum brought Mama home, he asked me to explain a couple things about Daonain relationships to you. He seemed to think you'd be more comfortable hearing this from another woman."

Relationships? "Hearing what?"

"Well, you know we don't have as many females as males."

Vic nodded, remembering Alec's painful explanation of why they couldn't get involved. "Right."

"Our customs altered because of that. Human monogamy is so a guy is certain he fathered the children. But we don't care who begat whoever, not when our race might die out entirely. So we rejoice whenever a baby is born, whether its parents bothered to marry or not—and our marriages aren't restricted to one male, one female."

Whoa. Orgy time? "Like a bunch of men and women together?"

"Nah. At least not in a lifemating. Females are too territorial, especially if we're having kids. Usually it's two or three male littermates and one female."

As Heather turned to dish up the stew, Vic stared blankly, wondering when her brain would catch up. More than one guy per woman. *Got it.*

Which meant the woman probably loved—and fucked—all the men in that relationship. *Wow.*

The men were usually littermates. Brothers. *Alec and Calum are brothers. Littermates.* Vic felt her jaw drop open.

Heather grinned. "Looks like you're catching the drift. There's more, but that's enough for one gulp. Think about it, and we'll talk again. For now, let's take this in to mother."

Vic followed Heather into the bedroom. Daniel occupied a rocking chair in one corner, a book open on his lap. "Hey, Vicki."

Sitting up in bed, Helen smiled at Vic. Her eyes were clear, and pink color had returned to her cheeks.

Vic gave a sigh of relief. "You look much better."

"Partly thanks to you, dear." Helen raised her eyebrows. "In fact, I hear you gave me all your clothes and walked back to the village completely naked."

Vic's jaw dropped. "Excuse me?"

Helen's pressed lips didn't hide her smile as she glanced reprovingly at her son. "I had a feeling he embellished a bit."

"A guy can dream," he said. His grin was fast, the sparkle in his eyes wicked. "Vicki did give you all the clothes on top except for a bra."

Vic felt her cheeks heat.

"Now Daniel, you're embarrassing her," Helen scolded. "Vicki, come here."

When Vic reached the bed, Helen pulled her down for a soft kiss on the cheek. "I thank you for the gift of warmth. Aaron said I would have died if you and the boys hadn't patched me up so quickly and kept me from chilling."

Vic moved her shoulders. "Yeah, well, you look really good now considering how much blood you lost." Vic frowned. Actually, Helen looked too recovered.

"Daonain bounce back quickly," Heather said, handing her mother the bowl of stew. "Aaron sent this over with Vicki."

"Bless him. I'm starving. You all excuse me while I rudely eat in front of you." Helen scooped up a bite. "Mmmmh, the man can cook."

"Any more of that?" Daniel asked with a pitiful look. "I worked hard today too, you know."

"Ah, poor baby. Did the wittle baby have to carry his mama who weighs at least a hundred pounds," Heather said in a syrupy tone.

"Fine, I'll get it myself." He stomped out the door. "And she's at least a hundred-twenty," came his voice from the other room.

Vic choked on a laugh as Helen and Heather broke into giggles.

"So, Vicki," Helen said. "Tell me about yourself. After you get adjusted to being a shifter, will you stay in Cold Creek?"

"I don't—" A knock on the front door interrupted her. Vic heard a murmur of voices, then Alec walked into the bedroom.

She gasped. He had spatters of blood on his face and hands, more on his shirt. She was at his side before she could think. "Where are you hurt? Show me."

He glanced down at his clothes. "Oh, damn. I'm sorry, sweetie. I should have cleaned up first, but Calum was worried about you."

Vic tried to move his clothes to see where the bleeding came from, but he took her hands. "It's not mine."

"Then—" Had he gone hunting and killed a deer? "Okay."

"Thank you, Alec," Helen said as tears filmed her eyes.

Heather was openly crying. "Thank you, Alec," she repeated.

Jesus fuck, he'd done something more than kill a deer. Vic kept her grip on his hand and yanked him out of the room. Her jaw was set so tight, she had to force out the words, "Okay, I think it's time we had a talk. In private."

"We will." The lines in his face had deepened, making him look another twenty years older.

When they entered Aaron's cabin, it was empty. Alec left her, wanting to wash and change, so she curled up in a chair by the woodstove. She should be getting all her ducks in a row to yell at him, but her thoughts kept sliding back to that little chat in Helen's kitchen. Had Heather really implied that Alec and Calum might marry the same woman? That's why neither of them seemed worried about fucking around with her? Calum had said, *"Alec and I often…share…our women. Alone or together."*

Wow. A weird feeling slid through her. She could screw them both, and no one would object? She idly braided a strand of her hair. It sounded pretty cool for sex and everything, but in a marriage? How bizarre must that be? Not like she'd ever find out—she had enough trouble just hanging out with a guy. To marry more than one? Not in a kazillion years.

Neither man had mentioned marriage anyway. Why would they? If shifters didn't care who fathered babies, then guys probably ran wild when single. Vic realized her jaw had clenched again. She sat back and told her muscles to relax. She wasn't jealous of the guys—not really. She just didn't want to see bitch one and two get their claws in them. Not possessive, merely competitive.

When Alec walked into the living room, she frowned at the paleness of his face. "Want some hot chocolate?"

"Thank you, cariad, but I'm not hungry." He dropped onto the couch across from her chair. The laughter that always lurked in his eyes had disappeared completely.

He'd called her *cariad*. *Darling*. She hugged the knowledge to herself. "Alec, you're exhausted. I can wait."

With an attempted smile, he shook his head. "I won't be able to sleep for a while, and I'd enjoy your company. Calum said you had questions and weren't happy with his answers?"

Her anger rose again. "He wasn't making any sense at all."

"What's the problem?"

"Why isn't someone tracking this...feral person? I asked him to loan me a rifle, and he said no. And that he wasn't sending a hunting party out."

"Ah." Alec scrubbed his face with his hands. "Some of our traditions come down from the Fae."

Here we go with the traditions again. "And?"

"The Fae used bows and arrows only when hunting game." He moved his shoulders. "Sometimes humans too."

"I'm not getting this."

"Fae fought other Fae hand-to-hand or with knives. Bow and arrows—basically, long-distance weapons—were only used on *animals.*"

"Oh." Vic frowned. "So shifters don't use guns or arrows on other shifters."

"Exactly."

"And a hunting party? You don't do that either?"

"If needed. But cahirs only."

Another fucking new word. She glared at him.

His lips twitched. "Sorry. We still use some bastardized Gaelic and Welsh from the old days." He gazed at the woodstove. Behind the glass door, a salamander, scales brilliant as the flames, spun in circles. "Cahir are those chosen to defend the clan. You'd say maybe warrior? Protector?"

Marine. And Calum had said to Alec, *"I'm sorry, cahir."* Alec was a cahir. "Your God supposedly gave Calum power—powers—whatever. Does a cahir get anything?" she asked only half-sarcastically, for she'd *felt* that power in Calum, as if a fucking current of electricity had hummed through him.

"Anything?" Alec's finger traced the blue-tinted scar high on his left cheekbone. "A couple more inches in height, muscle, strength. All at once. I was a cop and in good shape, but I spent the next twenty-four hours puking my guts up and trying not to scream like a girl." Despite his light tone, his eyes held the memory of some serious agony.

Nasty. "Are you the only cahir around?"

"We have four in the North Cascades since we're fairly isolated. Rainier is fighting hellhounds and have seven or eight."

Hellhounds. Not gonna visit that subject right now. As she studied Alec, her mouth tightened. She'd already known, there in Helen's house. The blood on him hadn't come from hunting any deer. She'd recognized that soul-weary look; she'd seen it in her own mirror. "You killed the feral, didn't you?"

He nodded.

That's why Helen had thanked him. "So the attacker is a

shifter who went crazy. And you can't…uh, treat them or something?"

"No. There's no return once the door is shut."

"Door?"

"At the cabin, we told you about a portal in your mind—the one you open to trawsfur." In the lantern light, his eyes shone the green of deep forest.

"Well"—she smiled in relief—"there's no door in my head."

"Close your eyes and look around. It's kinda in the back somewhere. Glows just a tad." His expression held a challenge she couldn't refuse.

She shut her eyes. Yeah, okay, it was dark. Everything was black. She pretended her gaze turned in a circle, from the front around to the… *Oh, shit.* Her spine stiffened like someone had yelled, *Attention!*

"Yeah. Thought so," Alec murmured.

"Oh. My. God." Her eyes opened and she glared. "There is a fucking door-thing in my brain."

He tried to smile, but she could see how much of an effort it was.

Another realization twisted her guts. "Did you know him? The feral?" she asked softly.

He nodded. "Fergus taught me to hunt when I was growing up."

Oh, God, there was no comfort to be offered here. *'To the legion of the lost ones, to the cohort of the damned.'* Vic moved to sit beside him, taking his hand between hers. "He was older?"

His fingers curled around hers as if to a lifeline. "About Aaron's age. He'd never lifemated anyone, and his only family, a littermate, died last week."

"Are you saying he wasn't mentally ill? Depression made him go feral?"

Alec kissed her fingers and enfolded her hand in his. "If a

shifter has no loved ones or family, no ties to pull him back to the human side, then some *turn*, and unfortunately, loneliness and grief warps them, driving them to mindlessly attack."

Holy fuck. Fear shot straight to her insides and clung there, claws digging in deep. She didn't have any family. No loved ones. So if she shifted, she might not come back. Helen must have known Fergus too—and he'd savaged the sweet woman. She shivered.

"Vicki, it's not really—"

"Oh hey," she said. "I'm supposed to help Heather make cookies." She rose and smiled down at him, her heart aching as if she'd already decided. "I'll bring you back some sweets."

AFTER HELPING HEATHER bake, Vic had been dragged away by Jamie to play cut-throat Monopoly with her friends. Vic had gone bankrupt, and she wasn't sure if she was pissed-off at losing so badly or proud of the munchkin for doing so well. "You have a head for business, kid," she told Jamie on the way back to Aaron's.

"I know." She gave Vic a smug look. "Daddy's teaching me to do the books for the tavern."

"Ugh. Better you than me." She'd rather fight a nice bloody battle any day. In the house, she stopped, staring across the room.

Sarah sat beside Alec on the small couch—where he and Vic had talked earlier. Cleavage was snuggled up to him so closely she was almost on his lap. Her dark head rested on his shoulder as they talked together in low voices.

Vic swallowed and followed Jamie to the kitchen where Aaron had his hands deep in bread dough.

"Where's Daddy?" Jamie asked, snatching a tiny piece of dough and stuffing it into her mouth.

Aaron pulled the ball of dough closer to him and continued kneading. "Gretchen came to get him a while back. They haven't returned."

Vic's lungs weren't getting enough air, and her hands felt colder now than they had outside. "Why don't you stay and help Aaron, Jamie? I'm going to take a break."

"Sure."

Vic ruffled Jamie's hair and left the room. *Okay then.* Apparently that was that. Her decision was made.

So why didn't she feel good about it?

Chapter Sixteen

CALUM COVERED A yawn as he walked into the kitchen early the next day. He and the Elders had stayed up most of the night, hammering out contingency plans in case the Daonain were exposed by the arseholes trying to catch shifters. Although well hidden, the Elders were the least mobile of the clan. Part of the reason he'd visited was to ensure they understood the seriousness of the threat and were prepared to run if needed.

Beside Alec at the counter, Jamie grinned over her shoulder. "We're making pancakes."

"Impressive accomplishment." Calum kissed the top of her head, smiled at Alec, and looked around. Aaron liked to sleep late, but Victoria seemed like a dawn riser. "Did you leave Victoria sleeping?"

Jamie had her lip tucked between her teeth as she concentrated on pouring the perfect amount of pancake dough into the frying pan. "She's already up."

"Ah. She probably went out for a walk."

The batter sizzled as it dropped onto the hot skillet, and the scent of pancakes filled the kitchen. Alec's stomach growled audibly. "I get the first one."

Calum tilted his head. "I believe that reputable cooks serve others first."

"But Jamie wouldn't let her beloved uncle starve, would she?"

She frowned from one to the other, and a sly smile spread over her face. "I don't want you arguing with Daddy, so I'd better eat the first one."

"Even in an emergency, she keeps her head." Calum grinned at Alec, his pride making his heart swell.

The breakfast, although he didn't get the first pancake, tasted very good. "You're turning into a fine cook, Jamie," Calum said. "Since you did most of the work, Alec and I will clean up. Meanwhile, you can pack. We'll leave soon."

"Oh, Daddy. Do we have to go?"

"I have a business; Alec is sheriff." He gave her a stern look. "And you have school."

"Well, poop."

As Jamie trotted to her room, Calum poured himself another cup of coffee, then studied his brother whose face was still lined, eyes weary. They'd both had to kill clanmates; it never grew easier. "Are you all right, brawd?"

Alec shrugged. "It'll take a while. Talking with Vicki helped."

Hoping to divert Alec from his grief, Calum asked, "Was Sarah as helpful?"

"You bastard, abandoning your own littermate like that. By the God, I'd rather put a leg in an iron trap than be alone with that female. Would you believe she bawled over Fergus's death, and a second later climbed in my lap?"

"For a cahir, you certainly get trapped easily."

"And you didn't?" Alec smirked.

Calum winced. Overly sweet females made his fangs hurt. "I eventually managed to scrape Gretchen off by siccing Maude on her."

A door slammed, and Jamie ran into the kitchen, waving a

piece of paper. "Daddy, all Vicki's stuff is gone! This was on the bed."

His blood stopped in his veins. Calum opened the note as Alec read over his shoulder.

I'm returning to my normal life. I can't risk being a feral.

Please don't come after me.

Give Jamie a hug for me,
Vic

Calum's hand crumpled the paper as an icy blizzard lashed at his soul. *She left us.*

Alec's expression held the same devastation. "My fault," Alec said, his voice hoarse. "I didn't explain well enough. Why would she think she'd go feral?"

"You did your best, as did I. It is her decision to make."

"Did Vicki go away? Without saying goodbye?" Jamie's eyes filled with tears, and Calum pulled her into his arms.

"She did. She returned to her own home, and I think it's time we went to ours."

SWANE WALKED THROUGH the shack he'd rented close to Cold Creek. Since Vidal couldn't leave his business in Seattle, it was only him and the old woman he'd snatched. What a shame—for her—that she and her fat dog had chosen to walk in the deserted park.

Although he'd had a tranq gun ready, she hadn't transformed when he'd kicked her dog or grabbed her, so she probably wasn't a shifter. Even so, the nosy biddy was friends with everyone in town. If any of those monsters lived in Cold Creek, she'd know.

He shoved open the door to the bedroom. Wasn't she a nice

sight, tied so neatly in the straight-backed chair? "Hello there." He tossed his bag of tools at her feet, then ripped off the duck tape that had covered her mouth. Some skin came with it, and blood oozed.

She blinked away tears. "Wh-what do you want? I don't have much money, but you can have it. J-just let me go!" Her eyes were terrified in the wrinkled face.

Swane's breathing sped up. He got a better rush out of anticipation than from snorting coke. Fuck, he'd missed interrogating prisoners. Maybe wereboy's resistance had been an ego blow, but this old bitch'd spill her guts within an hour. Not that it would do her much good.

"I don't need money, Mrs. Neilson." Considering he'd earn a cool half-mill once his boss learned to shift. He dragged over a chair and sat in front of her, knee to knee. "That's your name, right? Irma Neilson? You don't mind if I call you Irma, do you?"

She shook her head frantically. "But—"

He slapped her, open-handed across the face. "First—the rules. I don't hear your fucking voice unless I ask a question. Got it?"

A trickle of blood ran from her lip. Her eyes were shocked.

Probably never been hit in her secure life. And nope, she wasn't a werecreature or she'd have changed into a cat by now. "We're going to talk about monsters, Irma. People who turn into mountain lions. Know what I mean?"

From the slight widening of her eyes, the twitch of her fingers, she knew exactly what he meant.

"Tell me who they are." He picked up a pair of pliers from the bag. "Then tell me who they love."

Chapter Seventeen

WINTER CAMPING FOR days. This had to be one of the stupidest stunts she'd ever pulled. Vic's hood brushed against a pine branch and dislodged a flurry of snow onto her shoulders. Taking a moment, she oriented herself to the four gray, bare patches on a high, white-covered peak. They looked like claws, she'd thought, when they'd hiked to Elder Village.

That time seemed a lifetime ago. The first day had been sheer misery...and mourning...but then, she'd done better. It was as if the surrounding snow had drifted around her heart also. Soon, her life would go back to the way it had been before without the impossible dream of having a family. A place to fit in.

Maybe if the danger was only to her, she might have stayed. But the memory of Helen's blood splattering the snow made Vic's stomach tighten. *If I turned feral—what an ugly word—then I'd hurt others, not just me.* The risk that she'd turn into one seemed way too high. She had no home. No family. No ties to keep her human. She'd never really belonged anywhere besides the military. Although she'd briefly hoped to be one of the shifter clan, visiting Elder Village had taught her the futility of that— half the time she hadn't understood what they were talking about.

Of course, it might be fun to be a cougar with big teeth and claws and run into the Ice Queen or Cleavage. *Ohh-rah*, she'd give a whole new meaning to nasty feral. Now if bitch one and two were the only ones she might attack, she'd do that trawsfur thing in a heartbeat.

But apparently a feral didn't choose its victims. No one could hate Helen, yet Fergus had tried to kill her. *And if I attacked Jamie?* The thought of hurting the child, slashing, biting was gut wrenching.

Hell, the kid was probably already hurt. She imagined Jamie's face at finding the note and cringed inside. *Coward much, Sergeant?* God, she'd never imagined how enormously she'd miss the munchkin. So bouncy and loving.

Was I ever that carefree? Saying just what she thought, screaming with laughter, hugging people? *No.* Growing up in the Mid-East as a hated American had set an early curb on her tongue. Her mouth tightened. Her father had doled out love, praise, and hugs only when she'd proven useful in some way, like putting on a diplomatic dinner or returning with interesting market gossip. Maybe that's why Jamie's—and Calum and Alec's—easy affection was so disconcerting.

Dammit, she wasn't going to think about them. Her throat tightened as if a garrote drew tight around it. The sex had been…wondrous, but what she really missed was how the men touched her so often. So lovingly. The way Calum would run a finger down her cheek, or Alec tuck an arm around her waist and pull her close. As if she belonged beside them. She swallowed hard and blinked back tears, then bent her head and concentrated on the trail. Footstep after footstep.

On reaching the summit, she stopped to catch her breath. Fat puffs of snow had started falling, and the dark clouds warned of more to come. As her eyes rested on the forested slopes and the white-covered peaks, quiet wrapped around her.

Once she'd stopped crying and listened to the silence, she'd started to feel the strength that existed deep within the wilderness—and her connection to it. Like going into a firefight, and knowing your teammates had your back.

She shook her head. As she'd walked, miserable and trying not to cry, she'd felt it, pulling her in. Somehow this place was…was like a part of her. Like she'd found a piece that had been missing.

But she'd also acquired something else. Closing her eyes, she could see in the dark of her mind, that fucking door. It glowed now around the edges, like light seeped through from some other place. Five years ago, she'd gotten stranded in the desert. Drank the last of her water. By the time she'd reached the military outpost her entire body had craved fluids, and then a private had held out a canteen.

She wanted to open that door even more than she'd wanted that canteen.

Not gonna happen. She deliberately turned away from the inner door and opened her eyes. She sighed, her breath a puff of mist in the air. There was no way to win this fight. *"We have done with Hope and Honour, We are lost to, Love and Truth, We are dropping down the ladder rung by rung."*

Tears blurred the trail in front of her as she started down the other side. Toward a life she no longer wanted.

THE BROTHERS AND Jamie had returned a few days ago…without his little barmaid. Still residing in Calum's guest room, Thorson opened his book and tried to concentrate on Dumas's Three Musketeers, but D'Artagnan wasn't holding his attention. He returned to fuming.

Vicki had not only turned down his grandson's gift, she hadn't stopped to see him. Damn the girl, she was supposed to have come back—she was his family now. He'd finally figured out what Lachlan had wanted. The boy hadn't had a chance to mature to wisdom, but his perception of people had been unrivaled. Knowing he was dying, he'd sent Thorson a substitute grandchild.

Thorson smiled a little. Being Lachlan, he probably hadn't even considered that Thorson might go feral upon his death. No, he'd just wanted his grandfather to have someone to love. He closed the book with a thump and rose from the soft chair, scowling as pain lanced into his shoulder. Pulling the curtain back, he looked out. Snow hissed against the window and formed drifts in Calum's garden.

Had he lost another child before he'd even known she was his?

A knock pulled his attention away. "Enter."

Calum appeared in the door, his expression angry. "I—"

"First, tell me. Is she still up there?"

Calum knew exactly who he meant, and the lines in his face deepened. "Her car remains at her house."

Was she lost in the mountains? Dying alone?

"Joe, she filled her backpack with everything she'd need to survive." Calum scrubbed his face and admitted, "I'm worried too. If she doesn't show up by tonight, I'll call out the clan to look for her."

"Thank you, Cosantir. Now, what's happened to anger you?"

"Alec called. Angie found Irma Neilson's dog injured in the park. Pretty dehydrated as if it had been there a while—and Irma's missing."

"She'd never leave that fat sausage," Thorson muttered.

"Exactly."

"You think she got taken? Kidnapped?" Thorson scowled.

"Possibly. Just in case, people are searching the forest

around the park. But…" Calum's face tightened. "Alec has a list of recent rentals from one realtor and is trying to reach the other. The deputy is taking part of the list, but I'm going to check the ones outside town."

Thorson frowned. With the power of Herne ramping up his senses, the Cosantir could probably tell—smell—if Mrs. Neilson was in a house. But still… "The old woman is human, Calum."

"She lives in my territory."

And he protected anyone in his territory, clan or not. Herne hadn't chosen wrong when he made Calum McGregor the Cosantir for the North Cascades. Thorson bent his head in acknowledgment…and respect. "How can I help, Cosantir?"

"I'd like to leave Jamie with you."

Jamie peeked around Calum, her face puckered with worry, and Thorson pulled his features into a smile. "I'd be delighted to have company, especially if she'll play chess with me."

"I'd rather play poker."

Calum straightened. "Gambling? With Jamie?"

"The stakes are M and M's," Thorson said, knowing his tail was surely caught in a trap on this one.

But when Jamie boasted, "I beat him last time," and laughed out loud, Calum's expression changed. Lightened. The child had been a solemn ghost since returning from Elder Village. None of them had realized how much she'd come to care for Vicki…how she'd craved a female's attention.

"A card shark, indeed." Calum shook his head with a small smile. "In that case, try not to win all of Joe's candy. He might cry."

Jamie snickered and trotted into the room, kneeling to get the cards from the nightstand. Thorson sighed. At one time, her head would have come level with the top. *How fast they grow. How soon they shift.*

As though Calum heard his thoughts, he said, "Call me if

there's any signs she is starting—well, if you need me for anything."

IN THE DRIVER'S seat of his van, Swane smirked as he stuffed his cell phone into his pocket. "We caught a break—McGregor drove out of town a few minutes ago. The kid's at home alone."

"Good info you got from the old woman," Perez commented as he and Tank started gathering their gear.

"Seems like." Swane grinned. "If this doesn't pan out, she'll live long enough for me to ask more questions."

Perez laughed, although Tank looked a little green. The pussy didn't like hurting bitches.

"Let's make sure the cop's too busy to come home for lunch." Swane punched in a number.

"Cold Creek Police," said a woman.

"Listen up, cunt. I just wanted you to know, I planted a bomb…"

TWO MORE ROOMS to go. As Alec strode down the hall to the next classroom, he could hear the school children laughing and shouting outside the building. For them, the early dismissal had come as an unexpected treat.

Alec wasn't laughing. Hell, his heart was thudding inside his chest like a stereo's bass turned too high, and sweat trickled down his back. When he'd joined the force, he'd accepted the possibility of getting shot, stabbed, even dying in a car wreck.

Being blown into tiny bits hadn't been on the job description.

He visually checked the door for wires before cracking it open. Stepping into the classroom, he was engulfed in the scents of books, crayons, and glue. Splashy bright paintings covered the walls, a plastic skeleton hung in one corner and—he sighed—the room held lots of little desks. He'd have to inspect each one, over and under for the bomb. The *alleged* bomb which was probably some asshole's idea of a joke.

Moving around the room in the prescribed methodical fashion, Alec growled. Once he got out of here, he'd go after this bastard who had disrupted the school and terrified his dispatcher. Poor Bonnie had looked white as snow when she'd burst into his office, babbling, "He says he put a bomb in the school. It's supposed to explode at one o'clock!"

Involuntarily, Alec glanced at his watch. A half-hour to go. Hopefully. Could he assume a bomber would be able to tell time?

AS VIC STUMBLED through the drift, a root caught her boot and sent her sprawling. *Hell.* After shoving to her feet, she wiped off her face. At least the snow made for a soft landing; she'd had worse.

As she brushed herself off, she squinted against the flakes slapping into her face. Fucking A, this was almost a white-out. The trees broke the wind, but in every clearing, the snow piled deeper. Thank God, she was near town.

Looked like the slope had leveled off. She couldn't see the town through the blizzard, but she smelled it. Wood smoke, a hint of cooked food—Italian maybe, a touch of gas fumes. Her nose was definitely more sensitive these days.

She hefted her pack onto her shoulder and started the last leg of her journey.

CALUM FOUND NOTHING suspicious at the first two rentals. One had a family with children. The second held three young men, and he could smell drugs in the house. He'd sic Alec on them.

After pulling his car over to the side of the road, Calum looked at the third house through the blowing snow. The ancient mobile home sat on a few acres of land.

No vehicle in sight. He left the car and sniffed the air. More than one male had passed recently. But using human senses, he couldn't tell if anyone remained.

Detouring to a clump of trees, he stripped and shifted. As he prowled around the house, he sniffed at the windows and doors. Nothing. Then at a bedroom window, he caught the faint scent of blood. Urine. Sweat. A female. Human. Old.

Here.

DID THREE OF something beat four in a row? Jamie bit her lip and glanced across the card table she'd set up in her new grandfather's bedroom—her Grandpa Joe.

He'd been so sick and lonely after moving in, so she'd told him he had to be her grandfather if he lived here, no matter how long. His face had looked funny for a minute—and she'd worried she'd messed up bad—and then he'd nodded and tugged on her hair. And her daddy had smiled like he did when he was proud of her.

His finger tapped his cards which meant he had something good. But if she could get the ten of clubs, then—

Grandpa Joe cleared his throat. "Remember what I told you about a poker face? That's not it."

She made her face go all blank, and he gave a boar-like snort. "You look older when you do that."

"Good. I guess."

He studied her for a minute, making her squirm. "Are you able to see the door yet?"

Closing her eyes, she looked inside her mind and saw it clearly before it disappeared. She barely managed to close her mouth over the "Fuck" that Vicki would have used. She opened her eyes and nodded. "Then it goes away."

"Soon."

"I s'pose," she sighed and examined her cards again. They hadn't improved. "Hit me."

"You got it." He slid a card across the table to her.

As she picked it up—*ugh, an eight*—someone knocked loudly on the outside door. She jumped up.

"Go get it." Grandpa Joe made a shooing motion as he headed toward the bathroom.

The person pounded again. Like something was really important. But people always came here needing her father.

Or maybe Vicki had come back? Jamie flung the door open.

Two big men stood on the landing, both in dark parkas. One man's face had little holes in it like he'd had pimples when he was her age. The other one had a shaved head and mud brown eyes.

When they smiled at her, she got a creepy, spidery feeling and retreated a step.

The guy with the shaved head held up a shiny badge, and she saw tattoos all over the back of his hand. "We're with the FBI, Miss. May we come in?"

The government. This was bad. And the rules set down by Uncle Alec were never to be broken. "My dad isn't here. I'll call him and you can—"

They pushed into the house, forcing her back. The tattooed one looked at her with cold eyes, "Are you Jamie McGregor?"

What was she supposed to do? "Yes. I need to call—"

"Later." He pointed toward the office. "Perez, check out the place. I'll handle the girl."

"On it." The one called Perez disappeared into Daddy's den.

"Sit." His hand hurt her shoulder as he shoved her onto the couch. "I'm looking for Victoria Waverly. She worked at your dad's tavern. Where is she?"

Involuntarily, Jamie glanced at the window. The mountains had disappeared in the snowfall.

He followed her gaze. "Is she in the forest? Where? A town?" He put his face too close to hers, his breath ugly with coffee and onion.

Go away! Jamie looked at the bedroom. Was Joe out of the bathroom? "Grandpa Joe!"

"Shit! Who else is here?" The man grabbed her wrist.

She saw a gun holstered on his belt, and her breath clogged in her throat.

The bedroom door opened, and Grandpa Joe appeared, holding his chest. "Jamie? What—" He stopped. "Who the hell are you?"

"FBI. Stay put, and we'll get to you."

"In a pig's eye." Grandpa Joe came forward.

As the man turned to Joe, Jamie yanked free. Daddy needed to come now! Quiet as a mouse, like Alec had taught her, she snuck toward the phone in the corner.

"Give me your name. And your badge," Joe snapped.

"You're not Calum McGregor?" The man circled around Grandpa Joe like Daniel did when he was buying a cow. "Nah, you're too old. Nice scars you got on your arms there, dude."

As Joe's face darkened, Jamie picked up the phone. No dial tone. Her hands shook. She hit the OFF button. Then, TALK. Nothing. She repeated, over and over. The phone was dead.

Grandpa Joe glanced at her, and she shook her head *'No,'* before setting the phone down. He jerked his head at the door and stepped in front of the man. "Listen, asshole—"

Heart pounding, Jamie darted across the room. She had the door halfway open when the guy slammed it shut and yanked her back by the hair.

Tears burst from her eyes at the pain. She screamed, but a hand over her mouth muffled it. With an arm around her waist, he turned, dragging her with him.

The other man had jumped in front of Grandpa Joe, keeping him from Jamie. Growling, Joe hit him in the face and knocked him down.

As Jamie kicked harder, the one holding her gave a mean, horrible laugh. "Jesus, he's at least sixty, Perez. Finish it already…"

Head down, the Perez man lunged, hitting Joe in the stomach like a football tackle. Joe grunted and turned white.

That man hurt Grandpa. No. No no no. She struggled frantically, tearing at her captor's hands with her fingernails.

"Little wildcat, eh? I love 'em young." He pushed his body closer, rubbing against her bottom, and her stomach cramped like she was going to throw up.

Instead of pulling away, she turned in his grip and kicked hard at his leg. Her foot slammed into his shin.

"Fucking bitch!" Letting go of her mouth, he yanked her back by her hair and slapped her. Pain seared her cheek, and she yelled.

Grandpa Joe jerked around, and through the tears blurring her eyes, she saw Perez punch him. In the chest. He groaned and grabbed where his wound was, and red covered his hands. The man kicked him in the stomach. Joe fell back and the sound of his head hitting the coffee table was horrible. Blood pouring from his head, he didn't get up.

"Grandpa!" Jamie screamed.

He didn't move.

"Nooo," Jamie moaned, her legs crumpling beneath her. She

held her hand against her burning cheek, choking on sobs. She tried to crawl to him, but the man grabbed her collar, shook her like an animal.

Like an animal.

She closed her eyes, and there it was, the door, glowing an angry mean red. Calling her. She yanked it open and stepped through…into wildness.

She was on her hands and feet—no, on her paws. The world looked different, and she screamed in terror, only it came out a snarl. Tipping her head up, she saw the men, backing away from her, and the scent of their fear made her want, need something. Her pants bound one leg and she bit at the cloth and ripped it free. Snarling, she stalked forward and slashed at the one who'd hurt Grandpa Joe. She caught only his jeans, tearing them, but he jumped away from her grandfather.

The tattooed one grabbed for his gun. *Fear.* She charged at him, trying to get the gun. He screamed, jumping back. His shirt was in shreds, and blood started to pour from horrible slices on his stomach and chest. His face and arm were all scratched. The men bumped into each other as they ran out the door.

I bit that man? Clawed him? She hadn't even known she'd moved. She'd hurt him. *I want to hurt him again.* The fur on her back felt twitchy. Standing up. No, that was bad. *Daddy. I need Daddy.*

She padded over to Grandpa Joe and snuffled his face, but the smell of blood made her insides feel funny, and she backed away. She wasn't supposed to enter a house. Not as a cat. She needed to turn back to human.

But what if they came back?

The door was still open, and the wind swirled into the room. She took a step forward. In the distance, the mountain called to her, cried her name as clearly as Daddy would. She sprang out the door.

ALEC WALKED OUT of the school, pissed off as any man could be. No bomb—which was a good thing, really—but there'd been *no* damned bomb. He'd bent over desks, looked into dusty storage rooms, and checked bathrooms where little boys obviously had no aim. Herne help him.

As the wind-driven snow lashed his skin, Alec breathed in the clean air and headed for his car. The parents had picked up their children, but to his surprise, the principal and another teacher got out of an SUV.

Alec rubbed his face, glanced around. More snow had fallen while he'd been playing with fake bombs. "You still here?"

"Hell yes. You think I'd leave you in there alone?" Doug Banner humphed. In fact, Alec'd had to shove him out the door to keep him from helping. "What'd you find?"

"No bomb."

The little gray-haired teacher woman patted his hand. Mrs. Henderson was a human, but one so unflappable that everyone in town considered her their adopted grandmother. Jamie adored her. "Are you all right, dear?"

"I'm fine, Mrs. Henderson. Just annoyed." He turned to Banner. "If you have time, let's go downtown and talk about who this bas—" he glanced guiltily at Mrs. Henderson and continued, "—who this prankster might be."

"Good idea. I've tried to come up with ideas," the principal agreed. "Thank you for waiting with me, Hilda. Get yourself on home now and warm up."

Alec dug his phone out of his pocket and turned it on. He'd never heard of a bomb being triggered by a cell phone, but the way his luck was running, he hadn't wanted to serve as the first. The log showed two missed calls from the station, both within the last few minutes. He got the dispatcher. "I'm free, Bonnie, and I found no bomb. Did you need me?"

"God yes, Alec, 'bout time." Bonnie's voice was shrill, and Alec's hand tightened on the phone. "There's trouble over at Calum's place. Joe Thorson's hurt, and—are you alone?"

A Daonain problem then. He jerked his head at Banner to stay with Hilda and walked farther away, knowing the wind and snow would muffle everything. "Spit it out."

"Albert Baty was driving by the tavern and saw two men run out of your backyard, one all bloody. They jumped in a van. And a panther ran out and down the street. Al said he didn't recognize the cat, but the van followed it. He went upstairs to check things out and called here."

"And?" Fear made Alec's voice snap, "Is Jamie all right? Joe? They were both there."

"Al only found Joe, and he's unconscious and bleeding bad." Bonnie paused. "Alec? The cat was little—not full grown."

Chapter Eighteen

CALUM FLOORED THE gas pedal, and the car screeched around a logging truck. The oncoming car's horn blared as he whipped back into his lane.

Irma had been alive, a wretched lump handcuffed and lying in the corner of the bedroom. Blood everywhere and discarded syringes. Tortured. Drugged.

She'd opened her eyes when he touched her, staring as he'd called for an ambulance. Then had motioned him closer. "He wants your people, child. And..." Her brows had drawn together. "My head is all foggy. I think I told him about you. And Jamie."

Jamie. They were going after his child. The car skidded around a corner, tires squealing. No one answered at home.

He'd just passed the first houses in Cold Creek when his cell phone rang.

VIC STAGGERED TO her feet and rubbed her bruised butt as she scowled at the god-help-me shortcut she'd come down. Under all the snow, the slope had been steeper than she'd realized. Like a damn ski jump, and she'd skied the last half on her ass.

Brushing her jeans off, she squinted into the blizzard to get her location. Not bad. The path on the ridge led to the public park behind Thorson's Books. By abandoning the trail and sliding straight down, she could circle around town and get her car without being seen.

Her chest squeezed at the thought of running into Calum or Alec. Maybe when she'd put an ocean between her and the men, she'd not anticipate seeing them every moment.

Shaking her head, she pulled a cookie from the sack in her pocket. As she stuffed it into her mouth, she tried not to remember the warmth of Helen's house. At least the sugar revved her up, something she damned well needed, considering she'd run out of coffee two days ago and other food yesterday. She'd better not meet anyone, or she was liable to bite their head off. *Cranky much?*

So, she just needed to get to the car—damn thing better start—and head out. Her walk quickened as she remembered the next town over had a Starbucks. *Yes!*

A noise caught her attention. Running footsteps. Sobbing?

With a huff of exasperation, Vic stepped behind a tree. Honestly, couldn't a person take a quiet walk in a nice blizzard without being interrupted? She edged out far enough to stare up at the ridge high above her. Someone was running up the trail from town. Through the trees and snow she could see the flash of a girl's shape. Naked?

Vic choked on a laugh. Alec had mentioned how young shifters tended to pop back and forth before they established some control. This little shifter'd freeze her ass off if she didn't get into animal form. But why was she headed *away* from town?

A minute later, the smile froze on Vic's lips.

Jamie?

CRYING AND WHIMPERING, Jamie staggered up the trail.

Somehow she'd gone back to being a girl, but using two legs didn't work after having four, and she kept falling. Snot and tears ran down her face. *Daddy. Alec. Help. Please help me.* She shivered, her feet burning with the cold, as she grabbed a tree. The rough bark scraped her palms as she pushed off, trying to run again.

She looked behind her and a whine broke from her. *No no no.* The men were gaining on her. Two of them. She was breathing too hard to scream.

A black van had chased her through town, and she'd run and run and finally come to the park. Thinking the van couldn't go up the trail, she'd gone into the forest, but two men got out and followed her. One a blond. And the man with the pitted cheeks whose jeans she'd clawed. Blood had turned his pant leg dark red, and he was so mad, his face was scary-ugly.

They were so close. She staggered forward. Too slow. *No choice, I have no choice. Have to go faster.* She closed her eyes, forced herself to open the door. *Tingling. Trawsfur. Dizzy.* She shook her head, tripping on her feet. Paws.

"Jesus, we have her! Shoot, dammit!"

Something stung her shoulder like a wasp, and she snarled, the sound horrible. She sprang forward up the trail. Almost to the top. She could... The trees spun in a circle around her. Her legs—too many legs—tangled, and she crashed into the ground. She tried to stand, scrambling uselessly with her paws, but her head felt like a boulder.

With blurry eyes, she saw a pair of boots walk up to her. When the man kicked her hard, she could only snarl helplessly.

Daddy—I want my Daddy...

THEY SHOT JAMIE! Climbing frantically, Vic was only halfway back up the steep slope. She stopped to listen, cursing silently.

The trail that Jamie was on curved out of sight. Thank God the two men following Jamie hadn't gotten close enough to the cliff's edge to spot her, but they'd surely hear her scrambling up to them.

Vic slowed, moving more quietly, every muscle screaming to hurry. *Okay, okay. Jamie's down, but she isn't dead. There's time.* She pushed up to the next step. Her foot slipped. What a cluster-fuck. *Stay the fuck calm, Sergeant.*

Where the hell were all those shifter townspeople? What were they thinking, leaving Jamie alone? Where the hell was the kid's backup?

As the wind died for a moment, she heard them.

"Swane said, on these beasts, the tranq wears off in ten minutes or so. Way before we can get it down and into the cage."

"Then shoot her again when she wakes up, dumbass. Fuck, she's heavy."

"That was the last dart, dirtbag. You got rope?"

"Hell no."

"Jesus. The guy wants it alive."

"Fuck that, I'm not going to let that hellcat claw me again. Bash its head in. The daddy don't need to know that his kid's dead—he'll still do fuck-all to get her back."

Silence. "Yeah, that'll work. I'll find a fuckin' rock." Foot-steps. "You s'pose they change to people when they die?"

Vic looked up at the distance remaining to the top. It was too far. Too steep. *I can't make it in time.* She closed her eyes in despair.

And there, in the back of her mind, the little door glowed.

THE PATROL CAR bounced as Alec drove it up and over the curb, across the snow-covered park, following the new boot marks in the snow that led directly into the forest. He braked to a skidding stop at the tree line and jumped out. As he ripped his clothes off, he heard a heavy engine start up—and a black van raced away down the street.

He hesitated. One would escape. But he could smell more here. And Jamie. Fear. Ahead in the mountains.

Calum's car roared up behind him as Alec shifted. He didn't wait. Fresh blood made garish red marks on the white snow. With a low growl, he sprang forward.

Not a minute later, Calum shouldered past him. As they tore up the trail, from the mountain above them came the high shriek of a female cougar.

THE DOOR ALMOST begged for her to open it. Vic hesitated, and then stripped, fear bitter in her mouth. *If this doesn't work…* In her mind, she pulled the door open and mentally stepped into the blinding glow.

Fuuuuck! She dropped forward onto her hands and knees…onto her paws. Those were *her* golden-furred paws. She shook her head, unsettled by how close her face was to the ground. The brightness of the world blinded her, the noises sounded too loud, and everything smelled. Too much.

"Here's a rock, but I got to dig it out," came one man's voice from the ridge. "The bastard's frozen into the dirt." Thumping noises.

Her muzzle rose, and her top lip curled in a snarl she barely managed to suppress. Fury buzzed in a red cloud around her, tightening her muscles. Her first spring took her over ten feet upward, another and another, her paws silent in the snow.

Suddenly, she reached the top and scrambling over it.

"Holy shit!" A man on the trail jumped back, and she ignored him. The other stood over a small panther with a rock in his big fist. Vic screamed and launched herself across the distance. She hit him in the chest and knocked him over, landing on top of him. Her front claws ripped out his throat, cutting off his yell. A fountain of blood spurted up.

The remaining man tore down the path. Vic sprang after him, then halted, although everything in her wanted his flesh under her claws. With a growl of frustration, she paced back to guard the panther. Her little Jamie.

The sounds of the man's flight diminished, then he yelled, "No, no!" Horrible snarling raised the fur on Vic's spine, and the yelling changed to a scream and abruptly stopped.

Silence. She nuzzled the little cat, licked an ear. *Jamie?*

A second later, two huge mountain lions appeared, side-by-side, running full out. Her anger was unabated, and the scent of blood heavy in the air. Vic snarled at them, showing her fangs. She felt her fur rise. Her front paw lifted, claws unsheathed.

Both cats snarled back, but they stopped.

Fuck, what was she doing? These were shifters, here for Jamie. Her brain couldn't convince her body. *My cub. Mine to protect. Nothing will hurt my Jamie.*

Suddenly, the lions blurred. Calum. Alec. The men rose to their feet.

"I do not know you," Calum said, his voice so controlled, she could barely hear the underlying violence, but his pupils were completely black, and the air around him seemed to ripple. "That is my daughter who I love. I would care for her if you permit."

With his husky voice, his careful words, her anger drained away. Her paw dropped, and she forced herself a few steps away from Jamie.

Calum ran forward and fell to his knees beside his daughter.

Feeling herself sway, Vic shook her head. This being a furry-thing was majorly bizarre. And how the hell was she supposed to shift into a people-thing again? Had any of those bozos mentioned the way to get back? God, would she stay stuck like this for… She spotted it, up in the corner of her mind. *The door.*

She hurled herself through. *Whoa, major dizziness.* Blinking, she saw bare arms buried elbow-deep in the snow. Her arms. "Fucking-A."

When she looked up, Alec was staring down at her, his green eyes almost glowing. "Vixen? You shifted?"

Beside Jamie, Calum raised his head. "Victoria. I caught your scent, but didn't believe it."

With an effort, Vic pushed to her feet. Her legs wobbled like half-melted Jell-O as she dropped down beside Calum. The little panther's eyes were open, but glazed, and it was panting. "Oh, God, is she okay? They shot her—a tranq, I think."

Calum ran his fingers through Jamie's fur and yanked out a feathered dart. "Just one?"

"Yeah, their last. They were scared she'd wake up before they got her caged." Vic couldn't keep her hand from stroking the snow-dampened fur, needing to feel the warmth underneath and the comforting beat of the child's heart. She was growling under her breath—as was Calum. She jerked her chin at the rock lying beside the dead man. "He planned to bash her—" She choked, couldn't even say the words as the horror washed over her again. The absolute wrongness of the act.

Alec's gaze touched on the bad guy, followed her leaping trail back to where it disappeared over the edge of the ridge. "You were below, weren't you," he stated. "That's why you shifted?"

"Yeah. Too far away." She shivered at how close she'd come to being too late, and then shivered again at the bite of snow and wind on her bare skin.

At the sound of voices coming up the trail, Vic rose, placing herself in front of Jamie. The door flickered in her vision, reminding her she had other options. Alec stepped beside her, his shoulder brushing hers.

But the people that appeared through the swirling snow weren't more thugs. The grocery store owner, Baty, trotted in the front, carrying a pistol. Behind him, Kevin Murphy lugged a double-barrel shotgun, his brother, a deer rifle. After that came Kori and Angie, and they had, *halleluiah*, blankets.

Baty stepped over the dead man's body as if it was a log on the trail and halted in front of Calum. "Cosantir, what do you require?"

CALUM KEPT ONE hand on his daughter, unable to stop touching her, reassuring himself she was alive. Across from Jamie, Alec did the same. Bless the clan members who had arrived. He and his brawd could stay beside Jamie and still discharge their duties.

He glanced at the corpse behind him. The claw marks on the slashed throat were too obvious. The same on the man he and Alec had savaged and killed. Deaths from mountain lion attacks always made the news. The bodies must not be found. "Go through the wallets and get their information, then replace everything. Don't leave fingerprints, just in case."

Baty held up his gloved hand. "I'll take care of that." He knelt beside the dead body, calling to the women, "Kori, do you have a pen and paper?"

As Kori bustled forward, Angie spread a blanket over Calum's shoulders, then did the same with Victoria and Alex.

Victoria wrapped herself in it, shivering so hard her teeth chattered. Calum put his free arm around her and pulled her against his warmth.

"Cosantir." A man of few words, Kevin waited for orders.

Calum glanced at Alec. "Suggestions, cahir?"

"Cold water might preserve them too well. Best let the forest animals clean up the mess."

Calum nodded, then said to the Murphy brothers, "Wrap them in plastic to prevent a blood trail. Drop them from the steepest cliff into Dead Mule Canyon."

Cody gave a short nod. "I know the one you mean."

Alec added, "Take as much of the bloody snow with the bodies as you can manage. No need to leave extra evidence behind."

Kevin glanced at the gory mess around Victoria's victim and grimaced. "Gee thanks, Alec."

"Got your information," Albert Baty said, returning to stand beside Calum. "What next?"

"Thank you, Albert. I think Victoria abandoned her clothing and probably a pack, down below." Calum nodded at the tracks leading over the steep cliff.

Baty's eyes widened. He bobbed his head at Victoria. "Nice job of climbing, missy. I'll get your stuff for you, don'cha worry."

She smiled her thanks.

"Thank you, Albert." As the little shopkeeper bustled away, Calum bent over Jamie. Her eyes focused on him, and she was breathing normally. He stroked the fur on her neck. "Jamie. It would be best if you trawsfur. Do you remember how?"

Her muscles tightened under his hand, but he felt no tingle of magic. His mouth went dry. If she couldn't find the way back... He looked at Alec, unable to speak.

"Parents, so quick to panic." Alec stepped to where Jamie could see him. "Look at me, baby, not that ugly thing you call a daddy."

Jamie's gaze shifted.

"You're safe, sweetie. All the bad guys are gone. Find the door, and let's go home." He waited.

Jamie's muscles didn't loosen, and she was panting again. Fear whipped at Calum's control. The first few trawsfurs needed to be calm and quiet so the youngster wouldn't panic. A bad experience while an animal could make a child subconsciously avoid the vulnerable human form...and be unable to find the portal.

Although his brother's hand fisted, Alec's laugh was normal. "Guess you want us to carry you, eh? Now, isn't that just like a teenager?"

Calum bent to pick up his daughter, letting go of Victoria. Instead of rising, she elbowed him out of the way and took his place. She cupped Jamie's muzzle. "Hey."

Jamie's eyes fixed on Victoria's.

"You're scared," Victoria said. "Well, hell, that shows you're not stupid."

Calum growled. "Victoria, that—"

"Shut up, this is girl talk," Victoria snapped. She bent closer to Jamie and whispered, "Those guys were scary and big, and they had you trapped. I know the feeling."

Calum frowned at Alec, but his brother motioned for him to wait.

"Thing is," Victoria continued, "you can let your fear keep you from doing anything else in your life—yeah, I've seen that happen—or you can have the guts to move on. Isn't easy. Nope, it's hard as hell. But you know, if you shove the fear over to one side, you'll be able to see that fucking door."

She made a face. "An' looks like we have some studying to do on being furry things. God knows, I'd rather there were two of us doing it, so get your ass in gear and shift."

Before Calum could yell at her for the language, he felt the sparkle of magic under his fingers, and his little girl suddenly appeared. "Oh, thank Herne," he choked, his gaze blurred with tears. He managed to remain still long enough for Alec to wrap a blanket around her before he yanked her into his arms.

"Daddy, I was really scared," she whispered into his neck.

"Me, too."

Chapter Nineteen

CALUM NEVER STOPPED giving orders, all the way down the damned mountain, and Vic decided he was far past captain's rank. *Colonel Calum.* Yeah. Really, the man had a knack.

It was slow going, walking down in the heavy snow. Still, she hadn't been about to trawsfur into kitty form, not after seeing Calum's face when Jamie didn't shift right away. The men hadn't mentioned there might be a little problem—like getting stuck forever with whiskers and a tail.

They finally arrived at the Wild Hunt, and Calum carried his daughter up the back steps. He started toward his side of the house, but Alec cleared his throat and jerked his head at his own door. Calum paused, then complied.

Serving as rear-guard, Vic nudged Alec and raised her eyebrows.

"I haven't seen it, but according to Bonnie, a fair amount of blood got spilled," he said quietly. "Thorson was babysitting Jamie here."

Oh God, not Joe. Even as Vic's breath hitched, her fingers curved as if remembering the feeling of flesh tearing beneath her claws. Damn them. "Is he all right?"

"Don't know yet." Alec kissed her cheek and nudged her through the door.

"Let's get you some hot tea, more blankets," Calum said to Jamie, heading for a couch.

Vic frowned at the blood smeared on the kid's face and clotted in her hair. "No, Calum."

"What?" He stopped in the center of the room.

"A hot soapy shower first. Then tea and blankets." Already knowing the answer, Vic said, "Right, kid?"

Jamie looked at her blood-streaked hands, and a tremor shook her body. "I want to wash," she said, her voice weak, but determined.

"Ah." Calum's gaze followed his daughter's and his pupils darkened, although he remained as calm as usual. "Shower it is."

Not being slow on the uptake, Alec was already in the bathroom, adjusting the water temperature. "Maybe a bath—"

Vic shook her head. Blood looked really ugly in bathwater; didn't these guys know anything? "Who stays with you, Jamie? Calum or me?"

As Calum set Jamie on her feet, she reached for Vic. Her little hands felt like ice cubes. "You, Vicki. Please?"

"No problem. Pop on in." Vic jerked her head for the men to depart.

As they left, Jamie got in the shower. A squeak, "Jeez, it's hot!" And then the sounds of washing.

Vic moved to where she could see the smoked glass of the door. The kid remained upright, not going face first in a faint. Good enough.

After a minute, she stepped out of the bathroom, knowing Calum would be right there. The man gave new meaning to *overprotective parent*, but just watching him baby his daughter made Vic feel all squishy inside. *Go figure.*

"What happened? Is she—"

Vic rolled her eyes. "She's fine. She might be better if she had some clothes to wear?"

Beside Calum, Alec gave a snort of laughter and nudged his brother. "Thinking real clear, aren't we, brawd? I'll run over to your place. Jeans or robe?"

"Robe," Calum said at the same time Vic said, "Jeans."

She continued, ignoring Calum's frown, "Treat her like a victim, and that's how she'll see herself. She's not sick, and she did damned well against two big men. She's a fighter, Calum."

Calum nodded reluctantly.

"Jeans, it is," Alec said.

Vic checked on Jamie. "'Bout done?"

"Almost. I need to rinse the shampoo out."

Alec had handed in clothes by the time Jamie emerged, all pink from the heat. As Vic helped her dress, she checked over the damage. Bruises on elbows and knees, and a nasty one on her face that roused Vic's anger again. A few long scratches and scrapes from banging into branches. Her feet were abraded, but no frostbite. Shifters were hardy critters.

"You look good, kid." She got a smile that made her eyes burn. *Dammit.* After a breath, she followed Jamie out of the bathroom.

Alec stopped her and pushed another set of clothing into her arms. "These looked about your size. Have a nice shower, cariad."

The rush of gratitude was amazing. Jamie wasn't the only one covered in blood. And Vic's hands had begun to shake. "Thank you. Really."

He kissed her lightly, and the warmth in his eyes turned her all squishy for the second time. Oh, she was definitely losing it. "We'll talk after you're clean and warm," he said. "Calum is making tea."

She knew she was in pitiful condition when tea sounded better than coffee.

After turning the shower back on, she tossed the blanket to

the floor and stepped into the steamy blue-tiled enclosure. She ducked her head under the hot pelting water.

Shampoo and soap stood on a tiled-in corner shelf, and she vigorously scrubbed the dirt and sweat and blood from her hair and body. But as the pink-tinted water swirled down the drain, her stomach clenched. By the time she finished, her hands were shaking so hard she couldn't close the flip top on the shampoo bottle. Adrenaline overload and aftermath—her mind said even as her legs gave out. Kneeling on the floor of the shower, arms wrapped around herself, she shook uncontrollably. And cried.

She'd killed a man. Cut his life short in a horrible way. God, she could still hear the ghastly choking sound he'd made as he died. Because of her, he'd never grow old, never have a chance to mend his ways, never return to the people who loved him— maybe a mother, children, wife, friends. Whether he deserved it or not, his voice would no longer be heard anywhere again, and she had done that.

No matter how many times she killed, it never grew easier.

The water had cooled by the time Vic stopped crying, but at least her shaking had slowed. Only a fine tremor remained as she toweled herself off. She wiped the condensation off the mirror. Major mistake. She looked like hell. The days of camping in the snow had taken a toll—cold-chapped skin, gaunt cheeks, circles under her eyes. Add tangled wet hair and reddened eyes. "Aren't you just a vision of loveliness, Sergeant?" she whispered.

Life truly sucked.

Leaving the steam-filled bathroom, she followed the sound of voices and stepped into the living room. The room was all dark walnut and golden-toned fabrics. The fire in the glass-fronted wood stove gave cheer and warmth despite the wind howling outside. Half-asleep, Jamie snuggled into Calum's side on one of the matching cushy-looking couches; Alec sat on the other. The men had damp hair and smelled of soap.

Although Vic hadn't made any noise, Alec looked up and patted the couch beside him.

With a sigh, she dropped down beside him.

Cupping her cheek in his hand, he ran a thumb under one reddened eye. "You all right?"

She shrugged and murmured an honest answer, knowing he'd think she was kidding, "After I kill someone, I like to sit in the shower and cry."

"Of course. It's good to have traditions." He tucked her into his side as easily as if she were Jamie. The way he dwarfed her and the feel of his hard muscles against her were disconcertingly comforting. He handed her the cup of tea steaming beside him. "Drink. I dumped a ton of sugar into it."

She took a sip and choked; he'd also added an ample amount of brandy. It burned all the way down, and she wheezed a little before she managed to speak. "Thanks. I think."

His eyes glinted with amusement. "My pleasure."

Before she could drink any more, she had to find out... "How's Joe?"

Calum's face tightened. "He ripped open his stitches and has a concussion as well. He'll spend the night in hospital while they sew him up. Again."

Vic shook her head. "How did they know Jamie was a shifter?"

"They didn't. Just that Alec and I are." Calum's voice was mild. She'd have thought him indifferent if not for the blazing fury in his eyes. "Old Irma Neilson has lived here all her life and is one of the few humans who know about us. Someone tortured her for information about shifters—and our relatives."

Vic shuddered, thinking of the sadism Swane had shown. God, that poor woman. "Is she alive?"

"Oh yes, but she'll stay in the hospital for a couple days." Alec's mouth curled up. "I talked with her a few minutes ago, and her major concern was that fat poodle of hers. Good thing the dog survived."

Calum rested his cheek on Jamie's head. "They went after Jamie to use against me, but didn't realize Joe was with her. Then this little cat gave them more than they'd planned for."

"I didn't recognize the men. That means Swane and the suit are still out there," Vic said.

"We're searching records. We need to take out the person who is doing the hiring." Calum looked so tired that Vic saw what he'd look like as an old man—one of those coastal trees, the trunk gnarled and gray, still standing defiantly against the wind.

And God, she wanted to be standing beside him then. She concentrated on sipping her tea, pushing away the hopeless wishes.

Footsteps thudded on the stairs outside, and she set the cup down so quickly the liquid sloshed over the sides.

Alec pulled her back against him and murmured into her hair, "Relax. That's just Devin and Jody. They were cleaning up Calum's place."

At the rap on the door, Alec raised his voice slightly, "Come on in—it's not locked."

The man poked his head in, nodded to Alec, then looked at Calum. "All done. We removed the throw carpet, used special stuff on the…stains. Jody suggested we put down one of Rebecca's hand-crocheted rugs so it wouldn't look so bare."

The woman shoved the guy aside long enough to add, "The rug looks really good, Calum. Better than what you had, actually. You should buy it from her."

"I will do that. And thank you both. I owe you."

Vic would have done a lot to have earned that fleeting smile of Calum's. Apparently the two felt the same for they beamed back at him. Jody said, "We'll bill you for the cleaning, but no further debt is owed, Calum. The attack was targeted upon us all, even if it happened in your home."

Devin gave a loose salute to Calum, and they retreated, pulling the door shut behind them.

"It's going to smell like cleansers over there, brawd. I think you and Jamie should bed down here in the living room." Alec tightened his arm around Vic and gave her his crooked smile. "You know, I might have nightmares, so you'd better stay with me, Vixen. Just in case."

SHE'D LET HIM tuck her into his bed as passively as if she'd been Jamie, and it tore at Alec's heart how exhausted she looked. She fell asleep instantly, but he was wide awake, the anger slow to die within him.

Pulling a chair close to the bed, he studied her face in the flickering firelight. He'd felt her increased slenderness when she leaned against him on the couch, and now, he noticed the hollows below her cheekbones. She'd lost weight, and the dark circles under her eyes said she hadn't been sleeping.

His jaw set. She wasn't the only one. In the evenings, he'd missed the pleasure of hearing about her day and sharing some of his. Most people, human or shifter, saw only the burden and pain of being a cop. But somehow, this little female understood the satisfaction—the fulfillment—that came from protecting others. She might be female, but she had a cahir's heart. He'd known he wanted her as a mate—he hadn't realized how much joy she'd brought into his life.

When she'd said she'd left the trail to avoid seeing him or Calum, she might as well have cut his heart out. He leaned his elbows on his knees, trying to solve the puzzle. He was experienced enough to know she cared for him, even without seeing how she watched him with that soft expression and how she stood within his personal space, letting him into hers.

Why the worries about going feral? He studied her even breathing, the complete relaxation that spoke of trust. Did his Vixen really think she had no connections to anyone, loved no one? If anything, she cared too much. She was like an over-cooked marshmallow, crusty on the outside, all sweet and soft inside.

But she tried to hide how much she cared; didn't even believe she did. Something had made her think she was safer alone. So she didn't share her past or her emotions. He smiled, remembering how she'd wanted to keep their lovemaking shallow as well. How she'd failed.

It was time the little ex-human let the rest of her barriers down. Obviously it was up to him and Calum to teach her.

Reaching out, he drew a finger across her stubborn jaw, determination settling inside him. The gods had provided him and Calum another chance to win her—and they weren't going to fail this time.

VIC HEARD THE crackle of rifle fire, and a bullet hit the man beside her with a gut-wrenching splat. He grunted, falling back, his blood spurting across the rubble. *Dead.* Her face was sticky with sweat and blood, her mouth dry from the sand. The sun beat down in the cloudless sky, the heat like a weapon. She veered to avoid a pile of trash in the road; IEDs were everywhere. A bomb exploded behind her, another in front of her, and she turned, confused. *Where am I?* She looked down, expecting her ragged Baghdad clothing—but Jesus fuck, she was naked! And standing in the street.

A snarl cut through the gunfire, and a panther sprang out from between the buildings. An M-16 chattered, and the small lion slammed into the pavement, blood making a red river down the golden fur.

"Jamie!" She tried to run, but her legs wouldn't move. She jerked up. *Sitting?* She stared into the darkness, her hands clutching at blankets. A bed. *Where am I?*

"Hey, hey, hey." A man in the bed beside her.

Jesus, no. She struck out.

He caught her fist in a big hand. "A nightmare, baby. You're having a nightmare." His voice was low and smooth. Oddly comforting. "Shhh, Vixen, you're safe."

"Alec?"

"None other." Sitting beside her, he finger-combed her hair from her damp face. "C'mere, cariad. I'll hold you till the boogie-men go away." He lay back, pulling her down.

"Oh, God, that felt too real." Her heart still pounded, but her muscles slowly relaxed as he stroked her back. With a sigh, she laid her head in the hollow of his shoulder.

"There we go," he murmured, his voice resonant under her ear. "You want to talk it over or let it fade?"

"It'll fade," she whispered. Her lips curved slightly as she recalled one part. "You know, I've heard about it, but I've never been naked in a dream before."

"Ah." He grinned. "I didn't realize humans had that one. It's a common shifter nightmare."

"Yeah?" With a start, she remembered how on the mountain, she'd shifted from cat to human and found herself bare-assed. "Oh. I bet." She snuggled closer, laid one knee over his thigh, his warmth wonderful against her chilled skin. *Skin?* "You stripped me! No wonder I thought I was naked."

His laugh rumbled through his chest. "You didn't even wake up."

"But—"

"I stripped me too," he pointed out virtuously. As if that would make a difference. His voice lowered, took on heat. "And, as it happens, I like you without clothes on." His hand stroked her shoulder, down to her waist, and warmth followed in its wake.

Well. Her heart rate had slowed, but now sped up for a much better reason than fear. What nicer way to celebrate life than—

"Is everything all right?" Calum walked into the room, his gait as silent as always. He studied her for a moment, and then glanced at Alec.

"Nightmare," Alec said. "Jamie?"

"Brownies are on watch."

"Good deal." Alec slid backward, pulling Vic with him until she'd replaced him in the center of the bed. "You know, we were just discussing the fact that we're both naked. You're over-dressed, brawd."

What? Vic stared at Alec. "But—"

"I am indeed." Calum's rare smile flashed, and then he shed his clothes. Tanned skin. Sleek, hard muscles. He lifted the covers and slid into bed on her other side, sandwiching her between him and Alec. She started to sit up.

Alec held her down. "Vixen," he said quietly. "You've made love with both of us separately."

Shame silenced her for a moment. "I-I'm sorry. I shouldn't—"

Calum snorted. He gripped her shoulder and rolled her onto her back between the two men. Each was propped up on an elbow, looming over her helpless position. *Dammit.* Calum's hand held her down, and she shoved at it.

His eyes narrowed; his voice deepened. "Do not move."

Her fingers released involuntarily at the short command—and even more appalling, her insides seemed to turn to liquid.

He smiled faintly. "Very nice, cariad." He gave Alec a disparaging glance. "Clumsy bugger. You made her feel guilty."

"Hell." Alec took her hand and kissed her fingers. "I didn't mean to do that, Vixen. We wanted you to enjoy us separately— now we'd like to enjoy you together."

Her heart stopped. Sure, she'd gotten a clue when Calum dropped his clothing, but to say it aloud—"Are you serious?"

"Cariad, did not Heather tell you about Daonain's customs?" Calum asked, his brows together.

"Uh. Yes." She tried to remember what Heather had said, but Alec ran his hand up her arm and flattened his palm on her shoulder…just above her left breast. Her nipples tightened.

Calum stroked a finger down her cheek and over her lower lip. "Your heart is pounding, little cat. You've flushed, and I can smell your arousal. Your human mind may say it's wrong, but your shifter body wants us."

His eyes had turned to a molten gray that held her gaze captive as he cupped his big hand over her breast. When his thumb circled the nipple, everything inside her burst into flame. The corners of his eyes crinkled with satisfaction. He glanced at his brother.

"Vixen." Alec cupped her chin, turning her face toward him, and his mouth closed over hers. His kiss lured her in, teased her into responding, and filled her with warmth.

The mattress dipped as Calum sat up and cupped her breasts. His touch was firm as his fingers rolled the nipples, the pressure increasing, then he pinched the tips. She jolted with the sharp pain, and electricity seared straight to her groin. She choked back a moan.

Alec lifted his head, eyes hot with desire, yet dancing with amusement. "I've never met a woman so reluctant to be pleased."

"That's not true." She tried to sit up, and Calum's hand between her breasts flattened her back on the bed.

"Oh, it's quite true," Calum said. "You enjoy sex, but you're afraid to give up control. Seems we've been through this before in the cave." He lifted her face with a finger under her chin, fixing her with that look again, the one that turned her muscles to jelly. "We both know you enjoy submitting to me, don't we?"

A tremor ran down her spine. She managed a tiny nod.

"Victoria, do you have any objection to making love with us both?"

Put up or shut up, Sergeant. But God, she wanted them—wanted them both. If that made her a shifter slut, then so be it. "No, sir." The 'sir' just slipped out, a reaction to him jumping into officer mode.

A crease appeared in his cheek as he smiled, the amusement in his eyes showing he'd heard her slip. "Then with Alec's assistance, I will continue your lessons on releasing control."

He raised her arms over her head and bracketed her wrists with one hand, pinning them to the mattress. Since his weight was also resting on that arm, she tugged playfully, thinking she'd get free easily. His grip was like iron. Unbreakable. She pulled harder. Her breath shifted, increased. He'd pinned her down in the cave in various ways...but now? With Alec?

"Calum," she whispered, anxiety pulling at her, even as her temperature rose. Her breasts throbbed, her clit pulsing in time with her heartbeat.

"Shhh, you're safe with us, cariad," he nuzzled her cheek, and then glanced at Alec. "I believe I'll stay here."

"Works for me." Alec slid down in the bed, and she felt his calloused hands pulling her legs apart.

"Calum..." She tugged on her wrists again as her arousal rose terrifyingly fast.

"Yes, little cat," Calum said, and took her lips in a demanding kiss. His tongue ravaged her mouth and drove every thought out of her head such that Alec's fingers sliding into her folds came as a surprise. Her back arched as she gasped.

She tensed, pulled at her arms, tried to close her legs…without success. Hard hands pushed her thighs more open, and Alec licked over her clit, one long stroke of warning. As she moaned, satisfaction glimmered in Calum's dark gaze.

Alec's chuckle vibrated against her, then his tongue flicked over her clit, the demand obvious, unstoppable. Blood inexorably rushed to her pussy as he continued. *Oh God, I'm going to come.* She tensed as the pressure built to an unbearable level.

His tongue abandoned the top and circled the sides of the sensitive nub. Leaving her on the edge of a climax.

Calum smiled at Alec and lowered his head to kiss her breasts. When his warm lips closed over a nipple, her back arched. Alec's hands tightened on her thighs, Calum's on her wrists and shoulder, both keeping her where they wanted her. The feeling that she couldn't do anything, couldn't keep anything back seemed to release something wild trapped inside her.

Calum was watching her as if to check her response. Now he smiled, touching her cheek with light fingers. "I see you enjoy being restrained, little female. Then we will continue." The dark promise in his low voice left a trail of need in its wake.

He bent to suck on her nipples. Each time he nipped her lightly, a jolt of heat shot through her. And Alec used his wicked tongue, a slow slide around her clit, then his teeth closed on her folds in a light bite. Her breasts and labia became almost painfully swollen and sensitive.

Too much. Too many sensations, too demanding. Her head started to spin as the demands overcame her defenses.

A finger swirled at her entrance, then pushed inside, the friction wakening every nerve deep in her pelvis. Her hips tried to rise, a hand pressed her down.

The finger slid in and out, and then Alec added another one.

"I can't," she gasped, her world narrowing until only one sensation remained.

Calum rubbed his cheek over hers. His voice was rough and deep. "You can, cariad. You will take everything we can give you."

A bite on her tender inner thigh yanked her attention back to Alec. His fingers set up a compelling rhythm, sweeping away her sanity. As her whole lower half turned into one over-sensitive nerve, she was drowning in sensation. When Calum bit her nipple and laved away the pain, she could only whimper.

Alec lifted his head. She opened her eyes as Calum nodded at him.

Alec's lips closed over her clit, Calum's over one nipple, and they sucked, both of them, pulling at her, tongues swirling. Nothing could stand under that. She shattered into pleasure, the explosion tearing apart the stockade holding her defenses. Freeing her to simply feel. Wave after wave of pleasure ripped upward, streaming through her veins in a hot rush until she felt as if she glowed.

Calum lifted his head, and he caught her gaze, holding it as Alec licked her clit in one slow stroke. She spasmed again, then went limp, totally spent, as if her muscles had drained away and puddled on the floor.

The grip around her wrists disappeared, and Calum took her mouth, deeply. Sweetly. "You're very beautiful, cariad."

The bed jiggled, then Alec kissed her slowly in his way, like he had nothing more important to do. After a time, long enough that her heart rate returned to almost normal, he lifted his head. "Thank you, Vixen. I enjoyed that."

She sighed and opened her eyes. Two tough killers, yet their expressions held such approval that warmth filled her. "God, I've never...um." Why was this difficult to spit out?

"Go on, little cat," Calum said.

Fine. "I've never felt like that before. Or come so hard."

"I can't say knowing that bothers me any." Alec grinned.

"Asshole." Her brain had started to seep back into her skull. "What about... You didn't..."

Calum lifted her hand to his mouth and nibbled on her fingertips, giving her tingles like a Fourth of July sparkler. "We will. But you're exhausted. Sleep first, cariad." He gave her a look that didn't help her breathing any. "We want you alert when we"—he grinned at Alec—"take our turn."

"Oh sure, as if I can sleep after this."

They both simply smiled at her, as if amused. Alec's hand moved slowly up and down her stomach, petting her like a cat.

And before she could fight it, she felt herself sliding down into sleep.

Chapter Twenty

A WHISPER IN his ear woke Calum.

"I think it's your turn now." Soft lips grazed his cheek, and gentle fingers ran through his hair.

He looked up into her lovely eyes. Sometimes copper-colored, sometimes golden brown with arousal, like now. "Victoria."

She grinned, mischief in her face, and he had a moment of joy in her recovery before her fingers closed around his cock, bringing him to immediate arousal.

"Hell of a way to wake up," Alec muttered, and Calum realized she'd knelt between them and had captured Alec's shaft as well.

"And what do you plan to do with us now, little cat?" By Herne, she was a worthy shifter, a woman warrior with a tender heart. He stroked her cheek, cherishing the way she tipped her head into his palm.

A frown appeared between her eyebrows, and she released them. "I-I'm not sure. How do we do this?"

Alec gave him a laughing glance before smiling up at her. "You're going to have to work up to some of the fun, but for right now…" With the speed and strength of a cahir, Alec grabbed her wrists and pulled her forward, pinning one hand on each side of his hips, with her knees still in the center of the bed, now against the outside of his right thigh. His cock rose toward her as if catching her scent. "Brawd?"

Smiling at her startled expression, Calum moved behind her. Her firm ass was in the air, the fragrance of her arousal hardening him further. He could have positioned her with touch, but the animal in him reveled at the way she'd submit to his voice alone. "Open your legs to me, cariad," he said softly.

A shiver made her breasts jiggle, and then her knees edged apart. He remained silent, unmoving, and she widened farther.

He knelt between her open legs and ran his hands up and down her back, outlining her lean muscles. A lioness, she was, even before becoming to a shifter. *Our cat.* He moved lower. Between her legs, her cunt was slippery and swollen, ready for his use.

Her breath hitched as he gently stroked each side of her clit until it firmed under his light touch. She grew wetter.

"I want your mouth on Alec, little cat," Calum said. "He'll give you one hand back."

Alec grinned and opened his grip on her left hand. She balanced over him on her right arm, with his hand still braceleting that wrist. He glanced at Calum, eyes filled with pleasure and heat—and amusement.

In the Daonain, sometimes a littermate would resent the dominant one, but Alec wasn't one of them. He simply enjoyed.

Victoria's freed hand closed around Alec's thick cock.

Calum heard his sharp inhalation. She took his brother in her mouth, pulling him deep, and Calum's shaft pulsed as if in envy. Alec tangled his fingers in her hair and sighed. "Damn, Vixen."

She set up a steady rhythm, licking and sucking, the sounds enough to drive a male wild.

Calum swirled his cock in her juices, then entered slowly.

Hot and wet and as welcoming as the little wiggle she gave. The need to possess, to keep her, rose in him like a flood, and he fought it. There would be no lifemating until after a shifter's first Gathering.

But the rules said nothing about ties of pleasure, did they? Smiling, Calum put light kisses up her spine, leaning forward to balance on one arm. When he closed his teeth on the delicate muscle of her nape, her pussy clenched around his cock. Her back curved down to put her hips higher—welcoming his use.

He caught the flash of Alec's delighted grin before his brawd tightened his hand in her hair. "Harder, Vixen."

Reminded, she increased her pace, her rhythm breaking when Alec abandoned her wrist to fondle her breasts. Her breath held a low moan which she cut off.

Still fighting. If there was ever a female who needed to be controlled and overwhelmed with sensation, it was this one. Calum slid his shaft out slowly, then back in, rotating his hips to find the sweet spot. Low, he remembered from their time in the cave. It took a few more exploratory thrusts before her insides softened, while the outside ring of muscle clamped onto him like a wrench. *Right there.* He angled himself to rub over the spot with every slow stroke.

Her ass muscles tightened and soon, she moaned, long and low.

Alec laughed, tugging her head forward to keep her moving, while he played with her nipples, rolling them, pinching lightly.

Calum could almost see her thoughts fragmenting. He kept his movements slow and easy. "Suck Alec hard, little cat. Get him off now." He gave his brother a nod to go ahead.

Alec fisted both hands in her hair, guiding her. She sucked noisily, taking him deeper. Soon Alec growled a warning, pulling her head down for his release. As his hips strained upward, she swallowed frantically. Alec fell back with a long, happy sigh. His grip on her loosened.

Victoria made a "mmm" sound of satisfaction and brought him down gently with little licks as she stroked his stomach.

Her sweet side came out when she had sex, Calum had noticed, and it touched his heart.

Alec tugged her hair. "Thank you, sweetheart. You were magnificent."

Calum waited for her to catch her breath, then met Alec's eyes. As most shifters, they'd shared often through the years, yet nothing had felt so…right…before. As if Victoria fit perfectly between them. His brother grinned as Calum gripped her hips and surged into her. No longer slow and easy. He needed to take her, and he did, hard and deep, rubbing his cock over the sweet spot with each stroke.

Her thighs started to tremble, and a low keening came from her. Not nearly enough.

Alec bent and slid his head under her so he could suck on her dangling breasts. She shivered, and her pussy clenched on Calum's cock. Her hips pushed back against him, matching his rhythm. Not yet.

Calum released his grip on her right hip and reached around her waist. His finger wandered down her low abdomen and lower to rub her slippery clit.

She went rigid, and he grinned.

Alec apparently nipped for she yelped and tried to pull up. Instead of permitting it, Calum pushed her knees farther apart, increasing her helplessness, then drove into her, harder, faster, teasing her clit with each thrust.

Her whole body went tight, and her pussy closed around him like a fist. Her every breath held a whine of appeal and then her breathing stopped entirely—and he knew her world had poised…right there…waiting for his touch.

He hummed, knowing Alec would hear and increase his attentions, and then Calum took her clit between his fingers, giving it firm, unrelenting pressure as he slammed into her.

A hard shudder ran through her, and she wailed her release—the most beautiful sound in the world—each broken cry corresponding to the forceful clenching of her orgasm around his cock.

The buffeting sent him over. He grabbed her hips with both hands, stroking her deep, letting himself go as he growled and filled her with his seed. May Herne and the Mother bless them someday with young.

Silence for a minute. Her head hung low, her ribs heaving with her gasps. Calum kissed her neck, and then pulled her over onto her side, staying behind her—in her. Alec shifted around to sandwich her between them. With a sigh of contentment, she wiggled slightly to snuggle closer.

As their mate laid her head in the hollow of Alec's shoulder, Alec gave Calum a sleepy, joyful smile and a murmur of sound that translated to *ours*.

CALUM REMAINED AWAKE. As the curtains brightened with the dawn, he simply lay and watched the other two sleep, feeling the rightness of their joining. When Victoria tensed in a dream, Calum murmured to her, stroking her shoulder, and she eased, her breathing slowing again. She trusted him, even at her most vulnerable. *I'll take care with your heart, little cat.*

When sunlight showed beneath the curtains in the bedroom, Calum slipped out of the bed, took a quick shower, and made himself tea.

In the living room, Jamie still slept on the couch. The two knee-high brownies in the corner bobbed their heads at his quiet 'thank you' and disappeared. He'd have to buy them some extra-rich cream and maybe one of Angie's pastries to reward them for their vigilance.

He settled beside his daughter, sipped his tea, and simply watched her. Doing that a lot recently, wasn't he? But he'd come so close to losing them all.

With a careful touch, he brushed her hair from her freckled cheeks. Aside from a few scratches and bruises, she'd survived the fight in fine shape. She was tougher than he'd ever have thought, more like Victoria than Lenora.

Not too much later, Alec emerged from the kitchen, yawning and carrying his coffee and the morning paper.

Calum could hear the shower running; Victoria was awake also. Would she be embarrassed? Or, more probably, full of prickles to hide the fact she cared. "Brawd, we should clean out the guest room between our flats so Victoria will have space to call her own."

"Good idea. Her house is far too exposed." When Jamie grumbled in her sleep at their voices, Alec grinned. "She looks better."

"Yes. But she should trawsfur again. Soon. Having you and Victoria there would help."

Alec considered, nodded slowly. "Yeah. And it wouldn't hurt the Vixen to start her lessons."

"What lessons?" Victoria asked from the doorway, engulfed in Alec's dark green terry-cloth robe. Her face was a lovely pink from the heat of the shower, her cheeks reddened from beard burn, and her lips swollen. She looked well-loved.

When she met his eyes, her color darkened. Not prickly after all. Shy. He smiled a little, charmed at the thought.

She knelt beside the couch to check Jamie. "That's a normal sleep. She's okay." Her tenderness warmed him. She truly did care for his kitten, didn't she? After brushing a strand of hair away from Jamie's cheek, she rose, assuming a cooler expression—closing the gate on that gentle heart of hers.

He preferred she leave the barrier open. He stood, gripped her robe, and pulled her close enough to take her mouth in a long morning kiss. Soft, swollen lips, the fragrance of clean female skin. When he raised his head, her eyes looked dazed, and her hands gripped his biceps.

"Good morning, little cat," he said softly, brushing her lips again. He'd enjoy greeting her this way for the remainder of his days.

"Good morning," she said, obviously trying for composure, but her husky voice told him different. "Um. You were talking about lessons?"

"We'll coach you on shifting, control, and the tricks of being an animal," Alec said. "It's pretty strange at first."

"So I found out," Victoria said with a wry smile. "And you two are my instructors?"

"If you like." Calum ran his finger down her pink cheek. "Being asked to mentor is an honor, so if there is someone you would—"

"No," she cut him off. "I promised Jamie we'd learn together. Having the same teachers is only logical."

"Indeed." *Logical*. Bugger it, he hoped she liked him and Alec as more than just instructors. He wanted her in his life, in his arms, arguing with him over politics, brightening his days. Yet, she'd spoken no words of affection—and they weren't permitted to do so at this point. "I'll wake Jamie, and we'll get started after breakfast."

"Start this morning?"

Her nervous expression brought a smile to his face. She wasn't nearly as blasé as she tried to appear. "Yes."

FUCKING-A, THE AIR in the tunnel was freezing. Vic shivered even more, knowing the next step would be to take her clothes off.

"Strip," Calum said, and Vic choked on a laugh.

"My clothes go…?" She looked around the dark cave. No furniture, no closets, no hangers.

"Here." Alec took his shirt off and stuffed it into the wall where cubbyholes had been carved out of solid rock. Some had clothing in them already.

"Got it." She stripped, feeling her skin flush despite the chill. Yeah, okay, they'd seen her naked—hell, had kissed most of her—but still, there was something different about getting all bare-ass in the daylight. In front of *both* of them. She shook her hair to veil the front of her.

Jamie had no problem with modesty and shimmied out of her clothes without a second thought. Guess shifters must be used to being naked. Hell, if they went out on a hunt, the cave must look like a nudist colony. Weird.

Alec grinned, obviously aware of her reluctance. "It's best to strip before changing. Gets expensive otherwise, since you'll end up bursting the seams. But having the clothes rip is good. They'll fall off and not leave you all tangled up."

"Unless you're wearing elastic." Calum's smile flashed. "When we weren't much older than you, Jamie, Alec forgot to remove his clothing. Rather than changing back, he tried to claw his stretchy body shirt off. I think he still has the scars."

Vic snickered, and Jamie laughed.

"Thanks, brawd." Alec rolled his eyes. "Needless to say, Mr. Careful never forgot to strip first."

Jamie shoved her shoes into her cubby and turned. "I'm ready to trawsfur, Daddy." Her chin rose as she tried to look brave, but the quaver in her voice betrayed her nervousness.

"Me, too," Vic said. At least her voice didn't shake. Much.

Calum glanced at Alec, and Vic felt a tingle along her skin as Alec blurred, then reappeared as a massive cougar, his fur so golden it almost shone. His eyes were slightly lighter, almost matching the paler fur on the insides of his ears.

"God, you're pretty," Vic said involuntarily and could swear the cat smirked at her words. It—he padded over and rubbed his jaw over her bare hip making her shiver. Sure she knew it was Alec, but...that was a very big mountain lion.

"Behave yourself, brawd."

With a low feline chuff, Alec moved away to crouch at the tunnel entrance.

"Victoria, is the door clear in your mind?"

"Yes." It glowed even more brightly today.

"Good. After you trawsfur, find the portal again before you do anything else. It doesn't look the same from the other side, and you need to be able to jump back quickly if needed."

Jamie nodded. "It's scary when you can't see the door."

"So it is. For today, you will stay with me and Alec. We may shift back a time or two to point something out." Calum tilted his head at Vic. "Trawsfur."

Open the door. Step through. A tingling ran over her skin, starting at her toes, ending at her scalp. Her balance ruined, she fell forward, and stared at her very own fuzzy paws. *Cool.* As she sniffed the air, a sense of belonging washed over her, being held and loved and never abandoned. To her regret, the feeling dissipated like mist in the wind.

Alec padded over and butted her in the shoulder. The breeze wafted his scent toward her—a cat scent, but very, very male. She sniffed and found herself rubbing him, cheek to cheek. Damn, he smelled good. Pure testosterone.

Pulling herself together, she saw Jamie and Calum had shifted. She simply stared. Calum had darker fur than Alec, almost brown, and his eyes were a golden brown. Instead of just being lighter, his muzzle looked as if he'd rubbed it in snow, making her want to smile.

Jamie bounced around her father on her little paws, batting at his tail, then noticed Alec and Vic. She sprang between them, shoving and rubbing.

Calum followed and... Oooh, Calum smelled as good as Alec. Different though. Could a scent be less...friendly and fun? But richer? Deeper? Vic felt her tail swaying with delight. She rubbed muzzles with him and actually licked his jaw to savor him more. He laid a huge paw across her shoulders, holding her in place as he rubbed her with his cheeks and chin. When he was finished, their scents mingled so thoroughly she couldn't tell where hers began and his ended. And she was *purring*.

Jamie bounded over to the entrance and out, then Alec and Calum. As Vic stepped from the cave, the mountain called to her, a force pulling at every cell. *Run. Hunt.*

Ahead the others disappeared into the forest. Vic let her instincts take over and sprang after them, catching up easily. As long as she didn't think about it, four legs worked even better than two, and the feel of the wind ruffling her fur was a sensuous delight. She caught a scent, something rustled in the brush, and suddenly she was chasing a rabbit. Part of her screamed, *'wait, no,'* and the rest of her saw food.

Food?

She halted so suddenly her paws skidded in the snow. Jesus, she'd almost killed Thumper for breakfast. *Major ugh.*

Calum's deep chuckle sounded behind her, and she wanted to cringe. *Please tell me he didn't see me tearing after a damned rodent.* She turned.

Back in human form, he leaned against a cedar, arms folded across his chest. She couldn't look away. He was gorgeous, all muscle and dark skin, and an um-hmm...well-endowed male package.

Involuntarily, her belly inched lower to the ground, so her hips rose higher.

His lips curved, and heat flashed in his eyes. "Don't tempt me, Victoria. Unfortunately, we're here for lessons only." He knelt and beckoned with two fingers. "Come."

He'd put no power into his voice, but she sprang to his side instantly anyway, and he still smelled so good she had to rub her muzzle against him. He stroked her head with his warm hand, and the sensation almost mesmerized her. Her front paws started stepping up and down.

"Being an animal is overwhelming," he said, the richness of his voice soothing. "You must strengthen the part of you that is human, so, if needed, you can overrule the wildness." He scratched around her ears, up under her chin. Her eyes slitted closed in pleasure.

"However, rabbits *are* good to eat, and part of the joy of being an animal is the hunt. And the kill. It's permitted, cariad." The hint of laughter told her he'd seen her sudden halt. Dammit.

Jamie and Alec loped over to join them, Alec's ears forward, his tail in a question mark.

"Victoria found a rabbit," Calum explained. "Ah, I do need to caution you—we've found trespassers in our mountains, setting animal traps. The traps are of an illegal type—quite nasty with metal teeth—and we might have missed finding some. Be cautious."

His serious gaze went from Vic to Jamie, and then he smiled. "That said, off with you. Alec and I will follow."

Jamie bounced forward, rose on her hind legs to bat at Vic with her paws, and sprang away, obviously inviting a game of tag. Vic leaped after her, and they chased each other up and down the slopes, through snow drifts, and over icy streams. Finally, in a sunny clearing they stopped. Sides heaving, Vic felt her blood pulsing in her veins. She felt joyously alive.

Something snapped in the woods behind them. With a snarl, she turned and leaped in front of the smaller panther, ready to protect her.

At the edge of the clearing, Alec and Calum, still in cat form, froze. Alec's ears twitched at Calum, and the two panthers settled quietly down where they were.

I'm an idiot. She shook her head and shifted back to human. Hey, it got easier with practice. She walked over to the cats, shivering as the cold mountain air hit her bare skin. "Sorry, guys. I don't know why—"

Alec shifted, then hugged her. "You were just protecting her, Vixen. Your heart and your instincts know she's your cub."

Jamie trotted over and stropped herself against Vic's legs. One little panther, so cute she should be outlawed.

"Mine, huh?"

"Apparently." Alec nuzzled her neck and kissed her cheek. "There's nothing quite as distinctive—or dangerous—as a mama cat defending her baby."

"Yeah, I guess." Her words might have been nonchalant, but not her feelings. Every time she looked at the little panther, her heart surged with love, with the need to protect. And she couldn't resist bending to hug Jamie, rubbing her face in the warm fur. *Yes. Mine.*

Again, she felt that weird feeling rising through as a sense of love and protection blanketed her. "What the hell is that feeling anyway?"

Calum shifted to human and rose to his feet. "What?"

Straightening, she waved a hand at herself. "That feeling. It's not...me."

Frowning, Calum took Alec's place and put his arm around her waist. "Ah, that one."

Vic waited, then prompted him with an elbow into his stomach. He grunted, though she knew she hadn't even dented his rock-like six-pack.

"You should have let her eat the rabbit," Alec said. "Women

get testy when they're hungry."

Calum moved Vic's elbow from his ribs. "Impatience is not a virtue, Victoria."

"Neither is stalling."

"What you're receiving is your connection to…the being we call the Mother, short for Mother Earth. Gaia?" He waited for her puzzled nod. "As descendents of the Fae, we apparently…hmmm, feel her presence more strongly than the humans, especially when in animal form."

"I'm not a furball right now."

"Ah." Calum stroked her cheek with his knuckles, his gaze warm. "She is also very fond of mothers."

Mothers? *Oh.* "Um. Okay, then. So how did you know what I felt?"

One side of his mouth tilted up. "As Cosantir, I am bonded to the earth. To Her, although most of my power comes from Herne." He caught her blank look. "Herne the Hunter? God of the Animals?"

She rolled her eyes to cover her discomfort. Not only new shapes but a different religion too? Then again, she'd felt that surge of warmth, of…love. Hard to discount that one. "Is that why you could make that wussy bear-guy turn back to human even when he didn't want to?"

Calum nodded, then glanced at Jamie. "Unfortunately, with a first trawsfur, forcing the shift makes matters worse. The youngling will lose all connection to the door, and if they cannot shift every month—" He looked away.

Something horrible must happen. She reached for Jamie, needing to feel her warmth. *Change the subject.* "What happened down there when you made that guy shift?"

Alec snorted. "He wanted to win Farrah's affections—or at least her attentions. Battling another is a time-honored method of scoring, so to speak. But crippling your rival is forbidden."

Well, hell, they were more aggressive than off-duty Marines in a bar.

"Speaking of fighting," Calum said, "I want to teach you two some techniques."

Hey. She was a damn good fighter. "And what exactly do you think I need to learn?"

"We'll start with how to use your hind claws to disembowel your opponent," Calum said in a dry voice and shifted.

Oookay. Vic closed her mouth and followed suit.

"IT'S SWANE," CAME the voice on the phone.

Vidal had anxiously waited for word that they'd captured the girl. He'd told Swane he wanted to be there when they contacted the girl's werecat father. But all yesterday—nothing. "Why the hell didn't you call?"

"It was a total cluster-fuck. The little bitch turned into a cougar. Clawed the shit out of me. I'm calling from the fucking hospital."

"Have you got her?"

"Hell no." Swane swore foully for a full minute. "She tore out of the house and ran into the forest. I was bleeding like a stuck pig, so I sent back-up and stayed with the van. Two of my men followed the cat up a trail."

"Well?"

"The cop showed up, then the kid's dad. They changed into fucking cougars. Both of them."

"What happened to your men?"

"Don't know. No arrests. Jail's empty. They haven't called in. I haven't seen them anywhere. I figure they're lion fodder."

Vidal dropped into the chair. He'd known the shapeshifters were dangerous. But to have his hopes flattened so thoroughly. Depression rolled over him, blackening his thoughts. "It's hopeless."

"Those fucking creatures have killed my men," Swane snapped. "They're not going to get away with it, even if I have to take some explosives in there and flatten the town."

Chapter Twenty-One

"**V**ICKI?" HER FRECKLED face worried, Jamie looked up at Vic.

"What is it, munchkin?" Vic walked down the sidewalk, eyes alert for any problems. Nothing. A few kids on their way to school. A man burning leaves. A fire salamander joyfully danced in the bonfire. "Is something wrong?"

"Not...exactly." Jamie chewed on her lower lip. "See, I owe you for saving me, and I'm not sure how to repay you."

"Owe me?"

"Uh-huh. It's the Law of Reciprocity. Favor for favor, or favor for damage done. You know—to achieve balance between us?"

Seems like she'd run into that rule of theirs before, and the baby was dead serious. Vic scratched her nose, stalling for time. She sure as hell wasn't going to put the kid in debt for being rescued. "Okay, here's the deal. My rules say that grown-ups protect kids."

Jamie nodded solemnly. "We have that too, but it's not a *Rule*."

"I was only doing my job." When Jamie opened her mouth to protest, Vic held up a finger. "And it happens that I like to fight. So I think for our exchange, you should do something for me you like to do."

Jamie's face scrunched up, and then she nodded.

"Therefore," Vic tried to remember the words Calum and Thorson had used, "in balance, I figure you should make chocolate chip cookies, and I get as many as I want before Alec or your daddy have any."

"Or me." Jamie gave a little skip, then sobered. "The balance is fair. Accepted."

"Good deal." Relief that she'd successfully navigated another strange shifter custom vied with sheer greed. Chocolate chip cookies all hers before the greedy bastards got to them. *Score*! Grinning, Vic stopped at the entrance to the school yard. This would be the kid's first day back since the mess almost a week ago. Vic took her by the shoulders, studied her face. No fear, only a trace of anxiety. *Okay, then.* Ignoring the babble of children's voices, Vic ordered, "You're going to do fine."

"I know," Jamie said. Scowling, she kicked a lump of snow into the fence. "Only I've got to make up a stupid biology project."

"You'll manage. I'll see you this afternoon." Vic watched as the kid trotted into the school yard, and her friends swamped her. Yes, the girl would manage. Smart, sociable, with a big heart, and a hell of a lot of courage. She'd make a great Marine.

I was a great Marine. But that life had disappeared. No Marines, no Wells, and no CIA. Firming her mouth, she turned away from the children's laughter and headed toward the Wild Hunt. She'd report in to Calum who'd had an unexpected delivery for the tavern. After letting him know his daughter had made it all right, maybe she'd go see Thorson. Have some coffee or something.

It wasn't like she had anything better to do with her day. Or her life.

Dammit. Imitating Jamie, she kicked a chunk of snow, sending it flying into a nearby tree. A pixie clinging to a branch chattered angrily at her. *Oops.* She glanced up at the angry, tiny face. "Sorry. I forgot about you guys."

After clicking its nails at Vic—was that the way a sprite flipped someone off?—it disappeared back into the branches. God, her world had gotten bizarre.

Vic walked slowly down the snow-patched sidewalks. Calum said she needed to stay in Cold Creek for at least six months, to learn shifter rules, how to control the trawsfurs, let her body adapt fully. What the hell was she going to do during that time, and even after that? Being a barmaid was fun, but not for a lifetime. It would be like surviving on cake instead of real food. But she wasn't exactly trained for much. *I'm a Marine, dammit!*

Not any more. The gusting breeze tangled her hair, and she brushed it back impatiently. She needed to call Wells and tell him she wanted to muster out. The thought left an aching hollow in her gut. He'd recruited her into his special undercover unit years ago, arranged the covert-ops version of Special Forces training, then CIA agent training. They spoke the same language of duty and honor and loyalty, and in typical Wells' fashion, he'd known just what to say to get her on board. *"I need you."*

Now she'd lose him too.

Her throat somehow cut off her wind, and she stopped to breathe and look out at the snow-dusted mountains, soaring tall into the blue sky. Immovable and unchanging, so different from the weak humans below.

She inhaled, let the pain pass through her. She'd survive, of course she would. She started walking again, trying to formulate a plan. Calum didn't need a full-time barmaid, so somewhere in this place, she'd have to find a nine-to-five job. Selling cars maybe.

The thought made her gag.

Calum looked up as the door opened. Vic dropped her coat

on a table and crossed the room to join him behind the bar. "Can I help?"

He studied her for a moment. "Is something amiss?" he asked.

She knelt beside the box of bottles he was unpacking and handed one up for him to put away. "No. Jamie didn't have any problem with returning. She was drowning in friends when I left."

"Not with Jamie. With you."

What, did she have some sign on her forehead saying, *I'm unhappy*? "Nah. I'm fine." She held up another bottle, and he placed it on the counter rather than the cupboard.

Mouth in a straight line, he pulled her to her feet. His eyes were dark gray, the stormy color darkening fast.

"What?" she asked. *Weak, Vic, weak.* Questions were a stupid way to—

"I asked because I care," he said in a level tone, his gaze not leaving her face. "And I would *prefer* to have an honest answer."

God, he was even better than Wells at boxing a person in. She huffed a breath and looked away. The bastard didn't move, didn't release her, didn't talk...just held her in place...waiting. Like a fucking cat outside a gopher hole. She had a feeling he'd stand there until she replied.

"Fine, then." She stared down at the unpacked boxes. "I can't go back to my old job, and I don't know what to do now."

"Ah, cariad. Your whole life has turned upside-down, hasn't it?"

The question stabbed like a knife, and she choked on a whimper. Raising her eyes, she met his gaze. Understanding. Sympathy. Dammit, she didn't need...didn't want... The sob rising in her throat humiliated her.

He pulled her against his chest, holding her firmly, ignoring her attempt to push away. "Shhh. Let it come. You have lost much." The low rumble of his voice soothed; his arms enclosed her in warmth. Safety.

Sobs rose up, choking their way out in ugly sounds. She tried to turn, to hide, but he just pressed her face to his shoulder until she gave up and wept.

It seemed like forever that she cried, and past forever before she could stop. Little hiccupping sobs kept breaking free, but he stood, patient as a mountain, holding her as his warm hand made long, comforting strokes up and down her back.

"I'm sorry," she muttered into his shoulder.

"I'm not. You were overdue."

"I'm not a baby."

"Indeed no. You are stronger than any woman I know." His cheek rested on top of her head, the feeling comforting. "Alas, Victoria, no matter how strong, you are still only mortal. You needed to mourn, cariad."

Her breath shuddered out. "Okay. Well." When she pulled back this time, he released her. "Ah. Thanks. For...holding me." God, how embarrassing.

He had a slight smile. "My pleasure."

"Oh, sure." All guys liked a bawling woman.

Hand on her cheek, he bent and kissed the tears away, his lips like velvet. His scent washed over her, clean soap with a tantalizing hint of musky male. And then he threaded his fingers through her hair, hummed a little in pleasure, and took her mouth. Possessed and staked his territory.

Unexpected desire exploded within her like a bomb, and she pressed closer. Running her hands up his back, she savored the rock-hard muscles under his thin white shirt. He cupped her bottom, pulling her against him, and the bulge of his hard cock made her shiver. When he stepped away from her, her shirt somehow came right off.

"Hey," she protested. "I thought—Alec isn't here. How

does—"

"Not all sex has to be a threesome, little cat. And you need something to take your mind off your sadness." Pulling on her hair to tip her head back, he kissed his way down to the curve in her neck. Holding her in place, he undid her jeans, and then shoved her pants and briefs down to tangle at her feet.

"I have something I've wanted to do ever since you walked into my tavern." With firm hands, he lifted her and sat her on the bar top. The glossy wood felt chill under her bare bottom.

He opened her legs and stepped between her thighs, then hugged her. A second later her bra dropped away. Sneaky cat.

"Now wait a minute." Naked in a bar? Was the man insane? "No, Calum." She took his hands, thinking to control him.

His jaw set, and his expression took on a dangerous edge. He moved her hands to her sides. "Your hands will remain there. Am I clear, Victoria?"

God, when his voice took on that lethal note of command, everything inside her quivered. How could he do this to her when no one else could? She swallowed.

His lips curved up. "I see you understand." He pulled her forward and kissed her breasts, his mouth shockingly hot against her cool skin. His tongue circled until her nipples grew hard and throbbing, then he sucked one, then the other. Shivers ran through her, pooling in her groin like molten lead.

With a small smile, he set a hand on her sternum, pushing her back, forcing her to lie flat with her legs dangling off the end. "Oh, yes, this is exactly where I imagined you," he murmured.

What? The bar stood much higher than his crotch, how was he... He ran his finger down her moist cleft and followed with his mouth.

"Oh, God. Listen, this isn't—"

"Oh, this is." He nipped her inner thigh admonishingly.

"Calum. Please—"

"Be silent, little cat." With his free hand, he lifted her right leg up, setting her heel on the bar's edge, pressing her knees to the outside, and opening her farther. Exposing her fully. She felt vulnerable. Hot. Needy. His tongue circled her clit, flicked across it. With one hand, he gripped her knee firmly, keeping her open. With his other, he toyed with her nipples.

Her head spun with the sensations. His mouth nibbling, biting, sucking, licking. His fingers circling, pinching, stroking. Then he moved his hand from her breast to her pussy. One finger slid inside her. She was so very wet, yet she could feel each knuckle as it entered. Her hips rose.

He slowed, his tongue moving away from her center, leaving her tight, wanting, and she made a whimpering noise. His teeth nibbled on her thigh before he returned, and she realized, in this, as in everything, he was totally focused, careful. In control.

His tongue swept back over her, reawakening the nerves with a rush. He circled her core, rousing her until she was so ready, so ready…and then moving. Everything merged; every cell in her skin was sensitized, waiting for the next touch, the next lick. She bowed upward, all her muscles tight.

"Not yet, cariad." His breath puffed over her engorged clit as his finger moved slowly in and out, until her insides throbbed with need.

She whimpered, hands fisting at her sides as she fought not to move, not to grab his hair. She stared down at him and saw he watched her in return. Pulling his finger out, he pushed in two, filling her more fully, stretching her slightly, his eyes intent on her face.

"God, Calum," she whined, teetering on the edge. Needing more…just a little more…her clit so tight that it ached. "Oh please." *Please, please, please.*

"Yes, I think now." His mouth came down on her fully, lips

closing around her clit. He sucked, gently, then hard as his fingers drove into her. Once, twice.

Her senses exploded in brutal waves of pleasure, the dark ceiling turning bright white. Her hips tried to buck against his restraining hand, and ruthlessly he held her in place, licking gently over her clit, sending spasm after spasm of sensation through her.

Her heart hammered until she thought she'd choke with it. "Oh God, stop…" When he finally released her, she felt as if a Bradley tank had run over her body.

A moment later, she blinked as he walked up to kiss her. She could taste herself on him as he savored her lips. Fondling her breasts, he took her mouth more deeply as if he could brand her with his kiss.

When he lifted his head, she smiled up at him and pushed herself up on her elbows. Naked. He was still fully dressed. That was…a weird feeling. "That's quite a bartending skill, you have there," she said, trying for light.

"Thank you." He scooped her up off the bar like a glass of beer, ignoring her startled squeak. He walked toward the fireplace.

"Now, wait—" Fuck, she hadn't even thought about someone coming in. Where'd her brains go? "Calum—"

He laid her, stomach-down, across the back of the couch. Her legs dangled, and her elbows rested on the cushions. Her butt stuck up in the air like a target. "What are you—"

"Be silent, little cat." He slapped her bottom, and the sharp sting zinged straight to her clit which sent up a demanding throb. She moaned.

"Ah. I had wondered if you'd enjoy a little pain with your pleasure, cariad." His forearm across her low back, with his free hand he swatted her ass cheeks, his palm hard, the swats painful.

And yet, somehow the burning engulfed her pussy in dark

need. A frightening feeling. Panting, she squirmed, tried to kick.

"No kicking." She received a punishing blow that truly hurt and showed how much he was holding back. She groaned with the pain and the confusing pleasure.

His hand slid between her legs. "Ah, you are very wet. This is something Alec and I will enjoy exploring with you in the future. But for now..." She heard the slide of his zipper, and then he thrust into her so hard and fast that her breath whooshed out with a groan, and every nerve deep inside her joined in the pulsing chorus of need. When her legs kicked, he shoved his thighs against hers, his hips between her thighs.

He bent over her, his hard chest against her back. His groin rubbed her burning butt cheeks, the feeling disconcerting, hurting and yet pulling her deeper into need.

"Calum...please..."

"Let go, little cat," he murmured in her ear. "You cannot control everything—especially this." When he bit the back of her neck, his erection pressed even deeper, and shock waves coursed up her spine. Bent over the couch, she was helpless, could only mewl as he set up a hard, fast rhythm. His hand slid underneath her to massage her breasts, pulling on the nipples as he stroked into her, his cock so thick, it seemed to stretch her more with each thrust.

Her hands tightened on the cushions as the sensations increased, and then he straightened slightly. His fingers swirled in her wetness, making her wiggle. It felt so good, almost too much. But then, his slickened hand slid between the cheeks of her butt, and one finger pressed on her asshole.

"Hey! No!" She tried to move, to escape.

He gripped her hip firmly. "Victoria, Alec and I would like to enjoy you here."

But but but. This was so not what she had in mind. She'd considered it...maybe...way in the future. Certainly not now.

Now. His finger circled the rim, rousing odd sensations, and then pushed mercilessly inside.

Jesus fuck. A tremor ran through her as nerves sparked awake. The merciless way he held her, not letting her pull away, seemed to make her bones melt.

"Gently, little cat. Let your body get used to the feeling. After this, if you truly hate it, then we'll talk."

Her anus pulsed around the intrusion, and she felt…strange. Not just having a finger in her ass, but she'd actually let him do it. Did she want him to push her?

He rubbed her ass cheeks lightly, and then started to move. His cock pushed deeper into her pussy as his finger pulled out of her anus. Then he thrust into her pussy, once, twice, and retreated just as his finger plunged back in.

An electrical vise clamped onto her spine as the sensations rushed together, forming one huge dam in a river of pleasure that got deeper and deeper. Her vagina, her ass tightened around him…and then the dam burst under the pressure, and sensation blasted through her whole body. She screamed as her spasms hit the hard intrusions in her vagina and anus, rebounding back with devastating pleasure. Her fingers clawed at the couch as she buried her face in the cushions. *Dear God.*

Before the shockwaves had diminished, he pulled his hand from her ass and bent over her, pushing his cock even deeper. His hands gripped her hips, pulling her bottom up higher as he slammed into her. The rumble of his voice deepened, roughened as she felt the jerking of his release.

He wrapped his arms around her in a hard…comforting…embrace, making her tremble. He'd taken her, done what he wanted…and she'd let him. She tried to catch her breath, to move—*to escape*—and he growled a warning in her ear.

A shiver ran down her spine.

Yet his hands on her stayed gentle, his lips soft as he kissed her cheek. "Little cat, can't you trust me not to hurt you…in a way you don't care for?"

She bit her lip against the strangest need to cry and managed to nod. He hadn't hurt her. Pushed her past her comfort zone definitely, and yet, everything he did just turned her on more. And that was almost scarier.

"Thank you, cariad, for sharing one of my fantasies." He nipped her nape lightly, sending goosebumps down her arms, and added, "Alec and I will be interested in helping you live out some of yours. Tonight."

God, I might not survive the next few months.

VIC'S LEGS WOBBLED as she walked beside Calum down Main Street. The cold dry wind slapped her flushed face. "What was that for, anyway?" she asked. "You don't usually… I mean, it's daytime." And why did that kind of swamping sex always leave her feeling…little? Needy?

He stopped and turned her to face him. As if she'd turned into a toddler, he zipped up her jacket. "You break my heart when you're sad or in tears, cariad," he said gently. "I needed you in my arms." The crease appeared in his cheek as he smiled faintly. "Forcing pleasure upon you was just a side-benefit."

She looked away from his intent eyes. "Damned if I get how you can do that," she muttered. "I've never…"

"Never relinquished control. We know. I think you have long needed a lover to command you, but you don't trust—didn't trust—anyone enough to give them that power." His hand cupped her cheek, bringing her gaze back to him. "I am honored that you trust me with your surrender."

His words sank into her, starting a tremor deep inside her. Why did it have to be so…right?

Him and his fucking fantasies—so maybe she'd had a few

slave-girl dreams, but to actually live them out? Real life? Hell with that. No one would ever get that kind of control over her. *Except he had it already, Sergeant Slave Girl.* She pulled herself together and said lightly, "Hell, if your God trusts you with so much power, who am I to disagree?"

Amusement lit his eyes. "Your God now too, little cat. But if you truly become frightened or overwhelmed or are in real pain, a sincere 'Stop' will halt both me and Alec. Then again, if you're simply saying 'no' without a true objection, then I will know." His smile held a wicked tilt. "And since you seemed to enjoy it, I will probably punish you."

God. Her body jerked back to life at the thought and she swallowed hard. *Let's talk control, not punishment. Please.* "The way you order me... Alec doesn't—it's not like this with Alec..." She wasn't sure what she wanted to ask.

"You and Alec are equals in bed." His devastating grin flashed as he stroked her hair. "But I am in charge."

The words sent a tingle all the way to her toes, one she tried to ignore. "You think."

His hand fisted in her hair, and he tilted her head back. She could escape—defensive moves flipped through her mind, but the sheer liquid feeling of her body and limbs kept her in place. He waited a second, then kissed her lightly. "Not think, little cat. I know."

He released her and pulled her against his side with an arm around her waist, before starting back down the walk.

"Did you have something to do in town?" she asked. He hadn't finished unpacking the boxes.

"I do." He ran a finger down her cheek. She was still so sensitive, she felt the zing all the way to her toes. Considering how his gaze heated, he could tell. "I'm taking you to Alec."

Alec. She closed her eyes as storm clouds of guilt piled up inside her. She hadn't thought about him once. Not once as she and his brother screwed like bunnies all over the tavern. "Calum." She stopped. What did she want to say? "Fuck, this is a mess," she ended up muttering to her shoes.

He ran his knuckles over her cheek so gently she wanted to snuggle back into his arms. "There is much you have yet to learn about shifter society and sex. It's difficult to explain, especially to a human raised without littermates."

"Like what?"

"For now, just know and believe that when it comes to mating, littermates feel as if they are one being. There is no jealousy if one makes love to a female, any more than your left hand would envy the right for touching a male."

"But you told me Thorson got scars from fighting for women—and the bear that night…"

"Ah." He gave her hair a tug and pulled her back into stride. "Littermates won't fight each other over a female, but everyone else is fair game. And we will discuss this further, but the center of Cold Creek is not a suitable location." He nodded at Rebecca Westerland who was leaving Albert Baty's grocery, then glanced down at Vic. "Alec will also demand his fair share of your attention as we each enjoy having you alone now and then." Without waiting for her to speak, he opened the door to the police station and ushered her in.

Alec sat in his office, head bent over paperwork. She couldn't help admiring his broad shoulders. There was something sexy about a tough guy doing paperwork. He'd left a rose on her pillow this morning. He was so sweet, and despite Calum's assurances, guilt lay like a stone in her belly.

He looked up. "'Bout time. You were due here an hour ago." His nostrils flared, and then his eyes narrowed as he studied Vic.

She flushed, knowing her lips were swollen. Hell, she probably smelled of Calum.

To her shock, he smiled with what looked like approval. *Well damn.*

He waved to the chairs beside the desk and waited as she and Calum sat down. "Vicki, Calum and I talked about how you're stuck here. Being a barmaid might be fun, but not for a prolonged period. Not for someone like you."

"Like me?"

"Smart, skilled, tough as nails, and dedicated to whatever you do. You need something more demanding than a fluff job," Alec answered.

"Well." She blinked, warmth filling her belly. Was that really how he saw her? "You have a solution?" And what would that solution be? Enlist? Join the Marines? *Been there, done that.*

"Yep," Alec said smugly. "Come and work for me."

Here? She looked around the tiny police station. Receptionist/dispatcher to one side of the door. Alec's office, the patrol officer's area on the other. A door to Alec's infamous two jail cells in the back. "Are you serious?"

"Very."

"Oh." Vic chewed on her lip. Police work. Protecting people. Using her brain to solve problems. "Don't I need some certification and classes and all that?"

"You will. But for now, until you decide if you like it, and I discover if you're any good, we'll call you an entry level sheriff's deputy."

"I don't know—you must know better qualified people."

"Hardly." Alec gave her an even look. "Qualified people rarely want to work in the boring boondocks. Of those that do, too many are arrogant bastards I wouldn't trust to take out the garbage." He ran a hand through his hair. "I have a couple of good ones now. Men who are here for the same reason I am— because this is where my family and friends live."

"Oh. Well—"

"With both Daonain and humans in an area, it works better when shifters handle enforcement." He grinned. "It's not appropriate to ask a human to calm down a pissed-off bear." Then his smile dropped away. "And if something happens like it did with Jamie, the standard human response is to get help from a higher authority. But if the government or military were called in…"

Calum growled under his breath.

Cold slid up Vic's spine at the deadly sound. "What do you think they'd do?"

Alec's eyes, so warm and full of fun, turned terrifyingly cold. *Please, never let him look at me like that.* "At least twice, we've rescued a shifter getting gutted on a lab table in a military site. Just another specimen to dissect. If they truly believed we exist?" His mouth thinned. "Humans have a long history of genocide."

"Oh."

His face cleared. "Anyway, with the problems recently, I could use another deputy. One who is skilled enough to handle deadly situations. Truthfully, Vicki? I need you."

There was a knot in her chest, one she hadn't even known was present until it started to loosen. She could have a job where she could use her skills. She was *needed.* She breathed in, worked for the right casual tone, "Oh, well then, sure. I accept."

EYEING THE PHONE, Vic sat on a chair in the bedroom designated *hers.* Each day, something new appeared. A quilt in soothing blues and greens. A handmade rug from a local craftswoman. A painting of the mountains above Cold Creek. The very comfortable chair she sat in now. She smiled. She hadn't spent a night in the bed yet, but to have a room of her own was comforting. She used it when the guys pissed her off, so she wouldn't rip their obstinate heads off.

She closed her eyes. *Stalling, Sergeant?*

She picked up the phone. Set it down. Picked it up again and dialed.

"Wells."

Dammit, why did he only answer when she didn't want to talk with him? But would this be the last time she talked with him? A place deep within hollowed out with emptiness. "Um. It's me, Vi—Sergeant Morgan."

She could almost see his attention move from paperwork to focus on her. Like a laser beam.

"Sergeant. I expected you in person."

"Well, yeah. I know." She grimaced. This was like having little pieces of her body—her soul—hacked off. "Something came up, and I…won't be returning. I'm resigning."

Silence.

"Um. Effective today. Sir."

He'd be narrowing his eyes now, as if he could see across the country. "Are you still in Washington state?"

She hadn't expected that question. "Yessir. Sir, I'm sending you the official paperwo—"

"Why are you resigning?"

Went right to the heart of the matter, didn't he? Sometimes she had to wonder if he and Calum were related. But she'd already thought of the answer to this—an honest one, oddly enough. "I fell for a man." *Men.* "It's serious and I don't want to leave him." *Them.* And it would be really awkward to turn into a fuzzball during a firefight. "Anyway, sir, I will be staying here."

"Cold Creek?"

"Um. Yes—how did you know?"

"I'm a spy, Morgan; it's what we do."

She snorted. Waited.

"You had a copy of your physical sent to you in Cold Creek," he explained.

She closed her eyes and thumped her head on back of the chair. *Dumbshit.* Swane had probably tracked her that way. Fucking-A, she'd done it to herself. "Got it."

"About that matter you wanted me to investigate—"

"That's been dealt with," she interrupted quickly. God, Calum and Alec would go ballistic if they knew a CIA muckety-muck was investigating Swane. "The local law enforcement took care of it."

"Then I won't waste my time."

Her sigh of relief was silent. "No need, sir."

She could hear his fingers tapping his desktop. Finally, he said, "All right, Sergeant. I can hardly keep you in service against your will. I'll get the paperwork started. And I wish you the best."

"You too, sir," she whispered to the dial tone.

It was done. She breathed out against the pain, feeling as if she'd cut out her heart. Would she end up as with the amputees she'd known, mourning the loss forever? But now she could move on.

And she wouldn't have to tell the guys what she'd done for a living.

She shivered as she remembered the frigid look in Alec's eyes, Calum's growl. Well, if she still knew them in a couple of decades, she might casually mention she'd served in the military.

But ever confess to being a CIA agent to this bunch of over-ly paranoid kitty-cats with claws? Never in a kazillion years.

VIDAL READ THROUGH the information on the new pill the doctor had prescribed. It might halt the symptoms of the Parkinson's...for a while. Then everything would go downhill.

At least, this bought him some time. He heard a knock on his office door. "Come in."

Swane. *At last.* Pale. Face tight with pain. Moving carefully. Long red marks on his cheek and neck had the ugly wrinkling of flesh glued shut.

"You look like hell."

Swane's grimaced, his eyes cold. "I'm eating enough antibiotics to choke a cow—after being on IVs for over a week. Fucking cougar bites and claws are bad as human bites. That's probably why we lost all those homeless people."

Vidal nodded. He'd have to remember to begin the antibiotics before starting the transformation. "Did you come up with a plan? One that will work this time?"

"Fuck, like I knew the kid would turn into a cat?" Swane ran his hand over his head, the scratching sound showing he hadn't shaved it recently. "We got information on a few wereanimals in town—the old biddy didn't know them all—but only the tavern owner has a kid."

Somehow that didn't seem right. Vidal regarded the ex-mercenary suspiciously.

"We can try again to grab the Morgan bitch if you figure it's worth it," Swane said. "But we don't know if she was changed into a werecat or how much she knows."

"I suppose you're right."

"Basically the kid's our best bet." Swane's eyes turned strange, sending a chill up Vidal's spine. "No matter what, I'm going to get the little bitch."

And that was what the problem was. Swane wanted the girl…and was becoming increasingly unreliable. But bringing in new help increased the risk. Vidal scowled. He obviously needed to keep a closer watch on what was going on. "They've seen your face."

Swane scowled. "It's a real bum-fuck town. Only a few people on the street, and they all know each other."

Vidal smiled slowly, his gaze on the picture on the wall. His uncle had pull with the movie industry in L.A. He could set up a shoot for a documentary—or anything, really, so long as there were cameras and people. "I can get a shitload of people on the streets. And lure the kid out too. No brat in a backwater will stay away from a movie being filmed."

Chapter Twenty-Two

LESS THAN TWO weeks after starting as a cop, Vic walked her beat, nodding to the people strolling the sidewalk. She glanced into the bookstore. It felt good to see Thorson behind the counter, like the world was right again. Tough old bastard.

She turned away when her eyes started to burn and scowled at two men who stood in the center of the street pointing at the mountains. Fucking movie people. Apparently the town council had given permission for some idiotic film shoot next week, and the flakes had already begun to infiltrate Cold Creek to map out where they'd do each scene. The townspeople were all excited at playing "extras". Vic shook her head. Having strangers around made her paranoid.

And not without reason. Swane and crew weren't about to give up. But maybe the shifters would find them first. They'd traced the dead guys to Swane and then to a mobster named Tony Vidal. Long list of suspected crimes, only a couple of convictions. She'd seen his picture—Vidal was the suit.

The shifter cop in Seattle had people watching Vidal's house and office, but the bastard had disappeared. Not good. Worry edged like a thin knife between Vic's ribs. Wells would undoubtedly have obtained the information faster, but if the CIA found out about the shifters… The thought of Jamie on some laboratory dissecting table made her crazy.

The sun had managed to come out for the afternoon, warming the air to a pleasant temperature. In the center island, Halloween bats and ghosts dangled from the trees, dancing in the breeze. Outside of Baty's grocery, a six-foot skeleton had replaced the wooden Indian, and Books' display window sported cobwebs from every corner.

Cold Creek took Halloween seriously.

So did her two men. Alec usually surprised her with flowers, but this morning, she'd rolled over and come face to face with a dark leering skull, a hand-sized chocolate skull. She grinned. *The idiot.*

Both of them were crazy, smothering her with attention.

Calum made her coffee every morning, although he hated the stuff and only drank tea.

Alec had given her a new knife...one so well-made she'd slit open her thumb just testing it. Laughing, he'd bandaged her up and kissed her owie, then searched out every bruise and scratch to kiss them too.

After Calum found out she loved M&M's, he brought out a bag one evening and given half to Alec. She had to provide a kiss for a yellow M&M, offer a breast for a red, and...dealer's choice for the brown and green ones. Her nipples crinkled as she remembered all the various positions and things they'd had her do. Inventive bastards.

Yesterday, Calum had come into her bedroom as she was dressing. He'd pulled a dark red, incredibly soft cashmere sweater over her head, stroked his hand over her breasts, told her that her skin was softer than the cashmere—and somehow she'd ended up back in bed.

God, she was out-classed and out-numbered, and she still didn't know what was going to happen. She cared about them— fuck-yeah, she cared—but they'd made no big *I-love-you* declarations. No one even mentioned the future.

Her stomach felt as if she'd swallowed a rock. Yes, they gave her attention, but was it because she was stuck in their home for the moment? Calum was so protective, he'd probably give a room to anyone in need, like he had with Thorson. Even worse, they acted so old-fashioned about women, they'd probably treat any…fuck-buddy…like they did her.

Her breath hitched as she realized that since they were old-fashioned, then if they were serious about her…well, they would have said so. Proposed or something. They hadn't. She rubbed her arms, feeling chilled. *Didn't even realize you'd started making wedding plans, now did you, Sergeant?* Pretty dumb. The men hadn't made promises. They probably considered her just…just a roommate with benefits.

Okay. She straightened her shoulders. They weren't the only ones enjoying the benefits. She was too. She simply needed to remember that's all there would be.

"Hey, you! Yeah, you—the cop," a woman shouted from the end of the block.

Vic stopped and almost looked around for a *real* police officer, but she was the only one downtown, so the lady was yelling at her. "Yes?"

"You're off-duty." A tall, lanky woman in tight jeans and sweatshirt walked toward Vic. "Let's go have a drink."

Vic recognized the woman's scent before her appearance—and wasn't that weird. "Heather!"

Heather put her hands on Vic's shoulders and gave her a slow study, then a hard hug. "You don't look too bad. Before you left, you looked like a horse that had been rode hard and put away wet.

"Thanks a lot." God, it was good to see her. "I thought you worked down around Rainier."

"I do." Heather linked arms with Vic and steered her the

other way down Main. "Daniel and I drove up for the Samhain Gathering."

Gathering. That's what Alec had called that orgy-style party in the tavern. Was that why the street was filled with so many people? "Where are you staying?"

"With Rebecca. She takes in boarders when something's happening in Cold Creek; makes a few extra bucks."

They turned down Aberdeen Street. Just behind Angie's Diner, Heather halted at a Victorian bed and breakfast. "C'mon, we can use the side door."

"Um. I'm still on duty. How about I come—"

"Like I said, your shift finished early today. Alec said so when he told me where to find you." Heather shoved the door open, glanced back. "I have a six-pack of Calum's fancy beer in the cooler. You in?"

"Definitely." Vic followed her up the steep stairs to the second floor and down a hallway. With oriental carpeting in rich reddish tones and rose-bud wallpaper, the room had a feeling of lush warmth. "Wow."

"Yeah. It's my favorite room here." Heather handed her a beer and pushed open the French doors. "Check this out."

A wrought iron table and chairs barely fit on the spindle-railed balcony. Heather set her beer on the glass-topped table, sat down, and waved at the other chair. "Best place to people-watch in town, especially during Gatherings."

The balcony was high enough to see over Angie's low diner to Main Street. Vic sat and put her throbbing feet up on the railing. "I'm beginning to see why they call cops *flat-feet.*"

I think you're crazy, Ms. Cop. Small pay, big risk, nasty people—what's there to like?"

"Maybe because I get to beat up on the assholes of the world?"

"There's a point."

A man's voice drifted up from the street, and she saw a middle-aged banker-type guy scowl at a portly man. A dowdy woman shook her head at both of them and walked away.

Heather glanced over. "Idiots. Like she'd look at either of them." She sipped her beer. "So how are you doing?"

Vic studied Heather. Here was someone who had no problem with giving open answers. "Forget how I'm doing. I want to know why all these people are in town. And what exactly is a Gathering?"

"Whoa, doggie, you're going to jump right into the pond?" Heather raised her eyebrows. "No small talk first?"

"Spill or I'll hurt you. Badly."

"Oooo, the kitty's got claws." Heather grinned and held her hands up defensively. "Okay, okay. Actually, that's why Alec let you off early—those two males keep leaving me all the tough explanations...like I bet they never mentioned that women come into heat with every full moon."

Vic choked on her beer. "Excuse me? *Heat*? Like a...a cat?"

"'Fraid so. It has to do with the Wild Hunt that the Fae held under the full moon. The time for hunting and partying and mating."

She sat up, forcing air into her lungs. "Are you saying I'm going to go howl in the street and let myself be raped by man after man?"

Heather whooped. "God, what an image!"

"But—"

Heather patted Vic's hand. "No rape, girlfriend. Never. If a guy can't smell that a woman is hot for him, his equipment doesn't work."

"Huh." Vic ran that around in her mind, and her muscles loosened. Like most female Marines, she'd experienced too many close calls. "They really can't?"

Heather's lips curved. "Really. I was damned shocked when

I went to college—human males can be total jerks, you know?"

"No shit." Vic rose to pace the length of the balcony. "So guys come to town to score with the women who are in heat?" *In heat*. God, that sounded nasty.

"And hopefully make babies. We can only get pregnant under a full moon."

"Huh. Gives new meaning to the rhythm method, doesn't it?" Vic said lightly, trying not to show how unnerved she felt. She took a sip of beer and watched a flower pixie in the rose bushes snatch a rose hip to nibble on.

"Unfortunately, shifter women don't get knocked up easily. But we almost always have twins, usually more."

"Jesus. I'm not sure if that's good or bad." What would it be like to be pregnant? As a Marine or agent, she'd never considered it, but now…the thought wasn't all that horrifying. Still, two or more at a time? A *litter*.

She shook her head. Then again, going into heat wouldn't be that bad with Alec and Calum around. "I think I get the drift. A Gathering is a good place to hook up."

"Almost." Heather looked…distressed. "It's more than just a fun time, Vicki. It's the law. All men and women attend Gatherings until too old to feel the pull of the moon. Or until they're lifemated."

Vic turned to look at her, cold trickling down her spine. "I'm not lifemated."

"No." Heather sighed. "You're not allowed to be yet. The Law states a Daonain—male or female—must experience at least one Gathering before…we'll call it marrying. A new shifter needs to discover how hormones affect her judgment before jumping into something."

Attend an orgy? One where her hormones would be in control? Vic stared at Heather in horror. "No way. I'm not going."

Heather gave her a sympathetic look. "Your body won't give

you a choice."

"My body does what I tell it to do."

"Well…the Law says you must attend the Gather, but if you can overrule your instincts enough to go home, more power to you." Heather reached across the table and patted her hand.

Okay. Then that's what would happen.

Heather glanced at the western mountains where the sun was disappearing. "We need to get dressed. Calum's going to do your introduction to the clan, and you can't show up in a uniform. C'mon."

Well, at least Calum had mentioned that. Just a general, *here's a new member.* Nothing formal, but yeah, wearing a uniform wouldn't be appropriate.

Heather led the way back into the bedroom. "Alec dropped off stuff for you earlier. Let's see what he brought." She started pulling clothes out and rejected most of them. A pair of jeans passed inspection. The tight suede boots were approved.

Vic scowled. "What's wrong with my shirts? They cover me—what more is needed?"

"Well, now, honey. There's covering"—Heather pulled a white top out of her suitcase and held it up—"and there's *covering.* Try this on."

"My bra straps will show"

"No bra. It's tight enough you don't need one."

"Uh-huh." After dropping her bra, Vic pulled the shirt over her head and walked over to the mirror. Silvery-white, low cut, almost a spandex material, the tank top clung to every curve and was snug enough to push her breasts up, displaying an amazing amount of cleavage. "Well. That's a little indiscreet."

Heather laughed and wiggled into a similar top in a golden color that set off her russet hair. "Tonight, we flaunt it. No underwear, sexy clothes. Tomorrow it's back to being ladies. Now, let's see. My mascara, liner, and shadow will work for you.

Use them."

"Sir, yes, sir," Vic muttered, obediently seating herself at the dressing table. As she stroked mascara on her lashes, she asked, "If the men are so hot for us, why bother with the getup?"

Heather started on her own makeup. "It's like this: no matter the ratio, there's still a lot of women in that room. And even if a woman wants a man, he can refuse her."

Vic shrugged. "So she finds someone else. BFD."

"Stop sulking and use your brain. You don't want to mate with just any guy; you want the best genes for your potential children. It's instinct."

"Mmmhmm." *I'm not fucking anyone; I'm not going into heat. Period.*

Heather set down the mascara and gave Vic a pointed look. "As Cosantir, Calum's at the top of the genetic heap. As a cahir, Alec is too."

Vic stiffened. *Now wait just one little minute*—women would be in heat and coming on to her men? *My men?*

WITH JAMIE BESIDE him, Calum leaned against the front of his bar, letting the clan chatter away. He'd given them a lot to discuss: Lachlan's gift to Victoria, the attacks on her and on Jamie, what was being done, what they needed to do. He'd told Heather to come late; Victoria didn't need to suffer through hearing about Lachlan again.

They would arrive any time, so he raised his hand for quiet. When a few people continued talking, he snarled. The ensuing silence was profound.

Alec, standing in his usual place at the end of the bar, gave him an amused look.

"To conclude on a more enjoyable note, shall we recognize our new clan members?" Calum said, and with impeccable timing, Heather walked into the tavern, followed by…Victoria?

"Herne's Holy Antlers," Alec whispered, echoing Calum's reaction.

His female—and she *would* be his female—wore tight jeans, and a…some sort of shirt that molded to her lush breasts and nipples that had peaked from the cold. Her lovely long hair rippling across her shoulders and down to her ass, and she'd done something to make her eyes darker, deeper, bigger. He could only stare and force his lust under control.

When he saw every man in the tavern gaping, he barely kept from snarling again. After clearing his throat, his voice still held a growl. "Just in time. Clan members. The clan welcomes Victoria, a werecat."

The room chorused back. "We See Victoria."

"The clan welcomes Jamie, a werecat." He smiled at his daughter, pride surging within him.

"We See Jamie."

"The clan welcomes Tanner, a werewolf," Calum said, and a blond teenager, standing beside his mother, grinned widely.

"We See Tanner."

"Rejoice, Daonain, the clan increases," Calum finished.

The meeting broke up with cheering. Some Daonain slipped out to run and hunt together on the mountain before the Gathering. Others greeted the youngsters and Victoria. Victoria seemed to have an inordinate number of men around her, Calum noticed, trying not to react.

"Timed it well," Alec said, joining him. He nodded toward the window where the gleam of the sun barely topped the western mountains. "You're improving."

Calum sighed. His first meeting had started late, and he'd foolishly tried to continue after moonrise when the females came into heat. The clan still laughed about it.

THERE WERE FAR too many people in the bar, dammit. The attention. The noise. The smells. Vic wormed her way to the back exit.

Outside, the air was crisp and cold. She leaned against the building, ears ringing. God, what a crowd. She hadn't realized so many shifters lived in the area.

For a few minutes, she watched the moon inch into the dark sky, sending a pale glow over the snow-covered mountains. Pretty. And it was time to get moving. She glanced at the second floor. A light was on—Jamie'd gone home. Apparently, she wouldn't go into *heat* until around twenty or so which was a good thing, since Vic would cripple any man who touched the girl.

Maybe the kid would like to play some poker. Vic grinned. Looked like she could leave too since, obviously, the female-in-heat business had passed her by. *Thank you, baby Jesus.*

The backyard entrance was around the building, so she walked along the side, scuffling her boots in the gravel. At the scent of wood smoke, she looked up. Someone had built a fire inside, and smoke puffed up from the chimney. A translucent air sylph danced in the updraft, its elongated body sinuous and graceful.

As Vic rounded the front corner of the tavern, she lost her balance like the ground had fallen out from under her foot. She put a hand on the wall to steady herself. The grain of the wood felt rough against her fingers, almost too rough. She straightened as her bare arms tingled with the slight breeze. As she took a step, her jeans scraped over her thighs…rubbed over her pussy. A tremor shook her. With her every movement, the slick material of her top sensuously slid over her breasts and hardening nipples.

She could hear the people inside. The men's deep voices

were tantalizing, their gruff laughter giving her chills. She wanted to hear them, see them, and her feet carried her that way before she'd even thought about moving.

At the front door of the tavern, she stopped, her hand on the heavy ironwork handle. She couldn't move. Everything in her demanded that she go within, to touch and be touched, and... *No, I'm going home.* Her fingers tightened on the door. *I'm going inside.* She shook her head. Her body wasn't doing what she told it to—this wasn't her at all.

"Somewhat intense, isn't it." Calum's deep voice washed over her and brought every nerve to full awareness. She spun around.

He stood so close her breasts crushed into his muscular chest, pulling a moan from her.

A low growl came from him, and he grasped her by the arms, his grip not cruel, just firm enough to send her head spinning. He was strong, so strong, and a leader, and every cell in her body wanted him.

"Now, I'd say you're having trouble because it's your first time, but I am experiencing a definite loss of control as well." His hands slid up and down her arms, and the muskiness of a man reached her. She inhaled, filling her senses with his scent.

He bent and nipped her jaw, sending goosebumps up her arms. "Victoria. Cariad, I would be honored to be your first mating of this, your first Gathering."

When she breathed, "Yes," he lifted her into his arms, carried her into the tavern, and up the stairs.

Chapter Twenty-Three

I N THE TINY room, firelight flicked over a sea of velvety brown cushions, and Vic shivered with need. *Put me there. Take me.*

Calum kicked the door closed and lay her down. His eyes were intense, his gaze a palpable touch, arousing her until she wanted to writhe. She pushed the urge away—*have you no pride, woman?*—and sat up.

His lips curved. "Strong little female." The rumble of his voice was like a hand running down her spine, and she bit her lip, needing him inside her so badly she almost burst into tears. If he didn't do something, she'd completely humiliate herself and beg.

He straddled her legs and lifted her chin, examining her face, her body. "Ah, cariad, it has you good." His thumb rubbed her trembling lips. "We will play no games this time then, little cat. You will have what you require."

With a sure touch, he stripped her of her clothes, and each movement of his firm hands ignited a new spark. Her pussy throbbed; the need for him was growing painful. A shiver ran through her as his masculine scent washed over her. So very male.

He unzipped his jeans. His cock sprang free, long and thick.

Like the trunk of a massive oak on his mountain, it held no curve at all. Her head swam, her needs fighting with her refusal to concede, and she didn't know what to do. Her fingernails dug into her skin, creating sharp pains to join the rest.

He knelt in front of her and pried her fingers loose. "I have never known a female as stubborn or as strong." With his palm, he cupped her cheek. "Look at me, Victoria."

When she met his razor-sharp gaze, her skin heated as if she'd stepped into a sauna. Her hands went limp in his. Smiling slightly, he put them on his shoulders and came down on her, crushing her in the cushions with his solid weight.

Her arms tightened. She smoldered with heat, her nipples so tight that she gasped as his chest flattened them. When his legs pressed hers open, the light dusting of his hair scraped her tender inner thighs. Everywhere he touched burned.

"Calum." The hoarse voice…was hers? She struggled against him for a second, terrified of losing herself completely.

But then his fingers touched her sex, and the feeling was…indescribable, like a band of excitement being drawn taut low in her belly.

His rumble sounded like a purr as he pressed her open. Paused…and then sheathed himself with one thrust.

Everything inside her exploded, the pleasure too intense, engulfing her, battering her. She screamed as the waves of sensation rolled over her mind, drowning her completely.

A second—a minute—a lifetime later—she stared up at his hard face. So strong. Needing to touch, she moved and realized her fingernails had dug into his back. *Wet*. She'd made him bleed. *When?* "I'm sorry."

"I'm not." Amusement rippled through his voice as he nuzzled the crook of her neck.

God, she felt great. All her tension had disappeared, and she'd had a fantastic orgasm.

His black hair lay loose over his shoulders, and she ran her hands through the silky tangles and lifted her face for a kiss. He took her lips leisurely, simply pleasing himself and her until she wiggled in enjoyment. And froze. He was still fully erect inside her. He hadn't come? "Don't you want to…?"

He nuzzled her neck. "I will wait for you."

She gave him a puzzled look.

"I give it about thirty more seconds, and you'll demand that I move."

It took only fifteen.

First her skin grew a billion new nerves until she could feel the slightest brush of hair against her legs, feel his chest rise and fall, how warm his hands were, and the calluses on his palms. The deepness of his voice made her insides clench and when she felt his cock there, still thick and hard, a riptide of lust tried to sweep her away. She clung to sanity. "Calum."

His eyes were hot, yet sparkling with laughter. "Let go, little cat," he whispered, and then…then he started to move. Oh God, she'd never felt anything like it before. A slow slide out and in, setting every nerve rippling awake. A pause. Such a quiet rhythm to send her senses spiraling upward.

The crease in his cheek deepened as he lifted her hips and slammed into her, hard and deep—a pounding shock that pushed her off the cliff into a mindless orgasm.

An hour later, he showered with her in the tiny bathroom, and she wasn't sure if she liked him or hated him. She'd had no control whatsoever over anything he did, yet he'd given her exactly what she wanted. Over and over. He'd set her feet on his shoulders and thrust into her in a hard relentless rhythm that she could still feel inside. Her climax had almost killed her.

But within minutes, she'd roused, needing more. He teased her with his fingers until she couldn't breathe as the orgasm shot through her. After, she'd contentedly snuggled in his arms, and then, as if a switch had turned on, she'd wanted him. He'd simply smiled, rolled her over with merciless hands, and taken her from behind, straight and hard, and she'd screamed her way through another orgasm. And yet again as he released into her, filling her with his hot seed.

After that, she'd felt so satisfied, she figured she'd sleep in the pile of pillows all night, but much too soon, the tingle began in her again. The need to be touched, to be filled. This time, when she'd closed her fingers around him, Calum had stood and lifted her to her feet.

"I've stayed with you longer than I should as it is, cariad," he said and pulled her into the shower.

The splash of hot water over her sensitive skin felt heavenly, and when he washed her back, her breasts...everything, her hips tilted into his hand. "More..."

But he ignored her, dried her off so gently, yet so thoroughly that she ached with need before he finished. Putting on clothes seemed the very height of insanity. "Let's go back to bed."

He shook his head, and she wanted to punch him. "Downstairs, little cat."

Cursing under her breath, she pulled on her clothes. He picked up her boots and socks. He took her hand and led her, barefoot, back down into the noisy tavern. Almost a quarter of the people had disappeared, she noticed. After tossing her boots behind the bar, Calum didn't release her, just moved her across the room to a destination obvious only to him.

"Where are you taking me?" she asked, planting her feet.

He frowned. "I hoped Alec would be here, but—"

"Well, now, he had some emergency that only the sheriff could deal with." Daniel walked up, a beer in each hand. As he handed one to Calum, he tilted his head as if asking a question.

Calum's lips tightened but he nodded. His voice sounded hoarse as he said, "'Tis harder than I thought it would be, but

I'm glad you're here, Daniel."

"Calum?" Worried, Vic ran her hand down his arm. God, he had great muscles. And his hands, the way they'd touched her… She blinked, remembered the question, "Is something wrong?"

"I am only regretting that I must leave you now to the care of others." His eyes had gone black, never a good sign. He framed her face between his strong hands. "But I will stay over there by the bar, cariad, should any problems arise."

Giving Daniel an unreadable look, he kissed Vic quickly and walked away. She took a step after him—

"Vicki, this one's for you, girl." Daniel slid smoothly in front of her and pushed a beer into her hand. When she tried to look around him, he shook his head. "He can't stay with you, sweetie. I'm sorry."

She sighed. "You guys have too many rules." Dammit, she felt lost without him, and she needed him and—

Daniel moved close enough she could feel the warmth of his body. She had to tilt her head to look up at him. He was a werebear, she remembered, and built like one. Big and powerful. His sleeves were rolled up showing forearms thick with muscle. "Muscles…" she whispered.

"I have a fondness for women with muscles too." He ran a finger up her bare arm over her biceps.

She shivered at the feeling.

"Don't you like the beer I brought you?"

"Oh—oh, yeah." She *was* holding a bottle, wasn't she? The cold malty liquid slid down her throat, and she closed her eyes at the marvelous taste of it. "That's wonderful," she murmured.

Opening her eyes, she met his intent gaze, his blue gaze hot as molten steel. He leaned forward and licked a few drops off her lip, the touch of his tongue velvety. His musky scent enveloped her, touched her skin as if he'd stroked over her with his hands.

"Um." She shook her head. *Get a grip. It's only lust.* Horny, she'd felt horny before, for God's sake.

Another man came over, nudged Daniel to one side, and earned himself a slight snarl. "My name is Harvey," he said, pressing a kiss to her wrist.

She snatched her hand back, all her tingles abruptly cooling. She scowled before conquering her irritation. "Yeah. Um. Nice to meet you," she managed, and glancing over at Daniel, her gaze locked onto his again. His lips curved slowly. He should put those lips on hers. On her.

Unable to resist, she ran her finger over his mouth, silky soft, then down over his square jaw. The slight rasp made her shiver.

"Upstairs?" he whispered, "or do you want to talk for a while first." His fingers toyed with her hair, the little touches like sparks against her skin.

"Tal—" *Hell with it.* "Upstairs."

How many tiny rooms did this place contain? This one had red pillows in every size and shape and texture. Taking her beer from her, Daniel set it on a table in the corner of the room. Just watching his movements with the slight swagger of a cowboy weakened her knees. She sank down to the floor. This was total insanity.

"Hey, hey," Daniel murmured, kneeling before her. "I know it's overwhelming the first time, especially for you, being new to shifter customs." He pulled her against his chest, stroking her hair. "We can go as easy as you like."

"How long does this last?"

"From moonrise to moonset. With dawn, everything returns to normal."

She could hear his heart, slow and steady, the feel of his hard muscles against her cheek. His scent. She frowned. His scent was wrong; his hands were wrong. *Not Alec; not Calum.*

Suddenly she pushed away, unable to find enough air.

He released her and didn't move, only tilted his head. His nostrils flared, and then he frowned. "One minute you want me, the next you don't."

"I…" God, she'd wanted to come up here. She'd led him on. "I like you. I do." Yet the thought of having sex with him totally turned her off. "I'm sorry, Daniel."

"Me, too." He gave her a wry smile. "But scent doesn't lie."

The lust faded from his face as he helped her to her feet, putting little kisses on her fingers. Who knew a cowboy could be so romantic and gentle? He led her back downstairs. Men crowded around her again, pushing him to the side. She saw Calum talking with one man in the corner and keeping an eye on the proceedings. To her horror, her need was growing stronger. She caught his gaze and glanced upstairs. Heat flashed in his eyes before he shook his head with a regretful smile.

Bastard.

She looked at the guys in front of her. Two older and a younger one with the look of a gaunt wolf. Then a man stalked across the room. Hard and rough-looking, like a younger Thorson with scars white against his deeply tanned neck and arms. At least six foot five, he wore black jeans and a black leather vest with nothing underneath. His dark brown eyes were watchful, prepared for anything, and every move he made shouted danger. Strength. He halted before he reached her, and she saw him glance at Calum, lift his eyebrows.

Calum tilted his head in approval or permission—she wasn't sure.

The man's shadowed eyes settled on her, and she couldn't move. Two of the other men melted away, leaving an older, harder man still standing his ground.

"I am Zeb of the Rainier Territory, and I would be pleased to fight you for this female, to show my strength and win her favors," the scarred one said, moving close enough that she could inhale his dark scent. His eyes never left his opponent although his fingers traced a slow path down her cheek.

She leaned into his hand.

The other hesitated, shook his head. "Cahir from Rainier, I regret. I've heard of you." And he withdrew.

"May I take you somewhere, share time with you?" Zeb lifted her wrist, pressed a kiss over her pulse, and inhaled. Smiled.

The wave of lust burst over her, and she closed her eyes, trying to find her footing. When she opened them, his gaze met hers, intent, watchful. "I—I seem to have trouble talking," she managed. "I don't know what's wrong with me." He hadn't released her hand, and the way his thumb stroked over her palm made her melt inside.

He stiffened. "I hadn't realized—you are the new shifter."

She managed a nod, feeling like she would drown in his eyes, in his scent. "I can't—"

"Tell me your name." He moved closer and wrapped an arm around her.

She purred at his touch. "Vicki."

His fingers ran through her hair, a gentle caress. His voice was still deep, yet gentled. "I have heard a woman's first Gathering is a downpour of heat and sensation." He smiled slowly, "You'll gain control with experience. But since you only get one first Gather, let us both enjoy." And he lifted her into his arms with a roar that stilled the room.

Upstairs, as he laid her on the silky green cushions, she cooled, filling with horror. *Dear God, I don't even know this man.* She rolled to a sitting position and pulled her legs to her chest. She didn't have to do this—she could stay in control. Really.

He touched her lightly on the hair, and then, after tossing his vest to one side, built up the fire. Once it blazed up, he sat back on his haunches and watched her, his eyes intent, reminding her of a wolf waiting for a rabbit to move. To run.

He had a scar like Alec's, a blue knife mark across his right cheekbone. Her gaze dropped, seeing the heavy scarring on his arms and shoulders. She frowned. The guy was a walking war zone. What had caused all that?

His eyes narrowed. "Do the scars bother you, little female? Do I scare you?" Before she could speak, he snagged her ankle and pulled her over the cushions to him like a captured puppy.

She was no puppy. With her free foot, she snap-kicked his hand off her leg.

The bastard not only didn't wince, he actually grinned.

"I'm not little." She rolled onto her knees. "I just wondered what caused scarring like that." With fingertips, she traced one thin white line down his shoulder. Thanks to Lachlan, she recognized the marks of teeth on his arms and other shoulder.

Lots of white scars, a few were tiny and thin, parallel like Alec and Thorson's cat marks, three very thick ones extended all the way across his heavily muscled upper chest. When she ran her finger over them, he hummed in pleasure, and his six-pack of abdominal muscles tightened.

"Many of the scars—like those—are from hellhound claws." His voice was low, a little rough. "Rainier Territory has hellhounds. So far few have invaded the Cascade Territory." He lifted her fingers to his lips and nipped from the tips up the outside of her hand.

"Mmmmh." Her senses started to burn, then cooled again, leaving her feeling as if she had hormonal whiplash. "What are hellhounds?"

"New little shifter, you are not only fearless, but are trying to fight your need. I'm impressed." His smile gleamed white in his tanned face before he wrapped a hand behind her neck and held her still, kissing her so thoroughly, her mind whirled. Before she could recover, he rolled her onto her back with relentless hands and straddled her.

"Hellhounds?" she managed.

"I enjoy teaching, so I will instruct you"—he clasped the bottom of her shirt—"as we progress. Hellhounds are magical, like the Daonain, only their ancestors bred with demons." His smile went savage. "They chose the dark path."

He set his hand on her breast and everything in her went still. Cold. *This is wrong.* He was wrong. He smelled wrong.

He froze and frowned down at her. Inhaled slowly. And suddenly he'd moved off to squat beside her, dark eyes studying her. "You no longer want me."

"I…" God, how could she do this to someone again? "I'm sorry."

He shook his head. "What is, is. But I had looked forward to having you."

"There's a lot of women down there." She felt like an idiot, trying to console a man for not being able to fuck her. "I'd think you'd have plenty to enjoy. The men seemed to be having fun."

"Many do, yes." His gaze shifted away. "I prefer the fighting."

Huh. There were times she'd rather fight too, especially when she felt her emotions were at risk. Odd how she could see that now—after Calum and Alec. With the thought, everything in her longed for her two men. She pulled her mind back with an effort. "Don't want to let anyone too close?"

From his flinch, she'd say she'd scored a hit. And, then he added a comment that almost broke her heart, "I scare women. If the shifter urge to mate with the strongest didn't drive their need, most would run screaming back to their caves."

"Wussies."

He barked a surprised laugh. His dark eyes held a warmth that would lure any woman in. He touched her cheek. "I like you."

Pulling her to her feet with one swift move, he led her back downstairs to the center of the tavern. She felt the snap as the men's attention turned to her, but Zeb wrapped an arm around her and stood in place. She glanced at him.

"Somehow you arouse my protective instincts," he said, frowning. "I want that you get someone worthy. From the way the Cosantir watches you, but doesn't claim you, I think he's already had you tonight?"

She stared across the room at Calum. His black hair was still tangled from her fingers, marks from her fingernails welted his neck. Arms crossed over his chest, he leaned on the bar top…a master of stillness, yet an aura of danger seemed to surround him. The memory of upstairs and how ruthless he'd been sent so much heat through her that the very air she breathed turned thick.

Zeb grinned, ran his fingers down her flushed cheek. "Oookay. Seems the North Cascade Cosantir is as good as his rep." He glanced to where Calum stood at the end of the bar. She could almost feel the impact when Calum's black eyes met his, and he grunted as if gut-punched. "I pity the poor bastard who pisses that Cosantir off."

His arm turned her in the other direction. "The rancher's gone, but maybe the wolves' alpha male? Ah, wait, there's another cahir."

Her gaze followed his. *Alec.* Powerfully built, big bones and heavy muscles. So very strong. He was leaning against a table in that deceptively lazy stance. People saw his easy smile, not the danger beneath it. Like a crackling fire, he looked all cheerful warmth…and could burn you to a crisp if you weren't careful. She wanted him—kissing her, on top of her, pushing inside. She took a step toward him.

"Ah, she approves," Zeb said. "I agree. He's a good choice—unless the brunette snags him first."

Brunette? When Vic spotted the over-abundant Sarah from Elder Village, her sensuous overload disappeared as if it had never been. The bitch was rubbing her breasts on Alec, touching him, trying to kiss him.

A snarl rumbled through Vic's chest and escaped. She heard Zeb murmur, "Uh-oh."

Men stepped quickly out of her way as she stalked across the tavern floor, rage searing her insides. She stopped behind the bitch.

Alec said, "I'm not participating tonight, Sarah. Sorry. I—"

But Cleavage wasn't hearing him. Her plump hand ran up his chest, and then that soft hand was in Vic's hard grip. Sarah gasped and tried to yank away.

"Hands-off," Vic gritted. "Mine."

Sarah gave a shriek like a wounded cow. "You can't have him. He's going to be *my* lifemate!" And the woman swung her free hand. Her open hand.

A girlie slap? Vic growled with outrage, blocking automatically. Then she punched the skanky slut so hard that the bitch took out two men on her way ass-over-teakettle. Still growling, Vic crossed her arms, glared around the room, and repeated, "Mine."

No one moved. Behind her, Alec was laughing so hard he was choking.

On her right flank, Zeb gave her a long look before saying to Alec, "I would that I was you."

"Thank you, cahir," Alec said, still gasping for breath. He grinned at Zeb, and then frowned. Sniffed.

"She refused me, and I believe the one before me." Zeb tugged a lock of Vic's hair. "Her choice seems to be made."

Alec didn't touch her, just stared at her. "You had no one tonight?"

She flushed. "Calum and I…did," she muttered. "Not the others. I couldn't."

As Zeb walked away, Alec lifted Vic's hand and bit her palm, sending a bolt of lust through her.

She stepped closer, rubbed her face against his, marking him with her scent. "Mine."

He tipped her head back and took her mouth so thoroughly, she sagged in his grip. "Yours."

Alec had taken her upstairs, and oh God, no problem with the heat disappearing. It rose so fast and encompassing that she'd actually begged him to take her.

He had, hard and fast, no teasing—he pounded her into a screaming climax. A few minutes later, he did it again. And again before showering with her as Calum had and leading her back downstairs. Damn him.

This time, even though men surrounded her, nothing happened. The heat simmered inside her, keeping her uncomfortable and wanting, but no one who approached made it rise. She wanted Alec. Wanted Calum. Every time she caught the sound of their voices or their scents, she clenched inside, hollow and hurting. Needing to be filled.

Finally, after forever, Joe Thorson strolled into the tavern. She blinked at him. Hadn't someone said he didn't attend Gatherings any more? He headed toward Calum, but an older woman abandoned the younger men around her to step into his path. When she imperiously held out her hand, Joe barked a laugh and took her upstairs.

Vic saw Calum and Alec exchange looks and grin.

When Joe came back downstairs, he went directly to Calum. They talked for a few minutes, then Joe assumed Calum's spot at the bar.

What was going on?

Calum nodded at Alec, then looked at her, his gaze dark and possessive. Hot. He stalked across the room, a predator focused on his prey. On her. She felt a shiver deep inside.

Alec closed in on her other side, dwarfing her with his size. Her gaze lifted, moving over his broad, muscular chest, shoulders twice the size of hers, his strong corded neck, to be caught by his heavy-lidded stare. Her need blazed, as out of control as a burning city.

"Victoria," Calum said, taking her other hand. "We're going upstairs. Together this time."

Both of them? As Alec lifted her into his steely arms, heat pumped through her veins until the air itself shimmered.

In a tiny upstairs room, he dropped her onto fuzzy yellow cushions, grinning when she bounced.

Her insides tingled as she laughed. Sex with him was always so warm and joyful, like making love in the sun.

Calum caught her gaze, and his aura of power—and danger—made her shiver. Sex with Calum was like making love in a forest at night, dark and shadowy and rich.

She wanted them both more than she could bear. She held her arms up.

Alec pulled her shirt off, and then kissed her, his lips teasing despite the hard grip of his hands on her upper arms. Calum dragged her jeans off. No boots, no underwear—and she delighted in how quickly they got her naked.

Pushing her thighs apart, Calum stroked between her legs, finding her center, skillfully teasing her until she moaned, her hips lifting to him.

"I need to taste," Alec growled.

"No," Vic shook her head. "I want you inside me. Now." She ached with excitement. "Hard and fast like before."

"Nope. Last time we went straight for the finish line. We're going slower this round." Alec stripped, taking his time, driving her mad.

Already unclothed, Calum sat down behind her, his legs around her hips, his feet on the outside of her knees. His rigid erection pressed into the crack between her buttocks, sending more cravings through her. His muscular chest rubbed her back. She was surrounded by his body. His heady masculine scent. *Oh God.*

His arms crossed in front of her, securing her in his grip, and he leaned back onto a pile of pillows, pulling her into a half-reclining position.

"Calum, no."

"Yes," he whispered in her ear. His big hands secured her so she couldn't move. "You will let Alec enjoy your taste. After that, we will have you as many times as it takes to exhaust you. And us." His teeth closed on her shoulder, painful and so erotic that she moaned.

Despite her resistance, Alec's strong hands pulled her legs apart.

"No, Alec, I want you inside—"

"Give me her left ankle," Calum interrupted. When Alec complied, he gripped her ankle, holding her leg high, opening her. The cool air brushed the wetness on her pussy and down the insides of her thighs.

Alec grinned. "Thank you, brawd. Nice and exposed." He slid down between her legs, his face over her pelvis. His fingers framed her sex, spreading her labia, pulling the hood up and away from her clit. "God, you're pretty, Vixen, and very swollen." When he blew on her, every sensitive nerve fired, and she arched.

He gave a growling laugh. "Your clit's sitting right out there for me to torture." And he slid his tongue over her, slow and hot and wet.

She choked on a scream and another when his tongue pushed into her entrance before sliding back over the tight nub. Her legs jerked uncontrollably, but he had one pinned under his weight and Calum held the other.

"Dammit, I want to be fucked." Her insides ached, needing more, and Alec's teasing would drive her mad. "You assholes," she spat.

When she fought to sit up, Calum's arm around her waist tightened. "You had what you needed earlier," he murmured. "Now we will enjoy our female…and you will take it." He closed his free hand over her breast, calluses scraping over the nipple.

More heat shot through her. She growled. "You fucking—"

"Alec, please reprimand her," he said.

Teeth nipped just inside her knee, making her jolt. Another bite. Another as he worked his way in a line up her inner thigh. It hurt, only with each sharp pain, her clit tightened more, throbbing in anticipation.

His lips closed over the exposed nub.

"Ahhh!" Her hips strained upward. God, his mouth was hot, his tongue… She was so close…

He backed off, the bastard. His tongue wandered down her labia and pushed into her vagina. She wiggled uncontrollably.

He stopped.

With a low hum that sounded like a purr, Calum fondled her left breast. His fingers rolled her nipple, squeezing until her muscles started to tighten with the pain, and released. His fingertips danced over the aching peak, sending fire streaking right down to her pussy.

As if following the fire, Alec licked circles around her clit, and then brushed his tongue over the straining top, putting her right on the edge. *Oh God, please.*

He lifted his head, and Calum moved his attention to her other breast, leaving the first swollen and tight. Over and over. Exquisite pain from Calum, unbearable pleasure from Alec. The air seemed thick and hot, and everything they did drew her closer to a climax, one she couldn't stop. Couldn't control. She was shaking in Calum's arms.

Almost….

Calum kissed her shoulders. "A little closer, but don't let her come, brawd. I want us buried inside her when she does."

Alec chuckled. "She's going to hurt you for this tomorrow, you know."

A nip on her earlobe made her jolt. "She'll be busy running."

She didn't get a chance to ask what he meant before Alec's mouth closed over her clit, the heat, the wet, his tongue flickering up one side and down the other. "Oh God." Her hips strained upward, and he set his forearm across her pelvis, keeping her in place. Her whole body shook as she quivered, needing…needing.

"That's about right," Calum said.

When Alec sat up, she moaned. Her clit felt as if it had grown too large for her skin, pulling painfully.

As Calum released her, Alec took her hands and pulled her down on top of him. "A soft female body. Very nice." He curved his hand over her nape and kissed her.

His cock was hard beneath her, jutting toward his stomach. With a groan, she squirmed on it. "Inside me. Now."

He snorted. "You have no patience at all, do you?"

"No." *Damn men. Have to do it all myself.* She moved to impale herself, felt the head of his cock at her center and—

"Not yet. Up you go, lass," Calum said. He lifted her up, so she straddled Alec on hands and knees, butt in the air and yay too far from his cock. She ground her teeth together. Dammit, she needed more, or she'd burst with her need.

Alec stroked his hands down her body, over her hips, then cupped her ass. To her shock, as he pulled her cheeks apart, something cold trickled down between them.

Lube. She stiffened. They'd both teased her there, slowly increasing from one to two or three fingers. But if he had lube… Her head came up. "Wait… No. No, Calum."

"You can do this, little cat," Calum said. His finger slid into her back hole, pushing ruthlessly past the puckered ring as Alec's hands anchored her. The finger moved slowly in and out, igniting nerves. Confusing her. Her instincts screamed for a cock in her vagina, not something…there. This wasn't right. "Calum," she whined. "No."

"Good girl," Calum murmured and pulled out only to add another finger. Two fingers, stretching her, nothing unfamiliar. She looked down. Alec was watching her intently. He gave her a smile of encouragement. When Calum withdrew, she took a breath.

More lube chilled her skin, making her jerk, even before Calum pressed the head of his shaft against her anus. Slick, but it still hurt as it pushed in. So big. Stretching and burning, and she shivered as he entered, so very slowly.

Too big. Not quite pain—she knew how to handle pain. This was more…primal. Having Calum take her was far more dominating than anything before, as if he'd removed the last bit of control from her. He'd left her nothing private, had made everything open to him. *He has all the control; I have none.* Somehow the realization was more erotic than anything she'd ever felt before.

She felt Calum's hands stroked her back, petting her. "Breathe, cariad. Take all of me." He pushed deeper.

Her head bowed, as the discomfort grew. Her fingernails dug into Alec's shoulders, and she moaned, her mind filled with confusion, need, and pain.

Finally, she felt his groin press against her buttocks. He was in. "Are you all right, little cat?" Calum asked softly. His hands replaced Alec's on her hips. He moved in and out of her ever so slowly, his gentleness at odds with his implacable grip on her hips.

Totally unsure, she nodded anyway, feeling…taken. Vulnerable. Terrified—and excited—by what they'd do next. Her bottom burned, overwhelming any other sensation, and a tremor ran up her spine, knowing Calum was deep inside that dark place.

As she trembled, Alec moved his hands, holding her face between them gently. His dark green gaze was filled with heat, yet so caring that tears pricked her eyes.

"Brawd," Calum said, "why don't you give her something else to think about before you start?"

Alec smiled. "Good plan." The fingers of one hand tangled in her hair, holding her face close to his. His free hand moved between them, right to her pussy. One finger swirled in her wetness, then up to her clit, teasing the hood, the top, until the nub engorged, overcoming any other sensation.

Her hips tried to tilt forward, but she was secured in place by Calum's shaft deep inside her, by his restraining hands. She shook as her need built up inside. Her insides tightened, wanting to be fucked, but there was a cock in her *ass*, so foreign and wrong. "Oh, God, I can't take this."

Calum deep baritone held amusement. "You will, cariad. For us."

Alec's finger circled her entrance. "You're nice and wet for me, Vixen," he murmured, and her eyes widened as his erection nudged at the entrance to her vagina.

"No." She was already too full. She tried to push away, but Calum was immovable behind her. In her. Her legs still straddled Alec's hips, holding her pussy open. Calum's hard hands tightened on her hips, securing her completely—and sending another wave of heat through her.

Alec pushed in, just an inch, and she gasped at the unbearable tightness. As the head slid in farther, the burning nerves from Calum's penetration joined with the ones sparking from Alec's slow slide. Everything down there throbbed and burned.

Alec worked in slowly against her resisting flesh, not stopping, never stopping.

She groaned. The stretch of her anus, the overwhelming sensations from being taken by two cocks, the hard hands holding her for their pleasure. It was too much. Every nerve seemed to be shooting off in different directions.

"Easy, little cat," Calum murmured. "Take a breath."

"Oh God, you—"

He leaned forward, his arm wrapping around her hip. He set his hand on her pussy. She jerked as he unerringly found her clit, exposed completely with Alec's cock inside her, holding her folds open. His slick finger rubbed firmly on one side of the engorged ball of nerves, and then the other until her head started to spin.

She wiggled, trying for more, for less. Alec fondled her dangling breasts, teasing her nipples, rolling them between his fingers until heat streamed down through her. When she clenched around two—two—cocks, it felt so different, so strange, hurting, and yet contorted the appalling pleasure into an overwhelming sensation. Too much fullness inside, her clit being stroked, her nipples pinched. Her hands fisted as everything in her blazed upward and even the slight pain turned to pleasure.

"Now, Alec," Calum growled, and he moved for the first time, pulling his cock almost out of her ass. Emptiness. Then as he slid back in, he drew her toward him…and off of Alec's cock. Different fullness, new emptiness.

Alec's hands tightened on her hips and yanked her down onto him—and Calum slid out. They controlled her, moving her back and forth between them, their thrusts growing in force even as she shook, the pleasure too much to bear, to process. The climax rolled toward her like an Abrams tank, crushing her mind under the massive wave of sensation.

"Oh God, oh fuck, ohhhhhh." She heard herself, and it

didn't matter as everything around her dissolved. Her world blew apart, brutal unstoppable pleasure shaking her like a rag doll. A minute later, Calum drove in hard for his release, and she could actually feel his hot seed fill her.

Then Alec yanked her down onto his cock, and he growled as he jerked inside her, sending more waves of pleasure to shake her.

She was panting and sobbing. Her trembling arms gave out and her shoulders dropped onto Alec's chest. His hands closed on her waist. "Roll, brawd."

Calum anchored himself in her, and tipped them all over onto their sides. They kept her sandwiched between them, both still deep inside. Softening, but serving as another anchor in their possession.

Alec kissed her lips, using his thumbs to wipe the tears from her cheeks. "Shhh, baby, shhh."

With her back to his chest, Calum held her firmly, and his arms around her felt as if he kept her from shattering. He was crooning into her hair, a quiet rumble of pleasure and soothing.

She never felt so vulnerable, so shaken... *So cherished.*

Chapter Twenty-Four

THE HEADY AROMA of coffee wafted through the cabin as Vic blinked awake. Morning, huh? The night had ended.

God, the way last night's events were hazed over, she felt as if she'd gotten drunk.

They'd eventually left the little room in the tavern and gone downstairs. She'd seen Heather in the hallway of the tavern. Her friend had waved and laughed when Alec and Calum had pulled Vic down into the cave. The men had stripped her naked and dragged her out into the freezing night, as she spit curses at them.

But then… She sighed. In cougar form, they'd played in the last of the moonlight, chased each other through the mountains and valleys, tussled in the snow, and run together—Calum on the right of her, Alec on the left. The world had been beautiful…magical.

Now morning had arrived. Magic all gone. Back to reality. She poked her nose out of her warm cocoon of blankets and considered the chill in the room. Maybe she'd give it another hour. Surely one of the guys would put a bigger log on?

"She's awake." Alec's voice.

"Do you suppose she will join us sometime today before the sun goes down?" Calum's dry tone.

Hell, that was known as peer pressure. And it worked, dammit. She flung the quilts back, shivering as the cold air touched her nice warm body.

The guys sat at the little table wearing only their jeans. God, would she ever get tired of looking at them? Alec's broad chest had a light golden furring over his thick pectorals. Calum's silky chest hair contoured his sleek muscles. Her fingers tingled with the need to touch—until she saw the red scratches across their chests. Bite marks on their shoulders. Had she done that?

Flushing, she rolled over and buried her head. Various aches roused with her movement. Her leg muscles complained that she'd run all the way up a damned mountain. Her breasts felt tender and swollen, and every private part down below was extremely sensitive. Her asshole held a lingering burn as if reminding her of how Calum had taken her.

Then the rest of her memories of the night returned with horrifying clarity. First she'd bedded Calum, and…she'd actually let Daniel drag her upstairs. Had wanted him, at least for a while. And the guy named Zeb… *Fucking-A*. She'd acted like some nympho with a broken on/off switch, and she wasn't sure whether she should feel guilty about going upstairs with Daniel and Zeb—or saying no to them. Hell.

How could Calum or Alec think she cared after she'd enthusiastically flirted with those other men? Although Zeb had told Alec that nothing happened, but why would Alec believe him?

Could she tell them she'd never realized there was a difference between fucking and making love? And, didn't that sound lame? But true. Because it wasn't just the physical stuff. Sex with Alec and Calum touched everything: her emotions, her spirit, her mind. Yeah, like they were the whole orchestra after listening to just the piano, changing a sweet melody to something rich and immense. But damned if she could explain that.

With a sigh, she knotted a blanket around her and rose to

her feet. Unable to face them yet, she held her hands out to the fire.

"Victoria?" Calum's deep voice.

She shook her head without turning.

"Told you she'd be embarrassed." Alec's footsteps padded toward her—and when had she become able to tell his gait from Calum's?

"Vixen?" He set his hands on her shoulders, and when she didn't answer, pulled her back against his bare chest. "You thinking about last night?"

Okay, she was braver than this. She wasn't a little girl unable to fess up to her actions. She'd done the deed—deeds—and now it was time to pay the piper. She stared into the fire and confessed, "I almost went to bed with Daniel. And Zeb."

When he heard the guilt in Victoria's voice, Calum closed his eyes. His littermate had been right. She was more than embarrassed; she felt she'd done something wrong. He crossed the room. A glance at Alec, and his brother turned her from the fire to face Calum.

Her lower lip trembled, but her gaze was level, and he could only marvel at her courage. He'd never loved her more.

"I went upstairs with Daniel and with Zeb too. Nothing happened, but…I wanted it to. At first." She looked away and back at him. "You two didn't…go with anyone else. But I did."

"Didn't Heather talk with you yesterday?" Alec asked, one hand stroking up and down her arm.

She nodded.

Calum frowned. Heather had promised she'd go over everything. He could have explained, or Alec, but they'd decided a female friend would be more believable than the two men who wanted her so badly. What would she have thought when they said, *Go to bed with anyone you want, especially us two—that's what shifters do. Really.* "Heather told you what happens during a

Gathering?"

"Uh-huh." She bit her lip. "But you two didn't—"

He dared to move closer and stroke her cheek. "When a female comes into heat, the need to join with a male can't be controlled, cariad. Your instincts are to mate, and to whatever males are the best. Or who appeal to you most. To limit yourself to one—or even two—is impossible unless you're lifemated."

When a frown appeared on her forehead, relief eased the tightness in his gut. She was thinking, not reacting.

"But you two—" she started to repeat.

He glanced at Alec, and his silver-tongued, cowardly brother jerked his chin for Calum to continue. "Indeed, we did not join with anyone else." He let a wry smile appear. "Males do not come into heat. The scent of a female's arousal is all we need. But as the years go on, the desire to mate with every interested female begins to flag. Alec and I are no longer cubs, and we are very much in love with you. Last night, you were the only one we could see."

The glimmer of tears in her eyes was shocking. Terrifying. What had he said wrong?

"I…care about you too. And Alec. But I still went upstairs with—"

Alec picked her up in his arms and sank down into the blankets. "You're not hearing him. Shut up and listen, Vixen."

She stiffened, her gaze meeting Alec's eyes, and then she sighed. "You're right. Okay."

Calum sat beside them. He pressed a kiss to her wrist, felt the tiny pulse throbbing away. "For our race to continue, a woman needs to mate with many, Victoria. And we recognize that. We honor that. The Gatherings are not only biological, they're traditional."

"I really didn't do anything wrong?" She bit her lip.

She looked so like a little girl for a moment that Calum had a flash of how appealing her children would be.

"And," she continued, "neither of you are mad at me? Or at Daniel, or—"

Alec gave a short laugh. "What's there to get mad at? You can't fight biology, Vixen."

"You really aren't," she said wonderingly. "Okay. Well, okay." She tipped her head back to kiss Alec and bestowed one on Calum.

"I very much needed that," Calum murmured. "I was quite worried there."

"Me, too." Victoria took a deep breath. "Where I come from, what I did—well."

"You wanted the other men—and then you didn't. That shows you've formed an attachment. To us." Calum nodded at Alec. His brother set Victoria gently onto the blankets, and went to rummage in the small pack he'd carried up the mountain.

Finding it hard to think, Calum continued. "Some people set up households. Much like human marriages."

"Heather told me. And that sometimes there were more than just one man, one woman." She stared at her hands. "I was glad, since I... I..."

Calum's heart gave a massive thud. "Since?"

She scowled at the floor, then at him, her hands fisting. "How can this be so fucking hard to say?" Her mouth firmed and her chin came up and she looked like Joan of Arc heading for the fires. "Okay. Listen up—I love you. And Alec. Both of you."

She pressed her hand over her chest, wheezing a little.

It took all Calum's control not to just grab her right then. Alec, finally, returned—the slow bastard—and handed Calum a lifemating bracelet, keeping one for himself. They knelt together, shoulder to shoulder, as they'd spent their life. The rightness of it made Calum's throat tighten.

Victoria's eyes had widened. "What—"

Alec cleared his throat, his eyes suspiciously shiny. "Vicki. We love you—both of us love you. And—"

Calum opened his hand, showed her the thin bracelet of tiny silvery discs held together with interlaced strands of special elastic. "Will you be our lifemate?"

Oh. My. God. Vic wrapped her arms around herself, unable to speak. The brothers knelt in front of her, Alec like a golden god, Calum a dark lord, both powerfully masculine. The most courageous, honorable men she'd ever known. Honest. Caring. *And they want me.*

She'd never thought she'd find a family outside of the military. But…they wanted her. Alec's eyes had no laughter in them, just…need. He needed her and Calum… His gaze was steady, controlled, but she could see—when had she learned to read him so well?—could see he needed her too. And loved her. They wanted her in their lives. Even as her throat tightened, tingling fireworks were going off in her chest. *Yes, yes, yes.*

No. Think, Sergeant. Could she accept? Really? But the idea of saying no was intolerable, and her answer escaped before she talked herself out of it. "Oh, yes. Yes, yes. Fucking-A, yes."

Alec grinned at Calum. "I think that means she accepts." He grabbed the knot on her blanket, yanking her forward to kiss her, oh, so sweetly. "I love you, Vixen," he whispered.

And then Calum pulled her toward him. He framed her face with his hands, seemed about to say something, and kissed her instead. Tender and yet with that unconscious demand that she offer all of herself. He raised his head and traced her wet lips with one finger, then said, "Give me your hand."

She put her fingers in his, and when he slid the bracelet onto her left arm and pressed a kiss to her wrist, her eyes blurred with tears.

"My turn." Alec cupped her face, using his thumbs to wipe

away the wetness. He took her hand and slid his bracelet onto the same wrist. "I've wanted to do this for so long," he muttered, making her laugh before she kissed him.

"Now you." Alec handed her two larger bracelets.

Her eyes widened. "I get to tag you as mine?" *Damn right.* When they offered their left hands, she slid one on each man, admired the glinting discs against the dark and golden skin. "Hey. What happens when we trawsfur?"

Alec's smile was almost lethal. "We'll show you. In a bit." Grinning, he hauled her out of the blankets. "Why don't you have something to eat? Calum and I need to chop up some firewood before we leave."

Leave huh? She sighed. Reality always came too soon. After she took care of necessities, washed up, and dressed, she found that they'd left a pot of soup simmering on the fire. Coffee. Soup. Not a bad breakfast.

As the men came back in, stomping snow off their boots, she blinked at the view through the open door. The last rays of the sun showed in the west. "I slept all day?"

Calum joined her at the table, nuzzling her neck. "We thought you'd never wake up. How do you feel?"

"Fine." Her eyes narrowed at his odd expression. "Why?" she asked suspiciously. Why were they watching her as if she was a fresh-baked chocolate chip cookie?

Alec came up behind her, wrapped his arms around her. "The bracelets show we're lifemated—married, so to speak. Tonight is"—he thought for a second—"kind of a bonus ritual. If everyone in the lifemating is the same animal, like we're all werecats, then there's a special magic for us."

"Like what?"

Calum glanced at Alec, smiled slightly. "You'll see."

"Let's go play in the snow," Alec said, his voice hoarse.

Again? "Excuse me, but it's really cold out there, guys. I don't feel like freezing my ass o—"

Calum's eyes were intent. "Strip, cariad. Now."

Her nipples tightened under the power of his gaze, and heat unfurled inside her. Protest? Hell, no. *Sir, yes, sir.* She pulled her shirt over her head, then the rest.

Following suit, the men dropped their clothing on the floor and dragged her out the door.

Fuck, it couldn't be more than twenty degrees. She shivered, her feet burning on the frozen ground. *Forget sex; find me a fire.* She backed up to the threshold.

Calum's eyes caught hers, darkened. "Trawsfur. Now."

It felt as if he'd shoved her through that weird shifter door in her head. How did he *do* that? The tingling washed over her skin, sank deep inside, and she could almost feel her bones changing. She dropped to all fours and chuffed a complaint at him. But at least the snow didn't freeze her paws. Her lifemating bracelets gleamed on her front leg, half-buried in thick tawny fur, and delight washed away her irritation.

Still in human form, Alec leaned over, stroked her back. As his scent curled around her, heady and powerful, she purred and butted her head against his bare leg. He put his hand underneath her muzzle. "Vixen," he said. His grin was carnal. Dangerous. "*Run.*"

Without him? It must be part of the ritual. So she leaped away, bounding up the mountain, the snow flying behind her. Her muscles stretched and warmed, and a minute later, she heard the men behind her. The scent of their musk on the wind changed something inside her and heated her blood. Her leaps grew longer, stronger.

A shadow—Calum's dark fur—flashed through the trees to her left. He ran in front of her, his powerful grace mesmerizing.

She barely saw a movement to the right before it struck, blindsiding her, and tumbling her onto her side. Her paws scrambled uselessly in the snow for a second. Too long.

Even as she rolled back onto her stomach, the golden cougar was on her. *Alec.* His teeth closed on her neck, holding her securely. His front paws wrapped around her, pinning her in place, and heat rose within her at the feel of his body on top of hers. She yowled, almost maddened by the all-consuming craving that roared through her. His purr deafened her ears as she lifted her hind quarters to him, need gripping her even more savagely than his claws.

He entered her, long, hot, and hard, almost painful with his urgency. She took him in, filled with him, the feeling dizzying. And suddenly, they were human, her breasts swayed with his thrusts, her hands buried in the snow. His grip—human fingers—tightened on her hips as he hammered into her from the rear, deep and fast. She braced herself on her forearms, pushing back to meet him. Each thrust sent shivers through her, the sensations more and more compelling, until she screamed as she exploded, coming over and over in massive shudders.

With the roar of a conqueror, he spasmed inside her, filling her with hot seed.

Shaken at the suddenness of the mating, the strangeness, she could only quiver under him and try to get her thoughts together.

As he withdrew, she hissed at the emptiness, the loss.

He rumbled a laugh. "Our mate." He kissed her cheek before standing. As the moonlight glinted over his skin, he blurred into a cougar again. She felt the tingle and without warning, she was in animal shape.

Confused, she started to turn to face him. *What the hell is going on?* He bit her sharply on her hind leg, then again, spurring her up the mountain.

Bastard male. Running hard, she left him behind. She didn't need him, didn't need anyone, only herself and her powerful body. The moon rose over the eastern peaks, flooding the snow-filled forest with an eerie glow. The air was sharp enough to cut and scented with pine. Her blood sang joyfully with the rhythm of her paws.

As she ran beneath a cliff, something moved on the overhang, and a dark cougar landed on her, pinning her flat.

Calum. His muzzle rubbed over her fur, engulfing her in his scent, before he sank his teeth into her neck. She lunged forward, trying to escape, and his claws curled into her sides in warning. His fierceness sent need sizzling in her veins even as his heavy weight pinned her in place. Heat blazed through her, and she lifted up to receive his savage thrust.

Oh God. His penetration blasted awake every nerve ending, and she pushed up higher.

As his cock hammered into her, somehow, somewhen, they shifted to human, and his bare chest rubbed against her back. His hands were implacable on her hips, not letting her move or evade him. He was hard and thick, filling her almost too full, and she was still sensitive from Alec's use. His fingers found her breasts, her nipples, pinching just enough to send hot jolts of pleasure to her core. The burning inside grew, pulsing with his thrusts, becoming unendurable. His knees pressed hers outward until she opened fully, and he could slide into her even deeper.

Panting, she tried to move, but one arm curled around her stomach to hold her in place. Growling, he slowed, each stroke sending her closer. And then, with one final intense thrust, he ground into her, so deep, and a blizzard of pleasure engulfed her, spasm after spasm, as his own release came.

Legs trembling, she sagged in his embrace. He nuzzled her neck, his beard shadow scratching and making her shiver. "Beautiful Victoria," he murmured. "Our mate." As he slowly withdrew, he kissed her nape, his lips soft against the burning bitemarks. And whispered, "Run."

Over and over through the night, she'd bound away, escaping in the moon-dappled forest. Each time, they'd trap her and then take her, shifting back and forth between human and cougar, giving her pleasure each time until the moon disappeared behind the western mountains. Until her legs in either form shook and she staggered.

As darkness crept across the world, the two male cougars joined her, one on each side, maneuvering her back to the cabin.

Shifting to human, she pushed the door open and stepped inside. Her legs gave out, and only Calum's quick grip kept her from falling. Lifting her easily, he carried her to the blankets.

As Alec tossed a log onto the fire, Calum pulled her into his arms. Alec snuggled on the other side, sandwiching her between them.

"You guys have a really warped notion of a honeymoon," she whispered, shivering a little at the memory of teeth biting her neck, claws holding her.

Alec's hand cupped her breast, comfortingly, possessively. "Only lifemates who are all the same animal get to mate in both forms," he murmured. "I love you, Vixen."

Calum's big palm settled warm against her stomach, his voice rumbled in her ear, "I love you, little cat."

Chapter Twenty-Five

M ARRIED. SHE WAS *married.* Well, yeah, so they called it *lifemated,* but it was really being married.

Vic turned off the shower and dashed into the bedroom. Calum had already left, and the clock said three o'clock. Talk about running really late, dammit.

It was this married stuff doing it too. *Married.* Over the past few days, she kept repeating the word, and her stomach quivered like fucking Jell-O each time. Whatever happened to planning out major life-altering events?

She'd never been so happy. Ever.

After yanking on a shirt and jeans, she smiled. Her life had started to feel almost normal—as normal as some bizarre furred-thingie family with two husbands could be.

With a ready-made daughter as part of the package. That was like…like…she didn't even have the words. Jamie had actually known about Alec and Calum's plans and cheered them on. She'd immediately started calling Vic *MomVee,* all one word. Vic smiled, her eyes stinging. *Hell of a name.* Funny how she'd felt so proud at earning the rank of sergeant. Yet this *mother* title was even more rewarding since Jamie's love had come with it. Vic couldn't get from one side of the house to the other without collecting a hug from the girl.

Or from the men either. She'd married *two* men. Or would that be two *cats*? That Mother goddess of theirs must have a truly odd idea of humor.

Then again, maybe She just had a well-developed sense of fun. Vic shook her head. A few days ago, Alec and Calum had woken her and Jamie up in the middle of the night to play in the forest—pouncing, stalking, and hunting. And how cool was that? Made summer picnics seem so yesterday.

She glanced at her watch and grimaced. Yanking on a white shirt, she grabbed a black jacket and ran.

Ten minutes later, she eased into the police station. With any luck, Alec wouldn't notice—

He looked up from his paperwork and fixed her with a dark green glare. "Miz Waverly-McGregor, you're late."

She couldn't remember the last time she'd arrived late for anything. "Um. I'm sorry. I ran into a …" She felt a flush creep up her face. She'd worked evening patrol all week because of the movie shoots, and had still been asleep when Calum came home for lunch. A bed was a very indefensible location, and his so-called *quickie* hadn't been quick at all. "I guess I lost track of the time. It won't happen again."

The frown on Alec's face was belied by the amusement in his eyes. "I realize you're a newly-wed, but this department expects its law enforcement personnel to show up on time. Our citizens deserve no less."

"Yes, sir."

He finally grinned. "I can't imagine what could have happened to make you lose track of time—except Calum called to explain."

She stared at him. He knew? "You sadistic dirtbag." She tossed her jacket over a hook on the wall and took a seat beside the desk. "I thought you were seriously pissed-off."

He ran a finger down her cheek, around a mouth swollen

from Calum's mind-blowing kisses. "Oh, but I am. Angry that I didn't get a nooner. You'd better plan on placating me tonight, or you'll be in big trouble."

"Oooh. Please, Mr. Sheriff, I'll do anything." Her blood heated as she thought of a few things she could do. She licked her lips, and her voice turned husky. "Anything."

His eyes grew heavy lidded, and then he snatched his hand back. "You were sent by the devil, weren't you? Toying with us weak-minded men, leaving us helpless in your wake."

She grinned. "Yep. That's the idea. So, what's on the schedule today?"

"First, join Jenkins and practice patrolling in a car. Then you're on downtown duty after five."

Watching over those empty-headed movie people. She sighed. "Yes, sir."

ALEC GLANCED UP when Calum strolled into the office with a manila envelope. Leaning back in his chair, Alec studied his brother with pleasure. Calum had never looked better. His eyes had cleared of the last lingering grief. "Being lifemated agrees with you."

"Indeed."

"But I'll ask that you stop making my deputy late." Alec used his foot to shove the spare chair over. "What brings you to my illustrious establishment?"

"Two things. First, Tynan O'Connolly sent more information. He managed to get some background on Vidal. Brawd, he grew up in Gray Cliff."

"Gray Cliff?" Alec frowned. The name seemed familiar. "The town in Rainier territory that the hellhounds decimated a few years ago?"

"Precisely. Vidal moved away long before it disappeared, but

I would guess that's where he learned of the Daonain." Calum's voice turned grim. "I don't know what set him in search of us now."

"We may never find out. I'll settle for him being dead. What's the other thing?"

Calum's eyes turned cold. "Swane is here."

Alec rose to his feet, fury rising like a forest fire. "In town?"

"Aye. Jamie caught a trace of his scent when the movie crew was filming, but too many people were there. What better way to hide than in a crowd of people?"

"Tonight's the last night for the shoot—they're leaving to-morrow morning." *Catch him. Kill him.* Alec forced the rage down. "Is she okay?"

Calum's words were tight. "She doesn't want to hide. She wants it over with. She's tired of the restrictions we've put on her and she said"—he shook his head—"ordered, actually, that she wanted to play rabbit to lure out the wolf."

By Herne, they'd raised a strong female. "You agree?"

"Not in the least." Calum rubbed his neck. "But she has a point. This way, we'd have control in springing the trap. If they remain at large, some other time they might get lucky."

Alec nodded. "Then we'll set it up."

"Don't tell Victoria."

"Why not?" The memory of a snarling cougar came to mind. Twice Vixen had acted—without thinking—to protect Jamie. "I see your point."

WELLS CONSIDERED CONTACTING her by phone. But no, the good sergeant was too adept at sliding past the truth. She should be, Wells thought with a bitter smile. He'd trained her.

A face-to-face. He hoped she had answers that would satisfy him.

After parking, he wandered down Cold Creek's Main Street, pleased with the old-fashioned street lamps that lit the sidewalk nicely. He window-shopped in the small stores that had closed for the night. A movie shoot had set up at the end of the block, and he deliberately moved away from the crowd. Eventually, he crossed to the center of the street and took a seat on an iron-work bench. People-watching was one of his favorite activities.

There she was.

Clad in a khaki uniform, looking very cop-like, Sergeant Morgan walked her beat, watching the people, alert to everything going on. She would make a fine police officer.

He saw the almost unnoticeable hesitation in her stride as she spotted him. She moved out of the light, so he couldn't evaluate whether she felt pleasure—or dismay—at his presence. When he ignored her, she did the same. Pride warmed his chest; she hadn't lost her skills. She was one of the best.

He stood and stretched, checked his watch, and then walked down the street toward her. He passed her on the sidewalk, eyes flicking to Angie's diner. There he could wait in comfort until she found an appropriate time to meet him.

FULL DARK. *SHOWTIME.* Swane smoothed his short beard, tugged his bus driver's uniform straight, and walked away from the vehicle like a man needing supper. Behind him the filming continued, and he almost grinned. The acting in the romance wasn't bad; Tony Vidal might actually be making a blockbuster movie. Wouldn't that surprise the asshole?

If he lived long enough to see it. Swane snorted in disgust. He'd finally figured out Vidal's problem. The shaking hands, his difficulty controlling his anger, choking on a drink, his weird gait. *Parkinson's*—like Swane's uncle who'd died in a nursing home. Vidal wanted to become a monster to keep from turning into a vegetable and would kill anyone in his path to do it.

Swane cracked his knuckles. Not a problem. But after the bastard got his wish, Swane would grab the half-a-mil coming to him and quietly disappear into a third-world country. Maybe he'd take his own pet pussy. Rip her claws out—and teeth too—and she'd do anything he wanted. He hardened and had to stop and adjust himself.

Avoiding the pools of light, Swane worked his way over to where the 'extras' from the town waited for their cue. Looked like most of the people in Cold Creek. They'd practiced their part several times last night until the director let them go, and tonight would be the take. According to the skit, when the villain started shooting at the hero, the panicking mob would flee through several streets. The very dark streets.

Nerves on edge, he watched for any mountain lion shapes and shadows as he walked to his position.

After the rehearsals last night, he knew his target's route. This time, as the small group of fleeing extras came past him, he'd trank her and toss her in the car. The trunk was already open. He'd stop on the road and administer a longer-acting dose, and be at the farmhouse shortly after. He might even leave her sedated long enough to…enjoy himself before getting down to work.

Fuck yes. There was nothing like the young ones with their high screams and terrified eyes.

The sound of a pistol split the night air, then several more shots. Screaming. Yelling. The filming had begun. The people scattered into the various streets. They'd been told to keep running since filming would continue here and there.

No camera was set up on this street. Vidal had been clear about his requirements with the director.

Swane listened, and a second later, the kid appeared out of the darkness. She ran toward him, trying to look afraid, not very effectively. That would change. A few more steps and then…she stopped dead. Sniffing and looking around. *What the fuck?*

Whatever. She was close enough. He aimed and heard a growl. Before he could turn, jaws closed over his hand. His skin ripped, his fingers breaking with little snapping sounds. He screamed and struck at the animal. Another huge, monstrous dog sprang on him.

Swane landed hard on his back. As he tried to rise, teeth snapped close to his neck. He froze, barely breathing. Spittle hit him in the face as the dog's fangs hovered an inch from his throat.

They weren't dogs. Wolves. *Werewolves.* The monsters weren't just mountain lions. Swane's bladder released.

From the sidewalk, the girl watched him, then looked past him.

Too terrified to move, Swane rolled his eyes in that direction. Two men were crossing the street. The cop. The girl's father.

Fuck.

VIC DIDN'T SLOW her pace, but her heart hammered like a 'ma deuce' machine gun. *Wells!* Here in her town. The thrill of seeing him had lasted one whole second before turning to worry. And dread. After some hard calculation, she straightened her shoulders and followed him into Angie's Diner. *I can do this.*

Supper rush had ended, and only two men in overalls and work boots occupied stools at the counter. Wells had taken a table near the corner, and he motioned for her to join him. Her footsteps on the old wooden floors sounded like a drum roll of doom as she walked into the room.

"Vicki, dear!" The owner, Angie O'Neal, came out from behind the long counter, hands outstretched in greeting. "I didn't get a chance to tell you how pleased we are for you and the men. You've been good for them, and for little Jamie."

Oh, this was so not the time for this. Vic forced a smile and let the woman squeeze her hands. "Thank you, Angie. That's sweet of you."

"What can I get you? The special tonight is meat loaf and mashed potatoes."

"Just coffee, thanks. I'm meeting a friend," Vic added, nodding toward Wells.

He stood as she walked up to the table, politely pulling out a chair for her. Attired in jeans, T-shirt and a dark brown corduroy jacket, he'd dressed to fit in. They waited until Angie had set two cups and a pot of coffee on their table and returned to her counter.

Face impassive, he studied her with clear blue eyes, then nodded. "You're looking well, Sergeant. Very healthy, in fact."

"Thank you, sir."

"I was in the area and had a notion to see how you're doing. Have you adapted to civilian life?"

In the area? Sure, you were. She summoned a smile. "I think so. It's been harder than I thought in some ways." There was something wrong here. His expression and body language were…off.

"I'm not surprised." He changed subjects. "As you requested, I investigated the ex-marine named Swane."

"I—I told you that the locals took care of it." She realized her mistake immediately.

His eyes turned cold. "But they didn't, Morgan. The homeless crimes are unsolved, and Swane isn't in custody. In fact, they don't have his name at all in conjunction with the case."

Oh shit, she was screwed.

"Your Swane is an 'enforcer' who works for a Tony Vidal. So I checked out Vidal. Typical mobster with some odd interests."

She kept her eyes down, pretending to watch her coffee. Pupil dilation, eye movements—Wells could read the smallest flicker. "Really." How much did the spymaster know?

"He's investigating rumors of people transforming into mountain lions."

Worse and worse. She turned her shock into amusement. "Excuse me? Mountain lions?"

"Odd isn't it? But about two months ago, he captured a young man…who transformed into a mountain lion when tortured. Vidal wants to know how to create more monsters. That is where using the homeless as specimens came into play."

"Are you serious?" *Please, don't take this story seriously. Laugh, dammit.* She saw her coffee lapping at the sides of the cup—her hands were shaking. Moving her hands back, she exhaled the anxiety out, inhaled calmness.

"Oh yes. He took recordings of the transformations." Well's lips turned up. "Keeps them on his laptop."

Holy fuck. Wells had documentation. "He's keeping all that information to himself? Why not give it to the National Inquirer for some big bucks?"

"His motivation is unclear at the moment. He's focused only on how the creatures are created."

"He doesn't sound sane, sir," she said lightly. If the information was still in one place, the shifters could destroy it. Calum needed to hear—

"Did you know the young man—the one who turned into a mountain lion—was captured nearby?"

Fingers of ice closed around her spine. "In Cold Creek?"

"That's why Mr. Vidal is holed up not far away. I intend to pay him a visit later tonight to discuss his recordings." Wells looked her straight in the eyes. "Do you want to tell me again why you're here, Sergeant?"

Don't do this, she wanted to say. "Because my life is here. I fell in love, married, quit the service, you know how it goes." She pushed to her feet. "And speaking of new lives, I need to get back to work."

"Gone over to the enemy?" he asked softly. "Would you like a charge of treason added to all your medals?"

The slash was quick and brutal. "I'm no traitor, dammit!"

"Then tell me about these animals. How many are there? How are they created?"

Created? Did he think some evil scientist had made them? She wanted so badly to give him the truth. She couldn't. "I don't—"

"You're lying, Morgan." His voice had gone flat, his eyes icy—he'd never looked at her like that before. "I'd never have believed you would betray your country—or me. I loved—" He broke off his sentence, breathed out harshly.

The pain surged all through her, hurting more with every pump of her heart. How could she lose him like this? After her first assassination, he'd showed up at her apartment. Ignored her shaking hands, her teary eyes. Stayed up all night with her, drinking coffee. Just being there. He'd always been there. Guilt shriveled her spirit.

"Vicki," he said softly. "Have you seen these creatures?"

A tried and true technique. Slam the subject over the head, induce guilt, be their friend again. She searched for some answer to give him, and then simply shook her head. "Sorry, sir. I haven't seen any creatures."

All the life drained from his face, and his blade-like voice hacked bloody pieces from her soul as he said, "They're monsters, Sergeant. However they're created. You get me the information I need so we can hunt them down, and there'll be a medal for you." His voice dropped to an almost inaudible whisper. "Otherwise you'll have your discharge, Morgan. A dishonorable one."

She stared at him, her jaw clenched. Dishes crashed behind her, the sound mimicking the shattering of her heart. *I'm sorry, sir.* Trying to find enough air to speak, she inhaled…and caught a scent. She turned.

Alec and Calum stood in the doorway.

"THEY'RE MONSTERS, SERGEANT. However they're created. You get me the information I need so we can hunt them down, and there'll be a medal for you." For the first time in his life, Alec cursed a shifter's hearing as the blood in his veins turned to ice. His heart slowed, each thud painful. His chest was squeezed too tightly to inhale.

Surely he'd misunderstood what the man had said. Surely she'd been misleading the human. Alec looked at Vicki and his hope disintegrated. Guilt showed clearly in her shocked face, her horrified eyes as she stared at him and Calum. Her color drained away.

"Vicki?" He couldn't feel his lips, but the word escaped anyway.

She'd lied to them, to him. Lied and lied and lied.

Knowing his brother had frozen, Calum stepped in front of him. Victoria's face was white, her eyes wide, the scent of her anger mingling with…guilt.

Guilt. What kind of traitor had they harbored in their midst? The man's words "*hunt them down*" hovered in the room like the vultures had hovered over his wife's body. *Demon. Monsters. "Hunt them down."*

Calum shook his head, trying to escape the images, as his fears and memories mingled into a terrifying brew: Thorson holding his bloody shoulder, Angie with open staring eyes, Lenora…so cold, all life fled, Alec torn apart like so much meat,

Lachlan lifeless on a steel table, his Jamie… Calum choked, drowning in horror.

Burning with fury at this female he'd thought he knew, who he'd brought into his home, trusted with his daughter. *Loved.* And all the time, she'd been setting them up as prey for Lachlan's killers.

"Calum—I—" the human female called Victoria held her hands out to him. She met his gaze and flinched, taking a step back. "I didn't. I didn't, Calum."

Hunt them down. A medal. The growl boiled up from inside him and as it escaped, so did his control. Wildness filled his soul, pulling at him, trying to change him into the beast.

Alec's hand closed on his arm. "Steady, brawd."

She looked at his brother. "Alec? I never—I didn't tell him."

Alec raggedly asked, "You're not a spy for the government?"

The question struck her like a blow, and she took a step back.

The sound Alec made was that of a mortally wounded animal.

As Calum scented his brother's despair, the door in his mind burst open. The mountain seemed to shake under his feet. Claws sprouted from his fingers.

"Dammit, get out of here before he kills you." Alec's words were hoarse as he yanked Calum against his chest.

Everything blurred. As Calum fought the trawsfur, he barely heard Alec's grief-threaded whisper, "And Herne help me, so will I."

"No," Vic whispered. This couldn't be happening.

Calum's face had distorted with anger, his eyes black as the pits of hell. Snarling…like a maddened animal. The tingle of shifting was strong in the air. He'd kill her. As furious as he was, he wouldn't be able to stop, and he'd tear her to bits.

Alec struggled with his brother. His last look at her had held only anger—none of the love, the tenderness.

When someone grabbed her arm and spun her around, Vic barely pulled her punch in time.

Angie's face was red and furious as she shoved Vic back a step. "Get out of here. I'd like to kill you myself, but if Calum does, he'll never forgive himself." When Vic couldn't move, Angie slapped her, the cracking sound followed by fiery pain.

Vic shook her head. She hadn't tried to block the blow and didn't fight now as Angie pushed her toward the back. And out. The door slammed behind her.

Blackness surrounded her as she stood in the alley, trying to breathe, staring at the building. Her ears rang; her head swam with pain and guilt. *Alec. Calum. God, no.* She hugged herself. *What can I do?*

Somewhere close, a car started up and moved slowly away. Without lights. *Wells.*

Breaking into a run, she headed for the police station.

Chapter Twenty-Six

"**E**ASY, BRAWD, EASY." Alec held his brother tighter, impending trawsfur tingling against his hands. "Stay human, Calum. Hear me? This is no time to lose control."

His words finally penetrated, and Calum stilled, his head bowing. The magic faded away.

"There you go. That's good," Alec soothed, not taking his gaze from the back door. The need to chase after her, yell, hold her, *understand* burned inside him, but he couldn't.

He wouldn't.

A *spy*. It was so plain he couldn't believe they hadn't put together the clues. Her fighting skills. That night she'd followed Calum through the tunnels to spy on him—they'd been suspicious until she drew them off the scent with her tale about Lachlan.

Those big brown eyes had sucked them right in, and, by Herne, he still couldn't accept her behavior was all a lie.

Calum straightened to stand alone, then ran his hands over his face as if to reacquaint himself with human form. "Thank you."

"You did it often enough for me." But no one had ever had to help Calum regain control. *Damn her!*

"This is…not good," Calum said, hoarse from snarling. "She

knows everything about us." The pain in his voice was as clear as that in his eyes.

And in Alec's heart. He felt as if something essential, like an arm or leg, had been ripped away; he couldn't seem to find his balance. "She fooled us completely. Agents will cover Cold Creek and Elder Village like flies on carrion."

Calum's eyes narrowed. "I wonder how much she told her boss. Did she share that *she's* a shifter also?"

"Well, damn, I bet not." The thought that followed hit Alec like a blow to the gut. "Brawd, if she doesn't have us anymore, is—" he choked, managed to spit out the words, "is she going to go feral?"

"It's…possible. Does that kind of person have friends?" Calum's dusky skin had turned gray. "Whether she does or not is irrelevant. She is shifter and has betrayed our clan to the humans. She will have to be killed."

Calum's stomach turned over at the thought of sentencing Victoria to death, and he leaned against the wall for a moment. He hurt like an animal with one leg caught in a trap. But the only way to escape the steel teeth was to gnaw off his leg—to kill his love for her. He closed his eyes. How had he not seen what she was?

"Cosantir?"

Calum opened his eyes to a room edged with red and black. "Angie. Is Vic—the female gone?"

"Out the back door right after her boss." Angie's mouth tightened. "What do you require?"

Calum's gaze met his brother's, but the cahir tilted his head, deferring control. Calum inhaled slowly, trying to force his mind to function. "Those with children—this is an excellent time to visit relatives in other states. Remind them to watch for anyone following, to change cars when possible, to avoid using any ID or credit cards. You all know the drill."

"We do, Cosantir. And the rest?"

"Stay alert. If there's an influx of strangers, if you feel anything is dangerous, escape to the mountains."

Alec added, "I'll send the Murphy brothers to the Village to warn them and help evacuate if needed. They can take Jamie with them."

"Good." Calum took a step, and then glanced at Angie. "Alec and I have a murderer to visit. If we don't return—"

She held up one hand. "Don't go begging for bad luck. We'll guard your cub. You be careful and come back to us."

VIC HAD STOLEN the patrol car from behind the station. She gave a bitter laugh, knowing how furious Alec would be. Wiping tears from her cheeks, she concentrated on the red tail lights of Wells' vehicle. The dispersing crowds from the movie shoot had slowed the spymaster's car enough that she'd caught up to him on the country road.

Her smile was bitter. No one tailed Wells successfully...except perhaps a shifter with a cat's night vision who could drive without lights.

Would he continue with his plan and go to Vidal's?

Everything in her wanted to simply turn around and leave, run away from the mountains where she'd been happy, the town where she'd actually found friends.

Where she'd given her heart away. A fucking sappy expression. Only, God, it was true. She pressed a hand to her chest and could feel the emptiness inside. All that remained was pain.

Dammit, Calum. His face kept wavering into her vision, reminding how his smile would appear in his eyes before flickering across his lips. His deep rough voice would sound in her ears...and then turn into the choking snarls of a wounded animal. In the diner, his pupils had gone black with her betrayal.

What had she done to him?

Guilt cut through her, ripping her up inside. Before she lifemated them, she should have told them about her past. They were so paranoid—and with good reason. But if she'd explained, maybe they'd have believed her now.

She scowled, anger fizzling along her skin. But fucking-A, after all this time with them, shouldn't they figure she wasn't out to get them?

Then again, the evidence had been damning. Fucking animal hearing. They'd caught Wells' offer of a medal…and obviously hadn't heard the threat that came after it.

And she'd just stood there in shock, looking as God-damned guilty as she'd felt.

Her jaw firmed. Her life here was destroyed, and it was her own fault. She'd taken too long to learn to trust. She couldn't blame Calum and Alec—*much*—she'd been the one doing all the lying. And Wells had made her look so fucking guilty.

Damn him anyway. She swallowed against the painful knot in her throat. He'd looked as if…as if he really cared for her. She'd never looked very hard at the careful roles they'd played over so many years, but the way he'd turned on her, so terribly angry, showed he'd felt betrayed. Yes, she'd wounded him…but his return fire had been far more destructive. Fatal, maybe.

Fatal? With the thought, horror blindsided her hard enough that her car skidded on the road. She fought for control. An oncoming car flashed past as she steadied, hands squeezing the steering wheel. She'd lost her lifemates, Jamie, her friends. *Am I going to go feral now?*

What if she turned into some monster Alec would have to kill? She remembered the agonized look in his eyes after he'd executed his friend, Renshaw.

He was so loving and big-hearted. And the way he looked tonight, filled with such pain and anger and betrayal—she'd done that to him.

"Oh, Alec," she whispered, "I'm so, so sorry." Of all the people she could have hurt, why Alec? He'd never given her anything but joy. And love. Like the other half of her soul, he understood her like no one ever had. In return, she'd cut him beyond healing.

Surely her loss wouldn't turn them feral...but no, they still had each other. And Jamie. Her little Jamie who called her MomVee. Becoming a mother had been like finding a coat hung by the door, just waiting to be slid on. Vic managed a smile and tasted salty tears on her lips. The thought of mothering someone had scared her spitless until she'd realized Jamie had enough love to forgive any stupid mistakes.

Maybe not enough to get past this. At least Vic hadn't had to see the betrayal in the kid's eyes. Or had to face Thorson. Would her honorary grandfather spit when he said her name now?

With that fresh pain, she realized she wouldn't turn feral. Her ties to others weren't gone. No, the bonds were still there and hurting so much they felt like burning brands on her heart.

Okay, then. She hiccupped a little and increased speed as the taillights in front of her turned left off the main road. Yes, Wells was heading for Vidal's place.

Because of her, Wells wouldn't have called in back-up or documented anything. He'd have wanted to give her the benefit of the doubt. So all the information he'd acquired would probably be on his laptop. Convenient. If Vidal's damning evidence disappeared, Wells wouldn't quit, but he'd have trouble getting anyone to believe him. After all, he'd never seen a shifter himself.

Vic sighed and made the turn after Wells. She'd screwed up, and before she took herself off to somewhere very far away, she'd do some damage control. She almost laughed. Her life might be in chaos, her heart broken, but the call of duty still sounded like a fucking trumpet. *Go figure.*

CALUM'S RAGE HAD died; now only coldness remained. Determination. A sick feeling down deep. It was far easier to kill when the blood was hot. He walked into the section containing the jail cells. Two cells. One occupied. "Swane."

Swane stood. As he looked at Calum, his eyes widened, and he took a step back. "Fuck, man, I only did what he told me to. No need to get all upset. Just promise to let me go, and I'll tell you everything you want to know."

Alec locked the station door behind him. He walked over to Calum, standing close enough that their shoulders rubbed. No heat here either, only cold as the cahir said quietly, "Tell us where Vidal is."

WELLS HAD PULLED off to the side of the tiny dirt road. Good thing she'd stayed back, Vic thought, as she pulled over quickly. Branches scratched the paint as she inched into the deep brush to hide the patrol car. She got the engine shut off a second before he got out of his car.

A short way ahead, lights glowed from the windows of a one-story building in the middle of nowhere. Vidal had obviously wanted an isolated location where no neighbors could hear penned up shifters. The nearest place was at least several acres away, and the tiny dirt road was private. Yeah, the city boy had done a fine job of ensuring privacy.

Wells worked his way toward the house slowly, barely visible even to her cat's eyes.

After unscrewing the overhead light, she waited. He could

scope out the situation first. If Vidal had guards, Wells might as well do her work for her.

She could only hope that this half-assed plan of hers would work. Damn the shifters and their reciprocity crap, but the need to pay back what she owed drove her hard. She'd definitely bought into their morals, hadn't she? Her chest ached as she remembered Jamie's solemn face. *"The balance is fair."* Or how Calum had forced Thorson and Baty...

She shook her head furiously. No time for regrets, for grief. She'd led Vidal and Wells to the Daonain; now she had to remove that danger. Leave emotions behind. *This mission is a go.*

The car stayed dark as she slid out. From her regular gear and the equipment in the trunk, she assembled a bag of necessities.

She stripped quickly, shivering in the rapidly chilling night air. Only patchy clouds covered the quarter moon in the east. More light than she liked. With a sigh, she tossed her clothes into the back seat and laid the keys behind the front tire.

Okay then. She closed her eyes, opened the mental cat-door, and flung herself through. She wasn't a one-toe-in-the-lake sort of girl after all. The eerie tingling covered her skin as if she'd stepped into an electrified puddle. She felt her connection with the Mother for a second, and her heart squeezed at the realization that Her love was unchanged. Then her whiskers quivered at the scent of deer in the night air. Rabbit. Shrew in the grass— very close.

No, no, mission first. She grasped the backpack in her mouth and shook it to get the feel of weight. Thank God Alec had once made her carry a kill—a small deer—so she knew how much she could handle. Kitties were damned strong.

She loped through the woods, made a lovely leap over a stream, and realized a chain link fence enclosed the property. She studied it for a minute. No additional electrical wiring. Piece of cake. She took a leaping run and bounded up and over, landing lightly on the other side. As she trotted away, she glanced back at the fence, shining faintly in the moonlight, and let her tail twitch slightly. *Damn, I'm good.*

The rear of the building had little cover. A couple of small trees, a few lilacs in one corner. In the shadow of the bushes, she paused. Two distinct human scents; one idiot at the near corner of the house chewed tobacco. She heard him spit. The other was quieter, a dark shadow leaning against the house.

After shifting to human, she opened her leather satchel and changed into stretchy black clothing. Quick cammo on any exposed skin, K-Bar strapped at her calf, Glock, reloads and other toys in a belt around her waist. The police nightstick she hefted a few times to get the balance and kept in her hand.

A glance at the sky. One nice thick cloud neared the moon. When the yard darkened, she moved, circling, coming up behind Mr. Dipping Tobacco. Hand over his mouth and a thump with the baton. He went limp, and she lowered him silently to the ground. Some precut strands of dark rope from her belt secured him quickly, and she finished with duct tape over his mouth and a quick pat on his butt.

The next was just as easy. It was almost insulting. She checked for guards in the front, but Wells had already taken them out. Four total... *You're a nervous guy, Tony Vidal.*

Would she find Swane here too? She could only hope.

The back door was locked, and someone moved inside the room. No entry there. However, the bathroom window wasn't secured. She slid it open. The opening was too small for a guy, but hell, her boobs and butt would squish. She landed on the floor in the bathroom almost soundlessly. Her nose wrinkled. Jesus, one of the guards must have had beans for supper.

She cracked the bathroom door slightly open. Wells sat in an armchair, head in his hands. The posture, so different from his erect one, gave her a pang. *Ignore it.* The chair faced the front door; his back was to her. Couldn't get much easier than that.

She coshed him. And ignored the tears that seeped from her eyes as she tied him securely. She started to duct-tape his mouth and stopped. He was congested; he'd suffocate if he couldn't get air through his nose. Hell.

She ripped the tape back off. If he woke up before she finished, she could always whack him again…assuming she had the heart. She did a quick search, relieving him of his pistol and the tiny computer in his pocket. The pistol went in her bag.

The room had a sitting area to watch television and the other half was a token office. A box of files lay on the floor. A laptop sat on the desk surrounded by papers. She dumped Wells' belongings beside it.

In a back bedroom, a tied-up Vidal moaned and groaned, only half-conscious. *Thanks, Wells.* A chill ran up her spine. This was too easy—something was bound to go wrong.

When Vidal opened his eyes, she considered killing him then, but she might need more information. She dragged him to the living room and stashed him out of the way in the corner behind the desk.

All the rest of the rooms were empty.

Before starting a fire in the big stone fireplace, she removed her pack. *Flames and ammunition—so not a good thing.* Then she went to work. Folders and pictures. Vidal had accumulated information about her—a pleasure to burn. The blaze grew as she tossed in paper after paper, and when it was roaring well, she started on the DVDs and CDs. She didn't bother to look, just dumped it in. Hell, most of it was porn.

Black smoke and God, what a stench. She threw in Wells' micro-computer.

"It won't take long to collect more information."

Vic spun. Wells stared at her, eyes clearing rapidly. She must have pulled her blow. *Stupid, Sergeant.* "I know. But it will slow you down a little."

"You intend to eliminate me?" He struggled to sit up from where he'd slumped.

"I rarely tie up people I'm planning to kill."

"If you're hoping for me to change my mind, you are in error."

Right. Even as the words sliced her open, she had to smile. He'd been unconscious, probably had a splitting headache, hands and feet were tied, and he still had the same arrogance as if he sat in his own office. Damn, but she loved him.

The thought brought her hand to a stop in midair over the flames; the scorch made her jump. Loved Wells? *Well, duh.* She really did. Calum and Alec had managed to open the way to her heart, and now she could see all the ways love appeared. *Damn them anyway.* She grabbed a camcorder and threw the whole thing into the fireplace, sending up a flurry of sparks. And simply stood there, watching it burn.

"What are you going to do now?" he asked, breaking the silence.

"Don't know." *Don't care.*

"As I left, it sounded as if the werelions were unhappy with you for some reason."

She glanced at him as she slammed the laptop down on the desk, splitting open the bottom. "They heard what you said—cat ears—and reacted, oh, pretty much as you'd expect."

"Excellent."

Damn him. Even knowing it would hurt, she prodded at him like she'd picked at scabs as a kid. "Never seen you get so upset. Always thought you were so uber-cool."

Color surged into his face although his expression didn't change.

She pulled out the hard drive and the motherboard. Threw

them on the fire. "Did you feel betrayed by your favorite agent?"

He gazed at the far wall, a muscle twitching in his cheek.

While checking over the house, she'd found no info storage other than this room. *Information gone.*

One bad guy left. She should deal with Vidal without a witness. *Time to go back to sleep, boss.*

She picked up the weighted nightstick and hesitated. Wells had been her recruiter, her handler and more…. He'd trained her, been there for her when she needed him—although he'd pretended it was duty. He'd brought her junk food in hospitals with an expression of distaste, flown her back to the states against her wishes…just to make sure she was all right. Truly covert even in never showing that he cared.

It wasn't his fault Lachlan had turned her into a furball. In some ways, she *had* betrayed her boss. He was owed.

Damn the shifters and their fucking reciprocity law. Releasing a pained sigh, she knelt in front of Wells. With her K-Bar, she sliced through his bonds. So much for the easy part.

He didn't move, just lifted his eyebrows inquisitively.

"The kid you saw on tape—the one who bit me? Before he died in my arms, I made him two promises," she said softly. "I promised to inform his grandfather what had happened to him. I also gave my word not to tell anyone about the shifters. I did my damndest to discover whether they were a threat to humans or the U.S. If so, I'd have told you, broken promise or not."

His eyes narrowed slightly. He was listening at least.

"I…I couldn't figure out how to uphold my obligations and still not betray the kid. I didn't…" She felt her lips quiver and firmed them immediately. "I never meant to hurt you. You're—" After a breath, she managed, "You're more like a father to me than mine ever was."

His gaze lowered as he massaged his wrists.

Hell, she'd tried. She rubbed her face dry and started to rise.

Maybe someday he'd get past—

"I loved a woman once."

She froze, and then slowly knelt again.

"I'd just started in the CIA and was appallingly naïve. We lived together. I planned to marry her."

Unable to speak, Vic waited.

"I discovered… She was breaking into my briefcase every night. Selling information to the highest bidder. I confronted her, and she tried to kill me."

"Fuck."

His eyes were red, but the tiniest curve of a smile appeared on his lips. "Succinctly put."

"So you figured I'd betrayed you too." She shook her head, warmth melting some of the ice surrounding her heart. "Gee thanks, sir."

On each side of the front door, the windows shattered inwards with a crash. Two mountain lions landed, blurred, and shifted into human form.

Alec. Calum.

Alec's breath caught as he stood upright. Vicki rose, her big brown eyes wide with shock. The urge to take her into his arms and bury his face in her hair infuriated him. How pitiful could he get? Especially since he'd watched her and her spy boss chatting away a minute ago. His mouth twisted bitterly. "Ms. Waverly. Now, why am I not surprised to see you here?"

Her flinch was as satisfying as it was painful.

After an impassive look around, Calum left to search the house. And probably to get away from Vicki.

Alec glanced at the corner where a tied-up man lay on the carpet. "That's Vidal?"

Vicki nodded, mouth pressed firmly into a line. Alec had traced his finger over those lips… He winced away from the memory.

As he wandered around the room, he kept a wary eye on Vicki and the other man he wanted to kill. "Now what would a boss of spies be called?"

"The handler," the bastard said in a mild, somewhat snooty voice. Medium-height, lean like someone who naturally burns more than they eat, his expression seemed almost indifferent, but those clear blue eyes saw everything.

Over the smell of burned rubber, Alec caught the scent of distress from him—but no fear sweat. Too dumb to know his danger? Doubtful.

Calum came back in. "Nothing. What's in here?"

"Desk is empty. There's DVD and CD holders with no contents. Even the computer is gutted," Alec said. He knelt in front of the fireplace and stirred the contents with the poker. Flakey ashes from paper, melted plastic stubs, a shriveled green plastic board, and a metal box—probably from the computer also. He nodded at Calum, the beginnings of hope rising inside him.

Calum's eyes narrowed. He turned to Vicki, and power trickled through his voice. "Victoria, where is the information Vidal collected?"

She stiffened and shook her head...but answered, "I burned it."

"What happened to the information you were supposed to get your boss?" Calum asked mildly, although Alec could see the tension in his frame.

A flash of anger lit her face. "You jump to conclusions too fucking quickly. I'd already turned him down."

Calum walked over to the handler. "Had she?"

The bastard didn't agree or disagree. It was like looking at a statue.

They were all across the room, talking. In the corner, out of sight behind the desk, Vidal shredded the last rope with the glass from the shattered windows. His hands had slickened with his own blood, but he was free.

The creatures could attack quickly; he knew that. Their talk covered the sound of his crawling and then he had it—the pistol under one of the chairs, right where the fucking agent had knocked it out of his grip. Still behind the desk, he straightened. "Don't move, assholes. Hands in the air."

They jerked around, faces turning hard when they saw the pistol. As they raised their hands, he studied his haul. One man, naked, kneeling by the fire, then the bitch Morgan a couple of feet away. The cold-faced CIA agent who'd managed to take out his guards. Another unclothed stranger stood on the far side of the chair.

The government man spoke, his voice quiet. "Vidal, I suggest—"

"Shut up!" Vidal lined the pistol up with the agent's forehead, feeling his hand begin to shake. *Fucking disease.* But he had the cure, now didn't he? He smiled at the two unclothed men. "Swane described you. You're the cop and the daddy."

The dark one gazed back, pupils completely black, and growled.

A chill ran up Vidal's spine at the murderous anger radiating from him…from them both. He shifted his weight and ignored the creeping of fear.

"What happened to Swane?" Vidal asked, then shook his head. Didn't really matter. If the werecats were here, the bastard must have got himself caught—and spilled his guts.

He needed to get the hell out of here before more CIA or creatures showed up. He had only one cage though. It could hold two animals—but he wanted to keep the woman.

Vidal aimed the gun at the one by the fireplace. "I don't need you." He pulled the trigger.

Calum saw the man point the pistol at Alec. *No!* He shifted and sprang as the pistol snapped. He heard the gut-wrenching sound of a bullet hitting flesh and knew despair. On his knees, Alec couldn't have moved fast enough to dodge.

He hit Vidal from the side, knocking him down. The human tried to scramble away, but fury raging, Calum bit through his spine. With barely a shudder, the human died.

Lachlan was avenged. *And Alec.*

Calum shifted to human and turned, unsure if he could bear the sight of his brawd's lifeless body. But—

Alec was alive. *Alive!* It was Victoria, in panther form, who lay on the floor, incongruously still in her black clothing. The stretch top had a hole in it, and blood already pooled on the floor.

Kneeling, Alec ran a hand down her fur. "Damn, Vicki," he said hoarsely, "trawsfur back so I can get a bandage on that."

A blur, and she returned to human. She merely grimaced at her shoulder, but when she saw her handler's shock at her transformation, her face crumpled for a second.

His heart hammering, Calum went into the bathroom and grabbed a clean towel. He tossed it to Alec. "I thought he'd killed you, brawd," he managed to say.

"Me too. Vixen took—" Jaws set hard, Alec ripped the cloth into a make-shift dressing for Victoria's shoulder.

"It's a time-honored tradition—take a bullet for your buddy. You know I like my traditions." She shrugged and winced.

"How bad does it hurt?" Alec asked in a tight voice.

"Pain is weakness leaving the body," she said lightly.

"You were a Marine? I should have known." He put pressure on the hole, scowled at her back. "It went through. Change into cat form soon—that'll help."

Calum squeezed Alec's shoulder just to feel his warm skin, know he was alive. Then he touched Victoria's cheek. "Thank you."

She nodded, her lips curved up in a wry grin. "Next time,

consider using the door. Glass and tied-up men don't mix well."

"We will keep that in mind."

"Is Vidal dead?" she asked, her voice disconcertingly level, obviously familiar with violent death.

He should have considered the implications of that before. With an effort, Calum shoved his feelings to one side and reached for clarity. The jolt of seeing Victoria had been followed by too many others, and he could not afford to lose control…or his judgment. "He's dead. As is Swane. Irma will be safe, and Lachlan can rest easy in his grave."

Alec rubbed his face, sighed, and then asked, "What do the guards outside know?"

"They're Vidal's thugs. And they didn't see anything," she answered. "You're safe. There's nobody left who—"

Calum glanced at the handler. "Just one."

Victoria stiffened. "Calum. No."

He studied her for a moment. She'd burned the information, saved Alec's life. Hope tried to ease past his barriers as he looked at her. She'd used all those military skills to help the Daonain today. Maybe, just maybe, she wouldn't have to pay the penalty. His voice soft, he said, "Victoria, return to Cold Creek. We'll talk. Perhaps—"

She interrupted, "What are you planning to do to him?"

"He cannot retain his knowledge of us."

Her appalled expression grew. She looked over at Alec. "You said it worked good on one-time spottings. More than that, and you destroy big chunks of their memory. You can't do that to him."

"Vicki, there's no choice." Alec held his hands out. "He's with the government. They'll try to exterminate us."

Her face turned cold. "No. It's not a risk I'll allow."

Calum felt the tiny splinter of hope die.

"Vicki," Alec said softly, "don't. You can't win against both of us."

She slid a pistol out of the small black bag beside her.

Calum looked at her easy grip, the tilt of the automatic, and sighed. One more skill she possessed. "I do not think you will kill us."

Her finger tightened on the trigger, loosened. "Probably not." The pistol dipped lower, pointed directly at Alec. "But if you figure it's okay to damage Wells' mind, then I guess it's okay to blow out Alec's knee. It'd cripple him for life, Calum. There'd be no bone left there to heal."

Calum tilted his head in acquiescence, his heart turning to ash inside his chest.

She stepped backwards. "Bring your car to the front, Wells."

Silent as a cat, the man slipped out the door. Too soon, the hum of an engine came from outside the house.

Calum caught her gaze. "You are a shifter, Victoria. We're your people." *Please hear me. Don't do this to us all.* "If you leave with him, I will have to call for your death. Is this truly what you want?"

She started to speak, then shook her head. As she backed toward the door, tears filled her eyes.

But the pistol never wavered.

DAYLIGHT WAS BREAKING when Vic finally decided she'd driven far enough. She was high in the mountains, almost to the Canadian border, and miles down a tiny fire road. With a sigh, she shut the engine off and rested her forehead on the steering wheel. She'd cried enough, cursed enough…grieved enough.

After leaving the farmhouse, she'd dropped Wells off in a convenient town. When she told him she was keeping his car, he'd shrugged and called it a fair trade for his life. He'd said, as if he'd just discovered the fact, "You really are a werelion."

Almost able to smile, she'd given him Lachlan's words, hearing again the young voice saying, '*Some people call us* Daonain *or shifters. Me, I prefer werecats.*'

Then Wells had asked her what she'd do. His open concern felt…odd. Nice.

She slid out of the car and heard the engine ping as it cooled. She'd told him she'd be all right. Maybe, eventually, that wouldn't be a lie. She'd made errors over the past months, stupid mistakes due to her background, her fears. People had been hurt because of her poor decisions. She'd been hurt.

Breathing in the cold, clean air, she stripped, locked her clothes in the trunk, and gave herself a good scratch. She itched all over—apparently Alec hadn't bullshitted about the effects of being surrounded by metal. After pulling off her bandages, she checked the bullet hole. The bleeding had not only stopped, but the wound looked a couple of days old. Shifters healed fast. Good.

Time to move on. She'd fixed everything she could. Now she had to confront her own fears and decide what came next.

Through the long night's drive, she had remembered what Calum had said in the cave of the hot-springs, '*The silence of the mountains serves me well when I am troubled.*' Now, tilting her head back, she looked upward where the rising sun lit the snow-topped peaks of the huge mountain range.

And she shifted.

Chapter Twenty-Seven

CALUM PACED AROUND the shelves, unable to settle. At the front of the bookstore, Thorson sat at his desk, listening to Alec. With a jolt of pain, Calum saw how the newest grief had aged the old man. Last week, when he'd heard about Victoria's betrayal from Angie, Thorson had disappeared into the mountains.

He'd only returned today.

Calum paced back to the counter as Alec related the events at Vidal's farmhouse. "…after Vicki and Wells got away, we burned the building."

Thorson leaned back in his chair with a disbelieving expression. "You two couldn't catch a car on a dirt road?"

"We tried," Calum said. "Almost caught up, and then she threw something out the window. What did you call it, Alec?"

"A flash-bang. Good name for it."

Thorson snorted out a laugh. "I've read about them. Blinding light, deafening noise?"

"Precisely." Calum rubbed his ears, the memory still painful. "In cat form and at night, it's quite intense. By the time we could see again, they were gone."

"She's a cool cookie," Thorson said.

Alec slammed a fist on the counter as his temper, so long

under control, ignited like the bloody flash-bang. "Damn you, Thorson, she's not a cool *anything*. She betrayed us. And that spymaster she saved will do everything in his power to hand us over to the government. She chose him over us."

Calum understood his reaction. Seeing Victoria choose the enemy had knotted his guts like a meal of rotting carrion. And yet...

Thorson turned his head away, his face tight.

Calum leaned against the counter wearily. Too many sleepless nights. He'd tried to get over the pain of her loss, to see past his anger. The clan waited for him to declare Victoria's life forfeit, and he...couldn't. Something bothered him, kept him from taking that step, and he couldn't tell whether his emotions were swaying him or if he'd missed an essential fact. "If you don't mind, Joe, I would like to go through this together. I am not seeing clearly, I fear."

Thorson's face tightened, increasing Calum's guilt, and then he nodded. "All right. Start with when she first appeared. With my Lachlan."

"Swane and Vidal had captured him," Alec said. His hands were still clenched, but he was making the effort.

Calum moved up beside him, shoulder rubbing shoulder, and felt his brother's anger diminish. "Did she truly assist in Lachlan's escape or fake it to gain her entry with us?"

Thorson shook his head. "Lachlan Gifted her. The boy had the ability to read people. He wouldn't have made a mistake, and an enemy wouldn't have stood still for the ritual. Truth, Cosantir. It was a true Gifting."

Thorson would not have been fooled. "Yes."

"Got herself hired into the bar to collect information. Can't get around that," Alec said.

"She saved Jamie that day," Calum put in softly. He could never forget that. "But when we caught her the night of the

Gathering, she lied. She told us she was looking for you, Thorson. Not that she was investigating shifters."

"There's no law against killing two birds with one paw," Thorson admitted, the growl gone from his voice. "I do believe Lachlan gave her that task. There was no lie in her scent—or her sorrow."

Calum thought back to that night in Thorson's home where Victoria had first told them how Lachlan died. Her grief had been real. "Aye."

"My boy…he'd have been terrified of exposing us," Thorson said. "He probably made her promise to keep silent."

"But she's an agent for the CIA. She admitted that, and we know Wells is her handler." Calum's brows drew together. "So this spy has just found out about creatures she'd never seen before. What's her first action?"

Alec's mouth twisted. "Tell her boss."

"No, dammit," Thorson snapped. His eyes had brightened. "Stupid cub. Are we flooded with government agents?"

"No," Alec said slowly. "Aside from Vidal's men, only Wells showed up."

Calum leaned on the counter for support. "Could she have acted independently? Checked us out on her own?"

"You two know her better than I do," Thorson said. "Would that little werecat go running to her boss with a fairytale story? Especially if she promised to keep us a secret?"

Calum remembered when Jamie was two. *"Do it myself, Daddy."* Victoria would have been much, much worse. "No. I have a feeling she'd felt torn between her duties even before she turned shifter." He remembered her careful questions in Thorson's house, and her admission, *"If I thought you were dangerous, I'm not sure what I'd do."*

"But Wells said she'd get a medal for the information. That doesn't sound like someone on our side."

"I talked to Angie today." By Herne, he was still missing a piece of the bloody puzzle. "And this is what I want you to hear, Joe. I fear my own desires might affect my judgment," he admitted.

Thorson nodded. "She's your mate, Cosantir. You cannot help but be affected. Go on."

"Angie said Victoria and her boss had talked very quietly. Then Victoria stood up and shook her head as if she'd refused something. The man was furious. Angie was heading over there—right before Wells raised his voice—because she thought he might hurt Victoria."

"Vicki turned him down," Thorson said, massaging the old wound on his shoulder. "Just like she told you."

"Calum, I know you want... Brawd, she let him go free," Alec whispered. His face looked like stone, hardened with pain. "She chose him over us. You have no choice; she has to die."

I shouldn't have discussed this with him here. Calum squeezed his shoulder. Could either of them survive the death of their lifemate?

"When I wandered the forest, I wondered where she might run to for help." Thorson's gaze rested on the picture of his grandson. "You know, she told me once she didn't have anyone left either."

No family. But surely someone so loving as Victoria would have found a substitute... Deep in his chest, hope flickered to life as he finally scented the right trail. "Alec," Calum said, his voice hoarse. "We watched them through the windows before we jumped. Remember the look on his face?"

Alec frowned, and then his eyes narrowed. "She'd cut him loose. They talked. And he looked... His eyes were red as if he wanted to cry. He wasn't looking at her like an employer or a lover either." Alec rubbed his hands over his face. "And from the way she reacted to us hurting him, she loves him. Hell, he's probably like her daddy, and we wanted to do a mind-wipe on him."

"We didn't leave her many options, did we?"

"Herne, how could we have been so stupid?" Light bloomed in Alec's eyes as he reached the same conclusion as Calum. "But if he's family, sharing information with him doesn't break the Law."

Calum smiled. "Aye. Family can share."

Thorson barked a laugh, then jerked his head toward the door. "Cosantir. Cahir. Please fetch my granddaughter and bring her home."

FULFILLING THORSON'S COMMAND wasn't as easy as it had sounded, Alec thought, over a week later. The Vixen had disappeared as if she'd never existed. Well, that wasn't surprising, considering she knew the Daonain would kill her. Alec put out an APB, used every legal and illegal method he knew to track her. Nothing. That damned spy-boss had trained her well.

The shorter days of winter had turned gray and miserable, and he wanted her with an ache that grew steadily worse. Although he and Calum tried to keep up a cheerful front for Jamie's sake, they didn't succeed very well, and she was pining too.

Last week, they'd discovered exactly who Vicki's handler was. She'd made one slip in calling him by name.

Human channels of communication were too risky, but Calum had contacted Daonain on the east coast and arranged for the OtherFolk to leave a message for the man in his old Victorian house. House-brownies weren't averse to making calls when the bribe was big enough.

Alec had to wonder how the agent had reacted to finding a note on his kitchen table in his well-secured home.

No word, so far, but if he really cared for her like a father…

An hour later, the door of his office opened.

Alec's pen dropped as Calum walked in, followed by the handler. "Wells," Alec said in a hoarse voice.

Wells pulled a chair next to the desk, seated himself, and smoothed his dark gray suit. "You wanted to talk. I prefer to speak in person."

"Right." Alec glanced at Calum. Where to start? "We've been trying to locate Vicki."

A glimmer of amusement showed in Wells' pale blue eyes. "The Sergeant rarely sits still long enough for someone to shoot at her."

Calum poured them all coffee from the battered coffeemaker in the corner and set a cup in front of Wells. "You seem the type to take it black."

"Very perceptive." He leaned forward, his eyes like blue ice. "Why'd you change your mind about her, might I ask?"

"We managed to put together some of her actions, her motivations," Calum said smoothly.

"You do realize that she told me nothing about you? My information came from Vidal's recordings."

"Aye." Calum gave Wells a level gaze. "Your offering her a medal for her information came close to earning her a death sentence. I hope that gives you a sense of satisfaction."

Wells paled at the cold statement of truth. His fingers closed around the coffee cup and opened. "I didn't realize that until…afterward. I've handled it—her—badly."

Wells versus the Cosantir. I should take bets on the winner, Alec thought nastily. Then again, didn't women tend to mate with men like their fathers? He buried most of his irritation. "If that's so, maybe now we can stop playing these asinine games."

"Not yet. The Sergeant would get annoyed if I was mistaken and helped you—whatever you are—to hunt her down," Wells said and looked at Calum. "Why do you want Vic back?"

He answered simply, "I love her."

Wells' gaze turned to Alec.

Over the last week, he'd tried not to think of her, at least during the day. The tiny pebbles of memories—her laugh, her flowing grace, her scent—could so easily turn into an avalanche—the way she moved under him in the night, how she bit her lips as she studied the police manual, the emptiness of their home without her. As with Calum, the answer was simple, "I love her."

"She is, essentially, my daughter." Wells wrapped long fingers around his cup as if his hands were cold. "I would almost prefer you to be hunting her than to want her as your own."

To Alec's shock, Calum actually growled.

A hint of a smile crossed Wells' face. "But she loves you both, unworthy as you are."

"She said that?" Alec asked, the question escaping before he thought.

"Oh, yes, that very night." Wells grimaced. "In the same conversation where she made me give my word. I vowed to—" he shifted to an obvious quote, "'—*never ever, reveal, by any means whatsoever, anything about the shifters or anything that could lead to the shifters.*'"

Calum raised his eyebrows. "She threatened you?"

"Worse. She cried."

"Ah." Calum sighed. "She might as well cut your heart out with that knife of hers; it would hurt less."

Wells nodded, his eyes on the far wall. "I've never broken my word in my life, and at my age, I'm not about to start. Your people have nothing to fear from me."

"Or anyone else?" Calum asked.

"At the moment, there is no interest and no information about you that I can discover." Wells moved his shoulders.

"How long that might last is not up to me."

"Good enough," Alec said.

"I do have one remaining question," Calum said dryly. "Do you happen to know where we can find our lifemate?"

"No. I don't." Wells' face turned bleak. "I haven't been able to locate her either."

Chapter Twenty-Eight

H ER PAWS TOOK her south, and the rest of her agreed with the destination. She wasn't sure exactly how long she'd been in the forest now. The first week or so seemed a blur. Every time she'd change back to human, all the pain would return, and she'd simply kneel and cry like some abandoned baby.

But her grief had slowly eased, and now she'd shift to human during the day, sit in the sun, and think. Over the days, she worked through her choices.

She had a real tactical problem—how to keep the Daonain from killing her—that couldn't be solved until she answered the tougher question: *Go back or not?*

Oh, tough decision. She was a damned brave Marine. Yeah, shoot her to pieces, even kill her? *No problem.* Walk into a firefight? *You bet.*

But risk her heart? *Fuck that.* Talk about a scaredy-cat. Like a real coward, she hadn't even waited for the battle to start. Hell, she had run at the first artillery fire. But Marines had been known to desert the field of battle, and then manage to get control of themselves. To courageously return to the fight.

Could she?

The safest choice was to stay away. Live as an outlaw in the forests, or stay in the human world and hide her animal half. She could manage. Wells would help, even move her to a far-away country if needed. She'd lived undercover for years. Nothing new.

Or she could return. So, so much scarier. The physical risk: she could die, and—even worse—Alec or Calum might be the ones who killed her. Yeah, ugly outcome. But death was nothing new.

What really scared her spitless was the thought of fighting for the life—the love—she wanted. Of opening herself up to being hurt emotionally. Because—she took a hard breath—those two men could hurt her worse than even dying.

If it had been someone besides Calum and Alec in that restaurant, would she have run when Wells made her look like a traitor? *Hell no.*

If it hadn't been her lovers treating her like the bad guy in the farmhouse, would she have given up so easily? Or would she have told Wells to leave and stayed to battle it out?

With anyone else, she'd beat the crap out of them if they judged her without giving her a chance to speak. No matter how fucking overwhelming the evidence was. But because it was Alec and Calum, she'd caved, making herself look all the more guilty.

Why?

Because she didn't believe she deserved their love. Or the life they wanted to give her. Her stupid little subconscious had decided that no one could really love her enough to listen and work things out. After all, they must know how unworthy she was, how damaged.

Her subconscious needed to get its ass kicked.

But it had taken a while to see the idiocy of her behavior and then to admit that Alec and Calum really did love her. She hadn't put on an act. They knew her well. Maybe not her whole background, but definitely her personality, flaws and all. They loved all of her as she did them.

And she wanted them—everything—back again.

So she'd headed south. Best case scenario: they'd let her explain. They'd understand—and maybe even apologize for jumping to conclusions—and take her home. She'd love them and Jamie and...her chest went tight...and someday, might perhaps have a baby with them. Or a litter.

Worst case: she'd die.

She'd come up with a plan: walk her ass into the center of Cold Creek, create a scene—considering she'd lack any clothing, that shouldn't be difficult—and demand to talk with Calum and Alec. They couldn't kill a naked woman in front of the town, not when a whole bunch of the spectators would be human.

And she'd stand there and—quietly—tell them everything. What she had and hadn't done, how she hadn't known what to do, about how Wells had given his word and that she'd kill him personally if he broke it. Not that he ever would, but they couldn't know that. She'd promise to give them a ka-zillion babies if that's what they wanted. She'd beg forgiveness.

If they were fair—since they were men, fair wasn't a foregone conclusion—they'd acknowledge making a few mistakes themselves. She growled as she loped through the forest. Yeah, they could have given her a chance to explain, and worked with her on the Wells problem. But nooo, just had to jump to conclusions. Sure, she'd punched their paranoid hide-from-the-government hot button, but still.

So walk right into the firing zone, make herself a target, and hope for the best. One major invitation-to-disaster plan. But hey, even Wells might have trouble figuring a way out of *this* mess.

She leaped over a fallen log, scented a rabbit and paused, then continued. She was getting closer, she knew it. Sometime last night, a feeling had arisen in her, a sensation of being home, as if she'd been cold and someone wrapped a warm blanket around her. Each touch of her paws to the earth repeated that. *Home, home, home.*

This shifter shit is sure weird.

She lifted her muzzle, checked the scent of the early morning air. It even smelled like the right mountains, and the thought made her lope forward, her pace increasing and—

Snap! Pain. Horrible pain. She snarled, spun, fell. *Son-of-a-bitch.* A trap.

Her hind leg was caught in a heavy iron trap. She trawsfurred, then grunted as the metal teeth dug deeper into more tender human flesh. Fucking-A, that hurt. Mouth tight, she examined the trap. The sucker was huge, made of heavy steel. And those teeth were a real pisser. The bleeding wasn't too good either.

After managing to stand, she pushed down on the jaws with all her strength. Not enough weight. She tried again and again, and then slid back down to the ground. She couldn't open the damn thing. And nothing lay within reach to use to pry the teeth apart.

Could she yank it loose and carry it with her?

A few minutes later, she gave that one up. The hunter had pounded the anchor stakes so far into the frozen ground, they didn't budge at all.

Shifting back into cat form, she lay down and watched her blood turn the snow red. Dammit, in her few-and-far-between prayers, she had specifically requested a go-out-in-a-blaze-of-glory death.

This was so not it.

HOURS LATER, VIC'S ears swiveled toward the southwest. Something was approaching. With the wind blowing the wrong way, she couldn't catch its scent. Unfortunately, that meant it could smell her, blood and all.

Man or beast or shifter? An edge of fear prickled up her spine. It sounded like more than one animal. A pack of wolves? How delightful.

Dammit, weren't predators supposed to hunt only at night? Hadn't these animals read the rule book? The fur on her neck rose as she stood and balanced on three legs, trying not to growl as the trap pulled on her mangled leg. Fuck, if she tried to fight, she'd probably fall down.

Well, at least she was saved the embarrassment of walking into Cold Creek in her birthday suit... But she wouldn't ever get to see Alec and Calum again. And Jamie. And Thorson. And—

Just out of sight, a heavy animal moved through the under-brush. No, two animals.

The mountain lions burst into the clearing. The sunlight glinted on dark golden fur. And pale golden fur. She recognized them and snarled hopelessly. She was dead. She wouldn't even have a chance to explain, dammit—

With a resigned breath, she stood her ground. Going belly-up and begging? Not gonna happen. Anger at the unfairness of it all—at them—twined with her love and joy at seeing them one last time, and her cat instincts couldn't decide what to do.

Calum sprang first, straight for her. He landed barely out of reach. She raised a forepaw, showed her claws, and knew she wouldn't hurt him.

He stalked forward, ignoring her show of fight, and rubbed his muzzle over hers, purring loudly enough to make the trees shake. His giant paw landed on her shoulders, flattening her like a pancake, and he licked her ear, still purring.

Then Alec shouldered Calum to one side to do the same. Their scent engulfed her, mingled with hers.

They did know who she was, didn't they? The lifemate who'd betrayed them? But oh, she'd missed them. The higher rumble in the air was her own purring.

Calum shifted to human form. Kneeling beside her, he examined the trap and her leg. He glanced at Alec who loped away, returning with a large branch in his big jaws. He dropped it and shifted.

They had her leg free in minutes. Maybe the iron teeth hurt less coming out than in, but it still fucking hurt.

Calum frowned down at her. With one hand, he grasped her muzzle, forcing her to meet his very intent, very black gaze. "Trawsfur," he murmured. His power blazed through her, and a second later, she lay naked before him.

Alec wrapped his hands around her leg, putting pressure on it to stop the bleeding.

"Freeing someone from a trap before executing her is a little inefficient, don't you think?" she muttered, trying to keep her lips from trembling. She was a Marine, dammit; Marines didn't burst into tears. She managed to pull in a breath and almost sounded like herself as she asked, "How did you find me? This isn't exactly on a trail, is it?"

"There's a bond between a Cosantir and his territory. I know if a strange shifter sets foot in my mountains." The sun lines around his eyes deepened. "Or when a lost one comes home."

"Oh."

He stroked his knuckles across her cheek, and then his flickering smile appeared. "Cariad, did I not warn you and Jamie about these traps?"

Her breath caught. "I'm the enemy. How did I get to be a cariad again?"

Alec released her leg, waited to make sure it had stopped bleeding, then kissed her lips lightly. "Once we got our heads out of our asses, we figured out what had happened and what you must have been trying to do."

Hope made her eyes sting, reality made her look down. Calum lifted her chin. "Little cat, we doubted you. I doubted you. Can you find forgiveness for us?"

When she shook her head, his jaw tightened, his hand dropped away.

She grabbed his fingers. "No. I mean, I couldn't believe you'd forgive *me*." She sighed. "Not without a lot of arguing. It's my fault, I know. I—I didn't tell you all the truth." The next admission came slower. Harder. "I should have stuck around to have it out with you, but I…"

"Didn't think we'd love you enough to listen?" Calum asked gently.

She nodded.

Alec hugged her, his body hot against her cold skin. "We love you, Vixen, even if you're a tad insecure. Just like you love us, even when we're paranoid bastards."

"You do?"

Calum nodded, his eyes gentle. "We love you, cariad, and we *need* you. Come home to us."

Home.

Chapter Twenty-Nine

A month later.

COFFEE. *NEED MORE coffee.* Vic yawned, squinting at the mid-morning sun. She'd started work well before dawn. Alec had better take her off this fucking morning shift before she strangled him and left his body on the mountain for the coyotes. No—too classy. For the vultures.

As she cracked open the door to the bookstore, she reached up to quiet the bell before it rang. She liked practicing her stalking skills on Thorson; the old werecat was nearly impossible to sneak up on.

No one was in sight, but voices came from the sitting area. One was Thorson. The other was…Wells? When had Wells arrived in town?

Oh hell. She smoothed her hair back, scowled at her dusty boots. Sloppy, she'd gotten sloppy. With a frown, she pulled at her khaki uniform, trying to smooth the wrinkles Alec had created earlier when he'd locked them both in his jail cell and pretended to interrogate her as a spy.

She grinned, remembering the clothespins he'd used to torture her. *Nipple* torture. The man was completely warped. Good thing the jail had a shower in the back, or she'd have smelled like sex all day. She silently finished straightening her clothes, and then edged around the rear shelves for some recon.

Wells and Thorson sat in the comfortable chairs by the crackling fire. Each wore a scowl, but that was normal when the two of them got together.

Wells picked up his coffee, motioned to Thorson with the cup. "I've been thinking. It would be appropriate for you to perform that Death Gift ritual, and make me a shifter when you die. Considering your advanced age, that shouldn't be long now."

Thorson eyed him over the rim of his mug before taking a loud sip. "You annoy me, and you'll go tits-up first."

"I'm not planning to die until I see my grandchildren. Hopefully sometime this century." Wells frowned slightly as he stared into the fire. "The Sergeant said you shifters can take a long time, and that she's in no hurry."

"We leave that in the hands of the Mother." Thorson turned his head and winked at Vic.

Shit, he'd heard her. *Damn werecat.*

He turned back to Wells and said casually, "She'll name the first-born after me, of course."

Wells stiffened. "I doubt that. You're merely a token grandfather whereas I am her—"

The bookstore door slammed open, the bell jangling wildly.

"MomVee, are you in here?" Jamie ran between the shelves, spotted Vic, and wrapped her in a signature-Jamie hug.

"Is something wrong?" Vic lay her cheek against the soft hair. *My cub.*

"Yes. No. Not really." Jamie giggled.

Vic relaxed. "What then?"

"Daddy says there's probably going to be a fight, and since you're on duty, can you come and keep the bast—um, the bad guys from misbehaving." She whispered to Vic, "Daddy called them bastards, but I'm not supposed to say that."

"Do you need our help, Sergeant?" Wells asked, starting to rise.

"Nah, I can get it." Vic grinned at Thorson and tossed Wells a mock salute. It was good to be needed. Even better to be loved.

As she reached the door, she heard Jamie whisper to the men, "Daddy said Uncle Alec got more kisses than him this morning, and he needed MomVee at the bar so he could get his share."

Vic was laughing as she stepped out into the bright morning sunshine.

~ The End ~

Ready for more? Then try,

Winter of the Wolf
The Wild Hunt Legacy: Book 2

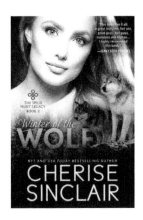

Available everywhere

Get *Winter of the Wolf* Now!

After years in foster care, Breanne Gallagher has the stable life she's always wanted, living with her foster-sister, working as a chef, enjoying her comfortable routines. Then one devastating night, a hellish creature invades her apartment and shatters her fragile existence. Shifting between monster and man, it slaughters her foster sister and assaults Bree. Alone, wounded, her beloved home tainted by gruesome memories, Bree flees to a tiny wilderness town, following her only clue to her past.

Shapeshifting warriors, Zeb and Shay move from one pack

to another, hunting the hellhounds which prey on their kind. Assigned to Cold Creek, they take over management of a decrepit fishing lodge for their "human" cover. Their first renter is a pretty human female who trembles at the sight of them—yet stands her ground. Furious at the hurt they see in her eyes, the protective nomads are drawn into helping her. Although no shapeshifter is ever attracted to a human, her scent is oddly compelling, and her ferocious determination to conquer her fears ignites longings neither loner ever expected to face.

Bree is healing, learning to shoot the biggest pistol she can find, and overcoming her fears, especially of the two deadly, disconcertingly attractive hunters. Her life is getting back on track…until she tries to save a little girl from a hellhound and discovers that everything she knows about herself is false.

I have read all of Cherise's books (several times over) and never been disappointed, but I have to say that Winter of the Wolf was one of my favorites. Magic and mystery abound with two tortured, lonely bad boys and an equally wounded heart in our heroine. Shay, Zeb and Bree find friends, family and a home in Cold Creek, things that have been sadly lacking in their lives. Their story is erotic and exciting, at times funny, and overall heartwarming. 5 Stars

~ You Gotta Read Reviews

Excerpt from

Winter of the Wolf

S HE SIGNED THE rental papers and handed over a check. God, three weeks sounded like such a long, long time to be away. After taking an ibuprofen—she'd really hit that wall hard—she showered and had to force herself to stop scrubbing. Would there ever come a time she didn't smell that creature's stench on her skin? Didn't feel soiled?

After unpacking, she lay on the bed, trying to relax and failing miserably. This wasn't her place. It was all wrong. She wanted to go home. *Not happening, so get over it, Bree.*

Then again, she'd never had a home as a kid, so maybe she'd skipped the homesick stage and needed to go through it now. Her lips curved in a wry smile. Naptime would be good right about now, too.

But she couldn't keep from staring at the metal bars on the window. They looked easy to open from inside, so could someone—something—open one from outside?

Unable to shake the thought, she raised the window, then went outside. Stretching her arm past the window and bars, she tried to reach the clasp that would let her push the bars open. Couldn't. She put her face against the glass to check how far her fingers fell short.

"If you're breaking in, try the door. It's open." The man's voice sounded like gravel.

She spun and bumped into the cabin wall. Pain ripped through her shoulder. Darn it. Bracing her feet, she raised her fists and got a look at the person.

Her spine chilled as if gripped in an icy hand. Willing her lungs to work again, she stared at him. The man was even taller than her landlord, and one cheek had the same knife-like blue mark. Sinister white scars marked his neck. His forearms. His powerful hands. His eyes were so dark a brown they were almost black with a terrifying coldness—like there was no human home in there.

The guy looked like he killed puppies for fun.

"I'm not breaking in," she said, trying not to act like a petrified rabbit. Slowly, she eased away from the wall and lowered her fists. "This is my cabin."

Straight black hair reached past his shoulders, and he had the dusky complexion of someone of mixed Native American descent. His brows lifted. "We have a renter?"

We? Please say this cruel-looking character wasn't her landlord. He wasn't anything like Shay. Well, other than being seriously huge. Shay'd been pretty nice, all in all; this guy looked like he could rip apart a bear. With his bare hands. "Shay rented me this cabin." *Not you.*

"I'm Zeb Damron. Shay and I run this place together." He loomed over her—far too much like her nightmares—and held out his hand. "You got a name?"

"Breanne Gallagher." She gritted her teeth. *I am fine. I am. I can touch him.* She'd been through this fear as a teen after Mr. Harvey tried to force her. She just had to gut it out again. So when his scarred-up, callused hand engulfed hers, she squeezed hard, trying to crush his bones and show him what a tough bitch she was.

His expression didn't change. "I make you nervous." There wasn't a shadow of a doubt in his voice, but no triumph either. Just a flat statement.

She jerked her hand away. "Well—"

"Don't lie." His nostrils flared. "Or would terrified be a better word?"

Definitely. Her teeth gritted together. "Maybe I just don't

like pushy guys." *Oh yeah, Bree, piss off the huge landlord.*

The corner of his mouth turned up slightly. "Sorry."

"I—" How had he gone from scaring her to making her feel rude? "You… There's no one around—" *Good going, dummy, point out how isolated this is.* "You're big. And a guy."

"No male would harm a female," he said, his wording uncannily like Shay's. His dark brows drew together, his eyes intent. "You don't believe that."

"I know it's not true." *The weight on her, pinning her down.* A shudder ran through her.

He folded his arms over his chest and studied her. The rolled-up sleeves of his flannel shirt displayed wrists as thick as her upper arms. "Little female, if you are bothered by a male, tell me. I'll take care of him for you." His cheek creased. "Part of the Wildwood service."

He was serious. He was really serious. How could a man scare her spitless and make her feel safe at the same time? But he smelled of clean pine forests and nothing like the monster. She managed almost a smile. "Um. Right. Thank you."

He nodded and moved back into the forest. Silently.

ZEB WALKED INTO the lodge and sniffed. The scent of beef and onion filling the air was enough to make a hungry wolf howl. He found Shay in the kitchen, stirring something in a Crockpot. Every counter was covered with vegetable peelings, meat, and dirty dishes.

Zeb tried not to wince. "Supper?"

"Aye. I found the grocery store. Tiny place in the center of town. And you're cooking tomorrow, *a mhac.*"

Zeb growled. Shay'd grown up in one of the more isolated Daonain villages that still clung to the older ways and languages. Over the last two years, Zeb had learned a few words. "I'm not your fucking son."

Son, my ass. Typical dominant wolf, going all paternalistic. He needed a pack to babysit, not a partner. "You're not even ten years older than me."

Shay snorted. "I feel older. By the way, I rented out the next-door cabin."

"Met her. Pretty little human. Scared though." She'd triggered every protective instinct in his body—only it had been him she was afraid of. Zeb checked the fridge. Shay had bought dark and light beer. Good male. He grabbed one of each and took a chair at the kitchen table, pushing away the scattered newspapers. Beer or not, having a person in his living space was weird. And this messy mongrel? Fuck.

"Definitely scared." After putting the lid on the pot, Shay sat down and rested his injured leg on an adjacent chair. "She acted like a trapped mouse when I blocked a door in the cabin."

The dark malty beer was cold with a smooth bite. "Huh. Figured it was me. I told her that."

"Zeb, you have all the tact of a dwarf."

Now that hurt. Dwarves were the rudest of all the Other-Folk, even worse than gnomes. "She said I was big and that the cabin was isolated. At least she didn't run away screaming." Zeb sipped his beer. Yeah, he'd seen terror in those big blue eyes, but she'd stood her ground. She'd even raised those little fists. Admirable.

Shay's brows drew together. "Isolated? Could she be afraid of *males?*"

"Maybe. She moved as if she was damaged, smelled of fresh blood, and not the moon cycle type. Then again, she's female—they're not designed to be understood." He never spent time with females outside of Gathering night.

"Aye. And human. Their mating patterns are strange." Shay rubbed his chin. "We should find out if she has a reason to worry. Wouldn't want some asshole coming here and bothering our first renter."

"You do the finding out. I'll instruct the male on manners."

"I'll talk, and we both beat the shit out of him."

Zeb scowled. Shrugged. Whatever. As long as he didn't have to try to quiz her. Tact wasn't on his short list of talents.

Shay set his drink down. "Supper's still got a while to cook. Let's do some scouting."

Be good to know what to expect before the next new moon. Most of the snow was gone, but tracks might remain in the wet dirt. Hellhounds were heavy. "Your leg up for it?"

"By Herne's hooves, do I look like I need a momma?"

They stripped and went out the side door into an area concealed by trees and bushes. The previous owner had been a careful Daonain.

The first quarter moon was high in the black sky. Carrying the chill of snow-capped peaks, the wind swirled the brush and made the bare tree limbs clatter. Zeb *trawsfurred* to his animal form, feeling the gift of the Mother's love run through him, hearing the siren song of the wild. He flicked his ears forward to catch the rustling of tiny animals in the dead grass, the slow flapping of an owl overhead. Shay's scent mingled with the fainter ones of deer and cougar drifting down from the mountain.

Shay shifted as well, turning into a big-boned, heavy wolf with light silver-gray fur.

Zeb glimpsed yellow light through the bushes, showing the little human was still awake. Good thing he'd barred her cabin windows. She'd be safe. Then again, hellhounds preferred shifters to humans, so she'd be ignored as long as it caught a shifter scent first.

Shay barked, getting his attention, and loped into the forest. Zeb followed.

Get *Winter of the Wolf* Now!

Also from Cherise Sinclair

About Cherise Sinclair

A *New York Times* and *USA Today* Bestselling Author, Cherise is renowned for writing heart-wrenching romances with devastating alpha males, laugh-out-loud dialogue, and absolutely sizzling sex.

I met my dearheart when vacationing in the Caribbean. Now I won't say it was love at first sight. Actually since he stood over me, enjoying the view down my swimsuit top, I might have been a tad peeved—as well as attracted. But although we were together less than two days and lived on opposite sides of the country, love can't be corralled by time or space.

We've now been married for many, many years. (And he still looks down my swimsuit tops.)

Nowadays, I live in the west with this obnoxious, beloved husband, a puppy with far too much energy, and a cat who rules us with a fuzzy, iron paw. I'm a gardener, and I love nurturing small plants until they're big and healthy and productive...and ripping defenseless weeds out by the roots when I'm angry. I enjoy thunderstorms, collecting eggs from the chickens, and visiting the local brewery for the darkest, maltiest beer on tap. My favorite way to spend an evening is curled up on a couch next to the master of my heart, watching the fire, reading, and...well...if you're reading my books, you obviously know what else happens in front of fires.

~ *Cherise*

Connect with Cherise in the following places:

Website:
CheriseSinclair.com

Facebook:
www.facebook.com/CheriseSinclairAuthor

Facebook Discussion Group:
CheriseSinclair.com/Facebook-Discussion-Group

Want to be notified of the next release?

Sent only on release day, Cherise's newsletters contain freebies,
excerpts, and articles.
Sign up at:
www.CheriseSinclair.com/NewsletterForm

Printed in Great Britain
by Amazon

80165229R00246